THE MAGISTER'S MASK

Deborah Fredericks

The Magister's Mask

ISBN 1-896944-16-7

CIP Data on file with the National Library of Canada

Dragon Moon Press
PO Box 64312
Calgary, Alberta, Canada
T2K 6J7
www.dragonmoonpress.com

Printed and bound in Canada

THE MAGISTER'S MASK

Deborah Fredericks

To Wendy —
Enjoy the read!

Deby Fredericks

To Daron, my one and only.

Chapter One
~ The Wind Knows ~

Laraquies Catteel of Nelnoor sat on his porch, enjoying the quiet of his garden. A sudden breeze made the treetops tremble. The birds, whose color and song he admired, stopped as if with one breath, and the soft mist that rose from his tea feathered away into nothing.

The leaves' whispered warning sped across Chalsett, City of Gardens. The silence reached the market, where the hubbub of merchants and hagglers faltered. On it went, over the docks and through the harbor, rippling away across the Jewel Sea.

A tense moment more, and the first brave bird ventured a strand of bright notes into the stillness.

The old man raised a small bowl to his lips with a hand as brown as the tea inside it. That was no mere wind. Those were voices from just beyond mortal hearing. Laraquies was a magister, one of the highest ranking sorcerers in Chalsett-port, and it was his business to hear such things. His dark eyes searched the arched fronds of a fern tree above him, as if he might see some answer there.

Bare feet patted softly over the cottage floor and out onto the porch where he sat. They stopped behind him, and a young woman asked, "Magister?"

"Oh, you're awake." Laraquies looked up into the face of his apprentice.

Shenza Waik of Tresmeer covered a long yawn with her hand. Like all people of the Jewel Sea, she was brown-skinned, with a compact build. She had thrown an apprentice's robe, striped purple and white, over the plain sheath she slept in. It half-fell from her shoulders as she pushed springy black curls away from her face. Shenza pulled it back up with a quick jerk.

Laraquies smiled at the self-conscious gesture. "Did you sleep well?"

"Yes," Shenza answered, "until just now."

"Then you should eat," he said cheerfully. "Get back your strength. You worked hard, Shenza."

A frown crimped the young woman's brow. She was very serious, Shenza, as the young often were. It amused him to tease her, the more because she would not let herself see the humor.

Shenza ignored his instructions and sat down beside him, tucking her knees neatly together. This rebellion was a good sign. For many years, the girl had been too much in awe to argue with him.

"Magister, what is happening?" the young sorceress asked. Her dark eyes did not leave his face.

Laraquies was forced to confess, "I do not know. It seems the spirits are troubled." He looked up again, past the green canopy of his garden. It had been a clear day, the air heavy with warmth and humidity. Now the faintest pall obscured the tropical sun. Or perhaps he merely imagined it.

"What touches them will affect us all," he said. "I expect we will be summoned soon."

Shenza stared at him with dismay. Laraquies did not blame her. The spirits who ruled the sea, sky and forest were the only creatures in the world more capricious and terrible than man.

"I woke up so suddenly, I didn't know what to think." Shenza rubbed at her eyes, then covered another yawn.

"That is why you should eat," Laraquies said. "You have been sleeping for two days."

A wry expression crossed her face. Laraquies raised a hand to stop her before she could speak. Shenza was always apologizing for some imagined lapse. She had worked hard in the last of her labors as his apprentice, but it seemed his teachings were soon to be tested. There was more bad news for Shenza this morning.

"You have completed your mask," he said. "Don't forget, this next investigation will be yours."

"Oh." From the stricken look in Shenza's eyes, she had forgotten. "This one?"

Her frightened tone pleaded with him to say no, not this one. She wanted him to face whatever made the wind blow, and give her the next inquiry that came in. Ah, but then it would be the next job, and the next after that. Laraquies tried to be a reasonable master, but some things must not be delayed.

"This one," he affirmed. "Now, child, I will prepare a meal and you will eat it. You're going to need your strength, I fear."

~

Shenza watched Master Laraquies stroll into the house and thought, "He can't mean it." But she knew he did.

Shenza stared across the lush garden, not really seeing the brook, with its artfully placed stones, or the small bath house on the other side. All was calm and cool here. Still, she could not forget the tingle of her skin that woke her, the cold burning like diving into deep sea waters. Then screams, which her confused mind soon translated into wind-tossed branches scraping against the roof tiles. Shenza nearly fell out of her hammock, came stumbling out to the magister seeking comfort. And what did he do? He told her it was not his problem.

She tried in vain to swallow her fears. Nature spirits were dangerous to begin with. It would not be a simple task to calm their fury. Now, in the face of some unknown disaster, Master Laraquies puttered around the kitchen, humming off-key as if nothing in the world was wrong.

The old man came back out of the thatched hut. He knelt and set a tray on the smooth boards of the deck, then eased himself down beside it.

"Eat now," the old man urged.

"Yes, teacher," she sighed.

The tea kettle, freshly heated, sat beside a drinking cup decorated with colorful fishes. A matching bowl contained sea-plums neatly pitted and cut into quarters. Shenza had to admit the tart fragrance was appealing. Laraquies' cup still sat on the deck, so she poured tea for both of them and took a slice of the juicy red fruit.

She eyed Laraquies as she ate. Despite his advancing years, he did not seem old to her. Waves of silver hair were caught in a rippling tail at the back of his bare skull. Dark eyes, set in his weathered face, reminded her of the sea—deep, and yet sparkling on the surface. A plain white kilt was neatly wrapped about his skinny mid-section, and over one shoulder ran the purple robe that proclaimed him a sorcerer. The casual drape of cloth belied its high importance.

Laraquies seemed satisfied to see food pass her lips. He stood up again and went back into the house. A sip of tea rolled bitter and sweet across Shenza's tongue. Her mask was finished. So, too, her time as a sheltered apprentice. Yet Shenza felt at a loss. To leave Master Laraquies and work on her own... She didn't feel ready for that. Certainly not now!

The old man returned, and placed something softly on the boards beside her. "This is yours. I had it made while you were asleep."

Shenza turned toward him and gasped. There, neatly folded, was the deep purple robe of a magister. Feeling her heart beat faster, she lifted the folded cloth. The color was so vivid, she knew it had never been worn.

"It's..." she began, and stopped. Shenza felt her chin tremble.

"It is a gift," Laraquies said softly. "I know you will honor it."

Perhaps he meant to reassure her, but he misunderstood. Shenza had been poor all her life, a daughter of illiterate fishermen. She could hardly remember having any clothing that someone else had not worn first.

"It's beautiful," she managed. And yet... Together with her mask, it seemed another reminder that her days as a student were drawing to a close.

"Come, then," Laraquies said. "I want to see you wear it."

With some hesitation Shenza put aside her apprentice robe, so familiar and comfortable. She straightened, holding onto one corner so the new one was pulled open. The harsh scent of dye still clung to the fabric. A loop of thread slipped over the bone pin that fastened her sheath. The robe passed once around her body, under her right arm, across her back, and up over her left shoulder. The cloth felt slightly stiff and heavier than she was used to. Master Laraquies smiled as he watched her settle the hanging end.

Shenza was adjusting the drape of the new robe when she heard a resonant chime from the front of the house. She turned, her heart in her throat. A client was here, her very first client. She was still eating breakfast. Her hair had not been combed. And she was barefoot.

Master Laraquies gazed into the treetops, his hands clasped loosely before him. The moment of hesitation stretched on. Then the chime sounded again. Shenza stooped, grabbed her bowl of fruit, and ran to the door.

She crossed the workshop, which occupied the front half of the round cottage. Though it was the largest room, that was not saying much, for the house was small. In the early days, she had wondered why a sorcerer of Laraquies' exalted rank was satisfied with such a modest dwelling. Nor had she any answer now, except that Master Laraquies placed duty before fleshly comforts.

She paused just inside the door, swallowing to clear her mouth, and reached through the strands of hanging beads that obscured the entrance. Light fingers touched a certain spot on the rattan gate. "Open," she murmured. The grille swung away, and she pushed through with a clatter of little shell beads.

Outside, jittering impatiently, was a tall young man who wore the deep yellow kilt of a peace officer. Shenza guessed he was within a few years of her own age. Black curls were cropped close to his skull, a cut she found unflattering combined with such a flat nose and wide mouth. A rounded club and short knife hung from a leather belt. The weapons were supposed to be ceremonial, though Borleek, the chief peacekeeper, was willing to look the other way if his men used force in execution of their duties. A light sheen of sweat across the man's broad shoulders hinted that one of these occasions might have occurred very recently.

The fellow stood near the bronze chime, which still hummed softly where it hung. Black eyes flashed eagerly when he caught sight of Shenza. He hung the leather mallet on its hook and jogged up the two steps to the porch.

"We need the magister!" he said, neglecting any other greeting.

Shenza bowed slightly, placing one hand on her chest and balancing her breakfast with the other. "We have been waiting."

He paused, impressed. "You were?"

"Please come this way." Shenza pushed the gate back against the outer wall and held the hanging strands aside for the man to pass.

Entering the cottage, the peace officer spied Laraquies and strode right over to him. Shenza followed, eating as quickly as she could. Reminded of his manners, the officer pressed a hand to the curly black pelt on his chest and made a cursory bow.

"Magister," he said urgently, "we have captured a criminal. Chief Borleek wants you to come right away."

"Really?" Laraquies answered mildly. Then he turned to his student. "I believe Magister Shenza should handle this."

The young officer gaped at Laraquies, then at Shenza, who swallowed a hard lump of fruit. She had been expecting this, but still her breakfast sat sour in her stomach. Just as she opened her mouth to ask what his need was, he blurted out, "But the first lord has been murdered!"

His words shocked her into silence. *Murdered?* Was that what awakened her so suddenly? She turned to Master Laraquies, whose expression was now grave.

"Borleek wants *you* to come!" the officer was insisting.

"And I wish Shenza to conduct this investigation," the sorcerer responded. A placid smile erased all concern. "She is no longer an apprentice, but a fully qualified magister."

"But, Magister..." he sputtered.

Shenza knelt, setting the empty bowl on the tray. She felt almost as frightened as the peace officer sounded. "Magister," she managed faintly, "this is a very serious matter. Are you sure it is appropriate..?"

"Yes, it is." He nodded cheerfully at her dismay. "If the first lord has died, then his successor must be located and ordained. And there is the spirit world to be treated with. Those shall be my tasks. The investigation, therefore, falls to you."

Shenza stared at him reproachfully. It wasn't fair. She was not ready to investigate a crime of this importance. Consecration of the new first lord could be done by any sorcerer—even she could do it. On the other hand, none of them were likely to challenge Laraquies once he made his claim. She supposed she should be glad he said he would deal with the spirits, at least.

"As you say, Magister." Shenza bowed to her teacher. "I will need a moment to prepare, officer."

"Now just a second!" The peace officer protested as Shenza walked into the house.

Shenza's room was a cramped wedge of space at the back of the cottage. It was mostly filled by the hammock she had abandoned just a short time ago. Shenza folded the thin sheet and rolled the mesh into a compact bundle. With shaking hands, she drew a sandalwood comb through her hair, restoring order to the tangled curls. With leather sandals tied on she hurried back into the work room.

"Light," Shenza commanded, softly but firmly. With a soft pop, oil lamps sprang to life. A pair of windows in the curved outer wall were screened with pierced wood to admit cooling breezes. Below them were a small cabinet and a low table decorated with carved vines and flowers. She knelt and touched the cabinet in two places. "Open," she said. The doors parted silently.

The young sorceress withdrew a flat leather travel case and opened it onto the table. Arcane sigils covered the interior, weaving about between straps for holding talismans. She sat back on her heels and stared at the many containers within the cabinet. How many times had she done this very thing, preparing Master Laraquies' tools? Yet now her mind was blank. She had no idea what she would need.

Shenza tried to think calmly, logically. She pulled out each tray and stared at its contents. The drawers held ordinary things: flat gray rocks, short lengths of bamboo, a handful of small, round shells. These were the magister's talismans, specially created objects of power.

All manner of spells could be stored in such commonplace items, to be released at need. They had to be made carefully, using just the right materials, gathered in the proper way and time, and prepared in exactly the correct manner. A good part of her training had been to learn their crafting. And now it seemed she was to depend on her own work, as she had not done before.

Strangely, that gave her little comfort. She had made these things. She knew them intimately. It shouldn't be so hard to trust them, but her hands would not stop shaking. She clenched both fists in her lap. Shenza blew out a breath, forcing herself to relax.

She started with the basics, a scroll of cloth, ink and pens for writing. Verity stones, for interviewing witnesses. A wand and powder for detecting spells. Another wand to dispel magic, though she did not know if she would need it. A knotted line for measuring. She slid these into straps and pouches shaped to hold them, and peered nervously into the cabinet's dark recesses. Had she forgotten anything? She was sure she had.

Behind her, voices echoed faintly as the peace officer continued arguing with Master Laraquies. His commander wasn't going to be pleased by the substitution, Shenza gathered, and the man thought it would be blamed on him.

She could certainly sympathize with his feelings. Murder was the worst kind of investigation, and rare. She had only seen Master Laraquies conduct one such inquiry, so long ago that she couldn't remember half of what he did. The only death they had investigated since was a drowning that was clearly accidental. And with this wealth of experience, she was to determine guilt in the death of a first lord?

Choking back her feelings, she closed her travel case and ordered, "Seal." Then she withdrew a plain wooden box from the cabinet. A slight push, a twist, and the concealed lid slid open. Within, cushioned on silk of a midnight hue, the gleaming face of her mask gazed up at her. She laid the box on the table and stared back.

The first layer had been new white cloth, pure feather-flower silk. At the public trough, on a rare moonless night, she washed and pounded the cloth, chanting rhymes to strengthen the fibers for the magic they would contain. Then, through more long nights, she rose when only the purple moon's rays shone under the eaves to set the careful stitches that joined in magic sigils of lightness, comfort. Then a layer of leather, boiled with rare herbs gathered from the shore of a tiny coral isle near

Chalsett's white shore. The soft leather was molded to fit her own features before spells stiffened it to steely firmness. Over the following days, a moon-shaped dagger, itself spell-set, carved more runes to repel danger. The eye pieces were pared from fragile mica, set with charms to make them see what endangered her, what was hidden. Next a layer of fine clay to join cloth, leather and stone. That was kept damp through weeks of labor as she sculpted a human likeness and added yet more runes into the pale, soft clay. These spells were intended to protect the mask itself from damage. Last of all, the kiln. For a day and a night she fed the flames, chanting the rhyme of transmutation. Finally, at dawn, she quenched the eldritch fires in a mixture of white wine and her own red blood. Afterward, she slept for days to recover from the exhausting campaign.

All that work, and she just wanted to smash it over her knee! But the spells were set, and physical violence could not touch it. And so, with firm words and purple cloth, her master shoved her out into the world.

With trembling hands, Shenza lifted the mask which would be both weapon and shield. The surface was a flawless pale gold. It glinted, though not as metal did. Despite the solid appearance it was feather-light, just as the spells decreed.

When she lifted it toward her face, Shenza could feel the mask bond to her skin, easily, eagerly, even without the word of command. She tensed momentarily at the weird sensation. Then she realized she was holding her breath. She released it deliberately. Warm air escaped from her nose, and cool air flooded her mouth on the indrawn breath, as if there was no obstruction. Blinking, she realized she could see perfectly. Cautiously, almost guiltily, she moved her hands over the exterior. The texture was slippery and firm beneath her fingertips, but she felt no sensation on her face. On the other side of the workshop, the peace officer was still arguing with Master Laraquies. Though they spoke in hushed voices, it sounded as if they were standing right beside her.

She knew what to expect, and yet it still confounded her. The spells worked!

Despite herself, Shenza felt a surge of confidence. If she had done this, then surely she could carry out her other duties. Then she would not be a disappointment to Master Laraquies or her family.

Shenza picked up the travel case and walked toward the two men. The peace officer, with his back to her, insisted, "But you know what he means. You can't play these games with Chief Borleek!"

Master Laraquies patiently answered, "Did I spend so many years training my apprentice, so that no one would turn to her in times of need?"

"I know she's your apprentice, Magister," the officer said plaintively. "But this is a murder—and the first lord! And she..."

Master Laraquies saw Shenza, and for a moment he went still. His face, regarding her, had an expression Shenza had never seen before. Then, as if nothing was happening, he answered, "My student knows all that I know. I have complete faith in her. If you cannot believe in her, then trust in me."

The man faltered beneath this logic. "I do, Magister, of course, but my orders..."

"It's no good trying to reason with him," Shenza said softly. The mask did not seem to move, yet the words were quite clear; another unaccustomed sensation. The peace officer's startled expression on seeing her wear the golden mask somewhat soothed her bruised feelings. "Shall we go, officer?"

"Chief Borleek won't like this," he warned.

"He is welcome to discuss it with Magister Laraquies," she answered, and was irritated by the old man's appreciative chuckle. Laraquies didn't think much of the chief peacekeeper, Shenza knew. The two of them had crossed words before, usually to Borleek's sorrow.

The officer must have known it too, for he flushed beneath his dark skin tone. Then he spread his hands and shook his head in surrender. Shenza paused, wanting to say something to her teacher, or for him to speak some farewell to her. No words seemed appropriate. She turned and hurried after the peace officer.

Chapter Two
~ The Moons Say ~

The peace officer led Shenza out Master Laraquies' front gate and into a narrow lane, paved with weathered gray stones, that hugged the natural contour of the hillside. The magister's small house was nestled in a quiet neighborhood on the city's third tier, just above the marketplace. It was not a fancy district, but close to the town center and accessible to any who might need his services. The tree-lined avenue curved to join with a larger way. Urgent strides carried the guardsman ahead, until he realized he was leaving Shenza behind. He jigged impatiently at an intersection where the street met a wide marble stair running up and down the hill. Plentiful foot traffic passed in both directions.

When Shenza realized he was leading her downward, toward the market, she halted. The disturbance she had sensed earlier came from uphill, not down. She was sure of it.

This time he was paying better attention. He got only a few steps farther before noticing Shenza had stopped. "The prisoner is this way," he told her, urgently gesturing down the stony flight.

"Is that where the crime took place?"

"No, it was at the palace." He sounded sullen, now. "But the prisoner is at the ward."

"You said he has been captured?" Shenza inquired. He nodded, an impatient frown knitting his brows. "Then I am sure he will be there when I wish to speak with him. Let us go to the palace."

"But the Chief..." he started, and fell silent, shoulders sagging in exasperation.

"Please be patient," Shenza said quietly, to soothe him. "I do not wish it said that I began amiss." That sentiment could be applied both to this investigation and to her career. "If you wish," she offered, "you may return to the ward and report what has happened. I know the way to the palace."

She didn't mean that as an insult, but he bristled at the words. "I'll go with you," he grumbled stubbornly. To keep an eye on her? Or to avoid bringing his commander unwelcome news?

"Then I will welcome your assistance," she answered frankly. "But let us begin at the beginning."

This time it was Shenza who led, and the peace officer who followed. To herself, she made a wry face. 'Begin at the beginning.' It was one of Master Laraquies' favorite maxims. Quoting him already... She wasn't sure if that annoyed her, or pleased her.

Unspeaking, the two of them mounted the wide steps. The pale stone gleamed, polished by the passing of countless sandaled feet. Two levels above, Shenza bore left along the rim of the fifth tier. She was aware of her companion's rebellious silence, and did her best to ignore it.

As it was, she could not mistake the tense atmosphere that belied the gaily patterned attire of the townsfolk. The news must already have spread, for brown feet paused, clustered in loose knots of conversation and worry. Shenza noted many stopped their talk to watch her or stood aside as she passed, a mark of respect for her purple robe and gilded mask. Or of curiosity. Or both.

Looking to her left, over a low stone rail, she had a good view of the town. Chalsett, City of Gardens, rose in marbled tiers up the three gentle hills that ringed the harbor. Terraces of white stonework, washed by daily rains, overflowed with verdant greenery that gave the city its name. Soft breezes from the harbor were scented with sea-salt and the mingled perfume of various blossoms. The water, far below, was a luminous, clear aquamarine that shimmered in the morning sunlight.

On the town's lowest level, serpent-prowed ships unloaded onto quays bustling with commerce. Most wares went directly into the marketplace, on the level immediately above the wharves. From this angle of view, the market was screened by vine-grown arbors that shaded the interior from the fierce tropical sun. The market was large, its selection of wares extensive, for Chalsett-port was a busy center of trade. Open canoes carried folk from the smaller nearby islands to conduct business here. On that same level were the civic buildings, such as the peacekeepers' ward, the public hospital and the general school.

Gazing down upon the crowded port, Shenza had a thought she didn't like. The calm gold mask turned toward her companion. "When does the tide rise again? Do you know?"

After a moment's thought, he replied stiffly, "Not until late tonight."

"Hmm." She accepted this information and said no more.

"Why do you ask?" he pressed.

"If the murderer had an accomplice, he might seek to depart on one of the merchant ships that will leave on high tide," she answered. Then she shook her head. "I am looking too far forward."

"But you're right." The fellow sounded faintly alarmed, and impressed despite his grievances.

Shenza was silent while they bypassed a cluster of women wrapped in flowered robes, who openly stared at her. "Let us keep this in mind," she concluded when they could speak privately again.

Ranks of homes rose up the wooded slopes above the town center. Modest thatch gave way to tile roofs, and small huts to larger buildings in the upper reaches. On the hilltops overlooking the town were the gracious dwellings of the three or four wealthy families who dominated local affairs. Most prominent of these was the first lord's sprawling estate. The palace's blue-tiled roofs lifted proudly among the treetops, colorfully decorated eaves flashing crimson and gold. And above... Her steps lagged abruptly.

Above the first lord's estate, the red moon Inkesh brooded heavy in the sky. It hung so low it seemed about to land on the peaked roof like some great, ungainly bird. Inkesh, the emblem of raw force and negative emotion—of bloodshed.

Stepping aside from the flow of traffic, Shenza paused to scan the heavens carefully. The sun was rising quickly. It was perhaps two hours until noon, and the day was growing more than warm. Gauzy clouds veiled the sky's deep blue vault. As the day went on, these would thicken and darken until they produced the evening showers that signaled the end of the working day. For now, she could clearly see three of the five moons. Pale golden Quaiss was just lifting a thin crescent of reason from the east. A happier sign was the green moon, Prenuse, nearly full and riding almost at its zenith. Purple Meor, the Sorcerer's Moon, should also be in the sky, though the sunlight overcame its faint silhouette. Only mottled Skall was absent. The little wanderer's unpredictable appearance signaled the blind chance which overset all plans. The death of a first lord would seem just such a circumstance, and yet... She eyed Inkesh thoughtfully.

It was a matter of endless debate among the more esoterically inclined scholars, whether the five moons actually controlled the forces they embodied, or whether they were themselves commanded and merely reflected some other, unknown will. The association of each with its own domain was clear, however. The emotional powers they represented might combine, or clash; that would determine much. If the intellectual Quaiss joined with the nurturing Prenuse to counter Inkesh's malevolent force... And Meor was neutral, but what of Skall? In any event, the heavens told an interesting tale. She would do well to study those movements further.

"What?" the peace officer asked, startling her. She had forgotten his presence.

Shenza hesitated to speculate. But, she decided, she wasn't Laraquies, and this man wasn't a student to be baffled with riddles.

"The moons," she explained. "Look at Inkesh."

"Yeah, I know," he grunted tightly. Broad features reflected a measure of superstitious fear. "I saw it up there this morning and I remember wondering who was going to..." He stopped, the unspoken word hanging in the air between them like a little moon, pregnant with force. He blurted, "This isn't just chance, is it?"

Shenza eyed the man for a moment, and realized he spoke gruffly out of worry, not disrespect. "I don't see Skall," she pointed out quietly. "Let's not assume too much. Omens can be useful, but what we seek is the truth. We cannot find that if our eyes are blinded by speculation."

He gave her a thoughtful look, but accepted her words without bridling this time. "Let's go, Magister."

She nodded, and he followed her back into the flow of traffic. Pondering, she realized that she was already lacking information. "Officer," she said, "I don't believe we were ever introduced."

The question startled a laugh out of him. "Juss," he answered, flashing white teeth against his dark face. "Juss Battour of Reiloon." Shenza nodded, recognizing a well established local house and line. "And, uh... I know the magister said your name, but I don't remember."

"Shenza Waik of Tresmeer."

"And this is your first assignment? By yourself, I mean?" he queried.

"Yes." Her soft tone held a wealth of meaning.

Juss sighed with gusty sympathy. "He chose a fine time to throw you out on your own, didn't he?"

"I am trying to have faith in his judgement," she answered dryly, realizing too late that she was once again quoting her teacher.

~

As they climbed, Inkesh appeared to retreat. It loomed westward, over the Inner Sea, as the two reached the first lord's gatepost. No one greeted them. A pall of smoke and a dreadful stench hung over the neatly groomed grounds. Through the haze a woman could be heard screaming, over and over; not a formal funeral keen, but shrill, uncontrolled cries. Juss tensed, ready to rush to the unseen woman's aid. He restrained himself when Shenza raised her hand.

She could feel sweat beading between her shoulder blades, and from more than the uphill walk. A low tone sounded in her ear, warning of magic nearby. No danger was imminent, however. Turning her head left and right, she found the signal was slightly more insistent when she faced left.

"Come." She beckoned, and they hurried forward. Juss all but trod on her heels in his haste, until her mask turned slightly in his direction with a silent rebuke. Sandals whispered over decorative stepping stones as they followed a winding path. Floral hedges screened and shaded the trail. Some were low, offering views of green bowers or the tiled roofs of the town. Others reached high, in artful disarray. The smoke grew thicker, the stench of burning stronger. The woman's shrieking subsided, as though her hysteria was abating, and a babble of other voices could now be heard.

"What is that smell?" Juss demanded under his breath, his features twisting with disgust. A fresh sheen of sweat glistened on his broad chest.

"Tell me," Shenza asked in return, "how did Lord Anges die?"

"Well, uh..." He faltered, swallowed heavily. "I don't know."

They crossed a low stone bridge over an artificial stream that flowed between the gnarled roots of a grand willow tree. On the far side were color and movement, and dense smoke filtering through the willow's graceful boughs. A series of smoldering blots—footprints?—crossed a grassy clearing and plunged down a gentle bank. Beyond that, Shenza could see a pond adorned with water lilies and thick clusters of reeds. On its bank was a milling crowd. Since they all wore blue mantles, these might be the first lord's staff . Pausing, Shenza looked back along the line of footprints, which appeared to have come from a residential wing of the palace. A hibiscus hedge showed broken branches and scorching, as if someone had forced a way through while carrying a blazing brand.

Juss made no comment, but Shenza could see he was as uneasy as she.

They descended the bank through a silent drift of smoke. The woman who had been screaming was now just sobbing aloud, comforted by half a dozen others. She had been stripped to a pale green sheath. Nearby, a pair of men was stamping out flames that appeared to have consumed her outer robe.

There was a general sigh of relief as Shenza and Juss were sighted. "Where is the magister?" asked an older woman whose hair was spun with silver. Shenza recognized her. Since the first lord had not been married, Alceme served as his head of household.

"I am the magister," Shenza replied.

"You?" Her composure seemed shaken. "But I thought..."

"I have been asked to conduct this investigation." Shenza spoke with firm resignation, wondering how often she would face such questions of her authority. "Please give us room to work."

The crowd parted hesitantly, and Shenza's breath caught in her throat.

"I want to go home," she thought with lucid panic. *"This is his job. I will make him do it."*

A man's body lay before her, resting on its side in the shallow water at the edge of the pond. Gusting waves of smoke and steam rose from the corpse. The water bubbled and hissed where they touched. Blackened strands of jewelry and shreds of scorched cloth still clung to the unfortunate man's withered and shrunken flesh. His eyes were gone, and his hair, but his mouth gaped wide in a silent shriek of agony. White teeth gleamed against the charred lips and tongue.

A wave of dizziness passed over her. Restraining her feelings, Shenza reminded herself that she had just been wanting respect from the onlookers. How could she expect that, if she shrank from her duty? This was a victim of murder. He was dead—no longer suffering, but waiting for justice. It was her duty to provide that.

Still, it was an effort to move her feet toward that pitiful, dreadful huddle of twisted limbs.

"Be careful!" Alceme cautioned, startling her. "Tio was trying to get my Lord out of the water and her clothes caught fire."

Shenza nodded, finding it was an effort to speak. "I see. Thank you."

The heat from the corpse was intense as she approached; a mocking death-grin confronted her. Juss, she noted, no longer followed her closely. The alarm in her mask sounded constantly.

Kneeling, she raised her left hand to touch a spot on its smooth jaw line. "Stop," she ordered. It was a relief when it did.

Aware of the watching crowd, she settled her purple garment self-consciously and laid aside her travel case, only then realizing she had been squeezing the handle with a painful grip. It was good no one could see her face beneath this mask, she thought.

Shenza breathed deeply in a meditative pattern. When she felt calmer, she lightly touched her fingertips to the base of her throat, gathering the power within herself. Then she stretched out that hand, feeling the angry heat that glowed against her palm. Concentrating, she focused her power. As it peaked, she murmured, "Fire, out."

Instead, the smouldering blaze rebelled. The onlookers gasped, stepping back as a column of ugly blue-red flames burst outward. The pond water sizzled violently. Shenza flinched too, turning her face aside reflexively. Her heart hammered in her chest. Yet the mask protected her. She could feel the heat, but was not burned.

Magic fire. And it was a strong spell, to resist her control.

Shenza knew she must look more calm than she felt as she turned slightly aside to find her instrument case. "Release," she told it softly. The lenses of her mask showed her a flare of light from the spell-set runes, and the leather case folded open. Shenza eyed its contents and drew out a bamboo rod the length of her forearm, as wide as her thumb at its base and tapered to a slender point. Mystic sigils were incised along the entire length. This was a spell- breaker, one of her most powerful talismans.

With the rod poised in her hand, she again breathed deeply and focused her power. The runes flared brightly. "Fire, out." She touched the rod lightly to the dead man's shoulder.

The crowd started again. With a blustering sigh, a burst of hot wind swirled past her. Then it dissipated. The water's boiling diminished to trembling ringlets. Forlorn wisps of steam arose from the blackened husk to fade in the air. It wasn't only the audience that sighed with relief.

Shenza looked at the corpse a moment longer, trying to see past its present, mutilated condition to the man it had recently

been. Who could do such a thing? She had not thought highly
of First Lord Anges. He was not a particularly good ruler, and he
often disagreed with Magister Laraquies. Yet neither was he so
incompetent that he deserved this grisly fate. She might doubt
her own abilities, she might question Master Laraquies'
wisdom, but she had no intention of letting this crime go
unpunished.

Returning the spell-breaker in its place, Shenza closed her
tool case and stood. Her knees tingled with returning
circulation as she faced the dead man's household.

"Is Tio hurt?" she asked, addressing the other possible
injury.

"No, Magister," the woman answered, though tears still
glistened over dark cheeks. "I was just scared when my mantle
took fire."

"I am glad." Squaring her shoulders slightly, she turned to
Alceme. "Are you in charge?"

The woman responded with a bitter laugh, spreading her
hands to indicate the household's shock and disarray. "As much
as anyone, I suppose."

Shenza nodded slowly. "To investigate this crime, I will need
complete access to the palace, grounds and staff."

"Of course, Magister."

"I hope you will assist me by providing a messenger," she
went on. "Magister Laraquies will personally make the funeral
arrangements. Summon him immediately." It would serve the
old man right to have this much turned back at him. "In the
meantime, it should now be safe to remove my Lord's remains."

"Very well, Magister." With a gesture, the elder dispatched
one of the watching servants. He favored Shenza with an almost
sneering glance before complying.

Sighing to herself, she turned next to Juss. Surprisingly, the
guardsman was looking pale beneath his dark skin tone.

"Officer Juss."

He started guiltily at her call, but walked aside with her,
obviously grateful to move farther from the first lord's remains.
Softly, so no other would hear, she told him, "I must ask you to
take another message for me. Go to Peacekeeper Borleek and
tell him to seal the harbor. No shipping is to go in or out until

my next order." Coming from a very junior magister, this would not sit well. She could see it in his face. "There are to be no exceptions," she stressed, "save for one.

"After relaying my instructions to your commander, go to the house of the sorcerer Choruta Ramli of Salloo. It is on the fourth level, almost directly above the breakwater. I would like him personally to find my Lord's family and bring back his heir. I believe they are in Porphery, City of Domes. Choruta is on better terms with the Eleshouri than any other sorcerer in Chalsett. Their aid will speed him on his journey."

"Borleek, then Choruta." Juss repeated briskly. He seemed to feel better with a clear, uncomplicated task. "What about you?"

"I will be here, receiving the testimony of the servants."

"Will that take a while?" he guessed, scanning the number of witnesses. The Lord's body had been retrieved from the pond. Several of the men had sacrificed their robes to wrap the charred carcass, and somberly bore it back toward the palace. The women went before and behind them, taking up an eerie funeral keen. The low, wailing moan was chilling despite its formal phrasing.

Shenza belatedly realized Juss was waiting for her reply. "I do not know," she answered truthfully.

"Well, I'll come back and tell you what Choruta said," he decided. "If you leave before I get here, just tell the mistress where you'll be."

Shenza angled her head at him, showing the puzzlement her mask concealed.

"You might need help," he insisted.

"Very well," she agreed. "Go, now."

He thumped his chest lightly in a salute. "Right away, Magister."

Chapter Three
~ Too Many Tears ~

Grateful for their shade, Shenza moved slowly beneath flowering trees. Gazing at a scroll of cloth in her hand, she tried to review and organize what she had learned. The sun, nearly at its zenith, added heat to a frustrating day.

The palace staff was nearly unanimous in their version of events, and the steady glow of a verity stone supported their account. The first lord had been sleeping, they said, as was his custom after entertaining guests late into the night. Unfortunately, none of them had actually seen the attack commence. Angry shouting from his chambers had first alerted them. Then the Lord's cries began, terrible cries, as Shenza could well imagine. Rushing to his aid, they saw him burst from his chambers, his body engulfed in blue-red flame. He was hotly pursued by an old man who bellowed with maniacal rage. No one had seen this man enter the palace, but his fury was clear.

"You cannot have my daughter," he howled. Or, according to Tio, "How dare you take my daughter from me."

Seeing the numbers that came against him, the attacker fled, shooting flames at any who tried to stop him. Men of the household gave chase, while others tried to aid their master by smothering the flames. In his extremity, the lord sought to quench the fire in the pond. His passage had left the marks that Shenza noted when she first arrived. But his final effort was in vain. Only magic could extinguish the greedy flames, and there had been no sorcerer to administer the counter-spell.

Alceme's son, Andle, reported how he pursued the madman over the palace wall, down steep slopes, over walls, through gardens. The old man had the strength of lunacy, Andle told her. Despite his advanced years, he stayed well ahead of the pursuit. 'Climbed like a monkey,' to use the servant's words. But finally, in the marketplace, he was borne down and captured with little struggle.

Shenza was frowning thoughtfully at the script on her scroll when the screaming began again. Startled, she turned to rush into the house. Before her foot struck the ground, she stopped, feeling foolish. That was a mourning wail, not a sign of fresh danger. She re-rolled the scroll, sealed it into the case, and turned her sandals to the palace at a more dignified pace.

The mourner certainly fulfilled her role, Shenza thought as she approached the open pavilion where the first lord lay in state. Even in the heavens, they must hear her desperate wails. Yet there was a tone of anger, as well—an emotion at odds with the expected sentiment.

"Mistress, be calm." A familiar voice spoke softly, attempting to soothe the woman.

"I don't want to be calm!" she shrieked as Shenza passed into the shade of the pavilion's tiled roof. "He is dead! Oh, my Lord! My love! Aaaah! He is taken from me! Aaaaah!"

Lady Innoshyra Sengool of Sengool had thrown herself across the first lord's body, which lay on a low dais, heavily swathed in a blood-red shroud. Shenza recognized her, because everyone in Chalsett-port knew this daughter of wealthy merchants. However, a recent inquiry which Magister Laraquies had conducted into the Sengool family business practices had not improved Shenza's opinion of her line. Innoshyra's head was thrown back, her lovely features distorted by the excess of her grief. With jeweled hands, she tore at her silken robes, just one of which cost many times the worth of Shenza's entire wardrobe. To either side, her attendants keened and swayed in a more temperate expression of grief.

"Dear lady, you must not harm yourself," Magister Laraquies reasoned patiently from where he stood slightly to one side. Draped over his arms were broad bands of white and gold cloth, embroidered with sigils ensuring the dead man would rest in peace. Due to Innoshyra's display, he was unable to install these in their customary places.

"My health doesn't matter," she sobbed loudly, tears overflowing to glitter against mahogany skin. "Nothing matters. He's gone. Taken from me! Aaaah, my love!"

Beyond the weeping lady, Alceme and Andle entered through the far side of the pavilion, followed by half a dozen others of the staff. Each carried a wicker basket bound with deep red cord. These would be the first lord's clothing and personal belongings, which would be sent with him to the next world. The two servants arranged these around the bier where Lord Anges lay. Afterward, Andle removed his outer robe, laying it reverently near the body's feet. His mother, too, methodically placed three bracelets, a necklace and an anklet— all of the jewelry she was wearing—atop one of the caskets. Unspeaking, the other servants added their own humble treasures. They kept a distance from Innoshyra as they worked, Shenza noted. Nor did she miss the contemptuous glance Alceme awarded the tearful lady.

Shenza hoped her mentor would be able to complete the arrangements before the ghost protested the lack. Nevertheless, she felt satisfaction in leaving him to deal with the situation. Her business, at the moment, was with Alceme.

Swift paces carried her around the pavilion, where the housekeeper and her son waited on her soft call. Together the three of them walked back toward the main house.

"Did Lady Sengool know my Lord well?" Shenza inquired, keeping a neutral tone.

"Not as well as she would have liked to," was Alceme's ironic reply.

"Mother," Andle murmured, shocked by her words.

"Please tell me what you mean."

Alceme now appeared embarrassed. "Oh, it's nothing. It's just that she was hoping to marry my Lord. She didn't say that, but we all knew." The asperity of her tone clearly told her opinion of such a match.

Picturing the spoiled Innoshyra as first lady, Shenza privately agreed with her. "Did my Lord also wish that?"

"Not him," Andle answered that with conviction. "He, uh..." The young man paused, obviously censoring himself, and concluded, "He wasn't ready to settle down yet."

Shenza nodded, smiling wryly behind her mask. Since Lord Anges' lechery was a local legend, that was putting it tactfully. From behind them, mourning cries continued their shrill echo. Hearing again the undertone of rage in Innoshyra's voice, Shenza inquired, "Was Lady Sengool angry with him because of this?"

A shocked glance passed between them as they realized what Shenza was implying.

"Yes," Andle admitted, "I'm sure of it. Though I doubt she dared say so to him."

"She is a great and gentle lady, you know," Alceme added, her disgusted tone returning. "She wanted to make sure we domestics all knew it. But she isn't really of noble blood. Her family just has money."

Shenza made due note of these revelations. "And were there any other ladies who might have been angry with him? Perhaps because he seemed to favor Lady Sengool?"

Alceme frowned. "No, I don't think so. What would be the point? He won't marry anyone, now."

An awkward pause followed this stark truth. The older woman turned away, and her son laid his arm across her shoulder, drawing her against his side. Even so, Shenza could not help thinking that the first lord would no longer betray a lover, either.

"Forgive me for troubling you," she murmured, moved more by their quiet grief than by a hundred of Innoshyra's cheated wails. She placed a hand between her breasts and bowed away, leaving the Lord's life-long servants their privacy.

She had been thinking of herself too much, Shenza realized. She dwelt on her own fears, on her irritation with Magister Laraquies and the slight personal inconvenience the first lord's murder had caused her. That was wrong. She would have to visit, pay her respects, and make an offering in recompense.

But as fresh sobs reverberated within the open pavilion, she decided that a later time would be better.

~

"Curious," Shenza murmured, realizing too late that she had spoken aloud.

Juss caught her up immediately. "What is?"

Kneeling and bracing herself on both hands, Shenza leaned over the estate wall. The turf came nearly to the level of the wall on the inside, but there was an eight-foot drop on the other side. A series of deep gouges in the hillside showed where the assailant and his pursuers had dropped down. The ground beyond was thick with trees, ferns of various sizes, dangling vines and shrubs. Long slithers of displaced leaves and soil hinted at the chase's progress down the slope, where the footing looked every bit as treacherous as Andle had described it.

What she could not decipher was which of the tracks had been left by the attacker, and which by the servants. She thought Andle had said three of the menservants gave chase. Adding one for the attacker, there should have been four trails. Granted, two of the men could have trodden over each other's traces. That did not appear to be the case, however.

Shenza sat back, reaching absently into her travel case. Extracting her scroll, she read carefully. The pursuers had been Andle, Ettrig and Hoon: three men. Laying the scroll in her lap, she again leaned out over the limestone wall.

Long staring did not alter the result.

A heavy hand fell on her shoulder, startling her. "What are you looking at?" Juss demanded, his forehead cramping crossly.

"Let go," she told him, sitting back quickly to regain her balance. The level coldness of her tone pleased her.

"Sorry, Magister." Grudgingly, he complied, though a frown still clouded his broad brown face.

"There should be four trails leading down the slope," Shenza explained coolly, "one from the attacker and three from those who chased him. I can only see three traces. Unless you know more of such things than I?"

Grunting to himself, more than at her, Juss followed Shenza's example and leaned over the wall to scan the forest floor. He had been this irritable since returning from his two errands. From his remarks, she gathered that Peacekeeper Borleek had been outraged by her instructions. At least Laraquies' old friend, Choruta, had understood the seriousness of the situation. Juss' attitude did not make her more inclined to share her findings with him. He was still Borleek's man, when all was said and done.

"Could the fourth one have flown?" Juss finally asked. "You said he was using magic."

Shenza considered that. "Andle specifically described him running, leaping, and climbing. If he had flown, Andle would have said that."

"Well, could he have been confused?" the peace officer persisted. "A lot was happening. Maybe he couldn't see it well."

Shenza sat quietly for a moment, until Juss stirred restlessly. Reluctantly, she admitted, "If he had flown, there would be no visible marks. But," she went on, "it should leave a faint trace of magic behind, on the ground or perhaps on the trees he passed near. I cannot see such a trace."

"It's dark under the trees," he argued stubbornly.

"No matter what the light, I would see it," she answered firmly.

Taking up her pen, she added this conundrum to her list. After a momentary pause, she included Juss' theory, and her reasons for doubting it. A gentle breeze, scented with blossoms, started the leaves above her whispering. Blossoms... or something else? Shenza felt the dark hairs rise along her arms. She looked around, and then skyward, but saw only thick white clouds drifting over the sun's bright orb. Nothing seemed out of place—except that her companion was staring at her impatiently. Holding back ill- tempered words, she restored her scribing materials to their places.

"Let us go."

"To the ward?" Juss asked, though he didn't sound very hopeful.

"To the market," Shenza corrected him. "I wish to see where he was apprehended."

She rose, brushing bits of loose earth from her robe. The treacherous hillside did not appeal to her. She left it, for now. If a more thorough examination was required, she would approach the site from the roadway below.

Juss' broad shoulders sagged, but he took the lead. Shenza followed more slowly, trying to make a logical tale from the fragments she had heard thus far.

She could not do it.

It was true that the most powerful sorcery was often commanded by the elderly. In magic, as in many fields, years brought cunning and experience. Sorcery could not, however, imbue an elder with abnormal abilities. Magister Laraquies had told her this many times, usually—she grimaced to herself—when he wanted her to take on some taxing physical duty. And so the fact remained that magic would not render an old man agile enough to 'climb like a monkey.'

Even if some kind of witchery enabled an elder to carry out the acrobatic feats Andle described, how had he been captured so easily? Shenza glanced at Juss' muscular back, for he had forged far ahead of her. The peace officers were strong men and numbers would overcome anyone. Yet Andle had said there was little struggle. Why go to so much trouble, casting potent spells, only to surrender without a fight?

Or, to put it another way, if someone planned to commit a murder, wouldn't they also plan an escape afterward? Unless he acted in the heat of anger, of course. Still, it seemed to Shenza that someone who knew such advanced magic should be able to do better than that.

Further, there was the stated provocation, that the first lord was somehow 'taking away' his daughter. None of the staff had known what that meant. True, Lord Anges had lustful appetites, but no one had ever accused him of taking a woman against her will. It was said he gave his companions rich gifts when he tired of them. Such brief liaisons were not uncommon among men of the noble classes. Some families even encouraged their comely daughters to bring them wealth in this way. So, if the first lord had tasted the charms of the assassin's daughter, that was hardly cause for such a gruesome revenge.

The whole scenario filled Shenza with doubt. There was something she didn't yet know, that was plain enough. She tried to console herself that the investigation had merely begun. 'Patience,' Master Laraquies always counseled. Despite all its powers, sorcery could not change facts. The answer was always there.

Chapter Four
~ Dead Fishes Tell ~

They had come to the market—to the beating heart of the town. On the terrace above the docks, overgrown arbors shielded the narrow stalls from the sun's relentless heat. All manner of goods were boasted beneath that shade: ceramic cookware, sandals of leather or hemp, bright bangles of metal, stone, shell. Virtually every surface that could display wares was occupied. Cloth of a hundred hues hung from ceiling hooks. Jewelry draped over poles. Farming tools stood in neat ranks. Vegetables were mounded on counter tops, next to wicker baskets holding doomed pigeons and geese. Even at midday, as the air grew thick with humidity, customers prowled the shady lanes carrying mesh bags that bulged with various purchases.

Wooing them was an endless chorus of competing voices. Some sounded bored, others confident and merry, and still more whined or cajoled. If the first lord's passing had cast a pall, that did not quell the essential vigor of this place. Nowhere else did the City of Gardens seem quite so much alive. It was good to be reminded of that.

Shenza knew that she should try to find Juss, who was lost in the crowd before her. Instead, she turned aside. When curious or frightened looks turned her way from the many brown faces she passed, she pretended not to see them. Just for a little, she wanted to lose herself here.

Shenza understood how the callers felt. She remembered the desperate need to sell—sell something, anything. Not so long ago, she herself made a living here. Her father, a fisherman, had been taken by the sea when she was just a little child. Her mother tended beans and vegetables in big clay pots behind their shabby thatched hut. In the evenings, she spun dried floss of the feather flower into silver-silken thread. Those products had been displayed in this very market.

As the eldest child, Shenza had been her mother's chief assistant. It wasn't long, though, before her true talents emerged and she spread a threadbare blanket beside her mother's stall. There the barefoot, ragged girl purified water, enchanted cook pots against breaking, or told fortunes— whatever brought her mother barter.

One day, as she bent nearly double in fierce concentration, condensing sunlight into perfume bottles to sell for lamps, a pair of passing feet stopped at the edge of her blanket. She scarcely glanced at the purple hem above dusty brown toes. No sorcerer ever stopped to buy from her. The humble powers she commanded were much beneath their notice.

When the enchanter didn't move on, she droned without looking up, "Buy some sunlight, good sir? Shines in the dark like day." A casual pass of her thumb sealed the gleaming vial with wax and spell craft. Not wanting to lose her concentration, she set it aside and reached for another.

"I think that I will," answered a cheerful voice. "You work very hard, don't you?"

This finally made her look up, for the first time, into the weathered face of Magister Laraquies. Even then, he had little hair, though there was still some black in the curling tail held at the nape of his neck by a copper pin.

"What are you asking?" he asked, a kind twinkle in his dark eyes.

"Twenty rukh," she answered. Even though she hadn't expected an offer, she didn't like the feeling that he was laughing at her.

"Oh? That much?" He seemed even more amused, and Shenza became indignant.

"It's good work," she retorted, "and glass is expensive." She lifted the thick little bottle in demonstration. "It'll last three months at least. You'll save more than twenty rukh on lamp oil, and if you bring the vial back, I'll refill it for ten."

Before he could reply to that, Shenza's mother fairly flew from behind her counter, bowing herself in half with abject apologies. That was Shenza's first inkling of her customer's exalted rank.

Shenza was distracted from her recollections by a familiar and appealing odor. Across the aisle from her, a vendor was roasting chunks of yam over a brick brazier. A crust of honey, crumbs and spices sizzled invitingly.

The scent reminded Shenza that she had not eaten since morning, and that had been but a light meal. A quick look in her travel case revealed a dozen copper rukh in a pouch. She felt a perverse irritation that Laraquies had anticipated her needs, but her feelings did not prevent her approaching the yam-seller's counter.

They quickly settled on a price, and she came away with a fine specimen on a wooden poke, still crackling from the heat of the fire. She raised the yam to blow on it, only then realizing her mask prevented it. The weight was so slight, she had forgotten she wore it.

Shenza quickly found a fountain in a quiet alcove sheltered by glossy, dark foliage. Seating herself on a marble bench, she laid her travel case down and raised a hand before her face.

"Release," she ordered.

The gold mask came away with a strange sigh, and the day's full heat suddenly bathed her from top to toe. She laid the mask atop her travel case and bit into her meal. The crisp skin crunched beneath her teeth. Sticky-sweet yam mingled with a mild burning sensation from the spicy coating. Shenza released a blissful sigh of her own.

Then a familiar shadow darkened the alcove. "So here you are," said Juss accusingly. "I've been looking all over the market."

Fortunately, the yam in Shenza's mouth provided a good excuse to hold back tart comments about having to account for her movements. When she had stilled her rebellious thoughts, she lifted a bamboo dipper from the fountain and sipped the cool water, thus clearing her mouth.

"Will you join me?" she asked mildly, and drank again from the dipper.

Recovering his temper, the peace officer said, "Good idea." He made as if to leave, then turned and stabbed a blunt finger at her. "But don't you move!"

"I am not through eating." She gently explained the obvious.

Snorting to himself, Juss strode off toward the food vendors. He returned shortly, carrying a much larger roast yam, two fish cakes wrapped in seaweed, and a mesh bag containing several small melons.

Noting her bemused glance, Juss grinned sheepishly around a mouthful of fish. "I'm still young, you know. Would you pass the water?"

She did. Juss offered one of his fruits in return, and Shenza gratefully accepted. They ate in silence that grew more comfortable as their empty stomachs were satisfied.

When there was nothing left but stained yam-pokes and melon rinds, Juss declared, "Now, that's better." Slapping his hands against his knees, he rose. "Weren't you saying that you wanted to see where the killer was captured?"

Shenza nodded. With another tiny gasp, her mask adhered to her face and she stood, settling her purple robe purposefully. "Show me."

Juss led her back to the main thoroughfare. They crossed an open plaza, where a huge fig tree reached skyward, then doubled back to follow the rank of booths closest to the rim of the tier. This time, she noted, he did not hurry and took care not to become separated from her.

Here, there was no densely-leafed arbor to protect the merchants and their wares from the sun. Instead, multi-colored awnings rustled and snapped in a light breeze from off the bay. Below, to their right, Shenza could see the clear sea and piers lined with shipping. There was still plenty of industry there. Perhaps word of the port closure had not spread. Strangely, however, the water was extremely low. Shenza could not recall ever having seen such a broad expanse of sand lying exposed. The receding waves had left a litter of rack and refuse. Almost all of the serpent- prowed vessels were partly or completely grounded.

The sailors had noted it, too. Among the toiling dock workers were clusters of ship-masters in plain brown kilts.

Hands on hips, they stared at the beached craft. Their consternation was obvious even across the distance.

"Magister!"

The young sorceress turned at her companion's hail. Juss stood at the last of the fish-sellers' stalls, on the end of the row. The occupant of the neighboring booth watched mournfully as Shenza strode to join him. She faltered as she drew near and the powerful stench of overripe fish assailed her.

"Pretty bad, isn't it?" Juss grimaced, guessing the cause of her hesitation. Shenza merely nodded and raised the bar that permitted her to enter the interior.

The walls were framed of thick bamboo poles, covered loosely with a heavy fabric that could be taken down and tied in various arrangements as the sun moved during the day. A chair of wicker and canvas lay tipped over on its side. Beside that was a ceramic jug, also fallen or kicked over. Otherwise, the smooth paving stones showed little sign of the struggle that was supposed to have occurred here.

Shenza glanced through the rear drape and saw a narrow aisle between two close-set rows of booths. Backing into the stall, she righted the chair, a simple folding frame with a sling-type seat of well-worn canvas. The jug was a common ceramic with a bland, gray-green glaze and a broad base to prevent it from tipping over. Liquid sloshed in the bottom as she handled it. The long neck was sealed with a plug of dirty rags.

Carrying the jug with her, Shenza returned to the counter. This consisted of several rough rattan poles lashed to the stall's frame. Beneath it was a row of three basketry bins, their weaving so tightly drawn as to be water-tight. Shenza knelt to inspect them. Woven into the baskets was a series of sigils. Activated with appropriate spells, these would ensure the contents remained fresh until sold.

Obviously, from the rank stench, the spell had failed. Her mask showed her no shine of magic, though she caught a glimmer from the neighboring stall. Only the faintest residue lingered from past enchantments.

The runes themselves appeared to be in good order. The sorcery must have been disrupted somehow. Steeling herself, she lifted the lid on one of the hampers. An even more potent

miasma of rot assailed her. With some effort, she forced herself
to coolly view the contents. Small, bloated fishes were heaped
within it. In the next bin, a mound of blue-black mussel shells
were cocked open in death. Shenza felt no need to try the third
container.

The mussels were small, and even without the whitish film
that coated their scales she judged the fishes were hardly prime
specimens. Perhaps not surprising, considering this booth was
at the far edge of the fish-market. Even so, this was too much
merchandise to just be left to rot.

Her lunch turned over restlessly in her stomach. Gratefully,
she let the basket lid drop and rose, wiping her fingers absently
on her robe. Shenza turned to Juss, who had retreated to the rail
and was waving his hand vigorously before his face. She tried to
speak, but had to swallow before she could find her voice.

"Were you here when he was captured, Juss?"

"No. We had some complaints of theft from the bead-
makers, and I was keeping watch on their lane. I came when I
heard all the yelling, of course, but it was all over by the time I
got here." He sounded almost regretful. "I heard all about it,
though. What do you want to know?"

"I could not accept hearsay," Shenza told him. "If I can, I will
speak with the officers myself, later today."

Juss shrugged, accepting this. "I'll show you which ones they
were."

"That would be welcome."

"Magister?" came a soft, slow voice. They both turned to
meet the sad eyes of the woman in the next stall. Of middle
years, she wore a simple sheath with a floral pattern in vivid
greens and blues. A matching band held long, curling tresses
back from a fleshy, dark face. Several brass bangles adorned her
arms. A silver hoop gleamed in one broad nostril.

"I was here," she said diffidently, almost as if she feared to
speak.

"Who are you?" Juss asked. "Did you see what happened?"

"I saw something that I didn't understand," was her reply.

"Just a moment," Shenza said, gladly leaving the reek to
approach her counter. The woman's stall was festooned with
smoked fishes, and a host of dull eyes stared from their little

withered faces. Opening her case, Shenza drew out a flat, grayish disc sized to fit the palm of her hand. Concentrating, she gathered her power and raised the talisman to her throat. The verity stone lit instantly, for she had already invoked its power several times today.

"Open your hand," Shenza instructed the shopkeeper, who tensed nervously. Hesitantly, she extended her right hand, showing a palm worn paler from a life of hard work. Shenza laid the verity stone in her hand. The lifeless gray disc now shone from within with a rich violet light. Two runes, fiery purple, hung suspended amid the translucent stone.

"Please tell me what you mean," Shenza said softly, to ease her. "Begin with your name."

For a moment, the woman gazed at the stone, as if it would speak for her. But the talisman remained silent. "My name is Nakuri Corteem of Cessill. I work here every day, just like Byben does... did."

Shenza raised a hand to stop her. "Is that his name?"

"Yes, Byben Calloob of Cessill. I can't believe the things they've said about him." On her free wrist, the bangles tinged together as she fidgeted thick fingers. "He just is... wasn't a violent man."

Shenza looked to Juss, who stood back, arms crossed over his chest. "He is still alive, isn't he?"

"As far as I know," he shrugged.

"Please do not worry," Shenza told Nakuri gently, "and continue what you were telling me."

"I heard the fuss coming across the market," she resumed, though appearing little reassured by Juss' statement. "Anyone would, there was so much shouting and carrying on. It was coming nearer, but I had a customer so I didn't try to look around. Then the matron I was selling to ran, like this —" with a louder clatter of bracelets, she mimed frantic backing away, hands raised to shield her face. "So I leaned out, like so." Nakuri extended her ample torso over the counter in demonstration. Straightening back up, she urgently exclaimed, "There were six men all on top of old Byben! They were all peace officers, like him." She gestured to indicate Juss. "He was crying and fighting, but they hit him until he stopped." Her fingers fluttered on the counter top. "Then they took him away."

The stone's lavender gleam remained steady throughout this performance. Shenza waited a moment, and then coaxed, "What was it that you did not understand?"

"They said he ran up to the palace and killed someone. With magic," Nakuri summarized eloquently.

"So?" Juss prodded impatiently.

"He couldn't do magic," the woman objected with indignant feeling. "He was terrible at it. Anyway, he was sleeping. He was always asleep by that time of day."

"It was only two counts until noon," Juss retorted. "Nobody sleeps at that hour. He must have left without your seeing it."

"I heard him snoring!"

Shenza turned her face toward her companion. "Juss, please let me ask the questions."

Under Nakuri's offended gaze and Shenza's inscrutable mask, the peace officer subsided.

Returning to the subject at hand, the young magister said to Nakuri, "You say that he is always asleep by that time of day. Do you know him well?"

"I thought I did," she mournfully agreed. "We're kin, you see—not close, not of the same line, but of the same house, the House of Cessill. I tried to look out for him, though there was little I could do, after all."

"Why did you think he required looking after?"

"Oh, the drink, Magister." Nakuri seemed surprised by her question. "Surely you saw his jug, over there."

"Drink?" Both Shenza and Juss turned to look at the jug, which still stood on the counter where Shenza had left it.

"I'll get it." Visibly holding his breath against the sour-fish odor, Juss stepped back toward the other stall.

"Thank you," Shenza said to his back. To Nakuri, she tried to keep a calm tone that did not betray her keen interest. "Did he drink often?"

"Yes, I'm afraid, Magister. He was always drinking. Since his wife ascended to the stars, I think it was his only pleasure. And then, after Xerema went away..."

Shenza wondered who Xerema was—perhaps the daughter that the attacker had mentioned at the palace? Keeping to the subject, she asked, "Did his drinking interfere with his work?"

Nakuri nodded, sighing with almost maternal despair. "He could never get down here in the morning to get a good spot. I try to save that booth for him, since nobody wants it if they can get one closer to the stairs. And he couldn't set a spell to save himself, Magister, as I've said. Usually I do it for him, once he's started dozing. I couldn't, today, because I was busy. But I don't like to see him lose the little he has to sell. With fishes and such, at least he can eat them himself in the evenings." She sighed again. "I don't know how he'd keep food on the table, otherwise."

"And you are very sure that he cannot perform even simple magic?" Shenza stressed.

"That over there, that's about the best of his work." Nakuri waved ruefully to indicate the stink in the neighboring stall.

Juss had returned with the jug. After waiting for Shenza to finish her questioning, he extending it for her to take. "Can I ask something?"

The gold mask gleamed as Shenza nodded. "If it is relevant, certainly."

"Well, so. If he's this poor, then how can he afford all the liquor?" Juss asked brusquely.

"He makes it himself, I believe. Trades some of his fishes for soft fruit, then mashes it up with a little water and sugar and a bit of yeast. Two days later, there you are."

Gingerly, Shenza picked out the stained rag that stuffed the narrow spout. She inhaled cautiously. In its own way, what she smelled was nearly as rank as the decaying fishes. For professional reasons, Shenza never drank alcohol, so she had little basis for judgement. From the faces Juss was making, however, the procedure Nakuri described did not yield a desirable product. She pushed the damp shreds of cloth back into the neck of the jug.

"I have just one more question," Shenza said to Nakuri, setting the jug on the counter beneath the dangling smoked fishes. "You mentioned someone named Xerema."

"Yes, Magister."

"Is that his daughter?"

Her dark eyes widened in amazement. "How did you know?"

"I had already been told that he had a daughter. And did you say that Xerema has left Chalsett-port?"

"Yes, Magister. Just a few weeks ago. She used to work up at the palace, as a cleaning maid, I think."

"And did the first lord..." Shenza hesitated, while Juss and Nakuri gazed at her expectantly. Shying from crude language, she awkwardly finished, "Did he make advances to her?"

Nakuri snorted lightly. "Probably, but she never mentioned it to me if he did. She met a young man who worked there. Subadeen, I think his name was. A very nice boy," she said with approval. "Honest, hard-working. He was a woodcarver, doing some decorations for the palace. He went back to Occida of the Fountains when his work was done, and Xerema went with him. She couldn't stand to see her father sink so low, she said, and went to make a better life for herself."

"And did Byben blame Lord Anges for his daughter's departure?"

The woman laughed sadly. "He blamed Subadeen! And he did, sometimes, say he should never have let his daughter go to work in such a household. But no, Magister, I never heard him blame the lord personally." Her laughter faded, replaced by deep concern. "He just kept drinking."

"It is kind of you to help him," Shenza said, placing her hand on Nakuri's plump one. For reasons of her own, she shared the woman's concern. "I will remember what you have said."

"Er..." Nakuri responded, surprised by her gesture.

Taking her verity stone, Shenza concentrated a moment to dismiss its power. The purple light faded swiftly. Replacing it, she closed her case. With both hands crossed over her chest, Shenza stepped back, bowing away. After a moment's hesitation, Juss followed her with the vessel of crude spirits.

The clouds were growing darker overhead now. The two of them moved slowly toward the central square. Shenza was deep in thought. It seemed Juss was learning her ways, for he respected her silence.

Beneath the boughs of the wide-spreading fig tree, Shenza paused. "I must record what I have learned," she told him softly.

"Please bring another peace officer and clear the rotten food from Byben's stall. You may throw the liquor away, as well."

"I wasn't sure if you would need it."

"It has told its tale," she assured him. "When you are finished, return to me. I will still be here."

"Whatever you say, Magister."

Shenza sat on a bench beneath the fig tree's shade and opened her travel case. Across the square, Juss cheerfully lobbed his burden into a refuse basket. The banners in the market rustled nervously, stirred by a gusting breeze.

It was difficult even to write what she now suspected. Shenza found the stylus rolling between her fingers, not moving across the scroll on her lap. It was almost impossible to believe that the old man, Byben of Cessill, had killed the first lord. That she was meant to believe so was clear enough. Yet it could not be true.

Ah, but these suspicions were not enough. It was her duty to seek the facts. And so, carefully, she recorded what she had learned. There was much time ahead of her for speculation.

Chapter Five
~ A Rock Above Raging Waters ~

"Now," Shenza said when Juss had returned, "we will go to the ward."

"It's about time," he grumbled, but cheerfully. Shenza followed him slowly. She was not looking forward to the next portion of her work and reminded herself that she would learn nothing if she got upset.

The peacekeepers' ward was just across the plaza. It was a large, circular structure with walls of bright marble. Pierced marble screens provided air to the interior. The main floor was elevated a full half-storey over ground level. Above, a double roof of dark gray tiles seemed to merge with the clouded sky.

As they mounted the steps, a gusting wind rustled the colorful banners that draped from the eaves. A young lad in the short kilt of an apprentice peacekeeper was scrubbing the steps to assure that no moss grew. The boy stopped, eyes widening, when he saw who was coming his way. Juss dropped back, letting Shenza enter first, and gestured that the lad could continue working.

It was even more humid inside the ward than outside. A broad walkway circled the room, giving access to many smaller private offices that ringed the building's outer wall. Shallow steps led down into a recessed central chamber, where scribes knelt beside low tables, recording city business. Six tall, cylindrical pillars rose from the floor through a gap in the lower roof. Cris-crossed beams supported the overlapping upper roof.

Shenza did not stop for the workers and peacekeepers who stared at her. After all, she had been here many times before.

Together, she and Juss turned left along the terrace and approached the narrow stair that led downward, to the prison. Her stomach tightened nervously.

The way was guarded by a peace officer who was both shorter and older than Juss. He was armed with a bronze dagger, spear and shield—a sign of the troubled circumstances.

"Magister," he said, with scant respect, as Shenza approached, "Chief Borleek wants to talk to you."

The last thing Shenza wanted was for the chief peacekeeper to control the terms of their encounter, for she knew he would not like what she had to say. She merely paused. "He may speak with me."

"But, Magister," the man protested, sounding worried as he realized she was not going to stop. "He wants to talk to you now."

"I am not his to command," she answered coolly. Sandaled feet whispered downward, into the dimly lit stairwell.

"You'd better go get him," Juss said behind her, smugly. She could not hear a reply over the quick beat of her companion's footsteps catching up to her.

The stairway curved to the right, following the building's foundation. At the bottom, a gate of stout rattan poles stood locked. A narrow bronze cylinder, girdled by interlocking bands, secured the latch. Extracting a tubular piece of shell from her case, she set it against the lock and concentrated. "Open."

The tumblers aligned themselves to release the pin, and the door swung free. Beyond the gate, a row of narrow windows at ground level provided illumination from outside. Since Juss loomed behind her, blocking the doorway, this was the only light. Fortunately, the mask sharpened her vision enough to see the outlines of stone walls and cells defined by more rattan bars. The air was tainted with blood and bile.

"Should I get a lamp?" Juss asked, startling her.

"No," she answered absently. Groping fingers quickly located a small leather pouch with a solid lump inside. With the fingers of one hand, she worked open the drawstring and drew out a little glass bottle. Piercing radiance streamed from the captured daylight, revealing the bare floor and walls in pitiless detail. There was blood on the floor in several places, some not yet dry, and other liquids better not guessed at.

Soft moaning led her to the only occupied cell, a shallow chamber barely wide enough to pace across. Lying on the floor was a dark huddle of bony limbs and rags. The prisoner rolled into the farthest corner, shying from the light like a worm suddenly unearthed. Incoherent cries took on an edge of panic, and the skinny form shivered violently.

Byben of Cessill had been stripped of his clothing except for a grimy loincloth. This meager covering displayed ample evidence of the beating Nakuri had described. Dark, swollen bruises were visible even through his brown skin, overlaying the ladder-like pattern of his ribs. Some of the weals oozed with darkly glinting liquid. Yet more blood was smeared on the floor.

Juss was right, Shenza thought. She should have come here sooner.

Reining in her feelings, she matched her shell tube to the end of the lock. The cylinders instantly turned, needing no word of command. The magister stepped into the cell.

"Grandfather," she said gently, using the common term of respect for one's elders. Ignoring the blood, she knelt just within the bars. The old man whimpered in his corner. "Grandfather." There was no response.

Shenza turned, to see Juss hovering behind her. To his credit, he seemed to flinch from the prisoner's plight. "Go for a curomancer," she instructed, her tone too even for condemnation. "Ask for Mistress Kafseet, if she can come at all."

"Yes, Magister." Juss sounded subdued. He hurried from the cell and went up the steps at a run.

Shenza tried again to sooth the prisoner. "I will not hurt you, grandfather," she said softly. "I am the magister. Will you speak with me?" There was no change in the narrow, trembling back. "I wish to help you. Do you understand?"

Finally, her words seemed to penetrate. Feebly, the old man tried to turn over. Beneath her mask, Shenza gasped at the ruin of his face. Byben's nose was pressed flat against puffy cheeks; his eyes, running with tears, were surely too swollen to see. Blood from a cut on his head had plastered the cloud-white wisps of hair to his head on one side. More bruises discolored his arms. His right wrist was too distended to turn. Shenza hesitated, trying to see how she could help him without abusing some already-outraged flesh. She quickly put down her travel case and vial of sunlight, supporting him under his arm pits, the only part of his body without visible injury.

"Magister?" He clutched feebly at her robes, his voice a sickly wheeze. How could anyone believe this frail old man capable of murder? So little strength could scarcely threaten the mussels he sold at market, to say nothing of jumping walls and the other feats ascribed to him.

"It will be all right," she heard herself saying. Shenza desperately hoped Mistress Kafseet would be available, for curomancy was a very different order of sorcery than her own and she carried nothing to comfort so many injuries. "Can you sit up? Let me help you. Try not to be afraid. I won't let anyone hurt you."

"They wouldn't stop hitting me," the old man blubbered. His front teeth were missing. Shenza found that she did not want to know if he had lost them before this morning. "I told them I didn't do anything, but they wouldn't stop. They wouldn't stop!"

"I know," Shenza said bleakly. In truth, she had expected some evidence of violence against the prisoner. After all, the first lord had been murdered and his servants could be expected to be upset. Nor would Borleek be bothered to discipline them, however often Magister Laraquies rebuked him. "It will be all right," she repeated helplessly.

Byben moaned on in incoherent sobs, his grizzled skull bobbing against her shoulder. Shenza stroked his back lightly, trying to avoid the lacerations, and said meaningless things. Her eyes stung with tears, but she sternly held them back. She should not have sent Juss for the curomancers, she thought. She should have asked for the names of the officers who made the arrest. Somehow, she vowed, she would see them punished. And Borleek as well, for permitting such conduct.

As if her thought had summoned him, she heard the peacekeeper on the stairs. No one else could make so much clatter by just walking. Her heart sank. From the sound of it, he was in a rare temper.

Well, so was she. And if he thought that he could roll over her, as he did everyone else, he was going to find out how wrong he was.

Borleek entered the room at full roar. "Who left this gate unlocked?"

Whimpering, Byben cringed back from the deep-throated bellow. Releasing him, Shenza rose deliberately, and turned toward the sound.

Borleek Surham of Bentei, the chief peacekeeper, towered over the heavily armed guards who accompanied him. Shenza had always thought he looked like a great sea bass, with his jutting jaw and little cold eyes. Deep, down-slanted lines from his eyes and the corners of his mouth were the only real sign of his age. There was no silver in his short, curly hair or the thick pelt on his chest, no fat or softness on his frame. Unlike the other officers who accompanied him, Borleek carried only a dagger. He was dressed in a yellow kilt with a short robe over his left shoulder. But after all, he did not need weapons, nor robes to identify him. He had served in his post for almost twenty years. He was an institution of himself, beyond any accounting—or so he must believe, Shenza thought, if he permitted his subordinates to go so far beyond bounds.

Heavy brows pinched inward, and Borleek stormed toward Shenza. "What are you doing in there? Get away from him! I ordered no one was to come down here!"

He did not actually raise his voice now, but spoke with the casual force of one who expects instant obedience. Shenza stepped forward and halted in the cell door, blocking his path. Though she did not doubt he could move her by force, she would not allow him to lay a hand on Byben if she could prevent it.

"My work requires that I speak with him," she answered with a calm she did not feel.

"What 'work!'" Shenza thought for a moment the man would walk right into her. He stopped at the last moment, scant inches from collision. "You've got a lot of nerve coming here, girl! I sent for Magister Laraquies, not you! This is no time for an apprentice to be playing at magister!"

Behind her, Shenza heard old Byben wheezing with fright. "Shall we talk privately?" she suggested, hoping to draw the peacekeeper away from his victim.

"We'll talk here and now!" Borleek's voice took on some heat. Obviously he was not prepared to be bossed by any mere girl.

"Very well. Magister Laraquies has assigned me this investigation..."

"Assigned, my eye! It's his job, and he has no right to delay it!"

Shenza might agree with that, but she had no intention of saying so. "Your Officer Juss expressed the same viewpoint, but Magister Laraquies chose to act otherwise. Since he is my instructor, I must carry out his wishes..."

"This isn't some classroom exercise!" Borleek's features twisted with anger. He leaned forward to roar in her face. "The first lord has been murdered! We have no government until the case is settled! And sealing the port won't help! That just hurts business at a time when everyone is already scared! Are you trying to ruin this town?"

Shenza was very glad for her mask, which concealed her expression. As long as she kept her back straight, she thought, no one would know what she was feeling. "I am not responsible for the economy or the government. My only duty is to learn who committed the crime."

Borleek growled deep in his throat when she did not quail before him. Shenza continued quietly, just as her Master would have done, "Now. Will you please tell me why the prisoner is bleeding?"

Borleek scowled over her shoulder at the whimpering elder. "He isn't," he grunted. "The bleeding stopped a long time ago."

Shenza paused for a moment, amazed by such callous words. "I had intended to question Byben about his involvement in the death..." She began, only to be cut off.

"What's there to question?" He blustered. "He burned Lord Anges to cinders—everyone saw it!"

"Were you there?" Shenza asked pointedly.

He paused, regrouped. "No. I didn't have to be, to know what happened!"

Shenza could not disguise her contempt for such a baldly ridiculous statement. "I assure you, Peacekeeper, the sequence of events is still very much in doubt."

"Are you saying he didn't do it? That my men are liars?" Borleek leaned forward, towering over her with real menace now.

"I am saying that they may have been mistaken," Shenza temporized slightly. She felt like a rock above raging waters, pounded and splashed by the waves.

"Mistaken?" He bit out a challenge.

"Since magic is involved, one's own eyesight may not always be trusted. But sorcery will reveal sorcery. I had intended to question this prisoner about his guilt or innocence." She paused, mastering her feelings. "But I now find he has been badly beaten..."

"So what if he was?" Borleek interrupted, actually sounding proud of the barbarity. "You witch-workers are always complaining."

"...So badly, that I cannot question him!" Shenza finished. Despite herself, her voice rose in anger. She was tired of being interrupted. "And it may be several days before I can! How then can I finish my investigation?"

The watching officers gaped at her temerity. For all the shouting he did, Borleek was not accustomed to being shouted at; he did not enjoy the experience. "Why, you..." His massive hands tightened into fists, and for a moment Shenza thought he might strike her. "What kind of excuse is that!"

"Magister!" Juss' voice rang in the stairwell. Sandals whispered and robes rustled as the newcomers drew closer. The knot of watching officers parted, letting their comrade pass. Behind him came two figures robed in vibrant green.

"Thank you, Juss." This time, Shenza was glad to be interrupted. She felt she was about to say something that would anger the peacekeeper even further.

"Who let them in?" Borleek demanded with fresh outrage.

"The magister sent for them," Juss answered defensively.

The peacekeeper goggled incredulously. "And you obeyed her?"

"Where is my patient?" snapped Mistress Kafseet, sweeping through the rank of armed men as if they were not there. The curomancer was a thin and angular woman, her raven hair plaited into a tight crown. Pearl earrings stood out starkly against the near-blackness of her skin.

"Here," Shenza answered. Despite her brusque manner, Shenza knew Kafseet Ikarys of Hei as both kind and competent, an excellent enchanter.

"Then get out of my way." Beckoning her assistant, a young man whose eyes rolled nervously at the air of tension, Kafseet moved forward purposefully. Even Borleek grudgingly stepped aside from her commanding air. Shenza also cleared the gate, bending to gather her travel case. She left her light where it lay, however.

Kafseet made a disgusted noise when she saw the prisoner's condition. Whirling on Borleek, she stabbed a narrow finger at him. "I suppose this is your doing?" The scathing words took in all of the peace officers. They shuffled restlessly.

Recovering himself, Borleek harshly countered, "And what if it is? I'll take the responsibility. It's just the start of what he's in for, anyway."

Behind her, Shenza heard a wretched wail from Byben. The younger curomancer moved quickly to comfort him.

"You're getting a bit ahead of justice, aren't you?" Kafseet queried irritably. He was two steps ahead, Shenza thought to herself. There was first supposed to be a verdict from her, as magister, and a sentence from the first lord. Peacekeepers were only supposed to carry out the assigned penalties, never to decide what the punishment should be. By permitting his men to beat the prisoner, Borleek had usurped both forms of trial.

"Like that matters," the big man scoffed.

Kafseet's gaze turned truly venomous. "Just get out," she answered furiously. "This is a sickroom. All of you—out!"

The men looked to Borleek, then among themselves, and slowly began to retreat toward the stairs. Their commander bristled, but stood impotent.

"Just a moment." Much as she hated to do it, Shenza had to antagonize them some more. "I agree with Peacekeeper Borleek that this area should be restricted." The Chief glared at her suspiciously. His countenance darkened further as she continued, "For the prisoner's protection, I order that no one shall enter without either myself or Curomancer Kafseet's permission and presence. Further, the prisoner is to be treated with respect as due his age."

"What?"

Shenza ignored Borleek for the moment. "He is to be provided with clean clothing, bedding, and decent food as prescribed by Mistress Kafseet. You will see to his comfort in all ways. Also, Mistress," she turned slightly to face Kafseet, who watched with amusement as Borleek's face contorted, "he has a dependence on alcohol. He may have only as much drink as you deem needful for his health."

"Drink!"

"Alcohol?" Kafseet, too, caught her up sharply.

"Yes."

"Then he can't..." the older woman stopped, giving Shenza a long stare.

"Please notify me as soon as the prisoner can speak with me," Shenza said, hoping that Kafseet would let it rest. Borleek was in no mood for a declaration of Byben's innocence.

"Fine," the healer mage agreed, nodding impatiently. Turning to Borleek, she snapped, "Now would you all please leave so my student can cleanse this room?"

"Yes, please." Shenza left the cell, gesturing for the officers to go before her. Reluctantly, they turned to obey.

"Don't think that I'm going to just put up with this," Borleek growled at her. Somehow, his taut, serious tone alarmed her more than his shouting had.

"I am the magister in this proceeding," she answered firmly. "If you object..."

"Of course, I do!" He reverted to shouting. "I'm going to talk to Laraquies about this, and..."

"You are free to do so," she replied, thinking that she knew what her master would say. "Until then, please do as I ask. I would hate to tell the next first lord that you did not cooperate in the investigation of his brother's death."

Rage distorted his face. Gritting his teeth, he hissed, "You little... You wouldn't dare."

"I hope I will not have to," she answered pleasantly, actually enjoying the sense that she had won a point from him.

"When the first lord gets here, I'll tell him of your incompetence! You won't even be an apprentice magister!" He thundered, exploding with rage.

"Sun and sea—would you both get out of here?" Kafseet's voice cracked like a whip. Each of them jumped.

With an incoherent snarl, Borleek stormed up the stairs and out of the prison. Shenza followed stiffly, slowly. Behind her, the curomancer's voice sounded briskly.

"All right, Satta, we've a lot to do. Let's get started."

~

When Shenza emerged from the prison into the humid interior of the ward, she found Juss waiting for her. Though this was far preferable to Peacekeeper Borleek waiting for her, she passed him without stopping. After a moment's hesitation, he jogged after her.

The sky outside was dark and the wind was gusting hard, tossing tree limbs and warning that the heavens were serious about their building storm. Shenza looked upward, seeking news in the moons' progress. The turbulent clouds blocked her view, save, she fancied, for a blood-red wash that hinted of Inkesh's enduring power.

Juss caught up with her at the bottom of the outer steps. "He can't do that, can he?" the peace officer asked, lowering his voice.

"Do what?" Shenza asked, distracted from her fruitless probing.

"Dismiss you. Can he do that?"

"No. He has already gone too far past his authority." With reluctant honesty, she added, "The first lord could replace me, however." His expression of dismay afforded her some comfort. "I must ask you a favor, Juss."

"What is it?"

"Can you find out which of the officers arrested Byben?"

"Well..." He faltered visibly.

"As you know, it is the peacekeeper's duty to administer punishments as assigned by the first lord. To treat a captive so severely on the mere presumption of guilt is a serious breach of discipline."

"That's true, Magister, but..."

Shenza sighed. "Never mind. I will not ask you to betray your comrades."

There was an awkward silence. "It's not that," he reluctantly answered. "But no one will want to talk about it, now. The chief would... Well..."

"I understand." Shenza kept her voice level to hide her disappointment. She felt very tired after the emotionally charged meeting with Byben and Borleek. "Go home, Juss. I will do no more today."

"Don't take it that way." His hand fell on her shoulder, startling her. "Look, it's about to start raining, and the market is going to close. Do you want to come with me for dinner? My wife won't mind."

Shenza hesitated, only then realizing she had no idea where she was going to spend the evening. She didn't want to see Master Laraquies at the moment. Still, she shook her head slowly. "That is kind, but I think it might cause you problems. Chief Borleek is already angry, and I would not want his anger to extend to you as well."

He made a face as she spoke. "It probably already does."

"You may be right. But more, there could be the suggestion of impropriety. That would not help either of us. No, I must decline," she decided firmly. "But I thank you."

So saying, she moved away from him, walking back toward the marketplace.

"I'll see you tomorrow," he called after her, hopefully.

Shenza could not answer that, for in truth she had no idea what to do next. How could she have planned for this situation? Her sandals carried her back to the boughs of the great fig tree, and she took shelter there momentarily. Her mask came away in her hand, gleaming amber in the dusk beneath the leaves. She stared at it, amazed that so great a burden should weigh so little.

Earlier in the day, she had wondered whether magic could make an old man young again. Clearly, there was little need to worry about that. Byben was no sorcerer. No one who drank so much could possibly be. Yet, if she could not demonstrate his innocence beyond all doubt, he might still be sacrificed at the first lord's funeral. Shenza felt anger stir in her heart again. What a sad end for an elder's life—a slave to drink, alone, poor, and victimized by someone who treated a miserable old man as a pawn.

Once again, Lord Anges' ruined visage passed before her eyes, and then Byben's, equally ravaged. Shenza shook her head to dispel the gruesome pair of images. She now knew that First Lord Anges was not the only victim. He and Byben both deserved justice, and she intended to deliver it.

But this still left the pressing question: who was the true murderer? Since the revenge motive assigned to Byben could be presumed as false as the accusation against him, why? Magister Laraquies would know what to do, of course. But it was he who had abandoned the question to her. (Was that only this morning? It seemed like days ago.) She was not ready to ask for his help yet. In any event, she thought he would expect her to try harder than this before giving up.

Still, her head felt heavy with weariness. The first rain drops would soon darken the pavement. Truly, there was no more she could do this day. Better to rest and hope her dreams would bring inspiration. Yet she was determined not to creep back to the roof of her sly old master, not while she still had family here in Chalsett-port.

Shenza had not been home for a visit for several weeks, not since beginning the final work on her mask. Today, she decided, was a very good time. Placing the mask back in its case, she set off toward the market. She would have to hurry, or there would be no gift she could bring her mother.

Chapter Six
~ Words in the Rain ~

The evening rain was falling as Shenza left the marketplace. Bare-faced, free of her mask, she at least did not feel quite so stared-at. She discovered far late that she was not wearing a head cloth; so much for preparedness. Not liking the feel of the cool droplets trickling down her scalp, she lifted the long end of her robe and with it improvised a loose turban. It was not the finest style, she reflected wryly, but it would suffice.

With the rain that signaled the close of business, the merchants were well occupied in taking down their displays. Some more frantically cried their wares, while others, either satisfied with the day's sales or giving up on them, merely glanced at Shenza in passing. A single enchantress with a basket of fruit was of little remark.

The sweet, dried dates were a peace offering. She had been a neglectful daughter during the crafting of her mask. Shenza wanted to buy dried fishes from Nakuri, but the booth was deserted when she returned there. Still, the fact that there was a gift was more important than its contents. Or so Shenza hoped. Grandmother could be unforgiving when she felt she had been slighted.

Back up the central stair she climbed, stepping carefully to avoid the many puddles. Looking upward, she could see the clouds, heavy with moisture, brushing low over the hilltop where the palace stood. With the steady rain falling, it nearly seemed that the sky was mourning, too. The treetops were in constant motion about peaked roofs, and the vapors seemed to swirl over the palace in a gradual rotation.

Shenza paused, feeling the raindrops chill her shoulders. It was unusual for the clouds to come so low. Likewise, she now recalled, the low tide of this afternoon was more than just unusual. It meant something, surely. She felt that she ought to know what it meant.

"Don't borrow trouble, Shenza," she murmured to herself, quoting Magister Laraquies yet again, and firmly turned away from the sight.

Now on the third level, Shenza walked southward into a district cluttered with small dwellings. The shabby little houses, built all of thatch, huddled close as if to give each other courage against the sorrows of the world. And there were many, for no one here had wealth. The young sorceress knew that well, for it was among these puddled lanes—infrequently tended by city workers—that she had dwelt as a child. Side-stepping the pools that grew beneath the steady rain, she chose a slanted way that ducked somewhat behind the gray roof of the peacekeepers' ward. The damp smell of rain mingled with smoke from cook stoves to form an oppressive pall in the air.

Another stair, this one narrow and crooked, led to the terrace above. Emerging at the top, she found herself approaching her mother's gate. A wall of bamboo stakes, shoulder-high, kept out trespassers. Two thicker wooden plinths, leaning slightly askew, formed the entrance. Shenza stopped, lifted a leather mallet from its hook, and tapped it briskly against a hanging metal plate. The resulting clank announced her presence.

Before her a walkway turned out of sight, toward the house. Light and dark cobbles paved it in a mosaic pattern. To either side were lattices, well grown with feather-flower vines whose spun floss now brought the family most of its income. Shaggy walls and eaves loomed beyond, dripping with the rain. A series of stone troughs caught the falling water and channeled it to nourish the thirsty vines.

"Welcome," called a familiar voice, and her younger sister dashed into view. Always in a hurry, that was Chimi. These days, she was looking more like a young woman than a girl. A simple sheath, patterned in red and gold, hugged her softly fleshed form. When she saw who was standing there, her teeth flashed in a smile. It lit her face, like stars in the night.

"Welcome! Come in!" Chimi dashed up to Shenza. The two kissed briefly in greeting.

"You're looking well," Shenza remarked.

"I am," her sister answered cheerfully. "Everyone's great. Oo, dates. My favorite," she commented with appreciation. The younger woman turned in place to call, "Mother! Grandmother!"

"Don't disturb them," Shenza protested.

"Oh, what do you mean," the girl scoffed as she dragged Shenza toward the house. Eagerly, she went on, "Your mask is done, right? Or you wouldn't visit us yet. Can I see it?"

Shenza hesitated. "Perhaps later."

The tardy daughter of the house stepped gratefully from the rain-wet garden onto a low deck beneath rush-covered eaves. She paused for a moment to drape her robe properly over her shoulder again.

This was not the cramped hovel of her youth. As her brother grew old enough to work and bring in money, the family had been able to move into these larger quarters. Though the dwelling was old, Shenza's spellcraft helped preserve the structure and kept vermin at bay. There was even a view of the Jewel Sea, its shining face dulled to matte by the falling rain. Little room was spared in the yard for anything but the vines. Only a very small fountain, its basin carved like a fishing vessel, caught the raindrops and tipped them into the irrigation system. A few more steps brought them around to the west side of the house, where a stretch of wall stood open to the garden. Within, the family sat on sturdy matts of woven reeds. On a table between them were mounds of silvery, raw floss to spin into thread. Baskets nearby held empty pods, from which the silk had been stripped. A mound of seeds, foundation of the next crop, glinted darkly in a separate bowl.

"Look who's here!" cried Chimi. Everyone looked up.

"Hello, sister." Sachakeen waved, and a tarnished brass armlet gleamed in the lamp-light. At nineteen, her 'little brother' was now taller than she, with wiry muscles over a sturdy frame. He had grown his hair a bit longer than she recalled, but still had an honest face, like herself and their mother.

"Shenza!" Giliatt Pallele of Tresmeer leapt to her feet and rushed to embrace her eldest child. "Welcome home!"

Shenza had never known her mother not to look tired. Years of supporting the family had lined her brown face prematurely. Her sheath and outer robe were thin and faded and both her daughters' garments were visibly newer than her own. More, there were shadows in her dark eyes, a tension that seemed never to lift. And yet she had never tried to hold her daughter back, even when her training meant long years away from home.

Her embrace was firm as ever, now. Shenza warmly kissed her cheek.

"I'm glad to be back. Here, mother, I've brought a gift for everyone."

"You don't have to do that." But the protest was merely a formality. Giliatt accepted the basket gratefully.

"But I want to," Shenza insisted.

"If you don't want them, I do," added Sachakeen with a smirk.

Chimi snorted back, "She didn't say that."

"I'll just wash these and bring them back."

"No, let me," the youngest offered, whisking the basket away before their mother could react. "You sit down and talk. Shenza's graduated, you know." Her voice retreated as she walked into adjoining kitchen.

Giliatt gasped with pleasure. "Did you? That's wonderful!"

With an inner start, her daughter realized that she felt little pleasure in the accomplishment. The day's events distracted her from it. She smiled anyway. "Yes. I can hardly believe it myself."

Her mother's eyes filled with tears. "I'm so proud of you."

The fifth person, Shenza's grandmother, had scarcely glanced up when she entered and returned to her spinning without a word. A soft humphing sound now came from that direction. When Shenza glanced her way, the old woman was hunched over her work. Ebony eyes glinted between folds of bronze skin. Black and silver hair was caught in a topknot like Giliatt's, but much tighter.

Myri Shingool of Tresmeer was her father's mother and the sole elder of the household. She seemed to feel this entitled her to badger and boss anyone younger than herself. The old woman had always been stern, as Shenza recalled, but in the early days she had at least spared a bit of kindness for her grandchildren. Since her son was gone, taken into the sea's jealous embrace, she sank more and more into her bitterness.

"Well, let's sit down, then." Giliatt tried to smooth the awkwardness between them. She dabbed at her eyes with the trailing end of her mantle, and the two women seated themselves beside the table. Shenza gladly laid aside her travel case.

Since there was no sense putting off the inevitable, she turned toward her grandmother and offered a half-bow. "You're looking well, Grandmother," she said neutrally. She had long ago given up on winning the elder's approval, but there was no reason to be impolite, either. "Does your back still trouble you?"

"It does. It does, and that curomancer can't do a thing," the old woman grumbled. She glanced at Shenza. The younger woman felt herself redden slightly. Master Laraquies had recommended Curomancer Gessaar especially.

"I'm sorry to hear that," she said quietly. Like her stolid mother, she was unable to be rude even when provoked. After all, this was still her ancestor. She owed a debt for her life—even if Grandmother demanded more than the just measure of obedience.

Sachakeen put down his spindle and leaned both elbows on the table. "So, it's true," he remarked, glancing sidelong at their grandmother. Though he was only a little younger than Shenza, he was starting to wear the same tired expression as their mother, these days. "You're a celebrity. We didn't know whether to believe it when Chimi came back from the market with all those tales."

Shenza bit her lip momentarily. She had hoped, perhaps selfishly, to have a little time away from her problems. But their curiosity was only natural, after all. She nodded slightly, resigned. "Yes."

"Was the first lord really burned alive?" Giliatt asked with quiet but genuine concern.

"Yes. It was..." Shenza hesitated, and finished with an understatement, "very bad."

All three stared at her, even Grandmother forgetting her grievances for a moment. Chimi padded barefoot into the silence.

"And you're really in charge of the investigation?" she asked cheerily. "That's exciting!"

'Exciting' was not the word Shenza would have chosen. She quickly ate a date.

"What's going to happen?" Giliatt asked softly.

An excellent question. "I am going to find out who is responsible," Shenza answered with more assurance than she felt.

Chimi plopped down beside her and helped herself to the dates. Beside her brilliant garb, Shenza thought, her own purple looked drab as raven's feathers. "I thought they caught him already. They sure took someone away!"

"I know." That was another unpleasant memory.

"Don't you think he did it?" Chimi pressed, her eyes wide with amazement.

Everyone thought they knew her job, Shenza thought irritably. "It isn't simply whether I believe it," she explained with forced patience. "I must be able to prove it to the first lord."

"So, are you not supposed to talk about this, or something?" Sachakeen frowned as he took a date from the basket. "You're sure not telling us much."

"It would be best if I did not." Especially since Chimi was sure to repeat whatever she said. "It is inappropriate to speculate."

"Then how long will the port stay closed?" he asked.

"Why does that matter to you?" muttered Grandmother. Sachakeen bristled. Myri had wanted him to become a fisherman, like his father and grandfather and ancestors before him. She had even arranged an apprenticeship, but Sachakeen refused. He wanted to work on land—and live longer.

Giliatt quickly put in, "We still have products to move to market, Mother. Remember, Lann may have found a new customer on Sardony."

Her reasonable tone did not sooth either of them. Lann was another difficult subject. A dyer, he had been buying their floss for years, but Shenza had long suspected it was more than a business relationship between him and Giliatt. She and Sachakeen privately agreed that he probably wanted to marry her. They liked the man, but their elder would not give permission. Grandmother humphed again, low in her throat, and Sachakeen gave her a bitter, sidelong glance. He was not yet old enough to defend his mother's interests as an adult.

Softly, Shenza said, "I will do my best to solve the murder quickly."

"Of course you will," Chimi declared, oblivious to the tension in the room. Shenza often wondered if she was truly unaware of the family's disagreements, or simply didn't think they were important. After all, Grandmother found no fault with her. Yet.

"I don't mean it like that," her brother hastily added. "There are many things we can do here while we wait."

Giliatt nodded to him approvingly. "We were a little behind on the spinning anyway."

Their brave words only made Shenza more aware that her order to close the port was having unintended consequences. 'You'll ruin the economy,' Borleek had said. And here was her own family, their livelihood disrupted by her decision. She hoped, silently but fervently, that the bullying peacekeeper would somehow prove wrong.

Sachakeen was saying, "I could go with Thell to cut bamboo on the dawn side of the island and fix the fence, Mother."

Chimi was smirking again. "Cut bamboo? You just want to see his sister Teesa. You like her, don't you?" Her black eyes gleamed with merriment.

"No! I mean..." their brother faltered, then recovered. Through his teeth, he said, "I just want to get some chores done while I have the chance. Don't go making this stuff up."

"Hmph," said Grandmother knowingly.

Shenza kept her mouth shut. She glanced curiously at Giliatt, and found her mother smiling indulgently. Well, this was an interesting development. Teesa, whoever she was, must be a true paragon if both Giliatt and Myri approved of her.

Thoroughly annoyed, Sachakeen opened his mouth to retort. What came out was a startled cry, as a gust of cold wind and rain came in from the garden. Silvery floss scattered from the table.

"Oops! Look out!" Chimi cried.

There was a momentary scramble as everyone fumbled to recover the fine, pale strands. Shenza gathered a handful of the precious fibers from her lap and placed them back in their basket. The wind continued stirring the air, blowing more raindrops into the room.

"Let's lower the shades, Sachakeen," mother directed with crisp, maternal authority. "Chimi, help Mother and me."

"I'll help Sachakeen," Shenza declared, and left the three of them collecting the floss from the floor.

Her brother was already at the open archway, unwinding the string that held up a roll of narrow bamboo slats. As he quickly released the tension the door shade uncoiled, forming a barrier against the weather. Side ties secured it against the blowing wind. Shenza, unwinding the shade next to his, gazed out into the garden for a moment. Falling water chattered on all sides, for it was still raining hard. The amber rays of sunset, battling between turbulent clouds, gave the evening a strange luminescence.

The evening shower was lasting longer than expected. Once again, Shenza wondered if something, somehow, had turned the weather awry.

"Hurry up with that," Sachakeen advised, startling her.

"I'm sorry," she murmured. The twine ran through her fingers and the shade fell, blocking the dusk-lit yard from view.

"I'll start work on dinner, Mother, if you'd like," Chimi's voice offered behind them.

"She needs the practice," muttered Sachakeen sourly as they tied down the sides.

"I heard that!"

Shenza smiled. "I'll help, too."

Giliatt, kneeling near the basket of floss, looked up. Hope sprang to life in her eyes. "Will you be staying for supper?"

"If I may. I don't want to cause trouble," she answered. An extra mouth to feed could be a problem at a time like this.

"It's no trouble," her mother declared happily.

"Trouble?" retorted Chimi in the same breath. "It'll be fun!"

And it was fun. The two young women chopped vegetables together in the kitchen, which occupied the center of the house. A waist-high wall separated it from the work room before it and the sleeping rooms behind. A smooth counter extended slightly into the kitchen. Beneath it were baskets not unlike those in Byben's stall, sewn with runes to preserve the contents from spoilage. In the center of the room was a low stove with a soot-stained chimney rising toward a smoke-hole in the roof above. The flat metal stove top was perfect either for warming ceramic pots or for cooking food directly.

Chimi did most of the talking, while Shenza tried to forget her worries by paying close attention. The younger woman seemed to know all about the neighbors' doings, and even something of the larger events of the town. Chimi had always been the most social of the three children. No more or less attractive, it was true, but she was lively and that gave her charm. She also had that trace of plumpness that men found alluring. Shenza and Sachakeen both favored their responsible, hard-working mother. At times, the younger child baffled them. Where did she get such energy? From their father, perhaps. Though, considering Myri's bitterness, it was hard to credit the blood tie.

Glancing toward her grandmother, Shenza saw her stealthily take a date from the basket that still rested on the table. She smiled to herself. Perhaps the relationship was not so impossible to imagine.

On the other hand, Chimi had no real ambition. She was already sixteen. Soon she would be content to marry and live through her children, while Sachakeen braved their elder's disapproval to choose his own path. And Shenza, likewise, reached for something higher. Or so she hoped.

Supper was a spicy broth with vegetables and spiral noodles, brown bread and watered lime juice. Contrary to Sachakeen's prediction, Chimi did not need cooking practice. She had a deft hand with the red pepper, in Shenza's opinion. The room fell silent as the family filled their stomachs. In the quiet, the rain finally stopped and the wind's whistle through the door shades gradually subsided.

Afterward Giliatt tapped a small keg of nut beer. Shenza reluctantly declined the mildly alcoholic brew, but she did find a few leaves of elitherium and peppermint to brew a tonic tea. She still felt very tired after all that had happened. Or perhaps it was merely the amount of soup she had eaten. A restorative seemed not amiss, in any event.

Muffling a mournful sigh, Shenza took her steaming cup to the porch and raised it to her lips. Behind her, her sister and brother took up their squabbling again. It was quieter in the shadowed garden, where the rows of vines seemed to whisper secrets to each other. From hidden places, crickets and frogs sang their songs to the night. Fireflies twinkled among the sheltering leaves. The falling rain had dissolved the clouds from the heavens, revealing a sky fabulous with stars. House-lamps of the dead, for it was there that the countless spirits ascended. Or so it was told.

Colored shadows cris-crossed the yard in shifting layers, Prenuse's green light mingled with the pale gold of Quaiss's rays, and ruddy Inkesh blanketed both of them where he would. Shenza stepped a little away from the house. Between the trellises, she could better see the moons.

She did not need to look for Inkesh. It still loomed heavy above the hill behind her. Quaiss and Prenuse, both faster-moving, had drifted significantly from their previous positions. The one she sought was Meor, the purple moon governing enchantments. Its fainter light was hard to see. When she finally found it, she frowned in concern. Rounding off a little from full, the sorcerer's moon hung very close to Inkesh, so near she could hardly see it. Within two days or less, if she guessed the orbit right, Meor would disappear completely... behind Inkesh.

In fact, there was a strong likelihood that *all* of the other moons might soon vanish behind the red giant. This was not unusual in itself, for the moons frequently crossed each other in various combinations. The symbolism, though, was disturbing. For Inkesh to completely block all other influences... At a time like this...

A nearby sound startled her, made her turn. It was a dry rustle, like the sound of wind-blown leaves and yet nothing like it.

Her restless gaze swept the shadows, finding nothing to cause such a noise. Lecturing herself inwardly for becoming so tense, the young sorceress began to step back toward the house and stopped, paralyzed.

A dark shape detached itself from the shadows before her. It was low, long, with round, glinting eyes and a forked tongue feeling the way before it. The shades of moonlight made its mottled scales seem to shuffle and disorder themselves. Instinctively she stepped back, and the creature halted, seeming to size her up.

A bamboo viper! Shenza knew the serpents well. They dwelt among dense thickets where she and Master Laraquies tried to avoid them on expeditions to gather arcane provisions. She had never seen one in the city before. They preferred wild land.

And yet, here it was.

She stepped back, hoping to avoid the venomed fangs. The serpent slid forward, maintaining the distance between them. The night-singing insects had fallen silent, and the air was unnaturally cool. Shenza stared down at the menacing reptile. Her family's bickering voices seemed to come from a very great distance, and the latticed vines loomed above her, blocking the light from the house. Only the softly shaded layers of moonlight defined the walkway, the serpent. She smelled a heavy fragrance that was not feather-flower.

Again she retreated, and again it followed. Acting on a guess, then, Shenza crossed both hands over her breast. She bowed very low, and slowly. If this was a normal snake she was endangering herself by its poison. But if, as she suspected, it was not, then her peril was already far greater.

"Well," said a voice, cool and disdainful. "Perhaps you are not completely without skill."

Shenza looked up sharply into the face of a... man? No, a spirit! Though she had never seen one before, she knew instantly what it must be. It was hard to say whether it was truly male or female, though masculine seemed to predominate. Shadows merely hinted at flesh, dappled as the serpent's had been. Hair the color of night curled like dark foam over sculpted shoulders. Its garb was of gauzy silk, utterly black. But the eyes... even in the dimness, she could see their eerie, impossible green.

"Eleshi," she thought. *"He is an earth spirit."*

Shenza was speechless before his alien beauty. She felt weak, cold, terrified. When she found her tongue, her voice sounded harsh as a gull's.

"Lord of the Boughs, this is a great honor."

"Yes," the spirit agreed with a casual arrogance that stung her like nettles.

The resonant voice made her pulse roar. "I am not worthy."

"I know." It sounded amused, now. Or perhaps not, for the next thing it said was, "Now be quiet and heed me."

Shenza did not dare to say a word.

"One of your men has 'died.'" It spoke the word *die* as if it were strange, alien. "This man shared in our blood. He held power through our will. But his life has been ended before its natural term. Do you know what this means?"

It seemed wisest not to speak. Shenza merely shook her head. Her hands, at her sides, trembled.

"It means that you have no right to be here." A graceful gesture took in all of Chalsett-port—the folk, their dwellings and boats. "According to the ancient agreement, there will always be one who shares in our blood, who speaks for our interests and assures us our due. What do you think will happen now that the pact has been violated?" It seemed more a threat than a question.

Shenza recalled the abnormally low tide, the unseasonable violent rain, and thought she had a good idea what might happen. She had a very little time, she felt, to bargain for thousands of lives.

"All of us are very shocked, great one," she said when it was clear the spirit was awaiting her response. The words seemed pathetically weak and awkward. "I can't tell you how seriously we regard this."

"You had best regard it seriously."

There was another clumsy pause, but Shenza would never dare to interrupt. The spirits were famed for their touchy dispositions.

"The first lord had a brother, Lord of the Boughs," Shenza faltered. "Word has been sent to him. He will soon return to take his brother's place as your representative."

"We know that. Our kindred of the sky and sea have lent their speed to the message. But what of this human who has dared spill our blood?"

"I will do all in my power to find that person," she answered fervently. "My efforts have not yet begun."

"And our vengeance?" The spirit pressed, accepting no mere words.

It was beyond Shenza's power to endure his burning pale gaze any longer. She crossed her hands and bowed again. "I am not permitted to decide what will happen to that person. The judgement of criminals falls to the first lord. As he is your voice to us, it may be that his justice will include your retribution as well."

"You had best hope so. We can't tell you creatures apart. Revenge may fall upon all of you." The bland, warning voice came suddenly fainter. "And you had best make speed. I wonder if you little crawling things can conceive how tedious it is to be held to one place, one time. But until this is finished, I am bound. Do not keep me so over-long."

Shenza straightened, feeling bile at the back of her throat. Abruptly as it had appeared, the Eleshi was gone. Her knees sagged with weakness. The vines thrashed as she clung to the trellis for support. Sweat made her body sticky, and yet her hands felt terribly cold.

Mere book-learning was no preparation for the power, the presence of the Eleshi. Indeed, there was very little written of these supernatural spirits. So little was even known. They were like the moons—constantly argued over without proof or result.

It was known that the spirits were of three kinds. Eleshi dwelt in the green of the earth, Elitheri ruled the open sky, and the Eleshouri domain was in the deep sea. Ever present, yet invisible, they dwelt in their separate realms and seldom crossed into human lands. It was Eleshi, like this one, who most often dealt with humans, for their domain was most like the mortal earth. Yet even they were tolerant only when approached on their own terms, with the proper rituals and offerings. Their pride must be constantly assuaged, and there was always the risk of encountering some cruel whim.

Most folk knew them only as 'spirits,' a word without parallel in solid experience. If they thought of the spirits at all it was as mere fable, or as the invention of sorcerers to end unwanted questions. Yet, by custom, there were places humans did not go, both on earth and sea. Their places. If fools ventured there without permission, they might return terribly changed, or not return at all. Most people did not take these legends seriously. Shenza now knew better. Never again would she doubt the spirits' power, or that they must be rendered whatever ceremony they desired.

From very near came a voice, clear and light, oblivious. Chimi. "Sister? What are you doing out there?"

She did not know how to answer.

~

Laraquies Catteel of Nelnoor stared at the bowl of food that sat forlorn on the low mahogany table. Millet with smoked fish and vegetables, fresh grapes, all lay cold and untasted. The rain was over, and it was well past sunset. Where could Shenza be?

After the peacekeeper's courtesy call, with his ranting and accusations, the old man had been looking forward to hearing what had really happened. His student, he knew, would never try to paint the truth in her own favor. And, much as Borleek might deserve an occasional curb to his unrestrained power, Laraquies had to admit that he was a little concerned. It did Shenza no good to tread on toes. She would need the peacekeepers' cooperation—if not now, then on later occasions.

More, he wanted to know if she was aware of all the supernatural activity. Laraquies himself had never been particularly gifted in treating with the spirit realm, but it did not take a great deal of skill to sense the astral disturbance that churned above the island city. As yet, it seemed unfocused, but for how long would that continue?

And still Shenza did not return. Nor would she, it seemed. Laraquies was beginning to think he had out-smarted himself. He hadn't realized she was this angry, or this stubborn. She still should eat, he thought with concern. She needed to recover from the ordeal of creating her mask.

Well, he told himself as he rose stiffly, stubbornness could be both good and bad. It was too soon for him to start wondering about her fitness for duty, especially if Borleek and his cronies already were. He would have to have faith in his student. After all—he smiled to himself wryly—he was asking everyone else to do the same.

Laraquies took the untouched food to the refuse bin beside the house and returned the empty bowl to the kitchen. After giving it a brief scrubbing with a rough hemp pad, he went to his hammock. Tomorrow would tell him more.

"Light, out."

All about the house, the lamps sputtered and went dark.

Chapter Seven
~ Flesh-Eating Ants ~

Old Byben floated in repose scant inches above the floor of the jail below the peacekeepers' ward. He was held aloft by a cocoon of pale green rays which emanated from four lamps carved with runes. These stood on the floor near his head, feet, and each hand. The old man's white hair had been washed free of blood. No bruises now showed on his body. He had been given a kilt and mantle, plain brown. The garments' edges trailed onto the floor. This was now so clean that it shone, reflecting the magical radiance.

At rest, he had a curious kind of dignity, more than Shenza expected to see when he awoke. After the restless night she had spent, the sorceress envied his healing slumber. Strangely, it was the gentle voice of Laraquies' garden brook that she missed. She had been awake half the night, it seemed, listening for it.

"He should revive by tomorrow," Juss told Shenza. He had been waiting when she arrived, a few minutes ago. "That's what they said."

By this he meant the curomancers, for it was they who brought the old man out of his cell and installed these wards. Normally, it would have been expensive treatment, far beyond his means to afford. And, if Shenza had anything to say about it, he would not pay a sekh for the care. Borleek should have that pleasure, since his men had inflicted the injuries in the first place.

Juss seemed to feel an apology was required, for he went on, "He'll be totally well, then. So Mistress Kafseet said."

"If that is the case, I must wait," Shenza answered, keeping her voice even to conceal her satisfaction. Contrary to what the peace officer seemed to assume, this was good news. The triumph she felt at facing down Peacekeeper Borleek had evaporated like the morning dew when the spirit confronted her. This delay gave her time to work, and that she badly needed.

"Oh, and there's something else. Something wrong with the sea."

"What do you mean?" Shenza turned to gaze up at him.

"The tide went out yesterday afternoon, hours before it was supposed to," Juss said.

"Yes, I remember," Shenza said. An image of sea wrack and stranded ships came into her mind.

"Well, it never came back in, I heard. They were all talking about it on the docks this morning. Nobody knows what to think." Juss shrugged, eyeing her. "I thought it might mean something to you, that's all."

It certainly did. But Shenza was not going to speak of such things here, where unfriendly ears might be listening. Softly, she said, "Come, let us go."

Ignoring the suspicious glances of the two guards at the top of the stairs, Juss and Shenza left the ward. On the steps outside, Shenza pleasantly asked, "Did the peacekeeper speak with you this morning?"

"Do you need to ask?" His broad features twisted at the memory. "I told him I was just trying to do my best yesterday, and that it was hard to know what to do without having any specific orders. And," he went on more quietly, "I told him we have to have someone near the case who you can work with. I think I convinced him, but he will probably expect reports from me. I hope you don't mind."

At the foot of the white marble steps, Shenza stopped and said bluntly, "There are details of this matter that cannot be repeated. Can I trust you?"

"Yeah." He shuffled awkwardly, hurrying on, "It made me think, seeing the old man beat up like that. That isn't what I wanted to be a peacekeeper for. Arlais agrees with me." Arlais must be his wife, Shenza guessed. Juss was nodding his head firmly. "Yes, Magister. You can trust me. And don't worry about the Chief."

"I am glad to know. And you do not need to be concerned about the length of Byben's treatment. If he is safe for another day, that is one less worry for me." Shenza hesitated, knowing that she really should be telling Magister Laraquies about her twilight visitor, not Juss. Defiantly, she began, "You see, I have had an interesting discussion as well."

"With who?"

Sensing something, Shenza ignored his question and pivoted sharply.

Standing nearby was an older man with thinning hair that receded from strikingly thick, black brows. Beneath their shadow his eyes were keen. The man appeared at first to be listening to them, but once she turned toward him he stepped forward confidently. Jewels gleamed about his neck and wrists, and his purple robe was studded with copper beads, which winked at her. A neatly knotted turban covered his balding head.

"Magister Shenza," he began. A smooth smile nearly erased the lines that crossed his forehead and circled his eyes.

Juss stepped up beside Shenza with unexpected aggression. "Who are you?" he demanded of the newcomer.

The man's smile did not waver, though something in his manner made it clear he was being magnanimous by tolerating the interruption. "Nurune Sengool of Sengool," he answered in a deep, cultivated voice, as if his mere name ought to be introduction enough.

Juss looked to Shenza, brows raised in question. She quickly stepped into the gap. "I remember," the young sorceress replied. She had met Master Nurune before, though at that time he had not deigned to speak with her, a mere apprentice magister.

Seeming satisfied, Juss stepped back slightly to stand behind her right shoulder, arms folded.

"You're looking well, Master Nurune," she commented neutrally.

"Thank you. And may I congratulate you on your elevation, Magister Shenza." He smiled with every appearance of sincerity.

"Thank you," she answered, awkwardly aware that she was repeating what he had just said. After his polished delivery, she felt like an ungraceful child.

Nurune of Sengool controlled a large coven including two partners, five junior enchanters, and nearly twenty apprentices. How a student could learn anything of value with so little personal instruction was unclear to Shenza. Nevertheless, the coven was by far the largest in Chalsett-port, and indeed one of the largest in all the Jewel Sea. Ostensibly, they sold protective services such as spells to safeguard merchandise against loss at sea. So many of their clients enjoyed extraordinary prosperity, however, that she was privately skeptical about exactly what kind of spells the enchanters were performing.

Still, their influence was extensive, and Nurune was not afraid to use it. He, much more than his two partners, moved in high circles. He was an influential vizier, and also a frequent guest of the first lord. The graven lines beneath his eyes were marks of jaded living, and the belly half-hidden under his robes hinted that he did not often perform his own spells any longer.

"And how does your business go?" she inquired politely.

"Very well, Magister." Nurune seemed aware of her uncertainty. The smile on his lips widened slightly. "It is kind of you to ask. And, since you mention it, there is one small favor, if I might impose on you..?"

Juss shifted restless in place, but Shenza had been expecting something like this. She gestured toward the spreading fig tree in the center of the market. It was still early in the day, but the sun was already bright in a cloudless sky. "I believe that I have a moment. Will you sit with me?"

"It would be my honor."

Shenza glanced up at Juss. "If you will assure that no one overhears?"

He glanced significantly at Nurune, who affected not to notice. "Yes, Magister."

The two sorcerers strolled casually toward the shade of the great tree. Juss strode ahead and pulled one of the benches slightly back from the neighboring row. He waited behind it, looking particularly burly with his arms folded across his chest.

"Actually, I am glad you came to see me," Shenza informed her guest as they sat together. "I wanted to ask you some questions, and I didn't know if you would be free."

The sorcerer nodded, his black eyes reflecting cautious interest. "Of course, Magister. I know how difficult your job must be, and now more than ever. I will do whatever I can, as is my duty." Nurune's tone was very sympathetic, almost fatherly. It made her nervous.

"But please, tell me your business." Shenza laid her travel case on her knees and silently gave the command to open it. While he spoke, she drew out a scroll and stylus and arranged them across her lap.

"I realize you must be very busy with your investigation, so perhaps this will aid both of us at once." He smiled as if conferring a favor upon her. "I would like permission to have one of my assistants speak with the spirit of First Lord Anges. Vesswan Sanguri of Zeell. Perhaps you have heard her name."

Shenza frowned beneath her mask. She had; the woman was a necromancer, a medium who communicated messages between the living and the dead. They were trained to summon deceased spirits, whether willing or not. It smacked of heresy, to Shenza's mind.

"For what purpose?" she carefully asked.

"I am acting on behalf of my niece, Lady Innoshyra, who is also my client," he assured her soothingly. "I thought too highly of my Lord to disturb his rest at such a distressing time, but Innoshyra is desperate to have an answer." With a slight stress on the word 'desperate' he seemed to seek sympathy for the grieving lady.

Remembering the woman's overdone mourning, and the servants' reaction to it, Shenza could not quite keep the coolness from her tone. "Go on."

Nurune leaned toward her, confiding. "Lord Anges and Lady Innoshyra were very close. She is distraught at his terrible fate. As you know, my Lord had many romantic interests. Their love was never consummated as she so dearly wished. All she desires now is to speak with him, to assure him that her feelings have not changed. Even though he has passed from life, she still yearns for their union. Her grief and devotion are so great." His rich voice trembled with tenderness and awe at a love that death itself could not sever.

It was almost a kind of hypnotic spell. Had Nurune tried any magic on Shenza, her mask would have warned and defended her. Yet clearly he hoped to evoke her feelings and sway her judgement. Shenza felt rising anger at the blatant ploy.

True, it was not unheard-of that living and dead should be joined in marriage. This was certainly not customary without a previous declaration of intent to wed. Of which there had been none, and Nurune knew that as well as she.

"And the necromancer would convey this to the first lord?" she asked dubiously.

"She has that ability. My Lord's response is his decision, of course. Vesswan is well trained and very experienced. And it would put my niece's mind at ease."

'Peace?' Shenza thought with disgust. More likely, Innoshyra's medium would attempt to compel the ghost's obedience. There had already been one complaint against Vesswan of Zeell for such malfeasance. The matter had been resolved without Master Laraquies' involvement, however, so Shenza knew no details.

Still, the brazen profiteering amazed her. Even in those rare cases when a marriage was celebrated posthumously, it was customary for a period of mourning to be observed, followed by a more conventional wedding to a sibling or some other close relative of the departed.

But that, of course, must be precisely what Innoshyra and her family hoped for.

Nurune's smooth voice interrupted her thoughts, pleading for understanding. "I know it must seem irregular, but these are very unusual circumstances. I assume that I have your permission?"

"No, you do not," she answered crisply.

The sorcerer straightened. The lines on his face deepened visibly.

"Forgive me, but it is impossible for two reasons." Shenza struggled to adopt a more conciliatory tone. "First, the seance would have to take place at the palace, where my Lord lived and his spirit will linger most strongly. But I am still searching for traces of the spell that claimed my Lord's life. If another series of spells were cast on the same site, it would obscure the information I seek."

"That is true," he quickly put in, "but it is not necessary to conjure the spirit at the palace. My Lord often visited the home of my brother, Lord Sengool. Perhaps there..?"

Where Vesswan would have even more control over the outcome.

"No," she repeated firmly. "Even without the investigation, I believe my Lord's family should be the ones to give their consent to raising his spirit. It is true I have a great deal of authority in the conduct of the investigation, but I fear I would overstep myself if I made such a decision."

Nurune placed a hand lightly on her arm. His brows curved upward in the center as he pleaded, "Is there no way I can appeal to you? Innoshyra will be most disappointed when I tell her."

"A messenger has been sent to my Lord's family," Shenza answered with compassion just as false as the other sorcerer's. She wished that he would not touch her. "They will soon arrive, and Lady Innoshyra can make a personal appeal to them. A little more time will not change her feelings, surely."

Nurune knew when to retreat. He bowed his head with forced grace. "I will tell her what you have said." Shenza thought she had not yet heard the last of this issue. To her relief, he lifted his hand from her arm. "Well, I am sorry to have bothered you." He prepared to rise.

"No, it I who must apologize," Shenza said very sincerely. Nurune was still a valuable source of information. "If you have just a little more time, there was something I wanted to ask you."

The magician hesitated, torn between frustration and curiosity.

Shenza said, "As you know, my training has been somewhat specialized. I'm sure that you know much more about the current events in Chalsett-port than I do. I hope I can call on your expertise."

Nurune appeared to realize that he was being flattered, but he chose to accept it and settled back onto the bench. "Of course, Magister," he replied, falling back into his former skilled manner.

"I appreciate it." Lifting her stylus, she cocked it above the cloth on her lap. "Magister Laraquies told me that in addition to being my Lord's vizier you often saw him socially. Is that true?"

"Yes," he answered with amiable arrogance. "I had that privilege."

"And are you familiar with his peers and habitual companions?"

"Naturally." His dark eyes gleamed with greed, not for gold but for information that might be of use to him.

"Had he quarreled with anyone recently? Someone who might have threatened him, or wanted revenge?"

Nurune sighed to himself, and all the lines on his forehead adjusted themselves as he pondered. "No, Magister." Modestly, he continued, "If I may say so, I assisted him with his affairs from time to time. Truthfully, Lord Anges always enjoyed extraordinary luck and seldom required my aid. He often gambled at dice, but there were no debts, so far as I know. He always had the means to pay promptly. To my knowledge, there was no one who did not like him. Even his business rivals, such as Lord Kesquin, personally enjoyed his company."

Shenza was skeptical of that, but noted his comments anyway. A subtle change had come over the man, Shenza was interested to note. His feigned kindliness had fallen away in favor of a more dry, urbane tone with a slight edge. This, she imagined, must be more the way the courtiers spoke among themselves.

"Were there any other business competitors, perhaps someone he had..." she paused over the word 'cheated' and finished, "defeated at some goal?"

"It was true, I suppose, that some must have envied his success. But no one ever threatened him," Nurune repeated.

"Could there have been any ladies who envied his special relationship with Lady Innoshyra." Shenza carefully kept her voice level.

Nurune gazed at her for a moment as if she were stupid. Recovering himself, he gently replied, "Certainly, but then why would they kill him? A love charm would have been more effective." He smiled drily. "Except that I happen to know he always wore an amulet to nullify such enchantments. I made it for him myself."

Shenza had been wondering about that, but she hadn't known how to ask without seeming crass. Now, she simply nodded. "In your opinion, Master Nurune, is there anyone at all with a reason to wish Lord Anges dead? Whether or not you believe the reason was valid."

"I have been thinking about that, Magister, since yesterday," the sorcerer informed her. The lines about his features took on a mournful caste. "He had no enemies. His family is free of feuds or blood-oaths. There simply is no one."

There must have been someone, Shenza thought rebelliously. It was a disappointment not to learn more from such an influential source. "My final group of questions, then. You must have heard that my Lord was burned to death by magic fire. Are you familiar with that enchantment?"

He eyed her warily, almost as if he expected an accusation. "I am familiar with the theory, though I seldom have any call for it in my line of work. But I thought the killer had already been arrested?" he asked.

Shenza did not want to repeat the tale of Byben yet again. Nor did the enchanter need to know the facts. Like Chimi, she suspected, he would be far too likely to repeat them. Yet it galled her to lie. She settled for evasion. "In a case of this magnitude, I would like to investigate every possibility before reaching a conclusion. Is there anyone you consider especially adept with that kind of witchery? Or someone who particularly enjoys magic fire?"

He frowned to indicate his ignorance. "The concept is widely known. Master Choruta would be my suggestion, since he maintains the flames on the low-water beacons. I never let my apprentices use that spell," he added sanctimoniously. "It is far too dangerous."

Choruta—but Shenza had sent him away the day before. She sighed to herself and tried her final hope. "I know it is difficult to judge, but is there any sorcerer you know who seems not to mind using magic to harm others?"

Nurune stared at her momentarily, possibly trying to decide whether she was insulting his coven.

Shenza continued quietly, "Clearly, someone is willing to do so."

The coven master's indignation gave way to sorrow once again. For a moment he seemed to forget his self-serving schemes.

"No one," he said, husky-voiced.

Shenza could not tell if his grief was genuine. Even if it was, she suspected it did not run deep. Controlling her dislike, she laid down her stylus. "I am sorry to take so much of your time."

But his head had already come back up, and the canny gleam was in his eyes. "Not at all, Magister. It is not just my duty but my honor to assist you. If there is anything else I can do, please do not hesitate to call upon me."

A few minutes later, all the courtesies had been spoken. Juss came around the bench and stood beside Shenza to watch the master sorcerer walk away. He muttered something under his breath.

"What?" Shenza asked, distracted.

"I said the flesh-eating ants are starting to gather," he answered darkly. "Him and that Lady Sengool. Each one wants a bite of the corpse. Sorry," he added, seeing Shenza's shoulders hunch in response to the image his words raised in her mind. "I'm glad you sent him on his way."

She closed her travel case firmly. "I should have realized there would be those seeking to benefit by the first lord's death. Do not worry. Magister Laraquies taught me better than to be used for such ends."

"Good," he grunted with satisfaction. "Where now, Magister?"

Before she could reply, another voice called sharply for her attention. "Magister!"

This time it was a man with a thin, frowning face who trotted toward her. He was garbed as a professional messenger, in a loincloth rather than a binding kilt. Over it was a mantle of brilliant blue, the shade worn by palace workers. A matching head cloth was wrapped fashionably aslant over artificially straightened hair. Both robe and head cloth were fastened by matching silver brooches, inlaid with iridescent shell. His skin held the deep bronze tone of one who worked outdoors, but a narrow chest and shoulders were oddly matched to his powerful legs. About his neck a charm hung by a leather thong. Its power glowed in the sight of her mask. It was a simple one, carved bamboo. Shenza could not see the sigils, but she guessed it was a luck charm, or one to attract wealth.

The messenger slowed when he saw he had her attention. He approached them breathing deeply, bowed curtly. The small patch of curly black hair in the center of his chest was beaded with sweat. "Magister," he repeated, clearly annoyed, "I've been looking everywhere for you."

"Show some respect," Juss directed indignantly.

"Do I have business with you?" came the sharp retort.

Juss bristled. "You're about to," he began threateningly.

"Juss," Shenza rebuked him gently. The messenger shot him a mocking look. "What is it you need of me?" she asked. Privately Shenza did not like the fellow any more than Juss did. She remembered seeing him at the palace the day before, just after the murder. He had been sneering then, too.

"Alceme wants you to come to the palace," he said in a grieved tone. "It's Lord Anges. His ghost came back last night. None of us got any sleep. Can you please do something?"

Ghost? Shenza felt her stomach tighten. Did Nurune know about this? But no, he would have used the information to support his request for a seance. Yet the coincidence sat oddly.

At least this gave some reason for the messenger's bad manners. "I will come. And would you please ask Magister Laraquies to join us there?"

The man's sullen expression clearly said he did not want to obey her. Still, he nodded. "Magister Laraquies is to join you at the palace," he repeated sulkily, confirming the message.

"Yes. Thank you."

Without acknowledging her, the messenger whirled and trotted off, disappearing into the marketplace throng. Shenza reminded herself that rudeness from such a meaningless person was really not important, and rose from the bench.

"You shouldn't let people talk to you that way," Juss told her bluntly.

"I cannot simply demand respect," Shenza reasoned. "I must first show that I am worthy."

"You're still a magister," he argued. She didn't know whether to be annoyed by his interference or flattered by his concern. When she silently walked off toward the Curomancers' clinic, he followed doggedly.

"That means people meet me at the worst times in their lives, Juss. I must disagree with them, or ask painful questions, or compel them to do difficult things." Just, she thought silently, as she had compelled Juss, the day before. "It isn't personal."

He contradicted her boldly. "You're being much too generous."

She sighed. "Try to think of it from his perspective. That man had a good job in a very prestigious household. Did you see how nicely he was dressed? But now his employer is dead. He probably doesn't know what the future holds for him."

"And that's your fault? No, listen." Juss strode in front of her and stopped. Shenza stopped, too, to avoid a collision. He jabbed his finger down at her as if she were a wayward apprentice. "You are the voice of the law to us. We don't honor you, we honor it. And nobody is entitled to scorn the law!"

Shenza hadn't thought of it quite that way before. "Yes sir," she said meekly.

He rolled his eyes, but smiled. "You're not listening to me, are you?"

She refused to pull rank the way Nurune did, casually, callously. "I don't have much pride, if that's what you mean. But," she switched topics, hoping to divert him, "I do appreciate your help. It was wrong of Master Nurune to listen when we were talking."

It worked. "He's that big-shot sorcerer, isn't he? I've heard of him."

From the sound of it, he had heard some of the same things Shenza had. She smiled slightly at the description, though Juss couldn't see it. "Nurune probably thought he could take advantage of my inexperience. I doubt he would have tried that with Laraquies. But he was wrong," she assured Juss, and started walking again. "He knows that, now."

"Marrying the dead..." Juss shuddered as he matched her pace. "I love my wife, but not that much!"

"Such an arrangement would not have brought any more stability to the town," she observed wryly.

"How true. I hope the new first lord can stand up to them."

Shenza nodded soberly. "I don't know what to expect of him."

Early in her tutelage, Shenza and the young lord had studied some of the same material, but they did not associate outside of Magister Laraquies' home. Nor should they, considering the difference in their stations. As a son of the first lord, Aspace had been trained by private tutors rather than enduring the crowded conditions of the General School. And he did not stay long in Chalsett-port after Lord Asbel died and his older brother took power.

"I hope he's smarter than his brother," Juss murmured. He glanced around warily, as if Lord Anges' wandering spirit might appear out of the greenery.

Shenza recalled that the murdered Lord had worn a charm against love spells and thought that Anges had not been a stupid man, merely lazy.

She led them briefly to the low wall at the terrace rim. As Juss reported, the sparkling water still lay far down the sand. It did not appear to have moved from yesterday afternoon. The wharves were crowded with shipping, small and large vessels rubbing together or lying a-kilter on the bare shore. Every available space was occupied. A few larger ships had been forced to anchor in the harbor. For the first time that Shenza could recall, rope ladders were required to reach the first terrace of the town. Heavy bales of goods were being lifted to the quay with pulleys on boom cranes.

Normally, there was traffic moving in and out constantly, and this prevented such crowding. With the tide so low, that was not an option. From what Shenza could see, the ship-masters were keeping their crews busy with maintenance, but yellow-kilted peace officers were much in evidence. How long could they keep tempers from flaring in the confined quarters?

"It's really something, isn't it?" Juss asked from behind her.
"Yes."

There seemed little more to say. Shenza turned away, seeking the relative coolness of the shaded market.

Sensing that she was holding back something, he pressed, "What do you think is causing it?"

She considered carefully before replying, "Eleshouri."

A half-snort of laughter broke off midway. "You're not serious, are you?"

"It isn't whether I'm serious, Juss. They are. A representative called on me last night."

"Was that the interesting conversation you were going to tell me about?"

She nodded. He gave a low whistle.

"Let us not speak of this to anyone else. It could cause a panic."

"Oh, most people don't really believe in those old stories." Juss tried to reassure her, but she noted his lips pursed nervously.

The two of them passed beneath an arbor on the far side of the peacekeepers' ward. On either side of the broad paved avenue stood large, rounded buildings—none so imposing as the ward, but still impressive—housing the port offices. The curomancers' clinic consisted of two long, low huts, roofed with thatch, running parallel to the street. Each was open along one side, and they faced each other across a narrow strip of garden filled with splashing fountains and flowering shrubs. Patients in loose white robes strolled there, since outward peace was held to improve healing. More lush greenery grew about the two structures, scenting the air and screening the patients from business on the street.

At the near end was an open area paved with cobbles and set with benches. A number of ill or injured already waited before them. There was a man with his wrist splinted and bound, and a woman held a baby which lay limp in her arms, moaning listlessly. An apprentice curomancer in a green-striped robe was helping her to give the baby water from a dipper. It was the same young man who had come to the ward with Mistress Kafseet, Shenza noted. As Juss and Shenza approached, both patients stared.

The apprentice bobbed respectfully. "I will assist you in just a moment."

"Certainly." Shenza stood aside to wait. The woman continued gaping at her, until the child coughed on the water and began to wail with more vigor.

Soon the young curomancer hurried over toward them. This time he crossed both hands and executed a full bow. He seemed much in awe of Shenza. "What can I do for you, Magister?"

"I would like to speak with Mistress Kafseet, if she has a moment."

"I will ask her right away." Bowing away backwards, he hurried off between the two patient care dorms. The infant's cries trailed off as his mother convinced him to drink a little more water. The man with a splinted arm now stared at the cobblestones between his feet.

The apprentice reappeared. "This way, please, Magister."

Shenza and Juss followed him along the nearer building. Most of the hammocks were not occupied, meaning that there were not many patients. That meant they would not intrude when the healers were busy. To their right, a shallow pond was studded with water lilies and basking turtles.

"I appreciate your help," Shenza said. "Satta, wasn't it?"

"Meersatta, Magister." The lad turned to answer her and stumbled. Shamefaced, he turned to face forward.

Meersatta led them to a central area where several curomancers sat on benches beneath blossoming trees. With mortars between their knees, they carefully ground and measured herbal remedies. Magic was not always the best solution to an illness.

Mistress Kafseet rose, setting aside a ledger she had been reading, and swiftly crossed the courtyard. She moved like a sandpiper, Shenza thought, quick and purposeful. She waved her apprentice away. "Thank you, Satta."

Dismissed, the young man hurried back toward the reception area.

"I hope I haven't interrupted," Shenza said.

"Not at all." Kafseet bowed crisply, with dignity. With open approval, she continued, "Well done, yesterday—facing down

Borleek like that. He's had it coming for years. You're old Laraquies' apprentice, aren't you?"

"Yes, thank you."

"I thought I recognized you." Kafseet was smiling slyly. "I would have expected no less of Laraquies himself. Well then, what can I do for you, Shenza?"

Aware of the other curomancers' curious gazes, Shenza gestured toward the water garden. "Would you mind walking with me?"

"I'd love to," Kafseet assured her.

"I've just been by the ward," Shenza said when they were out of the onlookers' hearing. "Your patient seems to be healing well."

The woman's lips thinned with displeasure, but she admitted, "Despite the number of his injuries, none of them was very serious. I put him into the cocoon more to remind those brutes that he's under my protection. It looks so much more impressive, you see."

Shenza glanced over her shoulder, but Juss showed no reaction to hearing his fellow officers described as 'brutes.' Kafseet herself appeared unaware of the lapse. Or perhaps she simply did not care.

"Well," Shenza began hesitantly, "I don't know if I should be asking you a favor, but..."

Kafseet snorted. "You can ask me anything. I'd like to hear what it is before I agree."

They paused on a low bamboo bridge, gently curving over the pond. Shenza remembered how she had despised Nurune for pulling rank, and wondered if what she was doing was any different. She sighed.

"It's just that, for his own benefit, it would be helpful if he stayed in that cocoon a little longer," Shenza said.

Kafseet frowned slightly, glancing at her. "Why do you say it would be for his benefit?"

"As soon as he wakes, Chief Borleek and the others will resume pressing for a conviction. He is a little safer while he is still sleeping. And it would give me time to find the true murderer."

"I suppose it wouldn't hurt him to rest a little longer," the curomancer said. "But," she cautioned seriously, "I can't keep him in there more than three days or he'll go into withdrawals. The cocoon can heal his physical ills, but nothing can protect him from that. Alcohol is terrible to be free of, once you're addicted. I can't decide for him that he must endure the process."

Shenza had forgotten about that. "I understand," she said reluctantly.

"Can I ask a question?" Juss cut in. Shenza nodded. "You keep going on about the drink. I know it's bad for you to drink too much, but you don't sound like you're talking about the same thing. So what's the big deal?"

Shenza regarded him with blank surprise. "I thought that..." she started.

With arched brows and asperity, Kafseet said, "You can't do magic while you're drunk. Everyone knows that."

Juss spread his hands, indicating helplessness. "I'm not a trained magician," he reminded them defensively.

"I apologize, Juss," Shenza said firmly. "Alcohol interferes with the power of concentration, which is essential to sorcery. Usually, spells don't work at all if attempted while intoxicated. Or if they do, they are likely to go awry. As a matter of professional discipline, most sorcerers do not drink at all."

"Besides," added Mistress Kafseet, "I heard Lord Anges was burned to death by magic fire. That isn't the kind of spell an average person would know. Why would he need it, working in a fish stall?"

"It is not a common spell," Shenza agreed. "A trained magician is most likely to know magic fire. But, and more pertinent to Juss' question, Byben was a habitual drinker. According to Nakuri's testimony, he was intoxicated at the time he is accused of murdering the first lord. And he was never a skilled sorcerer to begin with."

"Oh." Juss said. Then, with dawning comprehension, "So he's really not guilty. Not that I didn't believe you, Magister," he quickly added.

"I should have explained before," she apologized. "I really thought you understood."

He shrugged. "So then, who killed the first lord?"

The young sorceress shook her head. She had no answer.

Kafseet chuckled. "Boy," she said not unkindly, "we would all like to know to that!"

Chapter Eight
~ The Secret Wind ~

This time, when they approached the palace gate, a servant was present to greet them. Andle stood in a tightly wrapped turban and formal, full-length mantle of bright blue. Citizens were arriving to pay their respects, bearing funeral gifts wrapped in scarlet cloth or bound with cords of crimson silk. Considering how little care the first lord had spent on the public welfare, it was surprising how many wished to honor his passing. The people came anyway, both singly and in families, couples walking together and elders guiding small children by the hand. With a somber mien, Andle directed them to the site of public mourning.

As Shenza drew near with Juss at her shoulder, the servant bowed with both hands crossed on his chest. Both magister and peace officer returned the bow.

Shenza spoke first. "Has Master Laraquies arrived yet?"

"Yes, Magister. He is attending First Lord Anges now."

"Is that where the ghost was seen last night?"

"No, Magister." Andle sounded slightly harried. "The ghost first appeared in my Lord's private quarters. One of the maids was cleaning when someone pinched her. She turned, but no one was there. Shortly afterward, something grabbed her and tore at her robes. That was when she saw it was my Lord's ghost. She fled, and it pursued her into the servants' living quarters. There was a lot of destruction there, in the kitchens, and in my Lord's own chambers."

"I see." A line was forming behind them, and Shenza quickly bowed. "Thank you, Andle."

"Of course, Magister."

Once again, Shenza and Juss followed the winding trail of stepping stones. This time she knew where to go and they passed swiftly beneath the overhanging trees.

"Why would the ghost grope the maids?" Juss asked, glancing at her curiously. "He can't do anything about it."

"I do not know. I am not a necromancer," she answered absently, for her mind was already running ahead, planning what to do next. "Perhaps he is clinging to the life he had."

"Maybe," Juss assented, but doubtfully. Then, "And why destroy his own quarters? I thought wandering spirits were supposed to protect their old property and families, not attack them."

"Not always." Though this was a valid point. "Remind me to make a note of that, Juss."

"Yes, Magister." He sounded smug now.

The main flow of traffic was toward the palace, which consisted of several buildings clustered together. As the two of them neared a charming arched bridge, they could see the structures rising among the greenery on the crown of the hill. Their walls were of marble, with blue-tiled roofs overlapping like water lilies on a pond. The little bridge spanned an artificial stream which flowed between conifer and palm trees. Beyond it was an open expanse of garden.

The pavilion where First Lord Anges lay in state was set in the center. Funeral keening could be heard, low across the distance, and a throng of mourners tore at their clothing in ritual grief. Most of them appeared to be standing and watching something, however. A moment later, Shenza caught a brief glimpse of a familiar purple-robed figure, nearly bald except for a silvery tail at the back of his head.

"Hmph," she said softly, to herself.

"What?"

Shenza merely shook her head. She took Juss aside for a moment, letting others pass them. "I will go to the first lord's quarters. Please ask Magister Laraquies to join me there."

"Will you be all right?" Juss frowned, concerned. "If the ghost is there..."

"It should be dormant at this time of day. Or it may be inside the pavilion. They like to watch the ceremonies being held for them, I've heard. It looks like Master Laraquies is setting up a ward. If he is lucky, that will confine it to the pavilion until it is time for the funeral."

"All right. I'll see you soon." Businesslike, Juss strode across the bridge. Shenza watched for a moment, bemused by his insistence on protecting her. Well, it was certainly preferable to Chief Borleek's belligerence.

Rather than crossing the bridge, Shenza followed a damp trail beside the brook. She passed beneath a row of wisteria trees that wept delicate petal tears into the rippling current. Shenza quickly reached the source of the stream. A narrow splashing waterfall poured from the base of another marble structure. The path curved sharply left, ascended a few stone steps, curved right, and emerged beside the cottage's expansive porch.

As she rounded the corner, Shenza was surprised to see someone coming down the steps. She stopped, astonished. Innoshyra! There was no mistaking the extravagant robes and proud profile, despite the loose drape of cloth held over her head by a jeweled hand. The daughter of merchants trod softly but speedily, hurrying away to the right. She rounded the far side of the house before Shenza could give challenge.

The young sorceress gazed after her in shock. What was Innoshyra doing here? Tampering with something in the first lord's quarters? But what, and why? Shenza ran up the steps to the cottage.

To call the building a cottage was something of an understatement. This was the monarch's own dwelling, set far enough from the palace for privacy and yet near enough to place his bureaucrats and servants within easy call. Shenza had been here previously with her teacher when the lord summoned them. It seemed strange, now, to mount the steps alone and find the entry chamber so hushed and dark. It had always been brightly lit whenever she saw it, glittering with luxury and life. Shenza had never imagined it any other way.

The first chamber was, in effect, another pavilion meant for entertaining the Lord's guests. It was open on three sides, with steps descending for access to the surrounding gardens. From this prominence one had a sweeping view of the Jewel Sea, studded with coral islets and sparkling beneath the morning sun. Nearer at hand, she could see the towering willow tree of the day before. The pond shimmered through its branches. The first lord's scorched strides were clearly visible on the grass, permanently marring the tranquil scene.

Drawing out her vial of trapped sunlight, Shenza entered the house. It was hard to tell what Innoshyra might have done here, for the pitiless radiance showed many signs of the rampage Andle spoke of. The furnishings had been scattered. Tables lay upside down or at angles. A game board and pieces were strewn widely. Near the arched doorway she found two table legs, lying lonely. An alabaster lamp had cracked, dribbling aromatic oil down the wall and heavily scenting the air with sandalwood. Seeing this, Shenza was relieved she had not attempted to light the lamps. The spilled oil could have set the building afire.

What had not changed was the riot of colors and patterns both inside and outside the house. Thick carpets, extravagantly decorated, lay over a mosaic-covered floor. The furnishings and window screens bore elaborate carvings. Shades of purple and blue predominated, bringing unity to the otherwise chaotic collection.

Not all of the decoration was visible to the eye, either. Magic sigils were embedded in the tiles and window screens. They glowed violet in the sight of her mask. Most of these were simply protective, permitting the Lord to speak privately without fear of sorcerous spying. Others were more in keeping with his jaded lifestyle. Shenza felt herself flushing as she stepped past a cushion embroidered with emblems for carnal lust. It seemed strange that the first lord, who protected himself from love spells, saw nothing wrong with employing them for his own gratification.

But Shenza sternly warned herself to ignore that. There was no time to waste on what she already knew. What she needed was evidence of things she did not know.

The Lord's private bedroom was on a second level, slightly above his entry chamber. This was separated by a low rail of polished wood inlaid with brass. Shenza ascended the three steps and passed a row of painted screens (some of them badly damaged) which shielded the inner chamber from prying eyes in the room below. Now she stepped into unknown territory.

Here was no mere hammock, such as hers. Six carved posts upheld a framework of cris-crossing mesh, covered by a pad of feather-flower silk so no harsh cord could irritate the skin. This hung awry, since two of the support posts had been knocked away. More cushions had been flung about the chamber. Shenza spotted a table from the outer chamber, two of its legs missing, lying just below a great gash in one of the standing screens. The wardrobe had been thrown to its side and vari-colored robes were draped haphazardly about the room. This partly blocked the exterior door which permitted the Lord's staff (and paramours) access. The latch could be stopped from within, but she did not see an actual lock.

Even so, she could well imagine Lord Anges lying on such a grand bed. There had always been that sprawling indolence about him. Insolent, spoiled... Especially when Magister Laraquies was telling him something he didn't want to hear. Shenza had seen a captive marsh tiger once, in the marketplace. It lay with aplomb in the too-small cage, slitted amber eyes hinting of sudden cruelty. Lord Anges' eyes were like that, though his were green. Shenza felt herself shiver. Since the previous night, she knew who he inherited his eye color from.

Acting on a sudden thought, she went to the wardrobe. A quick exploration confirmed that the lord's jewelry was missing. There had been quite a lot of it, and some of great value. Could that have been Innoshyra's purpose? But no, her hands had been empty. Anyway, her family's wealth must offer no shortage of adornments.

Opening her case, Shenza drew out a stylus and noted that she must ask Alceme if all the lord's jewelry had been dedicated to his pyre, or if she had secured it until Lord Aspace arrived. Even among loyal servants, pilfering was not out of the question.

Straightening, Shenza continued her progress into the adjoining chamber, the first lord's bath. There was less damage here, since the stone walls and tile floor were impervious. A few drying cloths and toiletries had been cast about to drift in the bath. A deep oval basin was hollowed in the floor and paved with more tiles. Water continually poured into the bath from a ceramic wall spout shaped as a sea-serpent. Runes glazed into the tiles of the bath maintained a comfortable water temperature. Others warded against slips and falls. The towel rack was incised with a spell to prevent mildew. All of these enchantments appeared active and in good order.

At the lower end, a dip in the tile funneled water into a narrow outfall. In the quiet room, she could clearly hear the splashing of the waterfall where the stream emerged on the outside of the building.

"Strange," Shenza murmured. As she moved through the house, her mask's enhanced vision disclosed evidence of magic almost everywhere. There was much more than the lord's defenses and diversions should have accounted for. Returning to the dais above the entry, she saw lavender light clinging to the broken table legs and the seeping lamp. There had been quite a lot on the lord's wardrobe, as well.

She said again, "Strange."

This was not in keeping with what she understood about ghosts. They were not supposed to be magical creatures, and should not leave traces as witchery would. And if they had, there ought to be distinct marks, such as a hand print. She could see none of those. Anyway, Juss was right. It was odd that the ghost should attack its own dwelling. Especially since Lord Anges had been so house- proud, reveling in his indulgences. For him to destroy his home would be like disfiguring his own face. It was hard to picture the first lord, dead or alive, without his vanity.

Descending the outer porch, Shenza strode across the scarred terrace and looked back along the deceased Lord's trail. It appeared his flight was aligned with the steps to the second level. Advancing carefully, she concentrated on following the trail of magic luminescence in the footprints. Even the traces of such a powerful spell were already deteriorating. They seldom lasted beyond a day.

There was a way around that, however. On the porch, she set down her travel case and brought out a glass bottle whose contents glittered with pale light as she turned it. Removing the stopper, she poured a little mound of pearl dust into her upturned hand. Leaving the vial on the porch, she returned to the entryway. Cupping both hands together, she concentrated.

"Seek!" Shenza flung both hands open and upward.

The dust cloud sparkled, crackled with little lightnings, then scattered, swirling as if moved by some secret wind. It eddied, then swept downward and settled in a second burst of static flashes. A sheer coat of pearl dust, far more sensitive than her mask's detection spell, now clung to anything that had been touched by enchantment. The lamp, the tables, the spells embedded in the floor—all lay revealed. Her firm footsteps did not smudge it as she crossed the chamber, pausing twice more to cast pearl dust. She also took time to mark the dead man's fading tracks with ochre, since she wanted to distinguish them from the rest of the magic lingering in the chamber. When she reached the upper dais, the entire room below was glimmering. Shenza shook her head. Why was there so much magic in the house?

In the sleeping room, Shenza repeated the ritual of the pearl dust and methodically lined out the victim's path. Curiously, there was no sign of burning even though the trail ended (or rather, began) near the bed. It was possible the servants had already eliminated the marks.

Kneeling, Shenza removed enough of the scattered robes to examine the bed, cushion and posts. There was an area of heavy concentration that probably marked where Lord Anges was first struck by the fatal spell. Not on the bed, yet near it. Standing on that spot, she pivoted slowly in a circle. From where she stood there was a clear path from the exterior door. In all likelihood, the murderer had entered there to make his attack. Lord Anges must have had just time enough to get out of bed.

Shivering again, Shenza crossed the floor to shift through the fabric mayhem in search of the spell caster's trail. She could not move the wardrobe, but on the floor, the door and its posts, there was no sign. Just as yesterday there had been no traces on the wall where Byben was supposed to have left the grounds. Strangely, however, a small circle of dust had adhered to the ceiling above and to the right of the door. Shenza frowned up at it. The killer must have used some kind of spell to mimic Byben's appearance. Perhaps that had left this impression. Or, if he had been flying, as Juss insisted the day before, then he might have left traces on the ceiling rather than the floor.

Shenza did not intend to see this puzzle defeat her. She retrieved her travel case from the porch and laid it open on the side of the fallen wardrobe. Replacing the pearl dust, she drew out two large shells. The first was wide and flat, its interior gleaming with mother-of-pearl. The other was rounded, coiling to a blunt point and covered with brown and tan speckles. In order to use these charms Shenza had to lay aside her mask. She found, to her amusement, that it wore a thick coat of pearl dust.

She managed to find a patch of floor that was not covered by clothing, pearl dust, or ochre. This gave her a good view of both the bed and the exterior door, which was what she most wanted to see. Shenza seated herself cross-legged and closed her eyes. She relaxed her shoulders and let her breath flow slowly in and out. Languidly, she raised the speckled shell to her ear. She heard it roar as if the sea were trapped within it. When she opened her eyes, she let her gaze fall, unfocused, into the basin of the shell that was cradled in her lap.

It was like peering through a dense fog. The rushing faded to a soft hum. Overlapping layers of mist seemed to move toward her, brushing past her face like ghostly fingers. That comparison jarred her, and she nearly lost her concentration. But she steadied herself and relaxed again, letting the sea-roar lull her.

"Yesterday," she murmured in her mind. Given direction, the vision clarified itself into a dim tableau.

It was very dark. A faint, grayish light filtered through the window screens and crept beneath the exterior door. She could make out only the vaguest outlines of the furnishings. It must be early morning, for the sun had not yet risen. The faint glow through the windows and door reassured Shenza her past-sight was viewing the correct location.

There was movement, a dark form stirring in the darkness. Muted footfalls sounded in one ear. The door opened stealthily, silhouetting a female figure against the wan light from outside. She clutched a short robe about herself. On the bed, more movement came as a man rolled over, curling himself away from the intruding day. The bed ropes creaked. Then all was dark and silent once more.

So the first lord's companion left him to prepare for her morning's duties. And she had not latched the door behind herself. But this told Shenza little of use. Some minutes passed in blackness and the soft hum of silence. "Patience," she counseled herself. The light outside the room grew brighter as the Lord slept, indirectly defining the furnishings.

"Magister?" A new voice called as if from a great distance. "Hey! Are you here?"

Juss. Shenza ignored him, for at last her perseverance was rewarded.

The door swung inward once again, admitting a broad swath of light. Her eager eyes could see the trunks of wisteria trees, cascades of pallid blossoms, and the flagstones paving the small rear porch. Yet there was no one there. No shadow streamed in with the light. There was no sound, either, save for a low moan from the hinges. It must have been magic that opened the door.

Then she tensed. A small object dropped from above the open door and hovered a moment, framed against the green backdrop. She had the impression of a cylindrical form with a rough texture. It glided upward, into the deep shadows above the doorway. Flight! And it was hovering near the ceiling, just where she had observed the enigmatic patch of pearl dust. Straining, Shenza looked for it, but the bright light from the doorway overshadowed all.

"Magister?" Juss called again, nearer yet still faintly.

"Here," Master Laraquies' voice answered him. "She is fine."

In Shenza's vision, the first lord rolled upright in his grand bed. "What do you want?" he asked the empty air in a voice thick with sleep. Seeming not to wait for any reply, he swung both legs over the edge of the bed and groped for a loincloth to tie over his nudity. Dragging a handful of dark curls back from his face, he straightened, seeming to listen quizzically. Then he shrugged indifferently. "Which one is your daughter, again?" he asked in a tone of negligent familiarity that, Shenza had to admit, would make any father's blood boil.

Except that she still could not hear anyone else speaking to him.

Magister Laraquies' gentle voice once more intruded on her consciousness. "No, do not touch her. Let her wake naturally. And please do not step in the ochre."

"Sorry," Juss grumbled.

With something like panic, Shenza realized Lord Anges in her vision was strolling heedlessly toward the spot where death awaited him. She felt no need to witness this. With an effort, she squeezed her eyes shut and forced a heavy arm to move the shell from her ear. The phantasms gave way to a normal darkness. Shenza was cold, yet sweating, stiff in every limb. She could feel her own ragged breathing and the beat of blood in her ears.

"Magister?"

When she opened her eyes, it was to the welcome sight of a disordered chamber lit by a vial of condensed sunlight and pale scatterings of pearl dust. Juss crouched before her, concern written on his broad face. Master Laraquies stood behind him. The bald old man smiled obscurely.

"Are you all right?" Juss demanded. She merely nodded. "Then what happened?"

Shenza swallowed heavily, letting her mind re-adjust to reality. Slowly the fear faded from her eyes. "I understand now."

Chapter Nine
~ Written in Dust ~

Unexpectedly tired after the scrying, Shenza permitted Master Laraquies to urge her onto the porch. She sat on the upper step, leaning on the decorative rail and staring through the burn marks in the lawn.

Juss followed, frowning anxiously. "What were you doing in there?"

"I looked into the past," she said wearily.

"Did you learn anything?" He sounded impressed.

"I don't want to talk about it yet." And that was true. The implications of what she had seen were grave. "There is much I must think about."

"Well, fine." The peace officer set his hands on hips, exasperated.

Laraquies serenely observed, "It is past noon. Perhaps you should go to the kitchen and see if there is anything to eat. At least some tea. With elitherium, if they have it."

The old man's gentle words carried the weight of authority. Juss reluctantly complied. "I'll be back soon," he said meaningfully. Shenza sighed to herself. He behaved like a child who feared he would miss something exciting.

Shenza was surprised the morning had passed so quickly. But her teacher was right—mid-day clouds were gathering, tinged with the soft gray of rain. Inkesh leered through the obscuring veil, seeming to mock her. There was no comfort elsewhere in the heavens, either. The green moon, Prenuse, waned, all but eclipsed by Inkesh's carmine orb, and she could not see golden Quaiss at all. She let her gaze drop, feeling depression weigh her spirits. Behind her, Master Laraquies bustled about the pavilion, humming merrily and (it sounded like) straightening out some of the mess. Shenza was content to let him do as he wished.

After a moment he brought her mask and traveling case to her. She listlessly shook off some of the pearl dust and balanced the mask on her knee. White powder trickled down the purple cloth of her robe. The golden face gazed blankly skyward. That was how Shenza felt—blank, passive and drained.

She scarcely looked around when Juss returned. With him were four servants bearing containers of food. Alceme was there, and the messenger, who appeared distinctly annoyed at being pressed into double service. She did her best to ignore his sour demeanor.

Disregarding the informal setting, the staff served Shenza, Juss and Laraquies with all the flourish any noble of rank might expect. Despite herself, the junior magister watched with awakening interest as tea was poured and garnished with chopped mint leaves. Bowls of steamed millet were ceremoniously draped with steamed greens and then topped with dried fishes which were laid out in a fan shape, tails touching. Tiny cups of mustard sauce were provided for extra flavor. Completing the meal was a tray of mixed sea plum and pineapple slices, this last deposited ungraciously by the messenger.

Sad-faced but composed, Alceme oversaw the other servants in their presentation. "Is there anything else you need?" she asked in a deep, soft voice.

"This tastes great!" Juss muttered with enthusiasm around a mouthful of food.

"It is wonderful, as always," smiled Master Laraquies. "I compliment your kitchens."

"Tio will be pleased to hear it," the head of household replied warmly.

"If you have a moment, I would like to speak with you, Mistress Alceme," Shenza put in after swallowing her first drink of tea. "Privately," she added when the other three seemed likely to linger. With an offended sniff, the messenger spun and stalked off. The two women followed him more slowly.

Alceme tactfully inquired, "Has the staff been cooperating with your investigation, Magister?"

"Yes," she answered, reaching for a wedge of yellow pineapple. "Though I do admit I wonder if I have somehow offended your courier. He seems angry every time I see him."

The older woman chuckled understandingly. "You need give no offense, Magister. Makko has been that way since he arrived here. My Lord paid him well, yet he never seemed satisfied. He always puts on airs with the rest of us, as though such a small town isn't fit for his services. Now that my Lord is gone he's determined to find a more suitable position, but with the docks closed he must stay with us a while longer." The port again; Shenza winced inwardly, but Alceme was rolling her eyes with deprecating humor. "He doesn't much like enchanters, either. Magisters particularly, I'm afraid."

"But we magisters are so sweet and kind," Laraquies objected, smiling sweetly indeed. Alceme laughed again, her sorrowful manner lifting momentarily. Shenza stolidly chewed her food to avoid making any pointed remarks.

Juss regarded the servant over the rim of his bowl. "Why doesn't he like magisters?"

"I'm afraid I really don't know."

"Well, that does explain some things." Shenza laid down a thorny section of pineapple rind and picked up her bowl.

"Has there been a problem?" Alceme appeared concerned.

"Not at all. I was simply curious," Shenza answered firmly, mentally commanding Juss to keep his opinion to himself. She was also aware of Master Laraquies' probing gaze. "And now, there are a few details I wanted to ask you about."

The older woman nodded. "Very well."

"First of all, were any materials removed from my Lord's dwelling between yesterday and today?" It was possible, though unlikely, that Innoshyra had permission to enter the first lord's quarters for some valid reason.

"Just some garments that were too badly burned to be mended."

"What happened to those?"

Alceme shrugged. "If there were parts of the fabric that could be re-used, they were put aside to be sold. There are dealers in the market who salvage cloth." Shenza nodded. Since she bought most of her clothing from such merchants, she was aware of the practice. "Do you need to see them?"

"That is not necessary," she demurred. "I merely wondered where they were. And when I was in my Lord's chamber, I noted that none of his jewelry is there. I trust you have secured it?"

Alceme nodded vigorously. "Oh, yes, indeed, Magister. I wouldn't leave valuables out at a time like this. I've worked with most of our staff for years, but even the most faithful can be tempted."

"I am sure you are right." Shenza paused for another drink of tea. The flavor of mint was a novel addition. "Then please tell me how many of the staff have been admitted to my Lord's chambers since his death."

Alceme pondered for a moment. "Andle and I, yesterday, when we chose the personal items for the bier. Since then, only Juki and Saneen. I sent them last night to clean up and lock the chambers until Lord Aspace returns. But..." she faltered momentarily, "Juki was by herself when Lord Anges returned."

"Then all of this damage is from last night's haunting?" Shenza asked quietly, neutrally.

"Yes, Magister."

"Did you yourself see the spirit?" Alceme nodded, lips pursed to control her distress. "How did he appear to you?"

"Much as in life, Magister. He looked healthy and sound, except that his feet did not touch the floor. He was wearing a bright green kilt, the color of parrot feathers, with a blue and green mantle and a headcloth that matched. There were some of the parrot feathers in the brooch fastening the headcloth." Her voice became hushed. "He had just bought the outfit, you see, and was showing it off the night before he died."

"I see." Shenza was silent a moment, trying to remember from childhood tales whether the dead reappeared with marks of the wounds that killed them, or sometimes did, or always seemed just as they had been while living. She could not recall. "Did he pick things up and throw them?"

"Yes. He was shouting at us. It was quite frightening," Alceme explained with what sounded like a considerable understatement. "Luckily, no one was injured."

"I am glad to know that. And what did my Lord say?" Shenza asked, though she thought she might be able to guess.

The older woman hesitated before admitting, embarrassed, "He was demanding justice and wanted to know why his funeral hadn't taken place yet."

"I see," Shenza said for a second time. This accusation did not surprise her. She had expected such baiting. She chewed a mouthful of grain with what she hoped was some of her tutor's aplomb. "How much damage was done in the rest of the house?"

"Oh, not as much. Not what I expected. Small things were broken, but nothing that can't be replaced." Shenza nodded again, and Alceme nervously pushed the silvered-black hair back over her shoulders. "But I don't know whether to clean up now or not. What if the ghost comes back? Is there a way to keep this from happening again?"

For the answer to that, Shenza turned to her teacher. "Magister Laraquies?"

The old man was sipping his tea, but lowered his cup to reply. "I have installed wards that should confine the spirit to the interior of the pavilion. There is nothing there for him to attack but his own remains and the gifts left for him by his mourners. I don't believe he will disturb those. There should be no further problems."

He sounded soothing, but Shenza had doubts. Too much hinted at a non-spiritual source.

Relieved, Alceme sighed lightly. "That is good to know. Then, with your permission, Magister, I will send the maids to clean up again."

Shenza was caught with her mouth full and had to swallow quickly before answering. "If you would please wait a while longer. There are still things for us to discuss here."

"Very well," the senior servant agreed. "I will wait until you have gone."

"I appreciate it. And thank you for your time."

Alceme bowed and retreated down the steps, soon vanishing behind the far curve of the house.

Softly, almost to himself, Laraquies murmured, "But, you know, I put up a ward yesterday. The spirit should not have been able to pass it."

"So you were expecting something like this?" Juss asked accusingly.

Laraquies shrugged, unruffled by the criticism. "Knowing the first lord as I did, yes, I anticipated a tantrum or two."

"Let us not talk about that now," Shenza instructed quietly.

"Why not?" Juss demanded with his customary bluntness.

Shenza's teacher came to her defense. "Because magisters must eat. It is very important. And," he urged Shenza, "you should drink your tea."

"I am, teacher." It was hard to feel gratitude for his support when he nagged her so.

"You know, if you two would just say things out loud, this would only take half as long," the peace officer grumbled, not very good-naturedly. Shenza merely shrugged in response. She was not yet ready to speak of what she suspected.

The three of them ate in silence for a time. Shenza dipped her fishes into the mustard sauce, savoring its tang, then took a bite of the millet. The nutty flavor mellowed the burning sensation. None of this deflected the depression growing within her. Juss cleared the remaining fruit from the bottom of the bowl and looked around for more, but food did not truly interest her. She was simply eating to delay a little longer. The situation was worse than she had thought, and there seemed nothing she could do to improve it.

Eventually, she was left with no excuse. Both men looked up alertly when she set down her dishes. Heavily she told them, "Let us talk inside."

Gathering her travel case and mask, Shenza rose. Juss scrambled to his feet, while Master Laraquies stacked the crockery for the servants to collect later. Inside the glittering pavilion Shenza found three cushions neatly gathered beside the largest of the inlaid tables, all of these arranged within the first lord's circular ward. It no longer surprised her that the old man had anticipated her plan. She knelt within the barrier, while Juss seated himself on one of the cushions. Following last, Laraquies brought the half-full teapot and their three cups.

Once they were within the circle, Shenza pressed both palms to the mosaic perimeter. She could feel the crisp edges of individual tiles beneath her fingers. Concentrating, she gathered her power once again.

"Seal."

The glow of magic raced along the embedded runes, flaring brightly to a steady blaze. Visible even through the overlapping carpet and without the aid of her mask, it far outshone the lesser radiance of the pearl dust.

"What does that do?" Juss asked with some trepidation.

"It will defend us from spying," she told him, "either by sorcery or more normal means."

"That's useful!"

"Yes." The junior magister settled herself at the table, ignoring the tea cup her master pushed at her. Retrieving writing materials from the travel case, she asked of Master Laraquies, "Did Juss tell you what has been happening?"

"He mentioned a few things, but I wouldn't mind hearing it in order."

"All right." Shenza opened her notebook. Juss sighed audibly at the continued delay. She turned to him, primly annoyed. "We must now review all we know, and attempt to connect the facts to discover the truth. It would be best if we all had the same information, wouldn't it?"

He mumbled rebelliously, "Yes, Magister."

She was tempted to point out that Juss was not required to be present for their deliberations. And they were not required to allow him the privilege. His viewpoint had been helpful so far, however. She swallowed the harsh words.

Beginning in a dry, factual tone, Shenza recited portions of her notes from the beginning of her investigation. Her teacher nodded approvingly when she recounted her growing recognition that Byben of Cessill had been falsely accused. He listened with a gleam in his eye to her brief edition of the confrontation with Peacekeeper Borleek, and with gravity as she repeated the words of the spirits. Juss frequently added his own observations, making it harder for Shenza to concentrate. Master Laraquies clucked to himself when she described Nurune's importunity earlier in the day. She expected criticism for requesting Kafseet to delay Byben's treatment, but he did not. Then Juss interrupted with an indignant version of the messenger's rudeness, which Shenza would have preferred to omit. Sighing to herself, she drank her tea and waited.

"Now I understand your questions to Alceme," the old man said when Juss had concluded. "And so?"

"We returned here as requested," she resumed. "I asked Juss to locate you while I re-examined the site of the attack. I did this by first making a visual inspection." Her hand rested briefly on her mask. "It seemed there was a lot of residual magic. I wondered if my eyes were fooling me, so I spread pearl dust to manifest the remnant spells more clearly. As you can see, the initial impression was correct." She gestured, taking in the iridescent shimmer all about the chamber.

Juss grunted, looking around with new appreciation. "I wondered what that was."

"At the time, I could not explain the high number of magical traces. However, it did allow me to locate the actual steps Lord Anges took after the enchantment was laid on him. I then invoked the power of my talismans to see and hear past events, in order to witness the attack myself."

Juss gave a low whistle, his broad features reflecting mingled respect and dismay.

Shenza took a sip of warm tea to soothe a throat suddenly dry and tight. "I saw nothing."

Juss started to speak, but she raised a hand, forestalling him. "The first lord believed there was someone present. He was talking, but there was no one there. However, there was an object in the doorway. And it was flying," she felt obliged to add, acknowledging his suspicion of the day before.

Master Laraquies sat silent, thoughtful.

"A flying object?" Juss repeated, confused. "What kind of object?"

"It did not make sense to me, either, at first," Shenza explained. "I believe that the object was a semblage. That is a kind of talisman used to project magic at a distance, without the caster having to be present. The semblage was used to create phantasms—illusions, to use the common term." Juss straightened, his dark eyes widening. Heavily, she continued, "Scrying into the past can only reveal what was truly there and tangible. It cannot show an illusion. Thus, I could not see what Lord Anges saw, but I did see the semblage."

Laraquies seemed to sense her frustration, for he mildly pointed out, "You had no way to know his methods."

Shenza disagreed. "There were indications, which I should have recognized. In any case, Lord Anges saw the phantasm, and also heard it. I assume he thought it was Byben, since that is what all the other witnesses described."

"So he used this thing to set the Lord on fire?" Juss hazarded. "And he made everyone think the old man did it?"

"I believe so."

"And when everyone thought they were chasing Byben, they were really seeing the illusion. That's why no one could catch him."

She nodded. "If you recall, the attacker always remained just ahead of them. He moved over obstacles with superhuman agility. That is why we saw only three sets of tracks on the hillside. And, Master, it is also why the spirit appeared to escape your ward."

Eyebrows raised, he regarded her with placid curiosity.

"The ghost was never here," she said. "All this damage was done by the same sorcerer, casting kinetic spells through the semblage. Using his phantasms, he made the first lord's ghost appear to the maids."

Incredibly, the old man was smiling. "Clever. I hadn't suspected at all."

"That makes a lot more sense," Juss agreed, sounding relieved. "It just didn't seem possible that all of the witnesses were wrong!"

Shenza nodded slowly. "Although this explains much of what happened, I am still very concerned. This is not just an average sorcerer we are facing."

"How do you mean?" the peace officer asked.

Tensely, she explained, "Magic fire is not an uncommon spell. Though dangerous, it is not difficult. Neither is flight. Even someone like Byben could learn these spells."

"I thought you said he was a drunk," Juss objected.

Patiently, she replied, "That is not my point. In theory, Byben could have access to such spells. The semblage is a very different case. It is not something an ordinary person would be able to make or use. Likewise, phantasms are not common except among certain kinds of entertainers. This tells us our enemy is a highly skilled, professional magician. He has the resources to buy a complex talisman, or the skill to create it for himself. He can sustain several spells at once, for instance, flight, multiple phantasms, and magic fire."

Shenza completed this litany with dread. Just saying the words made the enemy seem much more real and threatening. It frightened her to admit how small her own powers were by comparison.

Frowning in confusion, Juss interrupted. "Multiple illusions?"

"Each phantasm is separate. Hiding the semblage is one. Making Byben appear is another, and mimicking his voice is a third."

"Oh." He paused a moment. "Is that a lot, five spells at once?"

"Yes." Shenza said simply, with quiet despair. She could only maintain two spells at a time, perhaps three if they were simple. Even if the semblage assisted, it was obvious they were confronting a wizard far more skilled than she was.

Then Juss caught his breath in realization. "What if they cast an illusion to make themselves look like you, and order the port opened?"

Shenza gazed at him in dismay.

Magister Laraquies had been listening silently. He now regarded the peace officer with new respect. "An excellent point. However, very few phantasms account for the sense of touch. If you suspect a false appearance, you can discover the truth simply by feeling it. Also, the deception is limited to details the enchanter knows. Someone would have to know Shenza very well in order to imitate her effectively."

"Unless they did not take the time to question," Shenza countered glumly. "Someone who ordered the port opened would be telling them what they already wanted to hear."

Juss was shaking his head in concern. "I'd better tell the Chief about this," he decided firmly. "Even if he doesn't believe it, he can't say later that we knew and didn't warn him."

Magister Laraquies nodded, approving of such pragmatism. However, Shenza had another worrisome thought. "The murderer does seem to know the details of the Lord's house fairly well. He was able to create phantasms that fooled the staff into believing Lord Anges' spirit was here. Considering this, I'm afraid we must conclude he holds some position close to the palace."

"You mean the killer could be someone on the Lord's staff?" Juss asked in a hushed tone.

Shenza nodded. "It could also be one of the functionaries who works in the palace. There are dozens of them."

"This is speculation," the senior magister interrupted calmly. "We must not speculate. We must deal with what we know."

Shenza glanced downward, flushing at the rebuke. It was a basic tenet. She should not have to be reminded. She raised her cup to her lips and found the tea had gone cold.

Unaware of her thoughts, Juss merely shrugged. "So, is there anything else I need to know about?"

Shenza paused, striving for professional neutrality. "Only that, although we know more of his methods, we still have no way of finding the murderer. Using the semblage has an additional advantage. It is impossible to trace the magic to the caster."

"You mean your powder stuff can't tell whose magic is whose?"

She smiled bitterly. "Certainly, if I know whose magic I am looking for."

"Oh." His shoulders drooped. "So they can strike at us whenever they want to, but we can't find them."

Wearily, Shenza agreed. She was beginning to wish that Juss would be quiet. "As long as he has the semblage, he can. If we could capture the semblage, we could locate him by using it as a link." Her low tone expressed how unlikely she thought this was.

Laraquies coughed gently, interrupting their speculations. "Now, Shenza, refresh my memory. Why would the murderer wish to destroy the first lord's home?"

Trying to hold a dispassionate tone, Shenza answered, "I first wondered if the vandalism was a distraction for robbery, but Mistress Alceme tells us the valuables had already been removed for safe keeping. I suspect the apparent haunting was intended to place the Lord's household under pressure. This would cause them to push for me to resolve the case more quickly."

"True," Laraquies acknowledged.

"Since the port is closed," she reasoned, "the assassin cannot leave. Presumably, if I declare Byben guilty the port will re-open and the murderer can then escape justice. So, teacher, I think we can expect more hauntings despite your wards. The enemy will wish to keep up the pressure."

"This may be true," he allowed.

Juss shifted in place, as if he wanted to say something, but held his tongue.

Shenza went on, "There is something else, though it may not be related to the murder. Did either of you see Lady Innoshyra today?"

Laraquies answered promptly. "Yes. She was grieving at the first lord's bier when I arrived today. She sounded hoarse, so I suspect she had been there for some time. However, she left not long after I got there."

Shenza thought about that, trying to calculate how soon her teacher had arrived after receiving the message that Makko relayed, and how this related to her visit with Kafseet.

Juss was asking, "Who's she? Oh, that fellow Nurune said she was his client."

"His niece also," she reminded him. "I declined their request to have a necromancer summon Lord Anges' spirit."

"Why?" the old man asked, surprised.

"To propose a posthumous marriage," Shenza answered with distaste.

"Then you rightly refused," Master Laraquies approved. Then he prodded, "Have you seen her today?"

Shenza nodded. "I saw her leaving this building just as I arrived."

"Here?" Juss frowned.

"She behaved as though she did not wish to be seen," Shenza mused, "but I can't think why. There was nothing of value here."

"Maybe she didn't know that," the peace officer said darkly.

Shenza shrugged. "As you say. And this may be irrelevant, but considering her interest in the first lord's fate, I am suspicious." If, for some reason, Innoshyra was involved in Lord Anges' death, she might seek to remove any evidence.

"But you are right to make note of it," Laraquies assured her.

His approval should have cheered her, but it did not. After a brief silence, Shenza said despondently, "If you have any suggestions, Master, I would like to hear them. I cannot think of anything else to do."

Her teacher patted her hand. "Do not be ashamed. I suppose what you did today might have been done yesterday, but that is no fault. You followed the correct procedure."

"Yes, teacher." The criticism stung, though he tried to soften it.

"Shenza, you are not listening," he chided gently. "I said you have done well. Closing the port was especially well thought of. I would not have done that. Now, the criminal we seek is formidable and well prepared, but you must not give up hope. There are three of us to his one, and many others will aid us."

"But he can do five spells at once," she thought rebelliously. And no one else would be held responsible for the results of the investigation.

Master Laraquies went on placidly, "If you are correct that this is a professional sorcerer, it is quite possible that others have encountered his work. I suggest that we request information from other magisters."

That was true, Shenza thought. An experienced magister like Laraquies already knew many of the other magisters, as she did not.

"How long will that take?" Juss wanted to know.

"From a few days to a few weeks."

"Do we have a few weeks to wait?" he asked doubtfully.

"We shall have what we require," Laraquies reminded him with a hint of steel. A magister had complete freedom in the pursuit of any investigation, no matter the pressure from others.

"But you must ask the Elitheri to aid you," Shenza felt obliged to point out. "They may forbid movement by air, as the Eleshouri have by the sea."

"Is that what you wish me to do?" the old man asked. After a moment's surprise, she realized that he was waiting for her permission.

"Yes. Please. I will rely on your contacts with the other magisters."

Laraquies seemed amused by her phrasing. Trying to shake off her gloom, Shenza said, "Let us review. The murderer is definitely a wizard. He may have a background in entertainment. He may have a background which permits him to work on the first lord's staff or government. He may be a professional assassin. He is willing to use others to shield himself.

"We should inquire about sorcerers who have had complaints of misfeasance brought against them. Tell them the enchantments the murderer has been known to use. Ask if anyone knows of a semblage being made by one whose motives might have been suspect."

"As you say," the old man half-bowed. Shenza glanced at him nervously while she began a fresh page of notes from this conversation.

"What else do you recommend, teacher?" she asked.

"Nothing," he answered mildly. "You must tell us what to do."

She gazed at him, feeling something like panic. She had just said she didn't know what to do!

"Well, I have an idea," Juss said. "You said we could find the killer if we got his semblage. I think we should wait here and see if he haunts the palace again tonight. That would give us a chance to grab it."

"That could be difficult," Shenza objected. "It will be disguised by phantasms."

"Can't your mask see through them?"

"I don't know," she admitted, feeling her depression return. "It was not made for that purpose. Also, no one else would have that benefit. The murderer will not let us take his weapon without defending it." Remembering the first lord's charred remains, she did not relish Juss' plan. "He may use his magic fire spell again."

"Don't you know a counter-spell?" he pressed impatiently. "We aren't going to solve this thing without taking some risks."

"Making an amulet would take weeks," she responded tightly, "even if the materials were available. I do not think we have that much time."

"If we have time to wait for all these answers..." he argued, only to be silenced by their elder.

"As magister, Shenza should be seen to work on the investigation," Laraquies returned. "However, it is a good idea to be protected. When we are done here, we should look in the marketplace and see if there are any fire amulets for sale."

Shenza looked up from her notes. "Perhaps we should ask Master Nurune for assistance," she reluctantly suggested. "His coven specializes in protections."

"I don't know about him," Juss said warningly. "He'll want more than the fair price, if you know what I mean."

"But we should not overlook any resource," Laraquies pointed out. "Since Lord Anges was a personal friend, perhaps he will agree to work with us."

"Perhaps you should handle that contact, as well," Shenza suggested, "since he respects you." She had no wish to bandy words with Master Nurune again so soon.

The old man smiled with a gleam in his eye. "I would be pleased to."

"Then," she sighed, "if we can secure adequate defenses, I would not object to returning this evening and seeing if the murderer continues 'haunting' the palace."

"Good," Juss said. "We have to take the initiative, not just wait for them to do something."

That was easy for him to say, Shenza thought rebelliously.

"Well," Laraquies remarked while she wrote, "even though we can't find our opponent, he is still trapped as long as the port stays closed. By drawing out the investigation, we may goad him into acting unwisely."

This slight advantage was not enough to reassure Shenza.

Chapter Ten
~ When the Wind Says ~

With patient hands, Magister Laraquies wrote out the last of the messages. A murmured word enchanted the fabric to preserve his words, and he passed it to Shenza. While the old man capped his ink bottle and rinsed the stylus in a bowl of water, she folded the dispatch into the shape of a butterfly and arranged it beside five others on the table before her.

When his materials were restored to their places, her teacher told her, "The first message is for the High Magister, Oksim Entook of Entook."

Shenza nodded, trying to relax as she knew she must. The effort made it harder. Briefly she touched the hollow of her throat, felt the power gathered there. Then she extended her right hand over the first of her fragile creations.

"Oksim of Entook," she repeated softly, deep in concentration. A hot surge of power moved down her arm. The artificial insect twitched. "High Magister. Porphery, City of Domes."

Beneath her palm the paper wings opened slowly, closed, and opened, as if it were a real butterfly drying its wings after a rain shower.

"Jiseppa Fahri of Tisbain, Magister of Sardony."

She moved her hand to the second artificial insect, and felt the pulsing warmth build again. "Jiseppa of Tisbain."

There were far too many islands in the Jewel Sea to inquire with every magister. Laraquies had selected these six because the larger towns were more likely to receive reports of unusual enchantments. Soon the messages sat in their ragged line, each flexing its wings to its own internal rhythm.

With a final pass that took in them all, Shenza completed the enchantment. "Go forth, creatures of air!"

There was a flurry of skyward motion as she withdrew her hand. Small wings slapped the air with a barely audible, crackling whisper. As commanded, each sought the one to whom it was directed. Against the green and gold of the garden they looked starkly, unnaturally pale.

Laraquies, in his turn, now knelt facing outward. Hands raised in supplication, he intoned, "Lords of the Air, great ones. Guard and guide these humble messengers with your mighty power, more swiftly to bring about the justice you desire." His voice was not loud, yet it seemed to resound. There was an answering tremor among the foliage of the garden.

As the little couriers reached the level of the cottage roof, a sudden wind snatched at them. The roof thatch whistled frantically. Shenza had a final brief glimpse of pale wings against the emerald arch of the fern tree and the cloudy sky beyond. Then they were gone and the breeze stilled as quickly as it had come.

"How remarkable," Laraquies commented softly. He seemed unconcerned by the direct response to his invocation. "It would seem our messages will have speed on their way. But," he quoted another maxim, "we sail when the wind says we may."

"More like," Shenza retorted, "when the wind says sail, we have no choice but to sail!"

~

As agreed, Juss was waiting near the fig tree in the center of the market square. His choice had been to look for fireproof amulets among the peddlers in the marketplace. Since he stood empty- handed, there was no need to ask whether he had been successful.

The big man explained anyway. "No luck. All the fire charms were bought up yesterday. Since word got out how the first lord died, everyone wanted one." His dark face twisted briefly in frustration. "I guess I shouldn't be surprised."

"That is unfortunate," Shenza said.

"I don't suppose there's any way we can find out who's got them and... borrow one or two," he suggested hopefully.

Shenza looked to her teacher, who responded diffidently. "That might be difficult to justify afterward. Did you ask Master Nurune, as well?"

Juss snorted. "I tried. He doesn't see anyone without an appointment. Besides, you said you would talk to him."

The old man smiled. "Then I shall."

Behind her mask, Shenza regarded her teacher with surprise. After telling her for so many years that she must never abuse her position, he seemed quite prepared to stretch his authority now. To Juss, she asked, "And have you spoken with the peacekeeper yet?"

The peace officer grinned. "Not until I have you to hide behind!"

Laraquies chuckled. "Perhaps you two should do that, while I see if good Master Nurune can spare a few minutes for an esteemed colleague."

"Very well," Shenza agreed reluctantly. She did not look forward to seeing Chief Borleek again. She glanced skyward, gauging the nearness of the afternoon rain. Perhaps if they waited until tomorrow... But no. The investigation was difficult enough without anything more hanging over her head. Master Laraquies was already turning away. "I will see you tonight, then."

He glanced at her slyly. "At home?"

"Yes," she replied patiently, "at home."

Smiling, the old man walked away. Aware of Juss' curious gaze, Shenza likewise moved off toward the ward's rounded bulk. It looked exceptionally dismal, she thought, beneath the low-hanging, heavy clouds.

The mood inside was little better. It was stuffy and crowded with a mix of peace officers, angry merchants, and sailors who apparently were finding trouble during their enforced idleness. Lines had formed before each of the scribes, who hurriedly recorded the complaints and took payments from a list of appropriate fines. The air was thick with arguing voices and body odors. With her mask's sensitivity, the babel was barely tolerable.

Shenza avoided the press and led Juss between along the elevated walkway at the rim of the chamber. Hurrying apprentices stood aside to let them pass. The peacekeeper's office was the largest one, with a screened window overlooking the central chamber.

"Let me," Juss murmured over her shoulder as they approached.

Shenza paused, permitting him to move into the doorway first.

"Chief?" he said, parting the drape of wooden beads that obscured the entry.

"What?" Borleek's voice snapped roughly. Then, "Oh, you. Well?"

"Magister Shenza to see you," Juss answered with neutral professionalism.

Borleek grunted something she couldn't hear. Shenza stepped through the hanging Juss held aside for her. Small black eyes narrowed with barely tempered hostility. "It's about time you showed your face," he growled.

Shenza quelled the impulse to explain her actions. "I wish to speak with you and your senior staff. Anyone you would trust to lead a watch or hold authority in your absence."

"Why?"

"There is something to discuss, relevant to the first lord's murder."

"Fine." He beetled his brows at Juss. "Get Shamatt, Pars and Rakshel in here."

"Yes, sir." The junior officer hurried from the room with beads chattering behind him.

This left Shenza and Borleek alone together, an event she had not anticipated. In the stillness, voices droned from outside the room. Borleek glared at her, seeming engrossed by the unblinking golden serenity of her mask. He could not see her face, and yet she felt keenly uncomfortable. Looking aside, Shenza broke the tableau. There was a cushion on the floor near his, much worn and flattened. Shenza seated herself without asking permission, opened her travel case, and made a show of reading through her notations.

But she would not be left in peace. "Are you ready to convict yet?" he asked baldly.

At least the man seemed in less of a shouting mood today. But Shenza did not wish to discuss particulars before the other officers arrived. "I am afraid not."

"I knew it!" he exclaimed with disgust. "Now, look. I want to make something clear to you." He jabbed a blunt finger at her. She tried not to flinch. "I am the law in this town. Everyone looks to me to maintain order. And I mean to do so. And I don't appreciate you undermining my authority." More jabs punctuated his words.

"I am not attempting to undermine your authority," she answered, holding firmly to her temper and dignity. "That is not in my interest. Yours are the hands which carry out justice. That is indeed important. But it is my place to voice the law, not yours." He gritted his teeth, anger darkening his bronze skin. Shenza pressed on, for as much time as she had before he exploded. "And remember, neither of us has the power to decide the punishment. That is the first lord's privilege. I realize Lord Anges gave you much freedom in pursuing your duties, but he is no longer here to delegate that authority. I caution you, your men have already overstepped themselves by beating the prisoner before he was convicted."

"Overstepped..." Borleek knotted his fists in the dark gold fabric of his kilt, as if to keep them from lashing out at her. "And just what do you call that —!" A great hand splayed out, broadly gesturing toward the harbor. "Hexing the port to keep anyone from leaving!"

"I did not..."

His loud voice overbore hers. "Do you have any idea how hard it is to keep order when everyone is on edge like this? They all feel trapped here, and who can blame them!"

Shenza said coldly, when he took a breath, "It is not my doing, Peacekeeper." The voices outside the office hushed momentarily. There was a soft rumble of thunder from outside, and the first raindrops pattered onto the roof above them. She could vividly imagine the officers and citizens listening to Borleek's half of their conversation.

He roared, "Don't give me that! Every magician in this town kowtows to you magisters. If you did it yourself or ordered someone else to do it, it comes down to the same thing."

"No *human* lowered the water," she stressed, hoping against hope that he would understand. "Those who did are beyond my command. I trust the sea will return when the case has been resolved."

"What's that supposed to mean?" he demanded suspiciously but, to her gratitude, more quietly. "'Those who did it.'"

She sighed, anticipating his reaction. "It is the Eleshouri, whose powers exceed any mortal's."

"Spirits! So you say," he scoffed. "Am I supposed to believe this nonsense?"

Shenza wondered how he could be so entirely without self-doubt, when she felt so overwhelmed. "If you choose not to believe me, I cannot compel you. But I trust that we will still be able to cooperate with each other."

The grooves along his fish-mouth deepened with disdain. "I want this thing settled, one way or the other, before the new first lord gets here. Your mumbo-jumbo is making me look incompetent, and I won't stand for it. This is my town, and I'm going to stay in control, and we're going to have the results waiting when the new Lord gets here. So you'd better be the one to cooperate, little lady. Is that clear?"

Behind her mask, Shenza regarded him with amazement. 'My town?' How could he not hear his own arrogance? Yet she had no guarantee that the new ruler, when he arrived, would not support Borleek's position.

"Please do not threaten me," she managed faintly.

"Then do your job, Magister." He spat her title with an obvious sense of victory.

She had no chance to respond, for three men in dark yellow kilts were entering the room. They were all very tall, from her seated position. None had Borleek's massive bulk, but there was still a muscular strength in their bearing. They sat down cross-legged. From their cautious regard, Shenza wondered what they had heard about her. The chamber, though it was the largest in the building, now seemed intolerably close. No one spoke, and the soft beat of rain on the roof was clearly audible.

Juss nodded tersely to Shenza and took up a position just inside the door. Borleek glared at him for a moment, and Juss returned his gaze impassively. Snorting under his breath, the peacekeeper turned back to his preferred target.

"Well?" It seemed to be his favorite word. "We're all here."

For a moment, Shenza felt she could not continue. But of course, there was no choice. Not quite steadily, she began. "In my investigation, I have learned something of the methods used to attack Lord Anges."

Borleek shifted, impatient with preliminaries. Another of the men, one with a haze of gray at his temples, asked quietly, "Are you still searching for an accomplice?"

She hesitated. "I do not think 'accomplice' is quite the word. Byben of Cessill was never involved in the crime. The murderer merely used him as a scapegoat."

There was a stir of skepticism among the listening officers. "This again!" Borleek growled in disgust.

"Please let me speak," Shenza rebuked, more sharply than she meant to. "There is a kind of talisman, called a semblage, which permits a sorcerer to cast spells when he himself is not present. This object was used to feign Byben's presence at the scene of the attack. This is why all the witnesses say they saw him murder the first lord, when in fact he was sleeping off the drink in his market stall."

The graying officer regarded her with interest. His fellows seemed more to look for Borleek's reaction before responding. Shenza continued more temperately.

"I do not mean to imply any laxness on the part of the peacekeepers who were confused by the phantasms." Borleek frowned, unforgiving. "This enchanter is highly skilled. Even the first lord's own staff were fooled."

"You mean, when the ghost came back to the palace?" the same man interrupted.

"You are well informed." Shenza studied his face for a moment. Unlike his Chief, the lines about his eyes spoke of humor, not pride or anger.

He smiled modestly. "I try to be, Magister."

"What are you talking about, Shamatt?" Borleek cut in, aware that he was missing something and not liking it.

"A phantasm that seemed to be the first lord's ghost returned to the palace," Shenza answered briefly. "I will not bore you with all the reasons I believe it was spellcraft rather than a restless spirit."

Shamatt rubbed his nose, hiding a smile at Shenza's choice of words.

"What concerns me," Shenza went on, "is that the sorcerer may attempt to fool you again by mimicking me and issuing false orders in my name. Or not just me. He could as easily counterfeit Peacekeeper Borleek, for instance."

There were frowns around the room. Borleek bridled. "If he dared..."

"He has already dared to attack the first lord," she answered with eloquent simplicity. "Fortunately, there are ways to reveal the phantasms. If a false appearance is suspected, the sense of touch will reveal the truth. I would also suggest an additional safeguard, so we can all know we are really dealing with each other."

"What did you have in mind?" Shamatt asked.

"A simple series of code words should be adequate. It would give the squad leaders a way to determine whether an order is legitimate."

"It sounds like a lot of bother for nothing," Borleek grumbled. "Do we even know this other magician —" his tone made it plain he doubted the man's existence "— will try this?"

"Do you want to take the chance?" Shenza asked, pleased to put him on the spot. It was a slight revenge, but satisfying.

The expressions of the other peace officers made it clear they did not wish to rely on luck.

"We were caught off guard once," Shamatt pointed out. "We owe it to everyone to take precautions."

Juss and the other two nodded in agreement.

The Chief waved him to silence. "Enough. If you have so much time on your hands, you can organize it."

The Sub-Chief appeared pleased. "Very good, sir."

"But I expect to be kept informed," Borleek warned sternly.

"Of course."

Borleek turned back to Shenza. "Anything else?"

"Yes. There is the chance that, if confronted, the sorcerer will defend himself with magic. I would not like to see anyone else share the first lord's fate," she said with feeling. "All of your officers should defend themselves with magical amulets."

"We've already been through the market looking for fire charms," Juss put in, speaking for the first time during the meeting. "There aren't any left."

This caused a murmur of concern among the listening men.

Shenza countered, "Magic fire may not be the only enchantment at his command. I would recommend the strongest general protection, rather than a specific one. Do the peacekeepers have any amulets on hand?"

The Chief grunted sourly. "We don't usually need them."

"I'll ask around and see if any of the men have them," another of the men offered. He was in his middle years, with nearly black skin.

"Do that, Rakshel." Borleek nodded grimly.

"If there are enough men with defenses," Shenza went on, "it may be possible to wait at the palace tomorrow night for the false ghost to reappear and try to capture the semblage. That would allow me to identify the murderer." The men brightened at the prospect. She cautioned them, "I cannot overstate the danger."

Borleek smiled without humor. "You let us worry about that, little lady. Pars, see about organizing it."

"Yes, sir," said the third officer, a broken-toothed man with a hint of lisp.

"I would like Juss to participate also," Shenza quickly requested. "He has an idea what it looks like."

The younger officer glanced at her curiously, but then his expression cleared. "I'm willing."

Pars shrugged. "Fine with me."

Shamatt eyed the young magister thoughtfully, but Borleek frowned at her. "We don't need you telling us. We know what we're doing."

"Very well," Shenza said. The rain droned softly on the roof as she quickly noted what had been decided. "And what shall our code word be?"

~

Later, Shenza sat on Magister Laraquies' porch, gazing out across the rain-wet garden and picking listlessly at the meal he had prepared. The rain had fallen hard and long, with a constant flicker of lightning and grumble of thunder. The eaves dripped steadily and the garden brook ran full under the muted glow of dusk.

Its merry babbling did nothing to cheer her. She felt she had accomplished nothing at all in the second day of her inquiry. That was untrue, of course. She had learned a great deal, but it brought her no closer to the conclusion that everyone wanted.

It wasn't just Borleek's blustering that bothered her. She could avoid him, if she wanted to. No, it was the faceless, unnamed enemy who taunted her. Even the greatest magic could not touch an unknown object. There had to be something, however small, to connect a spell's intent to its target. That link she did not have.

Worse was the specter of the spirits' impatience. Fitful bursts of thunder only hinted at their vast powers. Remembering the spirit's uncanny eyes, Shenza trembled inside. If she failed to appease their fury...

It was some consolation to realize there was someone in the peacekeepers' hierarchy who could be trusted. Shamatt, Juss informed her, was Borleek's second in command. They had worked together for some years. As Shenza had seen, Borleek usually heeded him. Juss had also gone out of his way to assure her the chief peacekeeper had not raised his voice to her any more than he did to anyone. He said most of the officers were so accustomed to Borleek's shouting they paid it little mind. That was hard for Shenza to believe. She certainly found the man impossible to ignore.

She also distrusted his temper. Considering he had stopped just short of an open threat, she had decided it would be prudent to remove Byben from the peacekeepers' ward as soon as he had recovered from his injuries. Juss was to make those arrangements with Mistress Kafseet this evening before he went home. Borleek would probably erupt again when he learned, but she was confident he wouldn't dare violate the curomancers' refuge.

Master Laraquies padded out of the kitchen and settled himself comfortably across from her. The porcelain kettle rattled gently as he poured yet more tea laced with elitherium.

"It can't be that bad," he said mildly.

Easy for him to say, Shenza thought mournfully. She had never seen anyone speak to Laraquies during an investigation as Borleek had to her.

"It was a good day," he insisted, with a swallow of the deep amber liquid.

His student regarded him incredulously. "Teacher, how can you say that?"

"You have learned much of importance," he serenely told her.

What she had learned was that she could not touch her foe, she thought in misery. Shenza opened her mouth, but closed it without speaking. She had always despised whining self-pity. Even in the hardest times her family had seen, she hated to complain when it served no purpose.

"Hm?" he prodded in his amiable way. "Come now."

"I just don't see where I can go from here," she finally had to confess. "The semblage is my only hope, but anyone who helped me would be so vulnerable."

Laraquies sipped his tea again, pensively. "I don't know what to do, either."

These words were not reassuring.

"Sometimes, the answer is not obvious. What's important is that you not stop trying, Shenza."

"I know, but..." The exasperating whine was back in her voice. She faltered, paused for a drink of tea, and lamely concluded, "I just feel so tired."

"There is a reason for that," her teacher reminded her. "It wasn't easy work, making the mask. And then the investigation came up so quickly."

"Then why..." she interrupted, only to bite down on further words. *Why don't you take it back?* But he wouldn't do that. It would be foolish even to ask.

"Don't be ashamed, child," he said to sooth her. "You're allowed to be tired. But perhaps it makes things seem worse than they are."

Simply being tired didn't change facts, Shenza thought wearily. After an inner tug-of-war between logic and emotion, she had to ask. "Master, why did you give me this inquiry?" He arched silvery brows at her, and she went on defensively, "You could have taken it yourself. Anyone would say you're more experienced."

"It is your final trial, Shenza," he answered, not without sympathy. "As soon as the mask is done, the new magister takes up their first inquiry. That is our custom."

"But..." Words burst from her, unbidden. "I was barely awake!"

"The tradition is important," he replied all too reasonably. "It usually isn't a capital crime. And don't forget, you aren't working alone. You have already gathered a strong team. I like that young man. He is honest. You should listen to him."

His tone made Shenza wonder what Juss had been telling him.

The old man went on, "Not only that, but you still have the advantage. Yes, you do!" he assured her, seeing her doubtful expression. "You are the magister. You have flexibility and resources your opponent doesn't have. It is simply a matter of finding a way to make him reveal himself. Don't be content to fight on his terms. Make him come to you."

"How?" she asked flatly, feeling her anger return. His advice was far too vague. "As long as he remains hidden, I have no way to touch him. And the spirits..."

"They can be an asset to you. If they have an interest in resolving the matter, you may be able to call on their powers." Chiding gently, he insisted, "You are taking the darkest view of everything, Shenza. No one knows what will happen tomorrow, or even in the next few hours. Sometimes you must simply wait for movement. Be patient."

What would happen in the next few hours, Shenza thought grimly, was that the first lord's 'ghost' would mysteriously break the wards and terrorize the palace again. Indeed, the unknown enchanter would continue to do whatever he wished. And she was going to be blamed for it until she brought him to justice.

Hardening herself against her fears, Shenza resolved to ignore her teacher's wisdom in favor of Juss.'

"I don't think waiting is what I should do."

"Oh?" Laraquies sounded keenly interested.

She rose, feeling stiffness in her knees from sitting without a cushion. "I will go back to the palace tonight. I will take a ghost-net and wait for the haunting spirit." She smiled tartly. "If I let them know I am there, he will probably not come out. But if he does, then I will take his weapon away."

"Possibly," Master Laraquies agreed, though not without concern.

"I have to try." The brave words did nothing to warm the cold fear squeezing her stomach. "I have to do something, and this is the only evidence I have."

She quickly crossed the cottage to enter the magister's work room. The building seemed empty and bare after the riotous furnishings of the first lord's chambers. Strange, that she should think so. She had never envied the man before.

"Light," she said firmly.

In the amber lampglow she opened her travel case and gave the contents a careful inspection. From the inlaid cabinet came a fresh verity stone and a vial of pearl dust, replacing the materials she had depleted in the past two days. A new length of cloth for writing, since hers was already half used. Then a feather-light bundle of enchanted spider webs: the ghost-net. Its fine strands glimmered a subtle silvery violet.

Shenza examined it, wondering how sturdy the net might be. Spider-silk was extraordinarily strong for its measure, so it was said. Yet the fragile length was meant to capture immaterial spirits, not solid matter. Would it hold the semblage's weight?

Laraquies sauntered into the room after her. "Weren't you going to leave this to the peacekeepers?"

"When they have adequate protection, I will," she answered quietly. "At this time, you and I are the best defended, and I haven't heard you offer to do it."

After a moment's hesitation, he gravely admitted, "I am no longer young."

"That leaves just me, then, doesn't it?"

Shenza controlled her depression by pulling open each drawer in succession. She found little else of use. The charms were all ordinary ones, not intended for dangerous situations. There had been no way of anticipating these circumstances.

The silence eventually wore on her. "I don't truly expect a confrontation, especially if I make sure the staff knows I am there. Remember, the enemy may be one of them."

He asked again, "Are you sure?"

Shenza sat on the bench built into the foundation and looked up at him. "Well," she said, "there are two possibilities. He may realize we know how he committed the crimes, and protect himself by not using the semblage while I am there. In that case, I will be quite safe. If he does not think we know, he may make himself vulnerable by using the semblage where I have a chance to capture it. That would be more dangerous, but it is a necessary risk, isn't it?"

"Hm," he answered meditatively. "Then should I come with you? The two of us together might be safer."

"I would like that," she said, "but I believe you should stay here." He frowned now, troubled. She reminded him, "Only you and I are safe because we have our masks. If I am in danger, then it is all the more important for you to remain here, where you have all your defenses." She gestured, taking in the little house and its layers of magical safeguards. "That is my judgement as magister."

Obsidian eyes blinked at her, bemused.

"Considering how carefully he planned to keep himself hidden, I doubt he will challenge me. It would be too reckless." She shook her head. "I don't believe he will take the chance. Even so, my presence will put him in a more defensive position. If that is all I can do, then I will do it."

Recovering from his surprise, Laraquies wryly agreed. "It is generally a good idea to keep busy."

"Do you have any other suggestions?" she asked.

The old man nodded. He bent before the cabinet and drew out a broad leather sash, stitched with runes to protect against decay in the humid climate. A series of loops had been sewn on, offering convenient storage for the smaller talismans. "Wear this," he said.

"Do you think that's necessary? I have my travel case."

"It's hard to say what will happen from here," he answered gravely. "What if your travel case is taken from you?"

His words brought the sour taste of fear back to her throat. She swallowed it harshly. "Very well."

Shenza loosened the drape of her robe and let the old man settle the leather sash in place. Quick fingers loaded a small arsenal of wands, shells and stones. In a few minutes he nodded, satisfied. With the upper end resting on her left shoulder and the lower end on her right hip, the sash was neatly concealed when she re-settled her robe over her shoulder.

Reminded of her teacher's rich gift to her, Shenza hesitated between embarrassment and her sense of indebtedness. Duty won, as always.

"I meant to thank you for this, Magister," she said softly, fingering the fresh, bright purple of her robe.

To her surprise, the old man gripped her shoulders and kissed her cheeks, each in turn. "You have been a fine student," he said simply. "I am very proud of you."

A lump came to Shenza's throat. She suddenly felt very tired, overwhelmed by all that had happened in the past few days. It should have been her own grandmother saying that, she thought. But Master Laraquies had always been more than merely her teacher. She could depend on him, when her own elder disapproved. Gratitude for his many kindnesses welled up in her. "Magister, I..."

Softly, he soothed her. "Do not worry about this little trouble, Shenza. It will pass soon enough."

She swallowed the lump in her throat, but now felt her eyes burning. "But..."

He chuckled. "Stubborn child. Do not doubt you will win."

She did doubt it. Even with his astute counsel and Juss' brawn behind her, the whole situation seemed too much for her. Still, her own sense of duty compelled her to press on.

"Thank you, master."

"Sleep well," he smiled at her.

Shenza bent and picked up her travel case. 'Do not doubt that you will win.' If she repeated those words often enough, perhaps she would come to believe them.

Chapter Eleven
~ The Wrong Chances ~

Shenza's unexpected return to the palace threw the staff into a happy turmoil. A guest house was hastily prepared near the first lord's former home, since that was where they thought he might return. Their gratitude at her presence reassured her in a way that Master Laraquies' measured words did not.

But there was no haunting at the palace that night.

She would have felt more vindicated if her own rest had peaceful. Though the small cottage assigned to her was by no means as opulent as Lord Anges's, it was private and her every desire had been anticipated. Shenza found it difficult to relax amid so many comforts. She lay restless in the unfamiliar bed, rousing at any whisper of wind in the trees.

When she did sleep, her mind was troubled by unruly dreams. In a midnight jungle, vines seemed to tangle her feet and pinch her wrists. Onyx spiders glided on dagger-sharp webs, their hairy heads crowned with luminous peridot eyes. Serpents hissed, lithely swaying; Shenza started awake with the vivid sensation of a narrow, sinewy body pressed against her side. Yet there was no movement in the chamber, only dapples of ruddy moonlight and the sound of her own harsh breathing.

Because of this, perhaps, she slept longer than she intended. Shenza woke to find streamers of daylight slanting through the window screen. A guilty rush carried her to the hot, perfumed waters of the bath. There she tried to sort through what she recalled of her nightmares. She found little sense in the garbled fragments. Shenza was left with the heavy feeling that she might face such dreams again, each night she spent in the first lord's house.

The servants must have been observing her, for a large meal was waiting when she emerged from the bath. Shenza quickly ate the boiled goose eggs, smoked fish and sea-plums, finding it odd to dine alone. She would have preferred to break her fast with the servants, who were honest workers like herself. It would also give her a chance to observe them, and perhaps see some hint of the murderer's identity. Perhaps tomorrow it could be arranged. Otherwise—she smiled wryly to herself—it would be far too easy to grow accustomed to their pampering.

There was also the comforting knowledge that the dark hours had passed quietly. Her guess had been correct. The unknown enchanter did not choose to test her mettle. Surely her mere presence was not so intimidating, Shenza thought wryly. Catching him out would not be easy.

Once more Shenza donned her mask. She sought out Andle and offered her thanks to the household through him. Then she quickly turned her feet down the hill. A cursory glance showed her the pale moons hanging above the town. Inkesh had slipped toward the western horizon, and Quaiss was waxing greater. Prenuse and Meor were not visible, unfortunately. Still, what she saw gave her some hope. Also, the sun's position in the cloudless vault reassured her that she had not slept quite as late as she feared.

Nevertheless, Juss was waiting for her beneath the great fig tree in the market square. From his restless pacing, it seemed he had been expecting her for some while. Nor did he give her time to explain her tardiness.

"You tricked me," the peace officer accused. His short black curls were closely wrapped by a dark yellow turban, its fabric matched to his kilt.

Taken off balance, Shenza politely replied, "I beg your pardon?"

"You sent me off to that curomancer lady and went up to the palace by yourself." A decorative fringe on his head cloth shook with his indignation.

Shenza sighed, feeling the night's weariness descend on her again. "There was no choice, Juss."

"You could have been in danger," he scolded hotly. "What do you think we would do if something happened to you?"

In that event, she thought, Master Laraquies would take over, as he should have in the first place. Patiently, she countered, "Did you have an amulet to protect you?"

Since his broad brown chest was unadorned, the answer to that was obvious.

"You still should have told me," he fumed.

"Human lives are not toys to be played with," she lectured in her turn. "You have been a good deal of help to me in this inquiry. Do you think I want to tell your wife why I let you die?"

He did not reply, and Shenza gladly changed the subject.

"Was Sub-Chief Shamatt able to find any amulets for the other peacekeepers?"

"I don't know. I haven't seen him yet," he said, still sulking. "What about Magister Laraquies? Did he get any from that coven?"

"As of last night, they do have protections available, but Master Laraquies thought the price seemed a bit high."

"I thought so," he grunted.

"I thought perhaps Shamatt should handle those negotiations, since he seems a prudent man. Or Chief Borleek, if they are completely beyond reason."

This drew a grudging smile from her companion. "The Chief would just take them and get us all cursed as revenge. I'll mention it to Shamatt. We ought to keep some on hand anyway."

Shenza nodded, relieved to see his humor recovering. "And what did Mistress Kafseet say?"

He shrugged. "We can take the old man out of the cocoon any time, but she thinks he needs to go someplace else than the clinic. It's too close to the ward, she says."

"What do you think?" Shenza asked cautiously.

Juss considered before replying. "She could be right. It's hard to say."

Shenza pondered for a moment. The safest place would be somewhere anonymous and unknown, so Byben could vanish for a time. No likely places sprang to mind. "I will have to speak to her about it."

"So what are your plans for today?" Juss asked.

Beneath her mask, she smiled at the barbed question. "I'm afraid I will have to impose on Master Nurune's coven for the use of their library." He frowned dubiously, and she explained, "I need more detailed information on semblages than Master Laraquies has. What of you?"

"I don't want to go there," he complained.

"There is no reason you have to," she pointed out. Juss regarded her suspiciously, and she chuckled softly. "You aren't going to miss anything, Juss. It's a library. I won't be in any danger."

"I don't know about that," he grumbled.

"I am glad for your help," she stressed when he continued staring at her, "but I shouldn't keep you from your other duties indefinitely."

"You won't," he answered, just a bit too quickly.

Shenza searched for a compromise, but before she could speak, a silent shock stilled her tongue. It was like the sound of crockery breaking and silk tearing, both together; it burned along her nerves like scouring sand. Yet it was neither a true sound nor a physical sensation. Instinctively her head snapped toward the source, the harbor.

"What's wrong?" Juss asked uneasily.

"Something's happening," she breathed with alarm. He leaned closer to hear. "Last time..."

Two days ago, a feeling just like this had brought her bolting from her hammock. That, she now knew, had been the moment the first lord died. She had felt the spirits' outrage with her magician's trained senses.

Now, again, their fury had been aroused. Shenza began walking swiftly toward the edge of the terrace.

"What do you mean?" Juss easily matched her pace. "Magister?"

"I don't know yet," she answered tensely, but she feared what might be coming. The spirits were already offended by Lord Anges's death. Now something else provoked them. She had to find out what was wrong and stop it before it was too late.

The young sorceress was almost running by the time she reached the rail overlooking the port. She caught herself against a marble pillar at the head of the downward stair. Shenza's anxious eyes swept the shallow water, and she drew in a hiss of breath through her teeth.

A pair of boats was moving across the enclosed lagoon, toward a gap in the breakwaters that sheltered the harbor. Sea-wet oars flashed rhythmically as the crewmen bent their bronzed shoulders to pull. Tall prows, brightly painted, skimmed away confidently before the bales of merchandise lashed to the decks. But the placid waters of the bay were beginning to stir, and the sky above dimmed ominously.

"That's it," Shenza said with grim panic. "Someone is trying to leave, and they know it. We've got to call them back, or —!"

Juss was already gone from her side. Plunging down the steps, he bellowed. "Stop those ships!"

On the docks and the exposed sand, other sailors milled among their beached craft. Some called laughing encouragement to the defectors. Others appeared to be considering a similar departure. Shenza watched the men on the piers give way nervously as Juss descended on them. A rough demand she could not clearly hear resulted in one of the ship masters offering his signal horn. The peacekeeper snatched it up and raised the mouthpiece to his lips. The long cylindrical shell sent three short, piercing notes skyward. After a pause, he repeated the call. And again. Then a threatening rumble overhead drew Shenza's eyes upward.

The morning sky had been sunny, clear and still. Now, from nowhere, clouds clumped and darkened, blotting out the daylight. A fierce breeze brought the air alive with movement. Its buffeting currents tugged at her robes, her head wrap. As Shenza watched, the clouds began a circular rotation above the town. The pair of unwise vessels began to dip and plunge as the same wind broke the bay's smooth surface into a coarse chop that grew worse as she watched.

Juss thrust the horn back at its owner. A harsh command carried to her on the wind. "Sound the call-back!"

Reluctantly, the man obeyed. His cheeks puffed out, and a new sequence of notes rang out. Ships carried these trumpets as a means of communication in fog or at night. They could also be used to pass messages along crowded wharves. Shenza had learned the basic code from her father. She remembered almost none of it now, but she did recognize the urgent summons back to port.

Shenza clung to the corner post as if paralyzed. How had this happened? She was magister. She had ordered the port closed, and her authority should have been unquestioned. And where were the peacekeepers? They had their own patrol boats, and could have intervened before the ships left. She could not see them on the water, and it was obviously going to take too long to gather a crew now.

There ought to be something she could do, Shenza thought frantically. But what? Against the power of nature itself, what could any human do?

Curious townsfolk were gathering around her to gawk at the commotion. Some descended toward the docks while others lined the terrace rail, murmuring fearfully up at the sinister clouds. Behind them, in the market, a second trumpet had taken up Juss' call, and farther off she heard a third high echo. At the same time, a dutiful ship master had taken to repeating the summons to the departing vessels. No reply came from the two renegade ships. Against wind and wave, they fought stubbornly toward the outward channel.

Thunder rumbled above. It sounded as if something heavy was about to fall on them. The harbor churned, its clear waters now dark with mud from the bottom. Ever larger waves slapped at the tide-bare shore. Yet the sea was receding swiftly down the sand. As if it were a hand drawing back to strike, Shenza thought.

That frightful notion dissolved her paralysis, and she pushed her way down the steps toward the piers, where one peace officer stood amid an indignant tangle of seamen and laborers.

"He's not answering," the fellow with the trumpet protested. "I can't help it."

"Juss!"

Her friend seemed almost glad to turn toward her. "The others will be here soon," he assured her, all business now.

"We can't wait," she answered tensely. "Get everyone off this level. Hurry!"

"I don't follow you," he said bluntly.

And another of the sailors burst out, "We can't leave our ships!"

"You'll have to," she informed them tautly. "Look at the water." Heads turned. An uneasy murmur was all but lost in the thunder from above them. When she could be heard, Shenza demanded, "Do you think it'll just keep going out like that without coming back in? Now hurry! I don't know how much time we have."

"But..." The ship master stood, horn in hand, paralyzed much as she had been. At another time, she would have felt sympathy for him.

Juss interrupted. "You heard the magister. Go. All of you." He started pushing sailors roughly toward the steps. In a louder voice, he bellowed. "Get off the docks! Everyone up to the second level!"

Another masculine voice shouted from above them. "Who sounded the call?"

A day ago, Shenza would not have believed she could be so happy to see the band of yellow-kilted men shoving their way down the stairs. The leader was one of the three men she had met in Borleek's office. Pars. Or was it Rakshel.

"Me!" Juss roared back. "We're clearing everyone off this level!"

"Why?" came the shouted question.

With a broad gesture, Juss indicated the blackening sky and foaming waters. "Does this look normal to you?" To those nearest, he urged more quietly. "Come on, move! Get up the stairs! You, too—go!"

"And get the people back from the edge!" Shenza called.

The squad leader started, perhaps having missed her among the throng. With visible reluctance, he began detailing his officers. At least, if he scorned her words, he would listen to Juss.

Putting that aside, she moved out along the nearest pier, beckoning to the seamen who still lingered on the widening beach. "Go in!" she called, over and over. "You're in danger! Get to high ground!"

When the dock had cleared a little, she gazed urgently toward the bay. To her intense relief, one of the two boats had put about and was struggling for shore. The other wallowed, oars in disarray. It could not steer in the turbulent swells.

The predicament was their own fault. They should not have disobeyed a lawful authority. Yet Shenza could not bring herself to turn from their plight.

There was a way you were supposed to address the spirits, she knew, with poetic phrases and rich offerings. But fine language had deserted her, and she had nothing of value to present. Feeling foolish and small, she set her travel case between her feet and stretched out her hands in supplication. Softly, almost to herself, she spoke.

"Lords of the Waves, have mercy. Pity these foolish ones. Do not punish their error."

The spirits' mood was not lenient. There was a brilliant flash, seemingly directly above her, and the heavens suddenly split with a violent burst of thunder. Shenza started, feeling a wave of hot prickles along her arms and legs.

Then a rough hand fell on her shoulder. "What are you doing? You come in, too!" Juss called above the angry peals.

"Juss, I have to try. The whole town could be destroyed." Turning from him, she raised her hands again. "See! The men repent of their error. Even now, they return to land. Lords of the Sky and Waves, be gentle!"

"What, you think they'll listen?" Juss demanded incredulously.

"Mercy, greatest ones. I beg you!"

"Come on, or I'll carry you!"

They were both cut off by a great boom that was neither thunder nor tide. Amid a geyser of spray, something huge broke the surface of the sea just beyond the breakwater. Thin shrieks came from the town behind them.

Here was another legend become real. It was shaped like an eel, narrow and long, with a many-fanged maw topping a powerful corded neck. Elegant, spiny fins threw plumes of spray in a hundred directions. Its hide was of a color with the sea itself, a green so deep it looked black in the gloom. When lightning flashed again, phosphorescent stripes blazed along its sides.

"That's a..." Juss choked.

"Taisaris," she finished for him.

It was said the Eleshouri created the sea serpents to control the currents and tides. But their monstrous forms housed a temper that could swallow up entire islands, and so they were banished to the utmost depths. Only sometimes they crept out to overturn ships and drag the hapless sailors below. Or they might be summoned by their masters, to punish some transgression.

The beast roared at the height of its arc, a bellow like the howl of cyclonic winds. Shenza stepped back and bumped into Juss. He steadied her, but did not speak.

Taisaris turned in the air with lumbering slowness, then collapsed back into the sea. Its fall raised a wall of spray that obscured the horizon. And then, what she had feared came to pass: over the breakwater, a long hump of water rolled swiftly toward Chalsett-port.

Shenza needed no more urging from Juss. She snatched up her travel case and they ran toward the safety of the terrace. Under their feet the boards of the pier trembled with vibrations that grew ever stronger and closer.

In front of them, dark-skinned backs of seamen and peace officers together dashed up the stairs. For Shenza and Juss there was no time left. The crack of splintering wood mingled with a greedy roar as the wave struck the lowest level of the town. Juss threw his arm around Shenza's shoulder, flattening her against the vertical face of the tier above them. A hard wash of cold brine pressed them against the stonework with bruising force. It came to her shoulders, nearly lifting her from her feet. A moment later the flow reversed. She could feel the suction dragging at them. For a terrifying moment her sandals slipped, but Juss' strong arms helped her keep her footing. Then the pressure lifted and the wave fell back with a cheated sloosh. Sea-foam hissed malevolently as the waters drained back over the edge of the quay.

Cautiously, Shenza stirred enough to look over her shoulder.

The sturdy wharves appeared more or less intact, but the port's shipping was in complete disarray. Frantic voices babbled on the level above, exclaiming over the wreckage. Boats and trade goods lay on the sand like scattered playthings. Debris floated everywhere. Many of the vessels were badly damaged, and a few of the smaller fishing boats had even been thrown up onto the wharf.

The harbor remained in turmoil. Neither of the departing ships was visible, though dark heads bobbed in two clusters among the waves. Farther out, beyond the gap in the breakwaters, a long, finned arch of back slid slowly into the murky water. Soon nothing but turbulence was left.

"How..." Juss choked hoarsely in her ear. "How can something that big swim in water so shallow?"

Trembling, she leaned on his strength for a moment. "The spirits do as they wish."

"Do you think it's safe?"

Juss sounded more like himself, but Shenza had no idea how to answer his question. Instead, she concentrated on the stranded sailors in the bay. She could not tell if any of men had been lost, since she did not know how many had been on the two vessels, but they appeared to be swimming. Wisely, perhaps, they avoided the breakwater, which was nearer to them but also closer to the sea serpent. The swimmers struck out for the shore instead.

Rubber-legged and dripping, Shenza began to walk toward the stair. "Was everyone off the docks?"

"I don't know. I was looking for you."

Shenza ignored his reproach. "We'll have to search for wounded, then."

"Yes, Magister."

The buffeting wind cut at her wet skin, and inky clouds still boiled above them, pressing lower toward the land. As she spoke, the underside blurred into pallid streaks. Shenza stopped, gazing incredulously upward. What more could happen?

Her unspoken question was answered as hail slashed down on the port city. Hard white pellets hissed as they fell, bounced off wet paving and ruined vessels. They stung where they struck bare skin.

With despair, she said to the sky, "I did what I could!"

"It wasn't your fault," Juss consoled her, but he winced from the lashing weather. "Come on, let's get under something."

"But I didn't stop it, either," she said mournfully. Hail stones crunched uneasily beneath her sandals.

"Don't talk like that," he urged.

"I should have."

She stopped again. At the top of the stairs, arms akimbo, stood Chief Peacekeeper Borleek. Water darkened his golden mantle as he surveyed the destruction. At his shoulder, Rakshel stood glaring. His bald head gleamed with rain. Behind them, the townsfolk scattered, fleeing the stinging hail. Shenza hesitated a moment, but there was nowhere else she could go. Weary legs carried her upward to the landing.

Before Borleek could say the words she knew he was thinking, she told him levelly, "I am sorry, but I must ask you to contain the looting. Someone must search for dead or injured as well." Even amplified by her mask, her voice barely carried over the clatter of the falling hail. "Also, please send someone to bring those men in from the water. I need to know as soon as possible if anyone aboard had paid them for passage. If so, I want to speak to that person."

If the enemy had bribed or threatened the crew into breaking the ban on travel, he could well be dead by now. She didn't know whether to hope for that or not. But she needed to eliminate the possibility, either way.

"I will leave the penalties in your hands." With no tact, she added, "But no beatings."

"Huh." To Shenza's surprise, he did not seem offended by her words. She began to move past, and he mocked her with a curl of lip, "What's the code?"

"Sea plum."

Still sneering, he nodded to Rakshel. "Do it."

"Yes, sir." With a parting glower, he hurried off.

Borleek rumbled down at her, "You can hardly blame them. Time is money, you know. This has cost them a lot of both."

Hot anger welled in Shenza's breast. How could he not see, even now, the peril the city faced? With bitter feeling she replied, "Well, time is life, too. Do you think money can buy back a life?"

Once more Borleek snorted to himself. Then the gaze of black fish eyes focused beyond her shoulder, on Juss. "And don't think you're running off again," he said with deliberate malice. "I need every man here."

Shenza started, stung that he would take her assistant away. But after all, she had to admit he was right. Even one more officer would help to control the chaotic situation. She glanced back to see her companion's face tighten briefly, but Juss controlled his feelings.

"Yes sir," he said.

What else could he say? Borleek was still the chief peacekeeper, and his commanding officer.

"Go find Rakshel and see what help he needs."

"Right." Juss nodded and strode off in the direction the squad leader had gone. Shenza hesitated a moment. The beating hail was giving way to icy rain which dissolved her anger as quickly as it came. The Chief's callous eyes were on her, waiting for some challenge.

Shenza knew better than to make one, not now and not here. Not speaking, she stepped forward into the murmuring throng of villagers. If only she could escape so easily from the disaster behind her.

Chapter Twelve
~ Many Times Welcome ~

Dripping and draggled, Shenza slunk through the market and toward the grand stair. She did not really know where she intended to go when she left the piers. Her feet simply carried her along the familiar route to Magister Laraquies' house.

It felt, somehow, like a cowardly retreat.

The punishing rain slacked off, though the sky remained dour and gray. The subtle sense of outrage still radiating from every leaf and vine of the overgrown market did little to reassure her. Nor the lingering mutters of thunder from overhead. The spirits's wrath was not so easily assuaged.

She was approaching the base of the stairs when Magister Laraquies came hurrying down them. It was unusual to see the old man move with such haste. He paused when he saw her, interrupting the flow of townsfolk hurrying toward the docks. A parasol kept his bald head dry and overshadowed the worried glint of his sable eyes. A swift, keen gaze took in her sorry appearance.

The old man moved beside Shenza so his parasol covered her as well.

"Magister," she said.

"I sensed a disturbance," he said through the drumming of rain against the parasol. "What happened?"

"Two ships attempted to depart from the harbor. The spirits were offended and struck out at the town." Perhaps Shenza spoke a bit too evenly but it seemed important, somehow, to set aside her private feelings. "They sent Taisaris, and it caused a great wave."

Laraquies started. "The sea's vengeance," he said.

Shenza nodded. "It has gone for the moment, but the port was badly damaged. Chief Borleek was organizing the search for wounded when I left. I do not know whether he would welcome your aid or not."

Her teacher stared at her, as if he could see her face beneath the mask. He quickly decided, "I am sure he doesn't need me. Come, you are wet through. I suggest a hot bath and a solid meal."

Shenza did not bother telling him she had already had both those things today. Her new robe hung sodden, clinging to limbs that felt coarse with sea salt, and her stringy curls dripped down her back. In her mind's eye, she could see the monster roaring from the churning sea, lightning blazing on its baleful countenance. She shuddered, remembering, and let Master Laraquies hurry her back up the stairs to home.

~

Shenza only picked at her lunch before dragging herself off to the little bath house behind the cottage. While she cleaned up from her unintended swim, Laraquies helped himself to the last of the tea. He was beginning to feel the need for a little elitherium, and she would not miss it.

Absurdly, despite the destruction his student described, Laraquies felt an inner glow of awe and pride. First the Eleshi, and now Taisaris! Creatures of legend walked abroad on a daily basis, it seemed. He wished he could have seen them!

And Borleek had been there. Had he seen the monster? Laraquies smirked to himself. That ought to change his attitude. It should, but it might not. The man was stubborn as a rock. He would probably dismiss the experience as the result of salt water in his eyes.

Laraquies had to wonder how many others would do the same. Humans did have an amazing capacity for rationalization, especially when confronted by frightening experiences. Most people did not believe the tales, after all. Human arrogance made it necessary to believe they, with their magic, were the greatest power in the world. It was easier to deny the spirits than admit the existence of forces beyond their control.

Still, it was not wise to reject the evidence of one's own eyes. Nor was Laraquies the only sorcerer who had sensed the surge of mystic energy and come running to find its cause. He only regretted that he missed seeing these things for himself.

The old man sighed briefly over his cooling tea. If only the port could have been spared. On the other hand, the emergency ought to keep Borleek occupied for a few days. Laraquies smiled wryly. This was one way to gain Shenza the time she needed.

~

It was well past noon when Shenza once again attempted her research in the coven library. She set out wearing a spare robe borrowed from Master Laraquies. The purple cloth she had worn so proudly hung drying in his garden. The angry clouds had thinned at last, and the penetrating sunlight raised wisps of steam from the roofs and streets. She could smell the damp warmth on the air.

The town seemed very quiet in this humid afternoon. There was little business in the market, since everyone was working to clear the wreckage from the harbor. Shenza still felt she should have prevented it, somehow.

There had been no word from Juss when she left. She had thought he might break away from his emergency duties, but he did not. If he did arrive, Master Laraquies knew where she would be.

Rather than taking the central stair, she moved northeast along the third tier and descended to the second level by a secondary stair. This brought her through a shady warren of commercial buildings to the coven office. The small compound was located on the border of the warehouse district, where many of its client businesses operated. A shoulder-height stone wall enclosed several modest structures spaced about a central garden. The construction was of marble, pale against the dark green foliage, with roofs of soft purple tile. In an open pavilion, she glimpsed a man in magician's robes lecturing a group of children who sat cross-legged before him.

At the gate stood an apprentice sorcerer, a young boy in a kilt and mantle of purple and white stripes. As she approached, the lad strayed into the street, peering toward the harbor through gaps between the buildings. When he saw Shenza, he scurried back and bowed with commendable poise for his age. "Welcome. How may I serve you?"

"I would like permission to use your library."

"And your name?" The boy stumbled a little, as if he was reciting the words from memory.

"Magister Shenza," she answered. It still sounded strange to use that title.

"Please come this way." Stiffly, trying not to gawk at his important guest, the apprentice led her along a short path to one of the cottages on her right. Within, a tight cluster of purple-robed men and women stood in furtive conversation.

"Magister Shenza is here," her guide piped up.

The group burst apart with obvious embarrassment. They must have been talking about the morning's events, she supposed with mild amusement. All were somewhat younger than herself, garbed in wizard's robes and turbans with tasteful adornments such as armbands or earrings. Some of these gleamed with magic in the sight of her mask.

One of the men, just slightly older than the others, stepped forward. "Thank you, Deets. You may go." He spoke kindly, though with a trace of condescension. Not waiting for obedience, he crossed his hands over his chest and bowed twice. "You are many times welcome, Magister. What may we do to aid you?"

Bowing twice was a bit too much courtesy, Shenza thought with instinctive wariness. Aloud, she merely said, "I apologize for interrupting you. I would like to use your library, if it wouldn't be too much trouble."

A flash of curiosity, quickly suppressed, passed among the sorcerers.

"Of course you may," the young man assured her warmly. "Our coven is honored to help you in any way. Please allow me to escort you, Magister." With a less formal bow, he gestured toward the doorway.

Direction was not necessary, since Shenza had used the library often as an apprentice. Still, she could understand why the order would not want strangers wandering around unattended. They were a business, after all, and had proprietary concerns.

"I appreciate your help," she said softly.

"Not at all," he insisted. "This way, please."

Shenza nodded to the other coven members before joining her guide on the brick path. He set a leisurely pace, passing under the shade of a vine-grown archway along one side of the garden. A fountain, as they passed, chattered merrily. On the opposite side, the tutor droned to his young charges.

In the broader daylight, she saw that her escort was a thin man, as befitted a working enchanter, with smooth dark skin and unusual, light brown eyes. Regular features, though not exactly handsome, were still quite pleasant. His hair, worn long, had been artificially straightened and swept straight back from his face. Shenza did not usually like this effect, but the sleekness seemed to suit him.

She sensed her companion glancing at her sidelong, pleased by her scrutiny. "My name is Tonkatt Sengool of Tindali," he began conversationally. "I hope you don't mind if I welcome you as a new magister. We'll probably be working together in the future."

"Thank you. I suppose we may," she answered neutrally. So he was a Sengool? That made him a relative of Innoshyra and Nurune, though not of the same household. She couldn't help thinking they might not be working together in quite the way he wanted, if the coven's business practices continued as they had in the past.

Tonkatt seemed to be hoping for some further reply from her. "It is still very new to me," she said.

"The situation must be difficult for you," he said with sympathy. His smile reminded her of Master Nurune's.

"Yes."

The look in his eyes made her feel warm all over, with more than just the heat of the day. Even with her features masked, she felt somehow vulnerable and exposed. Shenza thought it prudent to concentrate for a few moments on the ground where she was walking.

She looked up again, and stopped. Descending the steps from one of the buildings and turning onto the path just ahead of them were two of the last people Shenza wished to see: Nurune and Innoshyra of Sengool. They too paused, as if they

~ The Magister's Mask ~

shared her reluctance. Then, after what seemed a very long hesitation, Innoshyra pushed forward with her chin raised proudly. Nurune followed her.

"Good day," Shenza murmured diffidently as they drew near. The wealthy lady wore a mourning robe of deep red and a turban of the same cloth, with strands of pearls dangling against her straight black hair. Cosmetics had been so heavily applied that her eyes almost seemed to have been painted onto her face.

Innoshyra sniffed with brazen hauteur. "I have nothing to say to you."

Nurune's face remained neutral, but Shenza detected a trace of dismay in his mellow voice as he murmured, "Niece, we must give honor where it is due."

"If I thought it was due, that would be different, Uncle." Innoshyra ostentatiously did not look at Shenza, and moved to push past her. But Shenza did not stand aside. She might have to accept such treatment from the spirits, and even from Borleek, but not from this proud lady.

"Pardon me, Innoshyra," she said firmly. "I wish to speak with you."

"Have we been introduced?" the lady hissed at her for the presumption of using her name alone.

"Everyone knows of a great lady such as you," Shenza responded, imitating Master Laraquies' cool, mild tone. Innoshyra glared at her, wary of the compliment. Her eyes strayed toward Nurune.

Her uncle at once interceded. "My niece and I are on our way to an important appointment," he said, as if with regret.

Shenza almost enjoyed insisting. "Then I shall be brief. Come, my lady. Walk with me for a moment."

Innoshyra hesitated. Shenza was keenly aware of Nurune's bland gaze and Tonkatt's quick interest in the scene before him. For a moment Shenza thought Innoshyra would flout her instructions. Then she heard the rustle of fabric as the lady reluctantly accompanied her.

They strolled aside, passing between two small buildings and toward a sunny grove of palm trees. Now that she had her interview, Shenza was uncertain how to open the conversation.

Innoshyra did not know Shenza had seen her leaving the first lord's quarters.

Then her companion stopped, all but stamping a dainty foot in her pique. "Do you have something to say to me?"

Shenza regarded her for a moment. Why was she so angry? A sense of guilt, perhaps? But for what? Cautiously, she said, "Please tell me about your relationship with Lord Anges."

A sequence of conflicting emotions crossed Innoshyra's face as if, like Shenza, she groped for the proper response. Then she drew back, virtuously offended. "What do you mean? I trust you aren't suggesting something improper!"

"I would never do that," Shenza answered immediately, though she suspected the absence of impropriety was not due to lack of effort on Innoshyra's part. She managed to say, without inflection, "It is simply that your uncle told me of your deep feelings for my Lord."

"Of... Of course I loved him!" Innoshyra snapped, perhaps irritated that she could not refute this statement. She adopted a trembling tone. "We had known each other since we were children, and I... I suppose that I always loved him. Who could know him and not love him?" Shenza could. She carefully held her tongue against the rejoinder that sprang to mind. "Naturally, I hoped to win his love in return. After all, we are equals in rank."

That was untrue, but Shenza was not interested in disputing it. "Surely," she said quietly, "you were aware that there were others."

Innoshyra's eyes glittered like beads of black jade, and not all the color in her face was due to cosmetics.

"They did not matter. They were nothing! We were a perfect match." Hearing her vehemence, Shenza wondered if she was trying to convince herself, too. "After we were married, all that would have stopped. My Lord would never need anyone else but me."

Shenza studied her for a moment, unable to believe even this self-involved young woman could deceive herself so completely. If, indeed, she believed her own words.

This supported Alceme's and Nurune's contention that Innoshyra had no reason to harm the first lord, but it did not address the main question in Shenza's mind.

"I'm sure you must have visited his grave," she probed delicately.

"Of course." Innoshyra adopted a quavering tone, but a strident one, as if she wanted everyone in the coven compound to hear of her fidelity. "Every day. Twice a day."

"That is commendable," Shenza began, but Innoshyra was not finished.

"...And I will continue to do so until the murderer is brought to justice." Innoshyra scowled now, reverting to her former hostile manner. "I will not rest until my dear Lord is avenged!"

"That is my intention, as well," Shenza said. She sighed to herself. As loudly as the woman spoke, she might as well just invite the two men to listen to their conversation. They couldn't have missed much of what was said.

Innoshyra frowned scornfully. "Then what are you doing about it? Nothing!" she angrily declared. "You have had three days—three! The killer has been caught, but all you can do is stroll around asking irrelevant questions. That isn't what I call seeking justice!"

"I assure you," Shenza began, but Innoshyra of Sengool was not listening.

"And putting up wards! Wards that keep me from my darling's side," she complained bitterly. "I am suffering from a deep loss, and you wound me further yet."

Shenza stared at her, equally appalled by Innoshyra's nerve and her poor acting skills. Then she tensed. The over-loud protests had nearly distracted her from something far more important.

Innoshyra mistook her silence for defeat, and smirked cruelly. "If that is all, I really must be going." She brushed past, and this time Shenza did not try to stop her. She watched thoughtfully as the other woman stalked away.

It was the wards that really angered Innoshyra. And why? Because she wanted a necromancer to engineer her marriage to the dead Lord's ghost. Her intrusion into Lord Anges' quarters must have been for the purpose of securing some token that

could be used in a seance. The murderer had unknowingly
stymied her ambitions by his imposture, which resulted in
additional wards being raised. Not only was the Lord's spirit
prevented from wandering, it was protected from a spiritualist's
summons.

This was not something Shenza had planned, but it did not
displease her. In fact, it was almost funny.

"Let us go, Uncle," said Innoshyra loudly.

The two of them were walking off as Shenza rejoined her
escort. Tonkatt attempted to maintain a polite expression, but
his eyes gleamed as he glanced at her sidelong. He must think
her thwarted, humiliated. Shenza had no intention of revealing
how well satisfied she felt.

"Shall we also continue?" she suggested.

"Of course, Magister. This way, please." They walked on
toward their goal. The silence must have bothered Tonkatt, for
he inquired, a bit too casually, "Was Magister Laraquies able to
find the fire amulets he was seeking yesterday?"

So he knew a little of current events, did he? And he was
trying to find out more. She replied quite truthfully, "I do not
know. It would certainly be helpful if he could."

"We would be happy to help him with anything he might
need."

And make a profit at it, she thought, torn between irony and
his unexpected attraction. Censoring herself, she answered
lamely, "Yes. Thank you."

To her relief, they now approached another of the buildings
in the compound.

"Here is the library. Light." At his command, radiance
sprang from oil lamps along the walls.

The coven's library was much like Master Laraquies' but
considerably larger, filling an entire building where his was a
mere wall. Pigeonhole racks rayed out from the walls to
shoulder height, creating six wedge-shaped reading areas.
Cushions and low tables had been provided. A tightly wrapped
scroll rested in each of the many small, square compartments.
The familiar scents of old cloth and dust mingled with the
fragrance of lamp oil.

"Is there anything else you need, Magister?" Tonkatt offered pleasantly. "I can help you find what you are looking for." He was trying to make eye contact, but her mask prevented it. That was fortunate, for she was already keenly aware of his nearness. She wished he would leave.

"That is not necessary," Shenza assured him just as pleasantly. Cold instinct told her he did not need to know what she was doing research about. "I have worked here before and can find what I require."

"Very well." He sounded a bit disappointed, but bowed and stepped back. "I'll return in a short time, if you need anything."

"Thank you."

As his sandals whispered off behind her, Shenza quickly moved into the main room, choosing one of the study areas at random. She set down her travel case and let her knees fold in sudden weakness. She hoped Tonkatt hadn't thought her too brusque. Well, his fishing for information had been annoying. And yet, she knew that wasn't what bothered her.

What was wrong with her? It wasn't that she didn't understand her own feelings. To be truthful, her studies as apprentice magister had not left much time for personal relationships. To say she was unskilled in the ways of men would be putting it kindly. Even so, she did not normally respond to men this way. And how could she be attracted to Tonkatt of Tindali? He was the scion of an unscrupulous house.

No, it was unsuitable by any measure. Her quietly ordered life was already in disarray. There was no need for any further complications!

Before beginning her research, she quickly opened her travel case and made note of what she had learned of Innoshyra's scheme. Her opinion of the Sengool family had not improved in the least. Even their name was an affectation. Until very recently, Sengool was a line within the House of Kesquin. After a family quarrel, they set themselves apart as Sengool of Sengool. Such divergences were not unknown, particularly when money was involved. However, it was customary to petition the civil authorities, not assume the honor for oneself.

As for Tonkatt, his name was Sengool of Tindali, which meant his mother was a Sengool who married a man of the

House Tindali. That would make him a cousin of Innoshyra, rather than a brother.

But these things were irrelevant. With firm determination, she rose and went in search of information. As she had hoped, the library did contain some information on semblages, much more than the brief mention in Magister Laraquies' encyclopedia. Shenza quickly reviewed four scrolls in turn. Unfortunately, she found no easy means to destroy a semblage. Lacking that, she settled into a lengthy treatise detailing how a semblage was constructed, hoping to infer some way of severing the link between the sorcerer and his tool.

Twice Tonkatt looked in on her, and so did two other attractive young men. Each time she deferred their questions. Shenza wondered in bemusement if the coven had something to hide from her. She couldn't remember the staff being so attentive when she had studied here as a mere apprentice.

Despite their interruptions, the afternoon steadily passed. The shadows were lengthening when Shenza abruptly looked up from the list of arcane materials she was copying. The wind was stirring in the trees outside the library, and she felt her skin prickle as the hairs rose along her arms. The spirits were moving again.

Shenza re-rolled her scrolls and returned them to their places. With a growing sense of urgency, she snatched up her notes, stuffed them into the travel case, and all but ran to the library door.

In the compound, the class of children was gathered with a different tutor, a staid older woman. Other sorcerers hastened from the adjoining buildings in trios and pairs, wearing alarmed or confused expressions. Shenza's pulse skipped as Tonkatt hurried to her side.

"Magister, is something happening?" he asked, sounding a trace less sure of himself than he had been earlier.

She stood for a moment, merely listening. The unseen disturbance vibrated in the garden. The bushes and trees churned with the wind. Flocks of brightly colored birds flitted wildly. Bird calls rang out in a confused melange of chuckling, whistling and chattering.

"Magister?" Tonkatt repeated, nervously following her gaze.

Shenza was already moving past him. "I wish I didn't have to know," she sighed.

"But what is it?" he persisted.

In the quiet courtyard, shrill sounds pierced the blanket of bird calls. Horns! Many of them, sounding over and over. And below that was a building roar, harder to hear over the distance.

The coven members murmured around her—low, but she could hear. "Is it going to hail again?" whispered one of the apprentice boys to his neighbor. And a junior sorceress complained, "What now?"

Shenza told Tonkatt, "I sense no danger. It should be safe to continue your duties. I will have to go see what's happening."

Despite her assurance, Shenza was aware of the other sorcerers trailing after her as she swiftly crossed the garden. A growing stream of foot traffic passed outside the compound. Shenza joined them. All moved toward the insistent trumpeting in the marketplace. The folk were apprehensive, yet not frightened. Shenza too felt an impulsive excitement. With an effort, she held herself to a fast walk. The emotional pull toward the harbor was instinctive, irresistible.

What had seemed a dull roar became clearer as they moved among the market's crowded aisles. It was not another great wave, as she first feared, but the sound of drumming punctuated by high horn calls and human voices baying wildly. The drained atmosphere of the morning had changed dramatically. The crowds were almost giddy. Dark faces were split with wide smiles. Mixed with the growing din was joyous singing. Simple phrases, that everyone learned in childhood, fitted around the drumming. The hundreds of voices, raised as one, created an eerie effect.

As they neared the central square, merchants were passing out lengths of gaily pattered cloth for makeshift streamers. The dancing townsfolk waved these over their heads. In other stalls the vendors simply left their wares, taking up pots lids or wooden utensils and beating them together in an elemental rhythm. Whoever didn't have an instrument clapped along with the beat. Folk of all kinds mingled together, with no regard for kinship or class. They didn't seem to know why they celebrated, only that they must.

It was hard to keep her bearings as the press of humanity carried her along. By a steady effort, Shenza worked her way to where she could see into the central square. There she found the heart of the commotion. The crowd circled slowly in a kind of human vortex, dancing and singing, beating makeshift drums and blowing horns. At the center, above the maelstrom, rode a man in an open chair supported by bamboo shafts.

It must be the new first lord, she realized with a shock.

It was for him the people sang. His name, chanted over and over, set this spell on them. Lord Aspace had come to Chalsett-port.

The knowledge quenched Shenza's excitement, leaving cold dismay behind. She shrank back into the shelter of a covered arbor, feeling alone among the rejoicing throng. They thought, because the new ruler had returned, that everything would be all right now. But that was not true for Shenza. Her time to investigate was gone. All too soon, there would be hard questions, and she still had no answers.

Reluctantly, she made herself turn back to the jubilant populace. She could see very little of the new ruler, merely a man's dark-skinned form in a colorful mantle with matching turban. The chair shifted slowly, erratically, as if buffeted by strange currents. There were no carriers, she saw with concern. Instead, it was passed hand over hand by the mob. Everyone was eager to touch his chair and help bear its weight. The passenger's back was to her, so she could not see his face, but his general bearing seemed calm and poised. Metal jewelry flashed as he stretched out his hands to acknowledge the welcome, first on one side and then on the other.

What must it feel like, Shenza wondered, to be the focus of so much emotion? She shuddered, stepping back a bit further from the press of people.

Something brushed her shoulder lightly, startling her. She spun, and a small object fell, fluttering. It clung to her hip, bright white against the dark purple fabric. A butterfly, she thought. Then she saw the violet glow surrounding it.

Shenza quickly detached the magical insect from her robe and spread its fabric wings. A hurried scrawl read, *I am at the ward. Please join me here. Kafseet.*

Shenza winced at the reminder. The new Lord's arrival meant Byben also could be in danger if the peacekeepers decided to flout convention and bring him before Lord Aspace for judgement. Obviously Kafseet thought they could not delay any longer in removing him from the prison. Shenza herself was having doubts. It might be pushing her authority beyond its bounds if she released a suspect from custody. She did not want to give Chief Borleek any further grievances. There was also the lingering question of where to take Byben.

Still, this might be the best time to do it. With so much confusion, the peacekeepers would be distracted, less likely to stop them.

The crowd had carried the first lord's chair to the opposite side of the great fig tree. They now bore him toward the stairs. It seemed clear they would take him all the way up to the palace. Shenza hoped qualified bearers would step forward before the ascent began. The congested square was opening up as the throng followed the Lord's chair. Shenza was able to make her way across the flow of traffic and enter the ward.

The great central chamber was nearly empty. As she had hoped, most of the officers and scribes were outside among the revelers. A mere handful of gold-kilted men stood on the upper walkway in an excited conversation. They scarcely glanced at Shenza as she hurried down the steps into the cell block.

It was good to hear Juss' voice in the room as she approached. She had missed his presence during the day.

His broad back was to her as she entered the chamber. "Drink it slowly," he cautioned impatiently.

The peace officer was bent over a skinny old man in a drab brown mantle, who greedily sucked at the neck of a bottle. The angular Mistress Kafseet worked swiftly, gathering her rune-carved candle sticks into a canvas bag not unlike Shenza's travel case. She looked up sharply as Shenza drew near.

"Ah, you're here," she said briskly.

"I got your message."

Juss straightened, turning to smile wryly. "Busy day, eh, Magister?"

"Yes," she answered tightly. "How were things cleaning up at the docks?"

"Nobody died, and that's a miracle. As for the rest..." He shrugged, hands spread helplessly. "We were making good progress until the first lord got here. You should have heard the sea gulls! There were hundreds of them."

"Let's not waste time," the Curomancer cut in. "Where shall we take him?"

Shenza had no answer. Stalling, she asked, "How is your patient?"

Kafseet rolled her eyes irascibly. "Hale as he can be, considering."

The three of them regarded their charge, who remained seated, cradling his bottle protectively. Byben of Cessill blinked up at them nervously. Even in his prime, Shenza guessed, he had not been an impressive specimen. Wisps of silver hair framed a face as withered as old fruit. There was no sign of any bruising or swelling from his recent ordeal, but his wizened features gave him a look of sickness. Well, Kafseet had said all along there were some things her magic could not heal.

"Well," Juss began slowly, "I'd offer hospitality but the Chief knows where I live. It would be too easy to find him at my place."

"He needs someone to be with him, and I'm never home," Kafseet said. They both looked to Shenza.

"My family can't afford a guest," she protested. Although, she thought, perhaps times were not as hard as they had been.

"They would find him at the magister's—Master Laraquies, I mean—but nobody knows where you live," Juss countered. "What if Arlais stopped by and helped out? She wouldn't be watched."

Shenza squirmed uncomfortably. She didn't want to involve her family without their consent.

"Does the Chief watch your movements?" Kafseet questioned sharply.

"Not usually," Juss answered defensively. "For this, he might."

Speaking up for the first time, Byben whimpered, "Can't I go home?"

"No, grandfather," Kafseet replied, more gently than Shenza had heard her speak before. "Someone could find you, and there would be no one to protect you."

"It's only for a while," Shenza reassured him.

"But I want to go home."

"Soon, grandfather," Kafseet promised, extending a hand. Her tone turned crisp. "Come, I know you can stand."

Reluctantly, the old man let them pull him to his feet. He swayed momentarily, and took a quick draw from his bottle.

"Go easy on that," Juss cautioned sharply. "It's stronger than what you're used to, and I'm not going to carry you."

"Just a moment," Shenza said. If she was going to change her mind, she could not delay any longer. "Are you certain this is what we should do?"

Juss looked between the two of them. "Well, if you're not sure, Magister…"

"What do you mean?" Kafseet retorted.

"Chief Borleek will be furious," Shenza said. "I'm not sure I should antagonize him any more."

"Nonsense," the Curomancer snorted. Then she recanted. "No, I know it isn't. But I really do think it's best, Shenza. He shouldn't have to stay in a room where he was beaten up. He's well enough to move now, and we ought to do it."

"I don't want to stay here," Byben whined after her. There was quiet sloshing as he took another pull from his bottle.

"He's not a risk to escape," Juss pointed out. "We'll know where he is, even if the Chief doesn't." Shenza frowned slightly, alarmed at how quickly he dismissed the feelings of his commanding officer.

Then the young magister stiffened her resolve. Kafseet was right. Byben had been badly used by the peacekeepers, and he deserved justice. That had to come before her selfish wish to avoid problems with Chief Borleek.

She sighed, resigned. "I'm afraid this will cause trouble, but I will err in Byben's favor because of what he has already suffered. Come, grandfather."

Shenza turned toward the door, but Juss interrupted. "Wait. Let me go first."

Before she could answer, he jogged back up the stairs to the main level. A moment later he returned to murmur with a satisfied expression, "We're in luck. Shamatt just sent everyone home who isn't guarding the piers. We have to come back on duty for the coronation ceremony tonight, and this is our only leave time. As soon as they've gone, we can go without an argument."

Shenza nodded silently. Now she was left with the problem of how to ask her family's hospitality for an accused killer.

Chapter Thirteen
~ The Son of Legends ~

They arrived to find Shenza's mother and grandmother spinning floss in the waning afternoon light. The house was otherwise empty. Chimi had not returned from the market, where she had been when the first lord's arrival set the town a-tizzy. Sachakeen had gone with his friend to cut bamboo in the dense stands on the dawn side of the island. Since sea travel was forbidden, it would be a journey of some days by cart.

Shenza felt strange to address her family through the barrier of her mask, but there was no choice. She explained her request as delicately as possible. Mother seemed inclined to accept Shenza's word that Byben was innocent, and it was clear even at a glance that Giliatt was both taller and stronger than her guest. Grandmother was suspicious, however.

Oddly, it was Byben himself who settled the question. He had partaken liberally from his bottle during the short walk, and arrived in a happy frame of mind. His obvious delight at visiting another elder, especially a woman, did much to smooth the road. Juss assured Giliatt his wife would visit to help care for Byben, and Kafseet also promised to check on his health the following day.

With many thanks and apologies, Shenza took her leave. When they left, grandmother was eyeing the newcomer cannily, while he hugged his bottle and hummed to himself. The gleam in Myri's raven eyes hinted that she planned to wangle something for herself. Probably treatment for her persistent back pain. Shenza thought Kafseet would be able to handle the old tyrant, however.

By now the sun was sinking in a brilliant amber haze that seemed to merge sea and sky in its fiery depths. The young magister hastened back to Master Laraquies' house. She found him busy preparing a light supper. As he reminded her, there would be feasting in plenty after the consecration. Shenza set aside her travel case and took over the cooking so her teacher could prepare for his role.

The meal of steamed millet and vegetables sat uneasily in Shenza's stomach as she explained her decision to remove Byben from the ward. If Laraquies was concerned about the possible consequences, he did not show it.

"You are sure he is innocent, aren't you?" he asked. Shenza nodded. "Then it will not matter in the end." He patted her hand. "Eat, child."

"It will matter to Borleek," she gloomily predicted.

"As I said..." he smiled with a trace of malice. "You will question Byben, of course, for the sake of appearances."

"Oh." Shenza had completely forgotten about that. "Yes, of course. I will interview him tomorrow."

The old man's eyes twinkled. Shenza chewed her food with lowered head. Borleek was sure to challenge her before the new ruler. How would it appear to him if she exonerated the only suspect without even basic questioning?

"Has there been any response to our messages yet?" she asked in turn, hoping for even a grain of good news.

"Sadly, no. It is a little soon yet."

"I know, but I thought with the Elitheri's aid..."

"You must be strong for a few days more," her teacher said with compassion.

She winced from his coddling tone. "I will, teacher."

Chuckling, the old man shook his head at her gloom. After finishing the last bites of supper, he stood and stretched, then strolled back into his work room. Shenza ate without appetite, and methodically collected the dishes.

In her narrow room, she picked through her small wardrobe, trying to decide what to wear to the confirmation. She would have preferred to stay out of the public eye and away from the peacekeepers, but she didn't want to miss the ceremony.

On the other hand, she couldn't wear her magician's purple. Nor her mask, since she would not be attending on official business. It surprised her how much that unnerved her. Was she already so dependent on the mask to hide her face from the world? No, she decided. But it was a comfort to know she had its protection.

Shenza had few choices of attire, and soon settled on a mantle of clear yellow with a pattern of pink and lavender blossoms. The colors were suited to a glad occasion, and the fabric was only slightly worn. She quickly wound on the matching turban so that her unruly hair was neatly covered. She also donned a matched set of graduated chains with discs of polished white coral.

She would put aside her problems, Shenza resolved, and enjoy the evening. That alone would be refreshing after the turbulent events of recent days.

There was one more thing to do before she left. Her new robe was still hanging out in the garden, and it should be dry by now. Shenza quickly stepped onto the age-smoothed stones of the path which curved alongside the bristly thatched wall of the house. Dusk shadows now lengthened over the garden, where the little brook gurgled peacefully.

Her robe was a flat, dark patch in the deepening gloom. It rested over a rack of poles that showed pale as bone in the dim light. The fabric was indeed dry, and stiff. Shenza was in the process of folding it when her skin began to prickle. There was a windless rustle in the bushes behind her, trailing into a rasping whisper. Her breath caught in her throat. She waited a silent moment, heard no sound... And yet, she knew.

Shenza turned, clutching her robe to her chest, to confront the spirit's crushing presence. He was clothed in the dark of night itself, emerald eyes alight with an unearthly fire. As before, her voice failed her. He nodded, almost indulgently, in response to her deep bow.

"Your humans acted foolishly today." His voice flayed her pride from the bone.

She hoarsely stuttered, "They sought to depart without permission. I ordered their return..."

The Eleshi waved off her apology. She swallowed, the sour taste of fear thick in her throat.

"Did they learn anything, do you think?"

"Yes, Lord of the Boughs," Shenza said fervently. If the sight of that monster didn't teach respect, she didn't know what would. "They will not behave so rashly again."

A silvery, mocking laugh startled her. Trembling fingers knotted in the robe she still clutched against her chest. Staring at his divine perfection, she wondered how any creature could be so lovely and terrifying at the same time.

He told her, "We know that the heir of our bloodline is here. Because of this, we will tolerate a brief delay in our vengeance."

She did not dare to show her relief at this temperate mood. "We share in your joy, great lord."

"But we have not forgotten." His face again grew stern. "Do not squander our good will."

He did not ask for an explanation, and Shenza did not offer one. No description of legalities could placate a force of nature. Swallowing, she forced herself to ask, "If... If it will speed the punishment, is it possible to call upon your aid, great one?"

He shrugged, eyes narrowed lazily, and murmured obscurely, "We are always near."

It seemed a dismissal, and Shenza was afraid to press further. She bowed once more, and when she straightened her back he was gone.

Her knees sagged with relief, and she made rigid fingers relax their grip on the crumpled robe. The indifference in his eyes, that indolent shrug... She had seen Lord Anges make the same gesture many times. And why must it always be vengeance? Never justice, only revenge. As a magister, she was sworn to seek the truth alone. How could she obey such an inflexible command?

Shenza took a moment more to compose herself and walked stiffly toward the house. Her newly cleaned robe trailed over the ground behind her.

~

Everyone is very sorry for my Lord's suffering, Shenza prayed silently. *Please be assured that your servant is doing her utmost to bring about justice. She wishes my Lord very peaceful rest.* Hands crossed over her breast, Shenza bowed, stepped back, and bowed again.

It was early evening. Warm lamplight filled the pavilion where Lord Anges lay in state. It glowed on the ornate carving of the roof beams and the mounds of funerary offerings within the rounded chamber. At the center lay the body, on a couch of pale bright silver inlaid with glistening emeralds. Fine cloth of deep crimson completely wrapped the corpse, though a series of unwholesome bulges hinted at the form beneath. Lying on its chest was a copper talisman to prevent the remains from decomposing before the funeral. A series of white cloth bands, stitched with runes, had been draped over the lifeless bundle like so many festival streamers. Unknown to the casual viewer, these were Magister Laraquies's initial measures against the spirit roaming from its body.

At regular intervals between the pavilion's outer support pillars, flat discs of reddish stone, carved with more mystic symbols, hung in mid-air. Shenza could feel the tingle of invisible force. These were the additional wards Master Laraquies had installed after the appearance of the 'unruly ghost.'

In addition to the gifts already presented and inside the ward, new heaps were building up just outside it. Shenza glimpsed rich clothing and sandals, carved wooden goblets and platters, tasseled cushions and personal items such as a matched razor and mirror. When Shenza completed her duty, all this would be consigned to the pyre with Anges' body. It would furnish the lord's household when he took his place among the stars.

Mother and Chimi were waiting as Shenza turned from making her offering. It had been an impulsive decision to stop by their house on her way up the hill, but she was glad she could join them for such an important occasion.

"Come on, sister, we're going to be late," Chimi fretted eagerly. Slender brass bracelets chimed lightly with her enthusiastic gestures. The younger daughter was garbed in a white robe with an alternating pattern of broad blue stripes and green vines bearing bright red and gold blossoms. Strands of feather-flower silk were interwoven with the cotton, giving the fabric a shimmering overlay. Her hair, held back from her face by a band of white cloth, fell over her shoulders in sable waves. Despite her finery, Chimi seemed oblivious to the second glances of passing men.

"Settle down," their mother advised indulgently.

Shenza smiled at her sister's adolescent energy. "I'm coming."

Together, the three women walked past the short line of citizens waiting to pay their respects to the dead lord. Citizens of all degrees swarmed the estate to observe the succession. Shenza often glimpsed peacekeepers in dark gold mantles keeping guard where visitors were not welcome. She looked for Juss, but did not see him.

Mother and Shenza proceeded at a leisurely pace, while Chimi pressed a little ahead, her dark eyes brilliant with anticipation. Several routes were marked by lanterns hung from arbors or low tree branches. Chimi, typically, chose the most direct one. It soon opened out onto a sloping natural bowl in the westward face of the hill. Shallow terraces had long ago been cut into the banks to provide seating. A steady stream of people found places on the level grass. Some carried folding chairs and other comforts.

On the crown of the knoll above them, the peaked roofs of the palace rose against the stars. Interior lights illuminated the buildings with an almost surreal glow. Behind them, plumes of smoke showed where food was roasting above outdoor pits. The palace cooks must be frantic, Shenza supposed, for the feast preparations would have started immediately on the new lord's arrival. With the port still closed, they had to be worried about replenishing supplies. But there was nothing Shenza could do about it at the moment.

"Shenza, come on!" Chimi's voice interrupted. "We can get a good seat over here, if we hurry!"

"Oh. Yes," her sister answered, startled. "I'm sorry."

"Don't get too far ahead," Mother called after Chimi.

"I won't!"

Chimi eagerly threaded a path through the shifting masses, while Shenza and mother did their best to keep her in sight. She soon led them to a small gap at the edge of the fourth terrace, between two large family groups. The two girls helped Giliatt spread a bamboo matt, and Chimi sat with her feet dangled over the terrace rim. Giliatt and Shenza each insisted that the other take the place beside Chimi, with the better view. Shenza won the debate, to her satisfaction. She settled behind her kinsfolk, while Chimi recounted the first lord's arrival that afternoon. She was full of details.

Shenza envied the neighboring family their cushions, though not the bottle of fruit wine they were passing among themselves. From the noise the group generated, it seemed they had been celebrating the new reign in advance for some while.

With time to spare before the ceremony began, Shenza let her eyes roam upward again. The stars seemed especially bright, pulsating to an unknown rhythm, and nested among them were the many-hued moons. She was happy to see Quaiss waxing quickly, amber and serene, though it might soon be eclipsed by Inkesh. The angry giant still dominated the heavens. Ever stubborn, it was slow to give way. Purple Meor was not visible, for it would not rise until late night. Green Prenuse was full, though; a hopeful sign. Shenza wondered briefly if the moons exerted any influence on the spirits, as they were said to do on mortals.

She sighed to herself. The twilight encounter had changed her mind about bringing her mask to the palace. It rested inside her travel case, which was secured within the guest chamber she had occupied the previous night. If anything else should happen, she wanted her tools near at hand. A ward, not unlike the one on the first lord's pavilion, protected against any tampering.

Giliatt must have heard her trailing breath, for she turned from Chimi's prattle. Her sad face was concerned. Shenza squeezed her mother's hand reassuringly. "Just a little astrology. It's a habit, I'm afraid."

Giliatt nodded, and Shenza turned her gaze toward the bottom of the amphitheater, where a marble floor lay empty and expectant. A low wall arched along the rear of the arena, providing both a backdrop and an acoustic reflector. A line of wisteria trees overhung the barrier, dropping a petal here and there onto the pavement. Slightly behind the wisterias were taller fern trees whose trunks almost seemed like pillars supporting the starry night.

"Won't it begin soon?" Chimi wondered out loud.

"It should be any time." Shenza felt more anticipation than she expected. She glanced toward the two ground-level entrances on either side of the open floor. If she recalled from Lord Anges' coronation, the procession would enter from her left. She smiled to herself. At the time, she had been just the age Chimi was now.

But I was never so young, even then, she thought with wry amusement. *I had to be Chimi's other mother, and Sachakeen's big brother.*

Horns called for the third time that day. Shenza straightened, scanning the amphitheater eagerly. The notes were long and full, more harmonious than the morning's frantic warnings or the afternoon's giddy abandon. The audience began babbling more loudly around her.

"Here they come!" shrilled Chimi.

"Hush," Giliatt cautioned her daughter.

There was slow and stately movement at the ground level entrance on the left side. A double file of musicians in vividly colored attire took measured strides onto the marble floor. First came the trumpeters, then cymbal players, bells, pipers, and finally a group of bearers with fancifully painted drums. The musicians divided into two clusters at either side of the amphitheater.

When the drums added their deep voices the melody changed, assuming a quicker pace that throbbed with the excited pulse of the day. The audience began to sing as well, creating a remarkable resonance, as if the sound were a physical thing surrounding them. Shenza glanced aside at her neighbors, who joined in with more zeal than skill. She also sang, but quietly.

A new line of bearers appeared even before the first group were gone. Teams of six men supported each of three bronze statues, much larger than life size. Though they must have been heavy, the carriers did not strain. A subtle use of magic lightened the load.

The sculptures were town relics representing the legendary nature spirits. The Eleshi was entwined with leaves and blossoms, the Elitheri wreathed in clouds and lightning and the Eleshouri rose from waves and foam. They were very old, yet uncorrupted. The cool gray of metal flesh gleamed as if freshly cast, and the gemstones inlaid as their eyes glinted with more than mere lamplight. The images had been draped in silken robes and decked with adornments made for their size. Following each was a small, square altar. Plumes of incense gusted up from their vent holes.

The idols did capture something of the spirits's sexless form, Shenza thought. After her recent experiences, she felt she had a basis to be critical. The smug knowingness was there, and the latent cruelty. Still, even the finest craftsmanship could not truly portray their knife-edged mystery. Statuary was simply too static and limited.

The idols were carefully placed before the marble wall at the back of the floor, each with its altar before it. Wisteria blossoms surrounded them with perfumed adoration, and fern fronds extended over them like a sheltering canopy.

Last of all came the grand chair of the first lord. It was of dark wood with beaten copper fittings and a rich inlay of ivory and pearl. This was set, vacant, at the center of the stage, and the bearers withdrew. A file of people entered after the chair and stood in a loose line between the two groups of musicians. The statues dwarfed them all.

"Look, it's Master Laraquies!" Chimi exclaimed, turning to Shenza for confirmation.

She nodded, patiently directing her sister back to the ceremony. It was hard to see faces from this distance, but she would have recognized the old man even if she hadn't known he was officiating. Shenza had to admit her teacher's tranquil bearing was perfect for the occasion, serious and yet not too severe. With him were six ritual witnesses, all prominent citizens. There was a Curomancer she did not recognize, Arze the Harbormaster, Tatteel the general school's principal, Alceme and, to her consternation, Borleek and Nurune. Borleek stood glowering, arms folded across his chest. He must have felt naked without any weapons. Nurune looked very pleased with himself.

There was no sign yet of Lord Aspace. Shenza felt a twinge of disappointment. Chimi, in her unrestrained youth, asked about this out loud and was sternly hushed by their mother.

The music ended. Voices that had been murmuring in the audience suddenly quieted. Master Laraquies stepped forward into the pregnant silence. His voice, assisted by the arena's construction, reached easily to the farthest seats.

"In ancient times," he began, "years of years ago, ages of ages past, this world was troubled and dark." Dancers appeared from the side entries, men and woman garbed in short robes with many- layered veils covering their heads and shoulders. The musicians began playing again, soft and ominously. "The people were frightened, for the spirits were against them. Hideous creatures dragged their ships down into the sea. The sky was full of storms and the land was covered with jungles where fierce beasts lay in wait. The people wandered from place to place seeking food and shelter, and nowhere was safe for them."

Shenza leaned forward, staring between her mother's and sister's shoulders as the performers leapt and danced, acting out the ancient tale. She had forgotten phantasms were part of the ceremony. The dancers's flowing veils took on a life of their own, forming visions of the hapless people and the creatures that terrified them. The likenesses seemed very real, though perhaps a bit too colorful and dramatic.

Laraquies continued, "At this time there was an old man and an old woman. They had ten children, but all of them died. The couple wept, for they were alone. One day, they came to the shore of a tiny island. They went into the jungle to find food, but instead they heard the crying of an infant." The highest trumpet did a good imitation of the wailing. "They found a baby boy lying naked between the forepaws of a tigress."

"'Oh Tigress,' they cried. 'Have mercy on the helpless child. If you will spare his life, you may eat one of us instead.'

"The tiger stared at them with cold eyes. 'What is mercy?' it asked, and before their eyes it transformed into an exquisite lady." The spirit woman was a bit too amply bosomed, Shenza thought, garbed in garish emerald with peacock feathers trailing from her headdress. "Though frightened by the powerful magic, the elders again begged her to spare the child.

"'I will give you this trial,' said the lady. 'You will take the babe for one year. Bring him back to me well and happy. Then we shall see what becomes of you.' She resumed her tiger's form and stalked off into the forest. The two elders took the child and fled from that place.

"Thus began a strange year for them, but also a time of great happiness. Good fortune followed the family wherever they went. As long as the boy was with them, they gathered food in plenty. The seas were calm before their small boat, and the beasts of the jungle fled before him. The couple marveled at his abilities, but they did their best to teach him wisdom and humility, as if he were truly their own son.

"More wondrous still, the boy grew at a astonishing rate. For each month that passed he aged one year. At the end of the agreed term he was a lad of twelve, quick, strong and clever. With heavy hearts, the two elders brought their beloved son back to the isle where they had found him, for they feared he would be taken from them, or that one of them would die. On the morning of the appointed day, the tigress appeared from the shadowed forest. The boy walked without fear to meet her. Together they vanished into the jungle. The couple waited all that day with sinking spirits. In the evening the boy returned alone, saying they were to bring him again when another year had passed.

"The time again passed swiftly. At the end of the second year the boy had grown into a young man of twenty-four, a proud warrior who build his parents a sturdy house on an island with fresh water and fertile soil. Again his parents brought him back to the island and he went into the jungle with the tigress. At the end of the day he returned, saying they were to return in another year.

"At the end of the third year he was a man of thirty-six who had attracted a great following because of his judgment and valor. The house he had built for his parents was becoming a village. He had chosen a wife who bore him twin sons. Both of the boys grew with astonishing speed, just as he had. Once again, he traveled with his parents to the island. He consulted in the jungle with the tigress and brought back the same command.

"At the end of the fourth year he was a mature man of forty-eight who governed a prosperous town. They called him its lord. He had three wives and three more sets of twins. The two oldest sons had settled on nearby islands, taking their own adherents with them. Once more he and his parents went to the secret isle. He walked in the jungle with the spirits and returned with the same orders."

Shenza had heard this tale many times, as did all folk in the Jewel Sea. This time, she found herself wondering about the many details left out of the legend. Did the little boy ever skin his knees, she wondered, or speak back to his parents? And how did the wives feel about their husbands and children aging so rapidly?

But the tale was nearing its conclusion. "At the end of the fifth year he was an elder of sixty, nearly as old as his parents had been when they bargained for his life from the tigress. His town and family were still growing, bringing good fortune to all who followed them. High lord, he was called, and his sons who ruled were first lords. He and his mother returned alone to the island, for her husband was ill and could not travel. Once more he walked in the jungle with the tigress, and returned with the same instructions.

"At the end of the sixth year he was seventy-two, older than his widowed mother. High lord of all the Jewel Sea, he was frail and tired. Yet he was not too weak to travel alone to the island, and this time he did not return.

"Oh, woe!" shouted Laraquies, and the musicians gave a wailing blast. Shenza saw Chimi jump. The players clawed at their robes, miming the age-old gesture of grief. "Our lord is dead! Who now will guide and care for us? Who will speak to the spirits on our behalf?"

There was an eruption of chaotic music and dance, flickering images of violent waves and storms. One might well believe that disaster was upon them. Then from their midst a new figure appeared. He was tall and lithe, robed and turbaned in the brilliant blue of nobility. His sudden arrival drew gasps from the audience. When he raised his hands, the commotion died away.

"Do not be afraid." The newcomer was calm and self-assured. "I am Aspace Alshain of Alshain, the son of Asbel and Izmay. I will take up my brother's duty."

A cheer arose spontaneously, briefly overwhelming the music. Shenza could not recall such an ovation during the previous Lord's installation. The dancers, their part completed, leapt and darted toward the exits. Their veils, once more ordinary cloth, fluttered behind them. As they left, a group of servants came in, carrying bronze urns and platters heavy with bread, fruits and fishes.

After a long while, the applause subsided. Master Laraquies and the six witnesses bowed ceremonially. "You are welcome," they intoned a bit raggedly. "We greet you in peace, and wait to serve as your advisors and in every way you wish."

"I greet you in peace, and I accept your service for the welfare of the people." Aspace sounded not at all self-conscious, as though he was made a first lord every day and the ritual was nothing new to him.

Laraquies alone replied. "Now we give thanks to the mighty spirits, and we make an offering from the good things they give us. To them we pray for future prosperity."

Before the solemn witnesses, Lord Aspace turned to the approaching tray bearers. Some of the wine was spilled before each of the altars, and the food was distributed between them. With each offering he spoke his thanks. Those were whispered among the audience as well. Then the new monarch turned to face the populace.

Master Laraquies intoned, "Now take your place, Lord Aspace, as our first lord and ruler, whose wisdom shall guide us and whose power shall protect us. May you govern in peace and abundance."

"I will," he answered firmly.

First Lord Aspace walked to the empty chair and stood for a moment, looking out at the silent throng. Then he reached back, steadying himself on the arms of the chair, and sat down. The musicians again began to play. A second roar burst from the crowd. Many leapt to their feet, cheering, waving scarves, and tossing handfuls of flower petals into the air. Shenza stood, too, because she could no longer see what was happening below.

Four peace officers and four strong servants filed in with carrying poles. Together with the six witnesses, they positioned themselves before and behind the throne. In a smooth motion it was lifted to their shoulders. The witnesses, who were mostly elders, dropped back, permitting the younger men to do the real work. The chair rode smoothly toward the right hand exit. Master Laraquies, the dignitaries, and the musicians came after it. As they left the amphitheater, some of the audience began to follow. Flower petals and fluttering streamers filled the air.

The audience about Shenza began to stir and stretch, and she helped Giliatt roll up their matt. Chimi asked Shenza, "Was that a true story, sister?"

"Yes, Chimi," she answered. It certainly put her twilight visits in a new light.

"Nah!" One of their drunken neighbors interrupted. "It's a pretty tale, all mystic and symbolic, but it's really just to justify him holding power."

"I beg your pardon?" Shenza asked coolly.

"That's right," said another of the men, equally tipsy. "There's nothing special about their family. They'd just like us to think there is, right, brother?"

"Right," the first man agreed scornfully.

"And I suppose you think it was politics that came roaring out of the sea this morning and swamped all our boats and hailed on us," Shenza responded tartly. It was bad enough their noise disrupted the ceremony, without hearing their ignorant theories.

He waved in dismissal. "That was just a freak storm. Could have happened any time." Still, he sounded a bit uncertain. His brother took a quick sip from his bottle.

Chimi retorted hotly. "My sister's a sorceress, and if she says it's true, then I believe her."

"Oh?" answered the second man with a drunken leer. "Tell me about it, sweetie."

Shenza instinctively stepped forward, interposing herself between her sister and the intruder, while Chimi stepped back, repelled. The men laughed rudely.

Giliatt's stern voice interrupted. "Come along, girls."

Chimi flounced off, and Shenza was only too happy to follow. No wonder these men had no women with their party, she thought. They were too rude to attract wives.

Chapter Fourteen
~ Twice Tested ~

Dozens of lamps banished the night's darkness and made the moons glow pale. Beneath their radiance, a public feast had been set out: platters of roast fowl, rice, noodles, yams, cassava, steamed vegetables, and several varieties of fruit. Townsfolk swarmed around the tables, eagerly taking from the first lord's largesse. A constant flow of servants kept the tables heavy with food.

The banquet boards formed a rough perimeter about a wide circle of lawn. By good fortune, Shenza and her family found a vacant bench near the center. There was room for all three of them to sit together, and the height allowed her to see the area clearly.

To her right and behind her was the pavilion where Lord Anges lay in state. Across, and slightly to her left, the new lord's chair sat elevated on a dais with steps rising up to it. The troupe of dancers was performing in the cleared space before him, accompanied by a larger group of musicians. No more phantasms colored the air, but their athletic motions drew appreciative cries from the audience.

Despite this, Lord Aspace did not seem to be enjoying himself. A small group of women was seated on the risers below his throne, offering choice food and drink or charming conversation. It should not have surprised Shenza that Innoshyra of Sengool occupied the topmost step. Her deep red robe was resplendent, and her long hair had been plaited with jewels in elaborate twists that defied another woman to best her.

From her manner, Innoshyra was attempting to console the Lord Aspace on his recent loss. Shenza could scarcely credit her boldness. After so loudly declaring her grief for Lord Anges, she now pursued the dead man's brother. As Shenza watched, the woman fastened a jeweled copper chain about the prince's ankle with a caressing motion, at once suggestive and possessive. The other women seemed younger, hard pressed to compete with the sophisticated courtier. They pouted, jealous.

The Lord, for his part, accepted only foodstuffs offered by his staff. Perhaps he sought to avoid favoring any of the women over the others. Or it could be he was wary of Innoshyra's aspirations. Shenza was beginning to feel sorry for him, though perhaps it was not necessary.

The witnesses from the ceremony lingered near the throne. They chatted with him, ate tidbits from little bowls, or sipped from delicate cups. Others of the local nobility strolled up to join the elite social circle and were greeted with quick kisses. Lord Aspace nodded as they were presented to him.

Though Alceme appeared to be among this group, she was actually hard at work. Shenza noted her conferring with Andle and other servants at frequent intervals. Nurune, likewise, was in a close circle with several junior mages from his coven, including Tonkatt and the other two Shenza recalled from that afternoon. She felt her face grown warm as she realized the young men were even more attractive in the warm lamplight. She looked away, reminding herself Nurune and his students could not be trusted. They held no higher principles, but served whatever master paid best.

Despite herself, Shenza glanced back in time to see the elder dismiss his apprentices. He turned to greet his brother, Lord Sengool, as he approached the throne. With him was his distant cousin, Lord Kesquin. The sorcerer ceremoniously presented both men to the first lord. To Shenza's eye, it seemed the two noblemen were also keeping an eye on their daughters as they vied for the new ruler's attention.

Nearby, Borleek still stood with the sinewy Harbormaster Arze. Both men looked as though they felt out of place in such exalted company. The peacekeeper sent sharp glances toward Master Laraquies, who stood in a solemn discussion with the curomancer from the ceremony and another sorcerer, Choruta Ramli of Salloo. Choruta was gaunt even for an enchanter, and seemed tired. In just three days he had found Lord Aspace and brought him back to Chalsett-Port. That could not be a slight effort, even with the Eleshouri speeding the way.

"Here we are!"

Shenza looked up at Chimi's cheery voice. Her little sister had made a foray to the banquet tables while the others held her place. A delicious odor wafted from the steaming bowls she carried.

"This is for you, mother. And sister..." She quickly distributed even portions between three serving bowls. There was roast fowl in a skin of blackened honey, rice balls with diced fish mixed in, and spicy pickled greens.

"Thank you, daughter," Giliatt said, accepting one of the bowls and a bamboo fork.

"There's lots more," Chimi assured them, seating herself between the two women. "I want to try the fruit soup next."

"This looks good," said Shenza. She could feel her tardy appetite returning.

A shadow fell over their group, and she looked up to see her teacher beaming down at her. "You're eating more," he approved. "Good."

Both Shenza and Chimi quickly rose. "Please take my seat, Master," Shenza said.

In the same breath, her younger sister told him, "You can have my place."

He chuckled. "No, no. It isn't necessary. I'm merely stopping by."

"It is good to see you, Master Laraquies," Giliatt said softly. "I want to thank you for everything you've done for my daughter."

To Shenza's surprise, the old man actually looked abashed. "I'm sorry I haven't visited to tell you about her progress. I suppose you must have heard by now that she has nearly completed her studies."

Chimi chattered, "Isn't it exciting? I want to see her mask! She was wearing it today, but I missed it." She made a teasing pout.

"Commit a crime," Shenza retorted. "Then you'll see it."

"No, thanks! I'll wait," her sister laughed.

As Shenza seated herself, she absently noted a nearby servant offering tiny cups of fruit wine to the guests. He wasn't able to move far at a time in the crowded area. It was Makko, the messenger. He directed a dark glare at Master Laraquies. When he saw Shenza looking at him, he started defensively and then forced a thin smile.

Mother was saying, "You'll have plenty of chances, Chimi."

Laraquies smiled indulgently. "I'm glad to see you're all looking well. And you're growing into quite a young beauty." Chimi straightened, beaming. "But where is Sachakeen tonight? At home with your guest?"

"He and a friend went to the jungle to cut bamboo for some household repairs," Giliatt explained. "Grandmother stayed with Byben, since he was asleep. She said she didn't want to walk so far."

"Sachakeen is taller than I am, now," Shenza said quickly. She hoped no one nearby had heard the name of the accused murderer.

Laraquies nodded. "Young men grow quickly at that age. I'll bet he's eating you out of house and home."

Giliatt laughed. "That he is, Magister."

"He's got a girlfriend," Chimi put in, slyly eager to share what she knew. "Grandmother likes her, too."

"Oh?" Laraquies' silver brows rose.

"Don't make fun, Chimi," her mother said sternly. "He'll repay you one day, you know."

The younger girl smirked, picking at her fowl with a sparkle in her eye. At that moment the dance music ended. Applause washed over the audience in waves as the dancers bowed to the first lord, backed away, bowed again and vanished into the throng.

"They were really good, weren't they," Chimi called over the clapping. "I wish I could do that."

A public entertainer? Grandmother would never stand for that, Shenza thought. Chimi did have the figure for it, though.

"It was an interesting performance," Laraquies agreed.

That reminded Shenza of something she had thought of after the ceremony. She asked, "Do you know who trains them?"

"That would be Aoress Ettacht of Kassant," he answered.

"Would it be possible to introduce us? There were some things I wanted to ask them." Their knowledge of phantasm could be helpful in her investigation.

"Right now?" Chimi asked bluntly.

Shenza gazed at her mother, who was obviously suppressing her disappointment. "No, not now," she answered quickly. "Tomorrow would be better anyway, I imagine." She looked a question to her teacher.

"Why don't I see if Aoress would be available then," he suggested.

"I would appreciate it."

With a parting bow, the old man moved off purposefully.

"I don't want to interfere with your work," Giliatt said softly, half apologizing.

"Mother," Chimi scolded. "You should hear yourself. Of course she wants to be with us!"

Shenza nodded, clasping her mother's hand firmly. "I am not working tonight. I promised myself."

A burst of loud music drowned any reply Giliatt might have made. All three women turned to see a new group of musicians enter the grassy circle, bobbing in time with a fast beat. Folk from the audience jumped to their feet and joined the snake-like line. Chimi straightened in her seat.

"Look, they're dancing! I want to go, too. Mother, can we?"

"Have you finished your dinner?"

"I will." The girl raised her bowl to her lips, scooping a last few bites into her mouth. "Come on, sister," Chimi urged.

Shenza regarded her half-eaten meal. "I'm not finished yet. You go. I'll keep our places."

"It's all right, isn't it, mother?" Chimi begged.

"Well..." From the lingering glance Giliatt directed at her own dish, Shenza guessed their mother was also still hungry, but as Chimi shifted from foot to foot, already dancing, she sighed softly.

"Wine?" Came a curt question from behind them.

Shenza looked up to meet the flat, unfriendly gaze of the messenger, Makko. His tray was nearly empty of the tiny ceramic cups that had occupied it. She was surprised he even offered them a drink. From the way he had been staring at Master Laraquies earlier, it gave him no pleasure to do so.

"I'd like some!" Chimi eagerly reached forward, but mother's raised hand forestalled her.

"You don't need it," Giliatt decided firmly.

"I agree," Shenza said. There was plenty of time for her to learn bad habits.

"But, Mother," Chimi protested.

"Come, daughter. You said you wanted to dance."

The servant did not try to hide a mocking grin as the disappointed girl followed their mother toward the line of dancers. His smile vanished as he realized Shenza was still looking at him.

"Do you have any watered lime juice?" she asked, keeping her voice soft and neutral.

"I'd have to bring you some." He sounded resentful now.

"If you don't mind?"

"Oh, very well," the man snapped. He whirled and strode off.

Shenza watched after him for a moment, saw the angry twitch of his narrow shoulders. She wondered if Makko knew her without her mask, or if, as Alceme had suggested, he was simply angry at the world. He certainly did seem to despise mages. What could have happened to make him feel that way?

But that wasn't important. She ate patiently, determined not to be antagonized. Instead, she savored her pickled greens along with a momentary sense of privacy among the busy throng. She felt more tired now than hungry. This had been a very long day.

A new voice intruded on her thoughts. "Pardon me. Aren't you Shenza Waik of Tresmeer?"

Startled to hear her name, Shenza turned in her seat to find Tonkatt of Sengool leaning over her bench. Her throat seemed to close as she gazed directly into his amber eyes.

She had been right. Tonkatt was even more handsome than she remembered. A short kilt and mantle, green patterned with bright gold, showed off both his long, brown legs and smoothly sculpted shoulders. Jewels gleamed from his ear lobes and about his neck, and a strand of small pearls was wound into the turban that held his hair straight back from his face. She felt like a threadbare peasant compared to his finery.

"I didn't mean to surprise you," Tonkatt said when she did not answer. His voice was soothing, yet it did not reassure her. "You are the new magister, aren't you?"

Too late, Shenza realized she was staring. Flushed with embarrassment, she nodded and stammered. "Yes, I am, although I am off duty now."

How did he know her? she wondered, flustered. She wasn't wearing her mask.

"I understand. But may I please join you?" He gestured to the empty bench beside her.

It was a bit forward of him. Unmarried men and women did not usually socialize without an introduction from their parents. Shenza wished, with clear panic, that her mother would come back. And Chimi. She was cute enough to distract any man. But neither of them was here, and she could not quite bring herself to refuse as she knew she should. Tonkatt was very handsome. And one couldn't say they were alone together, when so many guests swarmed around them.

"If... If you wish." Shenza moved over uneasily, feeling his body warmth as he slid down beside her. He was wearing a sweetly musky cologne. Swallowing, she edged a bit farther along the bench. Really, it wasn't fair that men were so much taller than women.

"Did you get to see much of the ceremony?" Tonkatt asked conversationally. She had the impression that he found her confusion amusing. That made her feel even more awkward.

Shenza nodded, swallowed her greens and feeling their spicy heat in her throat. "Yes. It was impressive." His brows rose at her unsophisticated assessment. She stammered, "Technically, I mean. The dancers and their phantasms."

"They are excellent, aren't they? I've seen them before."

Was that bragging? No, it was probably simple truth. The Sengool family was wealthy, after all. They could afford to hire such dancers. Remembering the cynicism of her neighbors after the ceremony, Shenza was tempted to ask whether he believed the legend. She stopped herself. That could lead to explaining why she believed the story was true, and she did not want him telling Master Nurune about her contacts with the spirits. If only he wasn't so good looking, it would be easier to guard her tongue.

Tonkatt went on, a bit condescendingly, "Aoress is a fine teacher, though the scope of her work is a bit limited. I'm sure she could do better on the Inner Sea than here." His tone seemed to dismiss Chalsett-port as unworthy of regard.

"Perhaps she doesn't want to be there," Shenza felt compelled to answer. "Her skill would be less valued. Some people would rather be important in small places than overlooked in larger ones."

"Oh?" Tonkatt smiled into her eyes, and Shenza realized he might think she was speaking of herself. "You're very empathic, aren't you? It shouldn't surprise me. After all, you are a sorceress."

It was hard to breathe when he looked at her that way. And she was staring again. Shenza focused her gaze on her empty bowl and the last kernels of rice stuck to the bottom.

"I was... merely speculating," she murmured.

"But it was so insightful," he insisted. "I can see why you would be drawn to the magister's profession. You ought to do well."

If he only knew how inadequate she felt... "Thank you." Shenza felt stupid saying that, but she didn't know how else to answer the blatant flattery. Would Mother never return? Shenza's eyes sought the crowded dance line, but to no avail. The music went merrily on, only a little muffled by the press of bodies.

The silence stretched uncomfortably. Staring at her plate was little better than staring at him. Shenza set the dishes aside, only to discover that now she had nothing to do with her hands.

"Is..." she began clumsily.

At the same time, he said, "Tell me... No, please go on."

"I was going to ask if your family is here tonight." That seemed a safe enough subject.

"My uncles are here," he answered easily. "Master Nurune and Lord Sengool, and their families." This was boasting, she was sure of it. "My own parents live on Amethan, to the south. My father is a jeweler, but he also mints coin for the High Lord."

No wonder he thought Chalsett was small. Amethan was a large island supporting two major cities and several smaller towns.

Tonkatt went on, "Mother is Master Nurune's sister. When they learned I had talent, my family sent me here to apprentice with him. Once I've completed the term of service I owe for my training, I'll return there. Eventually I'd like to start my own coven."

"I see." It was faintly reassuring to learn that Tonkatt would not be staying on Chalsett indefinitely.

A pleasant female voice interrupted. "Did you ask for the lime juice, miss?"

A young woman in servant's livery offered a porcelain cup to Shenza. Apparently Makko had delegated the unwanted chore to someone else. This did not bother Shenza at all.

"Yes, I did. Thank you for bringing it." She sipped her drink, savoring its mild bitterness.

The girl smiled cheerfully. "Not at all. And you, sir? I have wine as well." She indicated a tray laden with the small wine cups.

Tonkatt accepted one of those. "A bit of refreshment would be welcome." Shenza had the impression he was teasing her for her conservative choice of drink. Well, she needed her wits about her—especially now.

The serving girl departed, and her companion asked, "What about you? Is your family here this evening?"

"Yes," she answered, gesturing to the empty dishes which rested on the vacant end of the bench. "My mother and sister are here, but they are dancing."

He glanced at the weaving line of celebrants and smiled wryly. "I won't ask you to point them out to me. Perhaps I can meet them later." It was not quite a question.

"Perhaps." Shenza tried to keep her response neutral. It really wasn't proper that he asked to meet her mother, when they hadn't even been formally introduced.

Shenza took another sip of her drink, feeling bits of pulp glide over her tongue. It could have used more water. The lime was a little strong. A token of Makko's esteem, perhaps. Her stomach twinged in protest.

Tonkatt seemed to be waiting for more information. She haltingly explained, "My father was a fisherman, and Mother's father also. Father died at sea when I was young. Mother supported us by raising feather-flowers and spinning the floss. That is our family's trade now."

"That must have taken courage." Still, she could see he was disappointed by her lowly origins. She felt a second, stronger, pain in her stomach.

She drank again before continuing, "A magician came to the General School and tested the students for power. Once we knew I had it, I started working in the market with Mother. That's where Magister Laraquies first saw my work."

"And he decided to apprentice you from that?" Tonkatt eyed her over the rim of his cup with some respect.

Despite her misgivings about his interest in her, Shenza felt her face grow warm. "It was more of an acquaintance. He mostly chatted with Mother. Actually, I thought he was interested in her, not me. We kids were always looking for another father." She tried to laugh around the increasing knot of fire in her middle.

Tonkatt chuckled with her, appreciating the irony, but then said sympathetically, "It must have been hard for you."

Shenza shrugged. She did not often think about her father. He had been gone too long. "It happens. Fishing is more dangerous than you might think. It's not uncommon for ships to be lost. The widows help with each other's children, so all of them can work on some market days." But this couldn't be anything Tonkatt, with his wealthy background, would care about. "I must be boring you," she apologized.

"Not at all," Tonkatt insisted, leaning a little toward her. "I admire you for overcoming so much." His tone implied something more than mere admiration. Shenza felt a raw tightness in her throat. If only her stomach would stop hurting!

"Hey, sister! Who's this?" Chimi's bright voice shattered the moment.

"You're back," Shenza stuttered. She felt she had been caught at something improper, although really, they had done nothing but talk.

Chimi's mantle was slightly disarrayed and she panted a little, her dark skin glowing with perspiration. "Wow, that was fun! I'm tired."

Behind her came their mother. From her expression, Giliatt could not decide whether she was pleased to find her older daughter conversing with a strange man, or indignant.

Tonkatt rose and bowed, all grace, one hand touching his chest lightly. "I beg your pardon, Matron. My name is Tonkatt Sengool of Tindali."

Chimi's mouth made an 'o' at the sound of his name. She quickly dipped a bow in response. "Nice to meet you!"

Shenza quickly explained, "He is a sorcerer I met during my investigation." It was hard to talk normally. Her stomach churned restlessly. "This is my mother, Giliatt Palelle of Tresmeer, and my younger sister, Chimi Waik of Tresmeer."

Tonkatt smiled at the girl with obvious appreciation. "I am delighted."

She giggled in response.

"How do you do," Giliatt answered with a trace of wary reproach.

"Please be seated, Matron," he said calmly, ignoring her reproof. "I wouldn't take your place."

"Yes, please. You must be tired from the dancing." Shenza gathered the empty dishes, all too aware of their clattering.

"I'll get rid of those," Chimi offered, but Shenza guiltily demurred.

"No, it's all right. Please sit down, and you, too, Mother." She rose, keeping her lime juice aside. To her dismay, a wave of dizziness swept over her. Her throat and her stomach clenched as one. Shenza hesitated, assailed by an appalling hot and cold chill. Carrying the dirty dishes to the nearby collection table suddenly seemed like a very bad idea.

"Magister?" Tonkatt caught her elbow, supporting her. His hand felt uncomfortably warm. Shenza staggered a pace back to the bench and sat down abruptly, with a clink of dishes.

"What's the matter?" Giliatt's stern expression turned on Tonkatt, half-accusing.

"Are you all right, sister?" Chimi asked, all concern. "Here, give me those." She rescued the vessels from Shenza's sweat-slick grasp.

"I'm sorry, but I really don't feel well," Shenza croaked through her swollen throat. "I'll be fine in a moment." Inside, she winced from the poor excuse. It sounded as though she was trying to get rid of Tonkatt because her family was there. Her vision blurred alarmingly and she leaned forward, desperately controlling her nausea.

"She drank no wine," Tonkatt said, a little defensively.

Mother's work-hardened hand fell on the nape of Shenza's neck for a moment. The touch of her skin seemed cold as the depths of the sea. "She is feverish."

"She was fine earlier," Chimi whispered, frightened. "What could have happened?"

"It isn't his fault," Shenza choked out. "I've only had some watered lime juice since you left."

Calmly, yet with an undertone of apprehension, Tonkatt offered, "Shall I call for a curomancer? Master Hassangiri should still be here."

Shenza would rather have had Kafseet, but that didn't seem as important as the rebellion of her stomach.

"I'll go. Which one is he?" There was a faint rattle of crockery as Chimi made her offer.

"If you don't know him, then I will go." The young man's voice was already fading with distance.

Running off to tell Nurune about her weakness, Shenza thought uncharitably.

"But I want to help!" Chimi protested.

"Then put those dishes away and go find Master Laraquies," Giliatt ordered firmly. "And take this, too." A slight clink sounded as she passed over the remainder of Shenza's drink.

"Yes, mother." Light footsteps ran off.

Shenza blinked against the sweat that stung her eyes. She managed to turn her head and saw Tonkatt's tall form retreating into the busy crowd. Thank the heavens. She would rather have died than humiliate herself in front of him.

Now that they were alone, Mother let her worries show. "Do you want to lie down? How do you feel?"

"Sick," she answered succinctly. Lying down might have helped earlier, but it was too late for that now. "Help me off with this." Her hands were shaking with chills, but she managed to loosen her outer robe.

Even the slight straightening to remove her mantle proved too much. Her stomach twisted convulsively. Shenza fell to her knees, her mouth filling with hot, sour liquid. She vomited uncontrollably, coughed and panted between spasms. Mother's cool hands stroked her sweat-slick shoulders as she retched. There seemed no end to it.

Through her misery, Shenza cursed her own foolishness. How could she let herself get so upset over Tonkatt? Handsome as he was, she didn't really like him! And in the middle of an inquiry, too. It wasn't like her to behave so irresponsibly.

These bitter thoughts pursued her into unconsciousness.

Chapter Fifteen
~ Bound In Green ~

"Believe it or not," a man's voice murmured reassuringly, "vomiting is good for you. It's one of our elemental defenses. When you get sick, it means your body is taking care of itself."

"Ugh," Chimi declared.

"Hush, daughter."

Shenza was lying down. She was certain of that and of little else. A strange drifting sensation possessed her. Yet ironically her limbs felt heavy as iron bars. Her mind, too, was flaccid, weightless. What was happening? She tried to open her eyes. They did not want to obey. A vague green blur formed momentarily, then dissipated into darkness.

The voices seemed to be coming from a great distance. Had she been unconscious? For how long? Shenza's heart skipped anxiously, but still she could not move. At least, she no longer felt her stomach's angry protests.

"But what could her body be protecting itself against? She drank no alcohol." That was Tonkatt, sounding very defensive. A part of her quailed from the knowledge that he had seen her so helpless, and all because she was too frightened of his advances.

"So you say," Kafseet retorted. Shenza was relieved to hear her voice, though she wondered, in a hazy way, when the curomancer had arrived and why she spoke with such a cold cutting edge.

"I beg your pardon?" Tonkatt replied, clearly offended.

"Hmph," the healer mocked his indignation.

"Please, Kafseet," came the man's voice she did not recognize. Soothingly, the man went on, "Our treatment would be much more effective if we knew some details. Please continue, young man. I gather you were with her?"

"Only briefly," Tonkatt replied. "We talked for a short time. I don't know what she ate beforehand, but I saw her drink only lime juice. The wine glass was mine."

He seemed to want to be very clear on that point. From Kafseet's tone, it appeared she was blaming him for Shenza's illness. The sorceress tried again to open her eyes, but her eyelids were so very heavy. Was she somewhere in the palace? How did she get here? If only she could speak.

"The food she ate was the same everyone else had," Chimi said. "I brought it from the banquet tables myself. And she was fine all night. We sat with her during the confirmation ceremony. Nothing was wrong then. And nobody else got sick."

"Are we sure of that?" came Mother's quiet, worried question.

"I hadn't heard of anyone, but it certainly isn't impossible," Kafseet said in her brisk, dry way. "There are enough people here drinking the first lord's wine. What about you, Hasangiri?"

That was the name, Shenza thought, the curomancer Tonkatt had gone to find. He might have been the one who was a witness during the confirmation ceremony. She remembered him talking with Master Nurune near the first lord's throne.

"I was here socially, not to work, so I would not have heard," he answered regretfully. "But this is the new magister, isn't it? Perhaps the stress of her investigation overcame her senses."

Kafseet laughed at that. "Not her."

"Not my sister!" Chimi agreed.

"And you say she drank lime juice?" Master Laraquies' soft, thoughtful voice spoke up for the first time. Shenza felt relief. If he was here, everything would be all right.

"Yes, Magister," Tonkatt confirmed. "One of the servants brought it while we were talking. I assume she had requested it, since most of the staff were serving fruit wine."

"Do you know where her cup is?" the old man asked blandly. "There may be a residue that will tell us something. It seems unlikely, but we should not turn our backs on the possibility."

Despite his nonchalant words, Shenza recognized a subtle tone in his voice. She wondered, through her lassitude, what he was getting at.

"Good idea," Kafseet approved.

"I put it with the rest of the dirty dishes," Chimi reported. "I think I could find it again, if the table hasn't been cleared."

"A logical approach," Hassangiri agreed cautiously.

Kafseet seemed to brush aside his hesitation. "I have an idea what's wrong, based on the symptoms Giliatt described, but it would be nice to see what she was drinking when she got sick. Her condition is stable now, isn't it, Hassangiri? So we have time to confirm before trying further treatment."

"Yes, she is in lesser stasis. Her condition won't change until the spell is removed." He sounded a bit smug now. "I always carry one of those talismans in case of emergency."

Stasis? This explained why Shenza couldn't move. A creeping frustration soaked into her mind. They were all talking about her and she couldn't respond. Didn't they know she could hear them?

"Do you want me to go look for it?" Chimi sounded eager to help.

"Yes, thank you, child," said Master Laraquies kindly. He called, "Officer! Would you escort this young lady? I would like her to have access to the kitchen and scullery, if necessary. Oh, and if you see Juss Battour of Reiloon, would you please ask him to join us here?"

"Yes, Magister." The man sounded puzzled by the odd instructions. "After you, miss."

"I'll come back soon," Chimi promised fervently.

Mother gave her usual caution: "Mind your manners."

"I will."

In the darkness that imprisoned her, Shenza sighed. Chimi couldn't keep quiet when she was upset. She would babble everything within five minutes. Then, since the man was probably a peace officer, Borleek and everyone else in the Ward would know she was gotten sick. She cringed from the humiliation. They would never respect her now!

"Well," Hassangiri resumed as the footsteps retreated, "I don't want to seem disinterested, but I was called away from something. If this is your patient, Kafseet, may I leave her to you?"

"I'd like that." Kafseet sounded pleased. "Is it all right with you, Giliatt?"

Yes, Shenza thought. *Say yes.* She knew nothing against this Hassangiri, but she had no wish to be indebted to one of Master Nurune's friends.

"If you don't mind," Mother answered diffidently. "I don't want to cause a problem for you."

"It's no trouble," the curomancer assured her. "Don't worry about your talisman, Hassangiri. I'll have one of my apprentices bring it over to your clinic tomorrow."

"And thank you, Master Hassangiri."

"Not at all, Matron. Try not to worry. Your daughter is in excellent hands." Shuffling footsteps departed.

"I'd like to go as well," Tonkatt quickly added. "I fear I know little of healing magic. Good evening, Magister, Curomancer."

So much for his concern. Shenza was not surprised, nor could she blame him, though in a detached way she did regret it. She was below Tonkatt's social station, and she had the ill grace to get sick when he simply spoke with her. He'd want no more of her.

"Not so fast, boy," came Kafseet's austere voice. "I want to see that amulet you're wearing."

"I don't know what you mean," he coolly retorted.

"That pretty bauble right there," the curomancer pressed. "I want to see it. Or better yet, show Magister Laraquies."

There was a discernible pause.

Tensely, Tonkatt said, "It isn't what you seem to think."

"Prove it," Kafseet said, sharply triumphant.

"What is the matter?" Giliatt asked, baffled. Shenza wanted to know, too, but no one asked her opinion.

"You should not assume too much, Mistress Kafseet." Laraquies spoke up mildly. "May I see it?" There was a slight pause. "Please."

"If you have nothing to hide, then what's the problem?" Kafseet mocked sweetly.

"Oh, very well," Tonkatt said through his teeth. There was a rustle and a light clink. "There, you see? It's a good luck charm. There's nothing sinister about it."

"Did you make it yourself?" Laraquies asked meditatively.

"No, Magister. I bought it in the market. It's perfectly legal."

"Barely legal," Kafseet snapped, reverting to her normal brusque manner. "And that's no luck piece. Luck with women, I'd call it. I'm a woman. Did you think I couldn't feel it?"

'Luck with women?' If she had been able, Shenza would have sat bolt upright. Tonkatt had been wearing a love charm?

"Under some circumstances I suppose it might work that way," Tonkatt acknowledged uneasily. "And, I admit, I had hoped to have a pleasant evening tonight, including a lady's company. I did not know I would encounter Magister Shenza," he stressed. "I had no ill intention toward her."

Hot indignation swelled in Shenza's breast, even constrained by the spell of stasis. This explained so much—the irrational attraction, and her overwhelming response to his presence. Her mask had partially protected her during their first meeting. Tonight, without it, she had been vulnerable. And it would be just like Master Nurune to send his comely students to muddle her thinking.

"I'm sure," Kafseet was saying harshly. "You just wanted to be her friend, didn't you? For someone in your line of work, it would be pretty helpful to have a magister at your command."

"Please don't insult me, Mistress Curomancer." Tonkatt hissed.

Shenza felt a new surge of fury. How dare he act so wronged, when it was he who took advantage of her inexperience?

"Insult you?" Kafseet's tone was scathing. "We've had this kind of conversation before, haven't we? Did you think I wouldn't remember you, boy?"

Infuriated, Shenza fought the enchantment that bound her limbs. Her eyes snapped open.

Above her were the wide round beams on the underside of a tiled roof, tinted by a green haze that partly obscured her vision. As she had sensed, she was lying on her back. A folded garment supported her head. To her right an expanse of chamber floor lay open to the curved walls of a richly appointed chamber. To her left, a painted cloth screen separated her from the others. Her garb was a plain white sheath, decorated with damp splashes from her sickness. A square of cut jade rested on her chest, centered on the bare brown skin above and between her breasts. Incised sigils glowed with the radiant emerald of its healing power.

As Shenza oriented herself, she heard her mother gasp with horrified condemnation. "Young man! Were you addressing my daughter with a... a charm for lust?"

"No!" He tried in vain to laugh at the accusation. "I assure you, Matron, I had no dishonorable intentions."

Giliatt was not convinced. "Magister, is this truly legal?" she demanded fiercely.

Panting with effort, Shenza lifted her hand to clasp the talisman whose power held her helpless. Even lying down, her senses reeled, but her determined will conquered the darkness that assailed her. There was a sucking gasp, not unlike the sound of her mask, and the talisman's supernatural glow winked out. With it went the unbearable sense of pressure weighing her down. Shenza could move.

She could also feel again, a bitter dull burning throughout her body. She swallowed convulsively, feeling her swollen throat work sluggishly. Her lungs ached with each breath, and sweat chilled her form. Nevertheless, she sat up.

"Devices which control the minds of others are not legal," Laraquies was explaining quietly. "But, as Tonkatt says, this is not quite the same thing. It is an amulet attracting luck to the wearer. Its influence upon the actions of others is a secondary result."

"That's a pretty fine line," Kafseet observed disapprovingly.

"Yes, it is." It was impossible to detect the magister's personal feelings in his voice. "But, as you must also know, this amulet could not have caused my student's illness. That is my foremost concern."

Rather than risk standing, Shenza crawled from her resting place. The floor was covered with carpets, their colors obscured by the dull light in the room. It came from a single wall lamp, she saw as she emerged from behind the screen. She was still in the palace, for this was the chamber Alceme had assigned to her the night before. Master Laraquies and Mother sat with their backs to the screen, while Kafseet and Tonkatt stood in attitudes reflecting their confrontation. All heads turned as Shenza crept to a stop. She put the inactive talisman on the carpet with an offended slap and sat up to rake the tangled black curls from her face.

"Shenza," Giliatt began, dumbfounded.

And Kafseet choked, "How did you..."

Ignoring them, she turned her eyes to Tonkatt. His sleek, self- assured air was gone, replaced by shame and indignation. But the magnetism she had felt was gone, and he was not nearly as angry as she.

"Go," she croaked harshly through her swollen throat. "Out."

She didn't know what he saw in her face, but he stepped back a pace. Then he bowed jerkily, both hands crossed over his chest, and stalked from the room.

Kafseet had recovered from her surprise. "What are you doing out here? You should be lying down!"

Master Laraquies simply gazed at her, silver brows making a double arch of surprise across his forehead.

"Shenza?" Mother repeated anxiously. "Are you well?"

"No," she said shortly. There was little satisfaction in ejecting Tonkatt. As her rage ebbed, the pain was growing worse. "But I couldn't just sit there listening to you talk about me."

"You were in stasis! You shouldn't have heard anything," Kafseet protested. "How did you break the spell?"

"You said it was a lesser stasis. When I got angry enough, I broke it." Shenza did not know enough of curomancy to offer another explanation.

"She is a trained enchanter," her teacher pointed out placidly.

"Even so..." Mother protested.

"Enough," Kafseet interposed. "If she's not in stasis, we'd better start healing her right away. How are we going to find your daughter?" she asked Giliatt.

"I can look for her, but..."

"You said you had a theory, Kafseet," Shenza said despite a constricting band of fire about her throat. A sweat-dampened lock of hair draped over her eyes again. Exasperated, she pushed it back. She desperately wanted to hear that Tonkatt's proximity, even with a love charm, was not what had make her ill. "What is it, please."

"Excuse me," another voice interrupted, steady and masculine. Shamatt stood in the open doorway, resplendent in a dark gold kilt and mantle. A feathered emblem of rank jutted from his turban. "May I come in?"

"It's about time you got here," Kafseet snapped.

"Nice to see you, too, Kafseet," he retorted.

"Likewise."

Shenza was left to wonder how they knew each other.

"I have many duties," the Sub-Chief continued, evidently accustomed to Kafseet's sharp-tongued ways, "tonight more than most. I heard that Magister Shenza was ill."

"I am," she answered, too miserable to be polite. "Kafseet?"

The curomancer nodded briskly. "Your mother said you had an upset stomach and your throat was swelling. That usually means you've drunk ant bane. If Chimi can find the cup you were drinking from, I could be sure."

"Ant bane!" Giliatt repeated, appalled.

The angular woman nodded. "You know how stubborn ants are. Once they start foraging in your kitchen, it's hard to get rid of them. Alchemists sell a crystal in the market that is harmless by itself, but when mixed with citrus juice produces a strong toxin. The sweet juice also acts as bait to attract the ants. Usually we see this poisoning when young children find the juice lying out and drink it by mistake."

Poison. Shenza had changed her mind. She would rather have thought herself the fool. Laraquies must have guessed this, too, she thought grimly. It was he who first asked about the lime juice.

"And you think Magister Shenza drank this?" Shamatt asked carefully. As she spoke, he crossed the room to seat himself opposite Laraquies.

"I had watered lime juice," Shenza confirmed absently. "I requested it from a servant, since I didn't want to drink wine."

The throbbing ache of her throat seemed ever worse as the implications unfolded in her mind. The killer was definitely part of the palace staff. In fact, it had to be one of the domestics. A palace bureaucrat would not have known she drank lime juice with her breakfast, and could not have prepared the bane in case she requested it again.

Shenza felt a sickening lurch in her stomach that had nothing to do with her physical condition. The enemy was becoming aggressive, seeking to remove her interference by murdering her as well. Her eyes turned to Master Laraquies, who nodded soberly.

Shamatt must have seen them. "Are you saying this came from the palace kitchen?" he probed, quietly concerned.

"What does that matter?" Mother objected frantically. She appealed to Kafseet. "How do you treat it?"

"Ha!" The curomancer laughed curtly, without humor. "You make them vomit, if they aren't already doing it. As my esteemed colleague, Hasangiri, pointed out, that is how the body gets rid of things you've eaten that are bad for you."

Shenza rolled her eyes with weary humor, pressing one hand to her fiery middle. "And after that?"

"My next recommendation would be a purative extract to remove the poison that has already entered your system, followed by a cure-all to restore the damage it's already done. I have the extract in my office, but the cure-all will have to be compounded specially," Kafseet added. "They just don't last."

"How long will that take?" Laraquies wanted to know.

"For the cure-all, a couple of hours. I'll need to make it down at the clinic where I have all my materials. And I'll have to find at least one of my apprentices. They're around here somewhere." Her impatient gesture took in the whole estate, where the distant sounds of music made it clear the celebration was still going on.

"I think my men can help you," Shamatt offered.

"I'd appreciate it. Meanwhile, you'd better go back into stasis," the curomancer said crisply. "You must be in pain, and it will only get worse. I wouldn't want to leave you unprotected, even if you slowed your metabolism through meditation."

"There are still things I need to do," Shenza objected.

"You'd better do them in the next few minutes," Kafseet answered without compromise, "because then I'm putting you in. You can't see your aura with a healer's eye, but I can. If you don't listen to me, you won't live to finish this case."

Shenza stared at her for a moment, trying not to hear her mother's strangled gasp. The investigation had to be resolved soon, or the city would suffer. Nor did she believe a stasis spell would shield her from the spirits' impatience. Yet she felt every bit as sick as Kafseet said she was. Reluctantly she nodded. "How long will I be unconscious?"

"Just until morning. I can dose you then. After that you'll have to rest for two days more." Kafseet's thin brown hand rose sharply, stilling her protests. "I won't be responsible otherwise."

There was a taut silence. Shamatt looked as though he wanted to say something, but it was her mother who spoke first.

"How much will this cost?" she asked, only a little tremble in her voice. Shenza bit her lip, adding one more item to her list of grudges against the unknown enemy. Money had always been her family's worst problem.

"Don't concern yourself, Giliatt." Laraquies said soothingly. "Shenza is a public servant. You are not responsible for payment."

"But she is not your kin," Mother protested, with guilt and relief in her eyes.

Shenza cleared her throat. This was using up her precious time. "While I am recovering, Magister, I will delegate my inquiry to you. I would like you to take testimony from Byben of Cessill, and also please ask Mistress Aoress if she can call on me here." She glanced at Kafseet for permission.

"A short visit late in the day," the curomancer allowed.

"I think it wise to place wards on this building while I am in stasis," Shenza went on. She refused to lie helpless when her assailant was still nearby. "This will eliminate the need for guards when they are already so busy." Laraquies bowed his head silently, approving her choices, while Shamatt raised his brows slightly at her phrasing. She turned to him directly. "Also, it would be very helpful if Officer Juss could be released from his normal duties to assist Master Laraquies."

"This is not unexpected," he murmured drily. "I think it can be arranged."

"What about that man?" Giliatt asked sharply. "I won't accept him hanging around my daughter while he wore that... thing."

"Believe me, Matron," Kafseet smiled with obvious relish, "it will come to the attention of his coven leader. Skirting the law like that makes every enchanter look dishonest. I won't put tolerate it, and I'm not afraid of Nurune of Sengool."

"Some other time, Kafseet, I would like to know what you meant about having this conversation with Tonkatt before." Master Laraquies added serenely. He fingered a bit of jewelry cradled in his lap.

"With pleasure," the curomancer said grimly.

Shamatt merely sat and listened, his dark eyes roving from one to another as they spoke. He obviously hoped for some kind of clarification. Before he could ask it, Shenza cleared her throat again. Her stomach was shooting pains that seemed to reach all the way to her fingertips, and she longed for the solace Kafseet offered.

"My final question is, who will investigate this attack against me? Master Laraquies has a clear conflict of interest, since I am his apprentice." She looked again to Shamatt. "Is there someone you can trust to do this for us?"

He placed a hand on his chest and bowed from the waist. "I would be honored to investigate personally."

"But you also have a conflict, since Chief Borleek has been criticizing Magister Shenza and you are his second," Laraquies pointed out.

"My interest is in punishing the guilty. Such a deadly assault, directed against the representative of our judicial structure, cannot be permitted." His expression was grave. "An investigation should be concluded expeditiously, but fairly."

"I have confidence in Shamatt," Shenza said quietly. Both men regarded her with mild surprise. Shamatt bowed again.

Shenza had not expected Shamatt to take the responsibility himself, but it pleased her. Considering how well informed he was on other matters, he might be able to discover new information while she was under treatment. "But I caution you, if he is willing to strike out at me, he will not hesitate to attack you, either. Protect yourself, and do not attempt to arrest him without Magister Laraquies."

"Of course."

"Shenza," Kafseet interrupted, "let Laraquies worry about the details. You're going back to bed. Come on."

Shenza didn't try to argue. She rose, with some effort, while the others watched anxiously. Kafseet swept up the jade talisman and helped her steady herself. Shenza summoned a smile for her mother's stricken expression.

"Try not to worry. I'll be over this soon."

"I hope so," Giliatt murmured. Her sad, dark eyes followed Shenza's progress behind the screen.

Kafseet helped her ease down on the matt. It was the same one Mother had brought to the ceremony, she now saw, and the cushion for her head was her wadded up mantle. Shenza muffled a moan as she sat back. There was no need to worry her mother any more.

Despite the constant, throbbing pain it was hard to face going back into stasis. The enemy was getting bolder. Each of his actions told her something about him, it was true, but the learning was so painfully slow! And she still had no idea what the criminal had gained by killing Lord Anges.

Kneeling beside her pallet, Kafseet began to chant softly. Shenza watched as streaks of wan green light gleamed between the curomancer's dark fingers. The light grew harsher, brighter. Emerald energy flared as Kafseet released the borrowed talisman. It drifted downward to hover over Shenza's chest, rotating as if it must align itself. Tiny lightnings raced along the smooth underside.

And then—nothing.

Chapter Sixteen
~ The Taste of Smoke ~

The world returned first in dull pain that defined the limits of Shenza's body. An overwhelming lethargy possessed her. It made thought difficult, yet she knew there was something she should be doing, something urgent. As her eyes trembled open, the sallow light of a lamp whispered hints of rich furnishings in the darkened chamber. Muffled sounds betrayed movement behind the screen that loomed to her left. A dim female form bent over her.

"Where..." Shenza began, and coughed as her aching throat objected to the exercise.

"Not now," came Kafseet's quick voice. "Drink this."

Oh, yes. She had been in healing stasis, waiting for the curomancers to formulate a remedy. Her mind fumbled. A remedy for...

A firm hand supported Shenza's head. As the slick edge of a ceramic cup pressed to her lips, thick fluid ran over her parched tongue. It tasted like the smell of smoke, heavy and harshly cloying. The stuff seemed to stick in her throat, choking her. Fighting panic, Shenza swallowed harder, forcing down a painful lump. The cup persisted until no more was left, and her head was gently settled on the cushion beneath her. Kafseet's shoulders shifted in the wan light, as if she sighed with relief.

Eyes stinging, Shenza murmured thickly, "Thank you."

"Don't thank me yet," came the wry retort. "You're going to feel worse before you feel better, I'm afraid."

"Impossible," she croaked, drawing a chuckle from the curomancer. Merely swallowing had inflamed her throat, awakening pain that pounded outward with every heartbeat. The medicine... Shenza slowly dragged the words up from her memory, the purative extract... It certainly didn't taste pure.

Kafseet turned aside, setting down the cup. "Wash it carefully, Satta," she ordered crisply.

A familiar lad appeared in the rim of Shenza's sight. "Yes, mistress." He bobbed obediently and disappeared.

The chamber was very quiet. The festival must be over. That meant it was very late at night. Kafseet must have used a stronger spell than Hasangiri, Shenza thought dully. She remembered nothing from the time she laid down.

Weakly she reached for Kafseet's knee. "How long was I static?" The ache in her middle had become an unpleasant burning. She longed for a distraction even more than information.

Kafseet obliged her. "Quite a while. Your mother and sister went home. Shamatt sent an escort with them, or I don't think Giliatt would have left. She's pretty worried about you. Not that I'm criticizing."

Then the peacekeepers knew where she lived, Shenza reflected wearily. Shamatt would soon know where Byben was, if he didn't already. It seemed somehow a petty concern. Yet it was the crux of the matter, wasn't it? Byben's safety. If she had felt more alert, she might have been able to think what to do about it.

"Laraquies and your officer friend have gone to Lord Anges' quarters to guard against that restless spirit," Kafseet went on. Shenza let her eyes slip closed briefly. Juss was not going to be understanding about this. "Shamatt found a couple of fire charms somewhere. Only the heavens know how. Juss has one, and I believe Lord Aspace got the other."

Sensible. If someone had a grudge against the first lord's family, it was possible they might also strike at Lord Aspace. That would be disastrous, given the spirits' attitude. Yet, her own experience showed the killer was quite able to use other means than magic fire. The precaution could prove meaningless.

And Shamatt, again, had been the one to provide the amulets. She didn't know how she felt about that. It was hard to trust any peacekeeper but Juss. Remembering how Kafseet had spoken to him earlier, Shenza cleared her raw throat. "Have you known Shamatt long?"

"Oh, most of his life. He was the little neighbor brat, two houses down from mine." Kafseet seemed to be smiling fondly in the shadows. "He was always tricking my brothers into doing something stupid. They never learned, either."

"What do you think of him now?"

"Shamatt?" the curomancer drawled thoughtfully. "He's a conniving bastard. Has his fingers in everything. I pity his wives." Despite her sharp words, she sounded complacent. "He's also the only one restraining that idiot Borleek from doing whatever he pleases."

"Would you trust him?"

"He's honest, if that's what you're asking. But trust him?" Kafseet chuckled again. "Not with my back turned."

"I see."

The burning in Shenza's stomach had turned to an itchy tingle, shooting through her body much as the poison had. She tried to put aside her growing discomfort and analyze the information calmly. She had thought from the beginning that the man seemed to know a great deal about events in the city. Yet so far he had not used his knowledge against her.

"Do you think he has told Borleek we moved Byben?"

"Did I say he was a fool?" Kafseet snorted. "He'll pick the right time, believe me. For his own sake, if nothing else."

"I suppose."

"How do you feel?" the curomancer now asked. The calm neutrality of her tone made Shenza uneasy.

"Itching on the inside," she answered truthfully. She was sweating, too, and it seemed she could taste the bitter, smoky flavor of the medicine in her pores.

"Good. That is supposed to happen."

Shenza nodded bleakly, feeling another wave of heat wash over her. It was not unlike the nausea just before she threw up. The reek of smoke on her skin became stronger, and she could feel her clothes growing damp with absorbed moisture.

Despite herself, she had to ask, "How long did you say it would take?"

Kafseet pressed a finger to her shoulder, stroking lightly. Her fingertip seemed to slip on the sweat-slick skin. "Not much longer," she said calmly. "Take a look."

Shenza raised her head, straining to see in the dull light. The natural brown of her skin was covered by a sheen of sweat, glinting darkly in the lamp glow. Sooty stains had appeared on the pale cloth of her sheath. Kafseet repeated her gesture, drawing her finger along Shenza's arm. To her surprise, the action left a visible stripe of lighter skin. Blinking, the sorceress let her head drop as her neck began to twinge. Shouldn't the area without the sweat be darker, rather than lighter?

But Kafseet rubbed her fingertips together in demonstration. "The purative is forcing the contamination out of your body. This is it." She wiped her hands on the trailing end of her robe.

Shenza nodded again. Learning about new kinds of magic was always a thrill, but in this case she would have enjoyed knowing more if the process didn't feel so miserable.

"Not much longer," Kafseet assured her.

Indeed, the burning suddenly began to fade. Shenza waited, afraid to relax too soon. In her ears, it seemed she heard a faint hissing. She lifted her head again, watching in bemusement as faint wisps of vapor rose from her skin. The burnt smell was already fading.

"Ah." The curomancer nodded, voicing a satisfied word. "That's the last of it."

"Smoke?" Shenza asked wearily.

"Yes, because there is no more bane. Now, let's get you cleaned up. Satta!"

"Mistress?" Kafseet's apprentice appeared around the screen. The dark and light stripes of his mantle were visible in the faint lamp glow.

"Help me get her up. No, not you," Kafseet corrected sternly when Shenza tried to stand. "Let us do it."

That was not an easy order to obey. Instinctively Shenza wanted to stand on her own, to prove to herself she was not beyond the effort. One on each side of her, the two curomancers assisted her into the bathing room. The light was brighter there.

Now she could see the oily sludge overlying her normal skin tone.

They reached the tiled margin of the bath. Shenza could feel smooth tiles and rough grout beneath her bare feet. Kafseet stopped. "Lean on me, Shenza. Satta, get her robe."

Shenza tensed as she realized the apprentice lad was undoing the bone pin that held on her garment. "No," she protested. The sudden movement made her head swim.

Meersatta hesitated, looking to his teacher. Kafseet rolled her eyes and snorted. "This is no time for modesty, girl. We're all healers here."

"But I can't..." she protested, remembering the ingrained stricture against lewdness. It wasn't proper!

"It's nothing he hasn't seen before. Unless you want to wear this soot for the next week, you'd better cooperate."

"It's really all right, Magister," the young man soothed her with a respectful voice.

Shenza averted her face, eyes tightly closed, and said nothing more as her sheath, and then her soft loincloth, settled around her ankles. The night air seemed uncomfortably humid as they helped her into the water. She shivered, mortified that a man had seen her nude before her marriage.

"The last chaste woman in town," Kafseet teased. Shenza glanced at her defensively, determined not to look at the male intruder. The curomancer relented. "I can handle it from here. Why don't you start the tea, Satta. The cure-all has decanted, hasn't it?"

"Yes, Mistress. Right away."

With intense relief, Shenza heard the man withdraw. Just a boy, really, but it was bad enough she felt so sick without being shamed as well. She lay silently in the bath while Kafseet rubbed her down. The warm water did feel good, and the healer's hands were gentle.

"There." Kafseet leaned back, wringing out her sponge decisively. She reached to retrieve a wicker tray bearing decorative jars of soaps and skin oils. "If you feel strong enough, why don't you wash your hair as well. Otherwise, just rest. We have one more charm to activate."

"Thank you," Shenza murmured, still mortified.

Kafseet patted her shoulder and strode from the room. Shenza lay in the water, half-floating, reluctant to move.

In the outer chamber, soft chanting began. Kafseet and Meersatta intoned together, a sonorous droning. The male and female voices mingled in a way that reminded her of the spirit's voice. That thought made her shudder, and she sat up to reach for the tray of soaps.

Washing did help her wake up a little, but it did not revive her spirits. Her worries returned, hovering in the air with the steam from the bath. It pained Shenza as much as the poison she'd drunk to contemplate her errors. She had thought she would be anonymous in civilian clothing, and therefore safe. What kind of fool would assume that? The adversary had found her easily enough.

And that Tonkatt, preying on her naivete. Juss was going to kill her, if he didn't kill Tonkatt first. And it wasn't her fault! None of this was her doing, yet she was responsible. She scrubbed at her face with the sponge, as if she could wash away the disgrace.

The room around her blurred. Hot tears mixed with the bath water, were swallowed and lost. Shenza despised herself for crying, but she could not keep her eyes from overflowing. She felt worthless and sick, and knew she was over-reacting. But even knowing the illness made her feel worse didn't help. If she had been more careful, she wouldn't be sick at all.

The chanting had stopped, she suddenly realized. The curomancers would be back soon, and she did not wish to be seen naked again. Shenza dragged herself out of the bath with slow determination. She could have used some of the skin oil, but it was more important to be decently covered.

Fresh clothing had been provided, which was good. Her old garments were blotched with sweated-out poison and other remnants of her ordeal. The full length mantle, adorned with butterflies and orchids, was more suited to a courtier than a public servant. There was no time to marvel at the softness of the feather- flower silk. Kafseet parted the bead curtain and entered the room just as Shenza was fastening a copper brooch.

"You must be feeling better," the curomancer observed when she saw her charge fully clothed.

Shenza refused to be baited. "A little," she acknowledged, though, in truth, the burst of activity had left her feeling shaky.

"Now that you're up and dressed, you'll have to come lie down again." Kafseet smiled, mocking the contradiction. "It won't hurt this time, but it will make you sleep. And then, so can we."

There were lines on Kafseet's face that Shenza hadn't noticed before, dark creases of weariness and concern.

"I am sorry to be a bother," she said.

"I volunteered, remember? Come, let's get you to bed."

Shenza followed her companion the short distance to the sleeping room, walking slowly but on her own strength. In the outer chamber, Kafseet's apprentice had taken down the folding screen and was spreading out two matts for sleeping. He nodded gravely as they passed, and Shenza fought her sense of chagrin.

It was a double relief to enter the bedchamber, where netting stretched invitingly between the bed's four posts. Shenza ached to lie down and begin a true recovery.

"Down you go, young lady," Kafseet said briskly. As Shenza obeyed, the curomancer poured a cup of tea from a plain porcelain pot. "Drink as much of this as you can, and then go to sleep. If you need anything, we're just out here."

"Thank you." Shenza accepted the cup gratefully.

"See you in a few hours." Kafseet smiled encouragingly and swept out of the room.

Shenza sat listlessly on the edge of the bed. *Tea again,* she thought. Master Laraquies had been pressing his tea on her for three days. She was tired of elitherium. Nonetheless, she drank.

It was not a true tea at all, she quickly discovered. She picked out the flavors of mint and other herbs, and underlying that a potent sweetness that was not honey. She found herself craving the taste, and the soothing warmth that seemed to encompass her. After draining two cups, she stretched out wearily with a half-full cup balanced on her stomach.

What a day! Tears stung her eyes again. It was hard to believe how much had happened. The morning's disaster at the port would have been enough. Or the Lord's arrival and inauguration. Or the spirit's second visitation. Or Tonkatt's scheming.

Just one of those events would have distracted her. Why did everything have to happen all at the same time? She had no idea how she was going to explain any of it, and she was sure the new Lord would want an answer.

But the problem went beyond even that. The bane had been meant to kill her, and she had not helped herself against it. She could have died because she wanted to impress Tonkatt so badly. She had not known, then, that he used illicit spell craft to attract her. But she should have. She was a magician herself. The attraction had been so irrational. She should have known it for what it was.

Shenza drank her medicine, determined to stop this whining. In the main room, she could hear the two curomancers talking softly. If only her tasks were as simple as theirs.

Her eyelids were heavy as sleep bound her in a different kind of spell. Rallying her wits, she murmured, "Light, out."

The faint lamplight yielded to darkness.

~

"It looks like they're all asleep," Juss reported. His voice came muffled over his rugged shoulders.

"Then all is well," Laraquies observed. "They would not be resting if there was anything wrong."

"I can't see Shenza."

"I believe she had a private chamber."

"Probably."

The young man stood with his wide back to Laraquies, peering through the faint haze of the defensive ward. He leaned as close to the plane of the ward as he could without touching it. The unpleasant experience of being repelled by the ward's power had taught him caution, yet he would not leave the doorway.

Just to the left of the peacekeeper's head, a flat black stone hung in the air, incised with sigils of protection. Several others ringed the building. No person—and no magic—would enter or leave until Laraquies removed the enchantment.

"We can but wait, now. Surely all is well," the magister repeated.

Laraquies had to admit he spoke partly to reassure himself. It was a real shock to learn an attempt had been made on

Shenza's life. And on her virtue, for he did not believe Tonkatt's protestations. It was unheard-of to attack a magister. Even wealthy lords and rulers respected their persons. In his forty years of service on Chalsett, Laraquies had never heard of such a thing. On the larger islands, where standards were looser, he supposed it might happen, but not in a town this size. It simply didn't happen.

Of course, the assassin had already invoked magic against a first lord, who should also have been sacrosanct. Considering that, Laraquies supposed he shouldn't be surprised by anything else. Still, it made him feel old.

Worse, this was sure to be another blow to Shenza's confidence. If he knew his student at all, she had spent her few moments of consciousness blaming herself. Laraquies muffled a sigh. It was too bad Chimi hadn't been able to find Shenza's cup. That could have told him so much.

Even so, he believed that the assailant had made a grave error by striking directly at Shenza. Shamatt had already come to her defense. Even Borleek had asked after her, though one could not exactly call his terse query a display of concern. 'Does this mean you'll be taking over the investigation?' he wanted to know. Taking over the investigation, indeed.

Well, no matter. The clever Sub-Chief Shamatt was a great asset to the investigation, and others would surely join in the search as well. Victory could not be far off. He had to believe that.

Juss was still loitering at the top of the steps, as if some new magic would let him see into the darkened interior. "Come along," Laraquies chided gently. "We'll have breakfast, and then call on Byben of Cessill for his testimony. There is much to do this morning."

Reluctantly, the officer followed as Laraquies turned away.

~

Shenza slept as though dead, rousing only once to relieve herself. She was vaguely aware of morning light creeping through the stone window screens, and two still forms on pallets in the main room. Blessedly, she felt no pain in her middle. But those things seemed much less important than the rest her body longed for. She crept back to her hammock and fell asleep again.

~

She dreamed that she woke with a crushing weight on her chest and opened her eyes to find a bamboo viper coiled there. Lidless eyes, burning emerald, stared from a body of living black marble. She could not move beneath the pressure of its mass. Outside her room, the curomancers were talking about her in low voices. They were planning her funeral.

She again woke, sweating with fright. The voices had dwindled to nothing. Shenza rose and walked through the guest house, but could not see anyone. Searching for Kafseet, she went outside and discovered the coronation revels were still in process. Crowds of villagers danced serpent-style, hands on the shoulders of those before them, to a strangely distorted music. Chief Borleek appeared suddenly among the populace, a squad of peace officers at his heels. They moved toward her purposefully. Shenza turned away, but a wall of dancers hemmed her in. Rough hands seized her, dragged her to the cleared space before the first lord's chair. Master Laraquies stood to one side, shaking his head sadly. Mother was with him, silently weeping.

She struggled, but to no avail. With a ripping of fabric, she was shoved forward to tumble onto the grass. Clasping her torn robe around herself, she looked up. At the foot of the stairs, Innoshyra of Sengool curled possessively against the first lord's knees. Just behind her were her kinsmen, Nurune and Tonkatt. All three regarded Shenza with insolent smirks. Seated on the throne was a dark-skinned figure wearing the resplendent robes of Lord Aspace. But beneath the jeweled and feathered head cloth was the withered face of the dead Lord Anges.

Shenza struggled awake yet again, and didn't know whether to believe she was truly conscious. Radiance pierced the window screens in narrow rays, but at a different angle than she last recalled. In the outer chamber, Kafseet was talking to someone, laughing wryly. A faint, appetizing aroma filtered in to her. She distinctly smelled steamed millet.

Shenza sat up, reassured by the physical sensation of the netting swaying beneath her. That could not be a dream. There was a rattle at the door, and she looked over to see Master Laraquies pass through the beaded curtain. Behind him loomed a familiar figure in a dark-gold mantle. Both carried covered trays, the source of the appealing smells. The elder sorcerer and the strapping young man looked an odd pair. It was both comforting and distressing to see them—an equally odd match in emotions.

"It's just us," Laraquies announced. He looked so cheerful and normal, she somehow felt cheated.

"Did we wake you?" Juss asked anxiously. Shenza had never heard him use such a subdued tone. He stared at her as if she might faint away before his eyes.

Shenza shook her head. The fading shreds of nightmare left her feeling muzzy and confused. She blinked, trying to orient herself. From the day's heat and the angle of the light, she estimated it was mid-morning, not quite time for the daily rain.

"Come have something to eat," her tutor urged, kneeling to set his tray on a low table. "I cooked it myself."

Juss lingered in the doorway, as if uncertain what to do with his tray. After a moment, he hurried to join Laraquies.

"Are you hungry?" Laraquies prodded when Shenza remained seated on the bed.

"Yes," she admitted. Shenza swung her legs over the side of the bed self-consciously, taking care to keep her garments in order. She sat beside her teacher. Smiling placidly, he divided the contents of the two trays into three servings. One was significantly larger than the others. Juss poured tea clumsily, as if he were unused to dispensing hospitality. Shenza felt her stomach rumble. She tensed, remembering her illness, only to realize it was just normal hunger muttering inside her. That was encouraging, as was the absence of pain. Shenza wondered how long she had been sleeping, and if, after eating, she could sleep a while longer. Without the nightmares.

The silence lengthened uncomfortably. To end it, Shenza asked, "Did you say you cooked, teacher? It looks good."

He nodded smugly. "I hope you'll like it."

"It's safer this way," Juss added bluntly.

"I know." Shenza sighed into her teacup.

"I don't mind," Laraquies said serenely, but his dark eyes were keen on her face, probing for what she did not say. Shenza drank from her cup, using bitter tea to fill the silence as she had seen him do so many times. The aftertaste of elitherium hardly seemed worth noticing any longer.

Gratefully she accepted the bowl of steamed millet and greens. The first bite tasted heavenly. But she was not to enjoy her meal.

"How do you feel?" Juss blurted suddenly.

Shenza stared at him momentarily, caught speechless by the tactless question. She didn't want to think about what had happened, let alone explain herself to Juss.

Holding to her dignity, she answered, "I am tired, but the poison is gone. I owe Mistress Kafseet a good deal." And she should apologize to Meersatta. But not now. Shenza applied herself to her breakfast, hoping he would let her eat in peace.

"Indeed. We will have to repay her," Laraquies mused, subtly smoothing over the awkwardness. "Perhaps a gift of some kind. One of those flasks that always pours clean water."

Either Juss did not understand what they were hinting at, or he chose to ignore it. "But what is going to happen now?" he wanted to know.

When Shenza did not answer, Laraquies explained. "Shamatt is investigating the attempt on Shenza's life."

'Attempt on her life.' It sounded dreadful when he put it that way, yet she could not deny that was what happened.

"Shamatt?" Juss sounded doubtful.

"Since my own student is involved, I cannot do it. There might be questions later about the fairness of the proceedings," the old man told him mildly. "I wouldn't want the inquiry compromised."

"I suppose."

Shenza was getting tired of having to justify herself. She sipped tea to clear her mouth. "He seems astute. I am hoping the results of his investigation will be relevant to mine."

Juss brightened. "The killer can't focus on both of you at once."

Shenza shrugged. She just wanted Shamatt to 'connive' in her favor, to use Kafseet's term.

"The chance is greater he will betray himself," Laraquies agreed. "Until now, I suspect the killer was working alone. He seems quite confident in his own abilities." Not without reason, Shenza thought. Her teacher went on, "For this attack he may have used another, either a willing accomplice or another pawn. That person may lead us to him. And by the way, Shenza, Shamatt would like to speak with you soon." He smiled apologetically.

"Whenever he wants to visit me." She certainly didn't feel like going anywhere.

Silence fell again, and Shenza took advantage of it to eat her fill. But there was no stilling the internal voice that plagued her. It was all very well to complain that she was tired of justifying herself, but she could not deny there were things she was going to have to explain, and soon. What would she say? That she was a miserable failure, unworthy of the magister's tutelage? That was unacceptable.

She swallowed hard, as if she could somehow digest and destroy this poisonous self-doubt. She had mistakes to make up for, it was true. But Shenza swore to herself she would no longer disgrace her master's teachings. No matter what happened to her, or how tired she felt, she would not give up. She would let go of this defeatist thinking and simply continue, one step at a time, until she was ordered to stop or until she prevailed.

With a deep sigh, Shenza pushed back her empty dishes. Both men regarded her expectantly. "Master," she said, sounding steadier than she felt. "What has been happening while I slept?"

~

Shenza found it comforting to return to her familiar purple robe and mask. The gaudy borrowed attire had made her feel ill at ease, as though she was pretending to be someone she was not.

Immediately after breakfast and Laraquies' briefing, Kafseet had insisted on a physical examination. No sooner was she satisfied of Shenza's health than Shamatt arrived to take Shenza's statement. That had occupied much of the morning. The peacekeeper was very thorough, especially where the details of her interactions with Tonkatt were concerned. It was interesting, in a technical way, to observe how his questioning differed from Master Laraquies's. Shenza had focused on this, rather than her embarrassment. She did her best to offer only facts, not conjectures or emotional reactions.

When at last Shamatt departed, Shenza felt as limp and faded as a robe that has been washed too many times. Even after Juss brought lunch, she found herself yawning. The day was sultry, and her tea was tepid. Shenza wanted nothing more than to take a nap. Just as she was about to say so, Juss spoke up.

"We have a visitor," he mumbled around a mouthful of rice.

Shenza followed his gaze and saw someone approaching across the garden lawn. It was a lady, draped in a robe of soft green. She carried a mesh bag at her side.

"I think I know who it is," Shenza answered.

Despite her assurance, Juss jumped up from the table. He met the stranger at the bottom of the steps.

"Is Magister Shenza available?" The lady pressed one hand to her chest and bowed. "Magister Laraquies asked me to call on her."

Juss glanced at Shenza for permission.

"Yes, it's all right," Shenza said, trying not to show her reluctance. Tired though she was, she shouldn't inconvenience someone she needed information from. "Thank you for coming, Mistress Aoress."

"It is no trouble, if it serves my Lord's memory," Aoress replied. She glided up the steps, bowed again, and sank down opposite Shenza with unusual poise and grace.

In truth, Aoress did not look exactly as Shenza had expected. She was not glamorous in the way someone like Innoshyra would be. Aoress wore a simple robe without fanciful designs. Strands of brown and white shell were draped around her neck. The dancer was older than Shenza had thought. Silver curls surrounded friendly, dark eyes. She had seemed far younger when she was dancing.

"I enjoyed your performance during the coronation," Shenza began. "Have you danced that tale before?"

"Yes," Aoress replied. "I performed for Lord Anges' coronation as well. But every dancer must study those roles.

There are many legends and tales local to the islands, but this one is used throughout the Jewel Sea."

Shenza nodded thoughtfully. Perhaps it was foolish of her to waste Mistress Aoress' time. It seemed unlikely that this peaceful art could relate to Lord Anges' violent death. And yet, there might be a link. Shenza reached for her note-taking materials.

"If you could, please describe a dancer's training to me. Clearly, there must be physical preparation, and magical as well?"

"You are correct, Magister." Aoress nodded approvingly. "Both my parents were dancers, and my training began during childhood. They started with games to develop my flexibility and sense of balance, and afterward assigned the more demanding exercises. Sorcery began later still."

"But," Shenza murmured as she wrote, "isn't the magic just as necessary?"

"Ah," Aoress murmured. "An insightful question, Magister. Yes, the shadows are very important."

"Do you speak of phantasms?" Shenza asked, glancing up. "Yes," Aoress said. "Shadow is merely our word for it. Shadows are the illusions which make our performance so real." She smiled, acknowledging the inherent contradiction of her words. "Shadow is also the measure of true greatness. One might be a very capable performer, but without the mastery of shadow..." She raised her hands, then let them fall to the tabletop, empty.

"Then, how do you accomplish this?" Shenza asked.

"We use a kind of talisman, as you might expect," Aoress replied. "I have brought an example."

The older woman reached into her bag and drew out a length of cloth. Shenza instantly recognized the silvery-cream of feather- flower silk, with its subtle gloss.

"This is the veil we wear when performing," Aoress said. She ran her hand between the folds. The fabric was so sheer that every line on her palm and the inlaid table top was clearly visible through it.

"Just a moment," Shenza said. She put on her mask and blinked as her eyes adjusted. The very threads were permeated with magic. Tiny woven runes floated in the cloth like foam on the sea.

"Is this fabric specially woven?" Shenza asked. She removed her mask, and the sigils vanished.

"Yes, Magister. We each make our own." Aoress caressed her veil with obvious pride. "It is one test of a student's skill."

"That I can understand," Shenza said, remembering the long effort required to craft her own mask.

"May I show you?" Aoress asked.

"Yes, please do."

Shenza set her pen aside. Juss, who had been loitering nearby, pretending not to listen, quickly turned to watch.

Aoress rose, again moving with exceptional grace. She said, "We wear it so..." The shimmering veil fluttered open. With a practiced motion, Aoress swirled it behind her so the gossamer stuff drifted over her head.

The veil was larger than Shenza had thought from its folded size. Aoress held one corner in each of her hands, yet the fabric swept the ground before and behind her. The dancer raised her hands and spun in place. Shimmering veils whirled around her.

Suddenly, as she completed the turn, it was not Aoress before them but the spirit woman from the coronation. Her robe was a deeper green, glittering with jewels. No longer was her hair streaked with silver. It flowed over her shoulders, black as a moonless night.

Aoress allowed them to see for a moment, then spun in the opposite direction. This time she stopped with shoulders hunched, and became the old woman in a drab gray robe. Shenza noted, as she moved, how the dancer kept her hands slightly raised so she would not tread on the fragile veil. Aoress turned again, standing up tall and square. Now they saw a young man in a yellow kilt, shield and club in his hands. Juss gave a grunt of appreciation.

Aoress bowed slightly, her eyes twinkling with humor. She carefully lifted the veil off and settled across the table from Shenza. Gently, Aoress began folding the veil into squares.

Shenza, watching, felt her heart sink. This showing off had little to do with her investigation. The killer had not used a dancer's veil, or she would have seen it in her scrying. And yet, surely she could glean something from a practitioner as experienced as this. Perhaps the spell itself held some clue.

"Does this answer your questions?" Aoress asked. The dancer had been watching her, Shenza realized. She must know that Shenza was investigating Lord Anges' death, and wonder what it had to do with her. But if Aoress was curious, she was too much a professional to show it.

"Could you teach me to do that?" Shenza asked.

Aoress' brows rose slightly. "It is not a technique for a casual student," she said.

"She won't steal your trade secrets," Juss growled.

"Juss, stop," Shenza scolded automatically, though she shared his frustration.

"It isn't that," Aoress quickly said. "Not many students can control a shadow the first time. Still, with your training, perhaps it is possible."

"It may help me to know what a shadow feels like," Shenza said. "Please show me. Teach me as if I was a new student."

"Very well," Aoress agreed.

She opened her veil again, spreading it over the table between them.

"Begin by calming yourself," Aoress said in a lulling voice. "Breathe deeply and let go of any strong emotion."

Shenza closed her eyes, listening. She remembered Master Laraquies saying something very like this, years ago. She had been stiff with nerves, unable to relax. Of course, Shenza had had no idea, then, how much greater her worries would become.

Since that day, she had also had much more practice in meditation. Shenza immediately relaxed, preparing herself to summon whatever forces Aoress might require.

The dancer seemed to sense her readiness. "Put out your hand and take the cloth," Aoress said. "Let it slip over and under your fingers. Feel it with your hands and your heart."

Shenza complied. The fabric was powdery and sleek. She suddenly understood why the veil was called a shadow. It felt as light and insubstantial as air. Then, with a start, Shenza realized she could also sense Aoress' spirit in the weaving: her exuberance, and the joy she felt in her body's strength and flexibility. Shenza's hand jerked as she shied from the unexpected intimacy. A moment later, she recognized that what she detected was only a remnant of the veil's making, not a true sharing of spirits.

"Excellent," Aoress murmured. "You may now attempt to change the shadow's color. Remember, you will not alter the veil itself, as in other spells you may know. Change only the color."

Shenza nodded, acknowledging the cautions. Her eyes were still closed.

"Fix a color in your mind," Aoress instructed. "Then, will the shadow to be that color."

Purple immediately came to Shenza's mind. She pictured the sober purple of a magister's robe and let that flow through her hands, into the soft veil.

"Ha," Juss snorted before Shenza was even fully aware of her choice. Aoress chuckled, as well.

Shenza opened her eyes. She was not surprised to see the veil was now a bright purple. This was exactly like the spell casting she was already familiar with.

"Is that all you can think of?" Juss teased.

Shenza shrugged, smiling despite herself. She could never get tired of magic, no matter what the circumstances. Aoress directed her through a variety of changes, creating wide stripes and then more complicated patterns of leaf and shell. Shenza followed her instructions, allowing herself to be diverted from her worries.

All too soon, Master Laraquies returned from his errands and Mistress Aoress took her leave. Shenza's sense of pleasure faded as soon as the dancer was gone. She feared that she had wasted her time after all. For, whatever the killer had felt as he cast his deadly spells, it probably was not the joy of making magic.

Chapter Seventeen
~ The Ugly Flower ~

Just down the hill from the cottage, a small courtyard had been leveled from the hillside. It was accessible from any of the loose ring of cottages, but the thick vegetation surrounding the enclosure gave the impression of quiet seclusion. Gratefully Shenza chose one of the two marble benches. At her elbow, fishes carved from the same pale stone spat streams of water into a shallow, mossy basin. Behind her, flowering vines draped over a retaining wall. It had rained at the usual time—a subtle reassurance, given the previous day's fractious weather—and their fragrance mingled with the scent of wet stonework.

Shenza set her mask aside to rub at her eyes. The nap she hoped for had eluded her. She had better concentrate on the investigation. Juss would scold her even more if she shooed him away for private time and then did nothing but stare into space. Shenza retrieved a thin scroll of cloth from her travel case and dutifully read.

Master Laraquies' notes informed her that Byben's testimony had been much as expected. His only daughter, Xerema, had left Chalsett-port three months before with her new husband. The old fisherman could not hide his bitterness and sense of abandonment, but the magister had not gained any admission of personal malice against Lord Anges. Byben freely confessed his abysmal skill with magic. He said he was indebted to his cousin Nakuri for his meager livelihood. Nor did he attempt to conceal his dependence on liquor. Shenza had to smile at Laraquies' recorded complaint that Grandmother would not let Byben drink as much as he wished.

Shenza leaned back for a moment, allowing weariness to wash over her. Borleek had to know by now that Byben was gone. She could imagine his reaction quite clearly. She smiled again, ironically. Perhaps this explained Shamatt's devotion to her case: it gave him a good reason to avoid his Chief. Well, she had better save her strength for another clash with Borleek. Probably in front of Lord Aspace. She couldn't expect to evade either of them much longer.

Nor the spirits. The sun was beginning to sink, stretching shadows across the paving stones, and a fog was coming in off the sea. Soon evening would purple the skies. Shenza fully expected another visitation from the spirits. If she waited here long enough, they would find her.

With a sense of resignation, she rolled up the scroll and returned it to her travel case. Laraquies had learned nothing she didn't already know.

As she watched, the first tendrils of mist curled across her lap, showing pale against the sober tone of her garb. Soon the vapors blanketed the courtyard, walling off the outer world with an intangible barrier. It was a little early in the year for fog, but nature itself was under Elitheri command. He... no, *it* should be here soon. Shenza closed her case and sat quietly.

A moment later she felt her muscles tense. The fog carried with it no floral perfume, nor even the sea's briny scent, but a damp reek of decay. It didn't smell anything like the previous two visitations.

Shenza rose, groping with one hand for the mask she had set aside a short while before. She wished with all her heart that Juss were here. He would know what to do.

"Who's there?" The demand was shrill, uneasy.

In answer, a flower of ugly, blue-red light blossomed in the unnatural gloom. Magic fire! Shenza threw herself aside, stumbling in her haste. A heartbeat later, the bench she was sitting on exploded in a spray of marble fragments. Stinging pains in her left arm and side told her she had not escaped the jagged shards.

"My travel case!" her mind protested as she scrambled away. Her talismans and records were inside. They could have

been destroyed. With feverish haste, she slapped the mask to her face. "Seal!" she ordered, and felt its magic bond to her skin.

She was just quick enough. A second bolt struck her as she was straightening to look around. Shenza was thrown, arms and legs cartwheeling. Lurid red and blue flashes quarreled before her eyes.

"Justice!" bellowed a voice like the crashing of wind and surf in a sea-storm. "Revenge!"

Shenza rolled to her knees, momentarily aware only of her head's answering roar. Dimly, she heard the melodious chime warning of strong magic nearby. "Enough," she hissed, silencing it. The alarm was a distraction, now.

Crouching, she glanced around. Through spell-filtered lenses Shenza could see the outlines of the courtyard. Something snarled and boiled among the fountain of carved fishes. Dense smoke from burning greenery mingled with the enchanted mist.

"Revenge!" A second howl originated from within the vapors.

Fight fire with water, Master Laraquies was fond of saying. Shenza fumbled for the leather sash hidden beneath her the folds of her outer robe. Her fist clenched on a small, hard object. Drawing a deep breath, she dashed forward, squeezed her eyes shut, and threw it down with all her strength. The seashell shattered on contact with the pavement. Condensed sunlight blazed outward. Hissing, the fog withered before its assault.

A moment too late, she realized this had left her exposed and face to face with her attacker.

Hovering in the restored daylight was First Lord Anges. There was no mistaking the unlucky man's twisted limbs. The seared black grin had been shadowing her dreams. The magic fire that had claimed his life shuddered in the air about him. Despite herself, Shenza took a backward step. No wonder the maids had been frightened! If she hadn't known better, she would readily have believed that the first lord's ghost confronted her.

But this was wrong, the rational part of her argued. Alceme said Lord Anges's ghost wore his new robes. Parrot green, with matching feathers. Alceme had not said he was burning, and it was not the sort of thing someone would forget to mention.

The specter lolled its grisly head toward her. "Give me justice," it seemed to growl, though the jaws were burned wide in a tortured scream. "Avenge me!"

As if she believed in the illusion, Shenza crossed her hands in a nervous bow. "My Lord, please return to your rest. You should not disturb the living in this way." Beneath her mask, her eyes darted frantically. The semblage had to be close. If she could capture it...

"Punish the one who did this to me," rattled forth from the ghoulish maw. "Kill Byben! Then I will be at peace."

"Byben of Cessill did not murder my Lord." While she delayed, her fingers closed over the silken cords of the ghost net concealed under her garment. "It would be wrong of me to..."

Shenza broke off as the phantasm hurled a shout like typhoon winds. "Then you must die!" Claw hands, wreathed in blue-red flames, stretched out to her. She knew it could not touch her, but reflex jerked her aside with a fearful yelp.

"Give me justice!" screamed the phantom, spinning to follow her movement. "I want to rest in peace!"

"Revenge is not justice!" Shenza backed away, yanking the ghost- net free. "Open," she murmured, and the mesh of enchanted spider webs splayed wide.

There was no change on the grotesque visage, but the 'ghost' abruptly retreated. Then it returned to a proven weapon. Gaudy fire wreathed its charred and crooked fingers. Shenza passed the net to her left hand and grabbed at the first talisman her fingers touched. She dashed another shell to the ground and dodged aside. This time dust billowed outward, obscuring everything in the courtyard. In that moment she rushed forward, hoping to get inside the magician's aim before the next fire bolt came. And it did, searing the space where she had been standing.

The dust cloud was not large. It had only been meant to reveal an intruder's footprints within a small area. Shenza emerged into clear air and stood scanning the court. She turned in place, searching the treetops, but saw nothing. The semblage had to be here. Precious moments trickled away. Where was it?

Instinct warned her, and she darted aside an instant before a fire bolt cleft the air. Scorched leaves and marble shards flew everywhere. Continuing her movement, Shenza whirled and swept the net toward the phantasm. "Bind and hold!" she commanded.

The glimmering strands closed upon the fiery corpse... and passed through it, as expected.

"Give me justice, or you will die!" The phantasm again lunged toward her with claws extended. Once again Shenza spun aside. Why didn't he try again to burn her? Could the enemy be exhausting his reserves? It was almost too much to hope for.

"My Lord must calm himself!" Shenza panted, keeping up the charade. She had to find the semblage! It seemed impossible that it would be near the illusion itself. That was far too obvious, but she hadn't eliminated the possibility, either. And the horrific appearance of the phantasm certainly served to distract her from anything else nearby.

In her past-sight, the semblage had been positioned above the fire bolt's point of origin, but within a few feet of it. Shenza forced herself to look closely. Yes! She saw the glow of magic, a crisp purple silhouette against the cloudy sky.

Shenza shook the net out roughly and cast again, aiming higher now. "Bind and hold!"

Incredibly, the ghost-net caught in the air. The magical cobwebs, curled tightly around something unseen.

"At last," Shenza breathed, pulling on the net. Not too hard, or she would tear it.

Something seized her from behind, a painfully tight grip around her neck. "Magister," a voice growled with deadly sincerity, "you die."

Shenza experienced a moment of terror. Her frantic mind bleated that a phantasm couldn't touch her. It wasn't real! Kinesis, then. How could she forget? The net twitched out of her fingers, pulled by the retreating semblage. She uselessly pulled at a band of force constricting around her throat. No words from the 'phantom' now. None were needed. Shenza struggled, kicked wildly, but could not break its grip. She choked, robbed of breath. If only Juss were here. Or the Eleshi.

It had said it would be with her. Didn't it know she was going to die?

But Shenza was not ready to die. A rune-covered bamboo rod snagged in her clothing as she desperately tore it free. Both hands clasped it to her chest, the slightly wider butt resting at the base of her throat. Eyes tightly shut, she summoned all of her power and silently appealed for help.

"Spirits, aid me! Spells, be gone!"

There was a deep report, like a lightning strike. A shaft of purple-white radiance nearly blinded her. The blast freed her. Shenza fell to the ground with the wand clattering beside her. She lay for a moment, thinking only of the sweet air rushing into her starved lungs.

Afraid to lie still too long, Shenza struggled to her knees. She blinked to see past the dark spots floating before her eyes. The courtyard seemed very quiet, or perhaps the blast had deafened her. Absently she reached for her wand, only to draw back with a startled hiss of pain.

The spellbreaker—for that was the wand she had been carrying—was nearly unrecognizable. The wooden rod was blackened and splintered, and it was very hot, as she had reason to know. The inscribed sigils were outlined with soot, in places scorched away. By the five moons, did it take so much power to dispel a semblage? She hadn't thought she possessed so much. And what would she do if she needed the spellbreaker again? It was obvious she'd get no more use from that talisman.

Shenza's weariness returned. It seemed all she could do to rise and survey the area. For the second time in two days, wreckage surrounded her. The bench where she had been sitting was completely shattered. A great swath had been scorched through the banks of glossy foliage. The fountain still flowed, but steam rose from the water. Two of the marble fishes were missing, and the cracked bowl wept polluted tears. Some kind of dark blot smeared the far wall. That, too, smoldered ominously.

There was no sign of the supposed ghost, but she hadn't really expected any.

A hasty examination showed where flying shards of marble had slashed her robe, even penetrating her tightly wrapped sheath. Several shallow cuts stung along her left arm and thigh, but none of these appeared serious. Shenza could feel broken rock beneath her sandals as she retrieved her head cloth from the rubble. Both hands ran through her dark curls, shaking out rock dust and crushed leaves, before she restored it to its place. Strange that it seemed so important, at a time like this.

Shenza paused a moment, trying to absorb what had happened. She had survived a second attempt on her life. The very thought made her heart jump fearfully. Impersonating the dead Lord had merely been an effort to frighten her into concluding the investigation. Or to cover her death, if she did not cooperate. She must have alarmed him when she caught the semblage in her net. Those last words, 'you die...' Surely that had been the killer's true sentiment, without the pretense of being Lord Anges.

Her neck still ached. She shivered, recalling the invisible iron grip.

Veering from that memory, Shenza prodded herself into motion. Her eyes fixed on the unknown smear on the wall. No charm of hers left that mark. Finally, she had some evidence to work with.

She located her travel case, half buried beneath fragments of the ruined bench. The grain of the broken rock grated against her fingers, but she managed to shift the largest piece away. The case dripped with water leaked from the fountain and there was a long score across one side, but the stitched runes gleamed steadily. Its magic held. Her relief was tempered when she shook off the coarse dust and heard something scrape ominously inside. Well, she had time enough to learn what was broken. For the moment, it was enough to know her notes had survived the onslaught.

The approach of excited voices distracted her. One she knew well seemed to be in the lead.

"Shenza! Where are you?" Juss called.

Flashes of color reached her through the thick vegetation, and other voices murmured anxiously, "Did you hear that sound?" and "What's all the smoke?"

"Something's happened to the magister," Juss predicted grimly.

"Juss, I am fine," Shenza answered, but he seemed not to hear. The bushes rustled vigorously, as if he were trying to force his way through.

"How can I get by here?"

"Officer, please don't do that." Shenza recognized the voice of Alceme's son, Andle. "Tanta, go get my mother." Sandaled feet went slapping off at speed.

"Juss, I am not hurt!" Shenza exclaimed more loudly. It was mostly true.

Now he seemed to hear her. "Where are you? What happened?" he demanded anxiously.

How to explain, without shouting it for all the world to hear? "I am in a courtyard. Please join me."

"We can go around the side. This way, officer," said Andle soothingly. The colored spots behind the greenery began to move along the path Shenza had taken earlier.

"You're going to give me gray hair, Shenza," Juss' approaching voice accused.

"Not before I get them myself," she thought rebelliously. She was the one who kept coming under attack, and all he could do was complain.

Andle and the peace officer rounded the bank of ferns at a brisk pace, but halted as one on the threshold. Behind them, two blue- kilted servants goggled in open-mouthed dismay. Juss stepped forward grimly. He was fully armed with shield, club and knife.

"I can't turn my back for a minute. Didn't I tell you to be careful?" Sharp words could not conceal his concern.

"I was careful," she said evenly. To Andle, she bowed deeply. "I am very sorry about the damage. I will mend it in just a moment."

"Please don't trouble yourself," he answered gravely.

Juss snapped, "Don't ignore me! And you've got to stop this business of sending me away and using yourself as a lure. How can I help you, if I'm not even here?"

"I did not do it on purpose," she answered, irritated that he would think so. And if she did, who better to take the risk? The enemy seemed unlikely to attack anyone else. "I told you I am fine, and there is something I must do."

"Fine? You're bleeding!"

"It's just a few scratches."

Juss caught at her arm, turning her sharply. "You call this a scratch?"

Shenza jerked away, rubbing her injured arm defensively. "Yes, but it does sting if you squeeze it that way."

He glanced at the small cut and rolled his eyes in supreme exasperation. "For a wise magister, you're pretty dense. Come on." More gently, but still forcefully, he pushed her over to the fountain. The cracked bowl gave it a drooling look.

"Juss," she said, holding to her patience, "you are interfering with my work."

"Just look," he ordered.

Against the mossy bottom of the basin, she could see the pale reflection of her mask gleaming back at her. The perfect features smiled inscrutably, but she was stunned to see a spider web of cracks raying out from a rounded dimple in the forehead. For a moment Shenza felt as ill as she had the night before. This couldn't be! She raised a disbelieving hand to feel the sharp edges and whispered, "No."

"I thought those things were indestructible," Juss said tightly.

Shenza did not answer. Her mind reeled with the shock. It must have been the fire bolt, the one that knocked her down. She hadn't even realized. Just like her spellbreaker—months of effort were ruined in an instant. The mask still retained most of its functions, or she would not be able to breathe, but that was small consolation. She needed her mask, depended on its powers. Without it... What could she do?

Andle asked anxiously, "Magister, are you sure you're all right?"

Before she could summon a reply, Shenza heard the second servant ask blandly in the background, "What's this stuff?"

She snapped back to awareness, whirling to shout, "Don't touch it!"

Andle and Juss jumped. Startled by her vehemence, the other servant turned from the blot on the wall.

The peacekeeper recovered first. "You don't have to yell," he told her, ignoring all the sharp words he had been using lately.

"This is what I've been waiting for," Shenza informed them coldly. If the remnants were contaminated, after all she had sacrificed, she might consider using the magic fire spell herself. "No one but me is to touch it."

Juss turned to Andle very seriously. "Nobody else can touch it."

"As you say, officer."

"Sure, Magister. Whatever you want." The servant edged away from the wall with exaggerated caution. Then he wrinkled his nose in disdain. "It stinks, anyway."

Meanwhile, Juss turned eyed the smudge narrowly. "So, is that it?"

"I will soon know," she said pointedly, "if I am allowed to work."

He snorted, almost amused. "So work."

"Thank you. I will. And will you please go get Master Laraquies?"

"No." Juss shifted his shield across his back and folded his arms stubbornly across his chest. "I am staying right here."

"Juss, I need his advice," Shenza insisted. Why must he choose this time to become unreasonable?

Andle offered helpfully, "Shall I send a messenger?"

"Thanks," Juss said before Shenza could answer.

"I'll take care of it right away." Andle hurried off, beckoning his fellows to join him.

Shaking her head irritably, Shenza walked away. The straps of her travel case were tightly clenched in one fist. She didn't know what annoyed her more, the attempt on her life, the loss of her two most potent talismans, or Juss talking so much. He acted like a bossy older brother. And she wasn't much better, losing her temper that way. Magisters should be calm, in control.

Marble splinters squeaked beneath her feet as she bent to examine the wall. A thick fluid was spattered across the stonework. Shards of a crude, reddish tan ceramic adhered to the sticky surface. Looking down, Shenza saw larger pieces scattered at her feet. As the servant had remarked, a faint, foul odor emanated from the mess. Just before the attack, the mist had carried a scent much like it.

Most of the pottery fragments were distinctly curved, with hastily incised sigils visible on some pieces. The original form would have been a short, wide cylinder, exactly the shape she recalled from her vision. Shenza could not restrain a surge of triumph. Finally, she had proof of the means used to murder Lord Anges. Even Borleek couldn't ignore it. Not only that, but she could use the fragments to locate the enemy himself.

"Is that it?" Juss' voice at her shoulder startled her. Fortunately, she caught herself before she touched the wall and contaminated the residue. "Sorry," he said, too late.

Breathing raggedly, Shenza sank to her knees and waited for her heart to stop hammering at her ribs.

"Well?" the man prodded.

When she could speak without swearing, Shenza answered him. "I believe so. Will you please step back? The sun is setting and I cannot see what I am doing."

"All right," he agreed, though grudgingly.

Trying to recover her composure, she laid her travel case open. The last of her elation evaporated as she saw a heap of glass fragments along the bottom of the case. Her bottle of daylight lay dull and shattered. It was not a serious loss, Shenza firmly reminded herself. Of all her tools, daylight was the simplest to replace. A quick exploration showed no other damage—one bit of luck, at last, among the disasters and frustrations.

Muffling a fresh sigh, Shenza drew out a leather pouch sewn with runes to contain any lingering malevolent influence. Gingerly, she gathered the clay shards into the pouch, moving along the wall to be sure she had them all. Something sticky clung to her fingertips afterward. Shenza vigorously rubbed the inside hem of her robe to remove it. Then, concentrating, she drew the leather band closed. "Seal." Sewn sigils flared with the light of magic engaging.

Since the daylight was indeed fading, she quickly drew out a palm-sized, flat jar with a wide mouth. Shenza could not immediately identify the substance sprayed along the wall, though she thought it reasonable to assume this was the resonating fluid described in the scroll she read. Through it, the sorcerer was able to link with his creation across a distance.

Exposure to air was drying the potion, solidifying gelid drips on the stonework. Using a tiny bamboo knife, she scraped a generous portion into the bottle and capped it tightly. "Seal."

Juss had been watching silently as she worked. Now he gruffly said, "Yeah?" Shenza turned to look over her shoulder.

A young boy with spindly legs and serious, dark eyes reported, "Mistress Alceme asked me to inform Magister Shenza that my Lord would like her to attend him in his audience chamber."

Juss looked to Shenza, his features rigid. She felt her heart skip anxiously, but managed a bow of acknowledgment. "Please say we shall come at once."

Bowing in return, the lad scampered off again. Shenza sighed as she sealed her travel case. The summons was expected, but it could have come at a more convenient time. And why had they sent this boy instead of the usual messenger? Was there some suspicion about Makko's role in the poisoning? It certainly seemed to her there should be.

Juss seemed to share Shenza's trepidation, for he muttered, "I guess we'd better get it over with."

"There is just one more thing I must do," Shenza responded, rising to shake the dust from her robe. The marble bench was shattered beyond repair. Still, she was determined to do what she could.

A few careful steps took her back to the fountain, which dribbled like a senile elder. She quickly saw that the crack was not serious. Shenza rested her fingertips lightly on either edge and chanted the rhyme of mending softly but firmly.

As she repeated the chant, the warm tingle of sorcery flowed down her arms. The marble knit quickly from both edges, leaving only a slight irregularity in the oval rim. Shenza passed her hands over the water, murmuring the chant of purification. The cloudiness disappeared, leaving clear, fresh water. At least, she thought, she could still do such a simple thing correctly.

"Let's go," Juss repeated tersely. The evening light gave his square features a grimmer look.

"Very well." Shenza took up her case and picked her way toward the exit. Juss settled his weapons and waited for her to pass. Then he strode behind her, a martial escort.

Shenza forgave him for speaking out of turn. Her strength felt as dim and faded as the evening light, but Juss' presence gave her confidence.

After all, she finally had what she was seeking. She had the semblage, and with that she had victory. It was only a matter of time.

Chapter Eighteen
~ Emerald Eyes ~

All too soon, they approached the first lord's hall. The moons' light crossed the gardens with green and gold, but mostly Inkesh's scarlet rays bathed the night in blood. It seemed that Shenza was supposed to remember something about the moons (an eclipse?) but she could not. Nor did she truly wish to. So much had happened. She dared not be ruled by superstition. Yet Inkesh was difficult to ignore. The ruddy giant hung low in the sky, nested among ghostly clouds. Its rim just touched the horizon, giving it a gorged and swollen look.

Soon the elegant palace loomed above her, blocking the emerging stars. Under its proud eaves, carved screens strained the light from within. Pale amber streaks scattered down the steps as they climbed. Juss, coming behind Shenza, was silent except for his breathing. They crested the stairs together and crossed the porch. A sweet chime sounded as they passed beneath an ornately carved doorway.

Immediately before them, as they entered, was a low rail of inlaid wood. Flights of steps led down in either direction. Shenza turned right, descending to the level of a walkway which circled the chamber at the base of the marble walls. Those who enjoyed the first lord's confidence could approach him directly along this level, for the throne was positioned directly opposite the entrance. Whoever sat there saw all who came in or out. Shenza did not count herself among the privileged number. She turned left and descended another flight of stairs. Slender columns rose from the sunken floor to support a double roof.

The floor, though bare of furniture or carpets, was richly inlaid with decorative scrollwork. Some of the interlocked designs spelled out words such as 'fidelity' and 'prudence.' Others, her mask revealed, concealed protective wards such as those in the deceased lord's private quarters. The interior walls were decorated with blue hangings. Woven through the cloth was a subtle pattern of feather-flower silk. When a breeze stirred the fabric, it made shimmers like sunlight on the sea.

Even more than these things, Shenza was aware of eyes upon her as she crossed the floor with Juss at her shoulder. It was all she could do to keep her chin level. Her gaze sought to stray to the floor, as if she were still a poor fisherman's daughter.

Before them, a broader flight of stairs led up to a slightly projecting terrace where the first lord sat on his throne. He lounged, really. The careless posture reminded her of Lord Anges, a comparison which unnerved her. Even worse, Master Nurune stood at the lord's left shoulder. Jewels gleamed over his purple robe. Even his head cloth had copper tassels. A calculating expression quickly gave way to exaggerated concern as Nurune gazed on Shenza. The shining fringe swayed as he leaned closer, murmuring gravely to the first lord. Shenza felt her stomach turn over. What was the vizier saying about her?

At the base of the steps were two familiar figures in dark gold kilts and mantles, fully armed just as Juss was. Shamatt's shrewd gaze was intent on the dais, while Borleek appeared bored. The muscles of his jawline tensed when he caught sight of Shenza and Juss.

But she was not here to see Borleek. Swallowing against a sour taste in her mouth, Shenza stopped at the correct distance from the foot of the steps. Her left hand still held her travel case, so she pressed her right hand to her chest as she bowed with deepest reverence. As she straightened, she took two paces more and bowed again. Echoing her motion, Juss dipped his spear in salute. From the corner of her eye, she saw Shamatt gravely bow in response. Borleek's head turned with a jerk to glare at him.

After her second bow Shenza looked up toward the ruler's throne. She did not quite know what to expect, for she had seen him only at a distance. Immediately she felt her throat tighten, her breath grow short. He had certainly grown up well from the coltish boy she remembered.

Aspace, First Lord of Chalsett, City of Gardens, sat aslant in the throne of his ancestors. He wore the latest style of the Inner Sea, with a cynical air to match. A brightly patterned mantle, sewn with pearls, was loosely draped over his left shoulder. The graceful folds of the mantle exposed a lean, brown chest and the edge of a close-fitted white kilt. A matching turban was fastened with a feathered brooch whose iridescent plumes arched sharply backward. Shell and metal ornaments glittered on both arms, his ears, neck and ankles. Shenza could not see the pretty chain Lady Innoshyra had so brazenly bestowed upon him. Strangely, this pleased her.

Though he did resemble Lord Anges, Lord Aspace was clearly the better favored. His face was simply breathtaking, with sculpted cheeks and a perfectly rendered nose. Black hair flowed over his shoulders in waves, like a night-dark sea. He had not had it straightened, she noted. Like the statues at the festival, he mirrored, but did not match, the unearthly perfection of the spirits. He had their knowing smile, and the eerie green eyes no human should possess. Yet there was no blending of the feminine. The set of his mouth was clearly masculine and also somehow very human.

The throne itself was even more impressive than she had realized, the dark wood fairly coated in pearls and silver filigree. Colorful pillows softened the back and sides. Incongruously, a pitcher rested on the floor beside the throne, within easy reach of the occupant. His right hand lazily swirled a copper goblet. It must have held something cold, for it was beaded with moisture.

Too late, Shenza realized she was staring. She became aware of the hall's stillness, in which she felt everyone must hear the drumming of her pulse. Shenza censured herself silently. Hadn't her disgraceful association with Tonkatt brought her enough trouble? Anyway, such a man as this was far beyond her reach.

Mustering all her poise, she spoke the formal words, "As my Lord commands, Magister Shenza Waik of Tresmeer has come." Her voice sounded a bit faint to her ears, and she wondered if her mask was operating properly. She raised her voice a little, feeling foolish. "Speak what you wish and I will obey."

Her stilted delivery provoked a flash of derision on Nurune's face, which the courtier quickly erased. He must have found the dutiful words quaint. But the lord himself leaned forward slightly, keenly appraising her in return. A subtle smile narrowed his strange, light eyes.

"That's very stylish," he said, sounding almost bored. Despite the space between them, she could hear clearly. A spell, much like that on her own mask, amplified his speech. Shenza had forgotten it was there.

When she did not respond, he went on, "Cracking your mask like that. Very original."

His voice was strange, honeyed and yet dry. Once again, Shenza thought of the spirits. He certainly had their breath-taking charisma.

Carefully, as if she addressed one of the spirits, she said, "I apologize for my appearance. I came at my Lord's first summons."

Something she said made him smile again, blandly. "How diligent. I wonder, will all of my servants come to me bleeding?" Copper gleamed as he sipped from his cup.

"If it is my Lord's wish, I would," Shenza answered. She felt he was mocking her, somehow. "Your servant was studying a report in the matter of your late brother's death. I was attacked, I believe by the same one who murdered him."

The men about her tensed. For a moment, even Borleek appeared to forget self-interest. But that moment quickly passed.

"Again?" the peacekeeper growled, as if he did not believe her.

Shamatt seemed to wince slightly at the Chief's harsh words. He asked, with genuine concern, "Do you need a curomancer?"

Shenza shook her head. "The wounds are superficial. Although my mask was damaged, it did preserve my life." Despite herself, she felt a bit gratified to say so. "I apologize again for my appearance."

Lord Aspace sat back, gazing at her levelly. And Nurune asked, with shock that seemed just a bit too sincere, "Did you see who assaulted you?"

"Regrettably, no." Shenza schooled her tone not to betray her distrust. "The enemy used his power of illusion to impersonate my Lord's brother. By good fortune, I was able to break the spell. There should be no further attacks."

Lord Aspace put aside his bored pose, showing fierce anger at the imposture. But Borleek demanded irritably, "And how much longer will this delay you?"

"It will not delay me." With difficulty, Shenza ignored his blatant questioning of her strategy. To the first lord, she quietly said, "I am very sorry that the criminal is not already in custody. I believe I am very close to an answer now. Despite the danger, this was a fruitful encounter."

After all, she had the semblage. She felt no need to boast of this in front of Nurune, however. Fortunately, Juss was staying silent. Though he did snort under his breath, so softly that she would not have heard him without her mask. Nurune, too, raised his brows at her claim, raising deep lines beneath his ornate head cloth. It made her wonder what else he knew.

Aspace shifted in his seat, one jeweled sandal kicking the air. He murmured lazily, "I'd love to hear all about this, but what I really called you for was to discuss the previous assault."

Assault? Beside the first lord, Nurune's mask of geniality slipped. His black eyes blazed angrily. Shenza suddenly realized that, despite his closeness to the ruler's ear, Nurune was not present as vizier. He, too, had been commanded. Somehow, she felt no better for this knowledge.

"Which of the two?" Shenza asked. "The poisoning, or..?"

Without even glancing at the coven master, Lord Aspace made it quite clear that this was about Tonkatt. His smile had the sharp edge of a knife. "Oh, all of them. But let's take it in order."

Saying nothing, Master Nurune bowed to the Lord, eyes cast down with a show of humility. It did not convince Shenza, and she doubted Aspace was fooled, either.

The first lord said, "Sub-Chief Shamatt, I'm told you were investigating."

The officer in question bowed at once and stepped a little forward from his Chief. "Indeed, my Lord. Magister Shenza requested my assistance, to avoid any accusation of bias if her tutor, Magister Laraquies, were to investigate. I believe she was wise."

"Is old Laraquies still around?" Lord Aspace interrupted, leaning forward a little. "Where is he?"

His tone was not exactly respectful, but Shenza quickly answered. "My teacher was summoned only a little while ago, after the latest incident. He should be joining us at any time." And she heartily wished for the serenity of his presence. She felt too tired to deal with Borleek and Nurune, and every time Lord Aspace spoke her concentration slipped.

"Excellent." The first lord pondered a moment, sipping again from his goblet. He seemed to realize they were waiting for him and waved arrogantly. "Continue."

Shamatt again bowed gravely. "To summarize: While off duty for my Lord's coronation ceremony, Magister Shenza was both poisoned and placed under a love charm. She was able to resist the charm, but the poison made her seriously ill. Her survival was in question until early this morning."

"So I've heard," Aspace drawled. In a way, his careless attitude was not unlike Master Laraquies's. Shenza wondered how much of it was ruse and how much real. "Were the incidents related, or not?"

Master Nurune looked as though he wished to protest, but he maintained his silence and his solicitous pose.

"Although both took place at the same time, I do not believe this represents a coordinated action," Shamatt reported. "The two events were counter-productive to each other. The purpose of the charm was to form an attachment or relationship with the magister, while the poison was simply deadly. If the magister died, there would be no point in forming an attachment with her. I conclude the poisoner acted separately, although perhaps taking advantage of the young man's presence as a diversion. Magister Shenza reports his advances were quite a distraction."

Nurune shot him a malevolent look. Shamatt must have seen it, but he chose not to respond.

"Distracting, eh?" The first lord smirked. His sly gaze rested on Shenza, and she controlled an impulse to squirm where she stood. "And so?"

The peacekeeper continued, "In the case of the love charm, it is quite clear what happened. The amulet was noted on the person of Tonkatt Akanti of Sengool by a sorceress, the Curomancer Kafseet, shortly after Magister Shenza took ill. It was confiscated by Magister Laraquies and is still in his possession if my Lord might wish to inspect it. Tonkatt denies any intention to influence Magister Shenza, but I interviewed colleagues who state Tonkatt has..." he paused momentarily, choosing the words, "...social aspirations. His denials must remain suspect."

"Sub-Chief, I protest!" cried Nurune with paternal dismay.

His rich voice was a thing of power, all reason and restraint. "Tonkatt is not only my student but my nephew. No 'social aspirations' are necessary. Our family already has higher connections than a magister. Asking your pardon, Shenza." He added the last carelessly, as an afterthought, but she bristled at the disrespect. How dare he address her by her name alone?

"Asking your pardon," Shamatt retorted sternly, before Shenza could respond, "that is disingenuous. Regardless of Magister Shenza's personal wealth or family background, she will occupy an influential position in the future. An enchanter with ambitions might find her useful, if he could control her."

Nurune gasped with every appearance of shock. "What are you suggesting?" Still playing at false emotion, Shenza thought bitterly. She hoped she would never sink so low.

"I did not realize we were on such familiar terms, Coven Master," she cut in, more coldly than she had believed herself capable of. She regretted it when Nurune gazed down on her with the sort of pity one might offer a fish caught for a meal.

"This is irrelevant," interrupted Lord Aspace, silencing all of them. The first lord had been swirling his cup as the two men debated. Shenza wondered if it amused or irritated him to watch them spar. The seasoned officer and the wily courtier seemed evenly matched in political skill and experience, though it appeared to Shenza that Nurune had under-estimated Shamatt.

In his silken voice, Aspace continued, "Love charms are forbidden for a very good reason. Their purpose is to influence the thinking and emotions of others, and that is a treacherous undertaking. Wearing such a device in a social setting is not an innocent or harmless act, no matter what he says his intentions were." Casually, as if he were merely discussing a boat race, Lord Aspace reached down to refill his goblet.

When he had replaced the pitcher, he mused on, "This may be an internal matter to your coven, Nurune, but I expect you to deal with it appropriately. And I warn you, if the punishment is not adequate, I shall take it personally."

The plumes of Lord Aspace's turban twitched as he shifted his seat again, putting his back to Master Nurune. The sorcerer appeared to fumble momentarily, shocked not so much by the decision as by the directness of the reprimand. From his expression, Nurune was just realizing that a new first lord ruled in Chalsett-Port, and he no longer stood close to the throne. Still, he had no choice but to bow and submit. It must have galled him to do so.

"Of course, my lord," Nurune said, his polished tone now somber and controlled. "All shall be as you command."

Lord Aspace sipped from his cup again, his perfect features impassive. He must have realized his ruling would have implications beyond this moment. Nurune had powerful friends. Yet Aspace showed no fear. Shenza regarded him with admiration. Even if she served as magister for as many years at Master Laraquies, she would never be able to speak her mind like that. And Giliatt would be gratified by his righteous judgement.

A chime broke the silence, the same that had sounded when Shenza and Juss entered the chamber. The entrance was behind them now, and they had to turn to see a familiar old man smiling calmly at the entrance. Borleek growled to himself, but Shenza felt the invisible weight of her fears ease.

Lord Aspace seemed to straighten a little in his elaborate chair. "You may go," he said, a cutting dismissal to Nurune. As the shocked courtier backed away, bowing and murmuring low words, Aspace turned his emerald eyes to Laraquies.

"Approach, Laraquies Catteel of Nelnoor. You will stand beside me."

Nurune retreated along the walkway at the level of the throne. Wounded dignity was clear in the set of his shoulders. Laraquies circled in the opposite direction, his steps unhurried. Shenza felt her chest tighten with pride. If Lord Aspace was wise enough to send Nurune away and take the magister as his vizier, she had more hope for his reign than his brother's. This also implied she would not be rejected as magister, though she cautioned herself not to over-interpret what could be a momentary whim.

With bows, Master Laraquies approached the first lord. "I am humbly at the service of my Lord. Speak any order and your servant shall obey."

Slouching a little, Lord Aspace gazed into the depths of his goblet. "You all keep saying that." He awarded the old man a cunning smile. "I will hold you to it."

"That shall be as my Lord wishes," Master Laraquies murmured gently.

The chime again sounded, announcing Nurune had reached the doorway. The Lord's eyes narrowed momentarily, watching him depart, then returned to Shamatt. "And the poisoning. What do you know of that, Sub-Chief?"

"I believe I know who is responsible," the peace officer answered somberly, "though he has disappeared and I cannot question him directly."

Shenza knew she wasn't the only one who stared at Shamatt intently.

"Unfortunate," the first lord observed drily. "Then how do you know he is guilty?"

"It is extremely unfortunate," Shamatt agreed. He remained composed but his Chief stiffened at the implied accusation. "That Magister Shenza has again been attacked raises grave concern, but it also reassures me that the culprit is still nearby. In time, he must be overtaken."

"So who is it?" interrupted Juss, startling Shenza. He had not yet spoken before the first lord. As all eyes turned to him, his jaw jutted with determination.

"Officer Juss, as you and Magister Shenza both suggested, the suspect is a member of my Lord's own staff. He is a messenger named Makko Kiliwair of Beerlama."

Lord Aspace sat forward, the arched feathers flickering behind him. "My brother's staff?" he demanded angrily.

"Alas, my Lord, yes. Many things remain unclear, but it appears he had arranged a situation here and was merely waiting to strike. What he waited for, your servant does not know."

A surge of heat passed over Shenza's body. Yes, it did make sense. Makko had been nearby on the night of the poisoning. He had never pretended to like her. She had been so determined to be fair that she ignored the obvious.

Juss could not restrain himself, and leaned forward to whisper, "I knew it!"

"Hush," she murmured.

"And how do you know this messenger is guilty?" the Lord asked sharply.

Shamatt explained, "The poison was brought to Magister Shenza mixed with lime juice. Only two of the servants had access to the drink, which was intended specifically for the magister. Makko, who received her order, and the maid who delivered it. But Jeema told me Makko gave her the juice already mixed and asked her to bring it to Shenza. Makko has not been seen since the night of my Lord's coronation. It is possible he was tricked by someone else and is hiding in fear of unjust punishment, but the conclusion remains until it is disproved."

Shenza felt compelled to interrupt. "Based on his interactions with me, I find the suspicion plausible. This person was always uncomfortable in my presence. Alceme told me he did not like magisters, but she did not know why. Clearly, if my investigation interfered with his escape after the murder, that would be one explanation. Also, we know the killer attempted to misplace blame for my Lord's death onto a pawn, who would suffer in his stead. If Makko was in Chalsett-port for some time, I suggest he was seeking to locate this second victim."

A harsh gust of breath warned her Borleek of Bentei was taking exception to her theory. Ignoring him, she turned to

Shamatt. "We must work together more closely, Sub-Chief. If I had known Makko was missing, I might have avoided his latest attack. Although, as a result, I do now have the means to locate him."

"You're a fine one to talk about cooperation," Borleek retorted angrily. He had, Shenza felt, merely been waiting for the pretext to vent his feelings toward her. With ferocious energy, the big man complained, "We've heard nothing but wild stories from you about Lord Anges' death. And then you released our prisoner without permission! And you dare to complain about our conduct?"

The outburst was not unexpected, but it still left her flustered. She waited a moment to compose herself before answering, evenly, "A magister's investigations are always confidential. Neither Master Laraquies nor I have ever been compelled to report our progress to you."

"Chief," Shamatt tried to interpose, but his superior silenced him with a curt gesture.

"And what about the city? The wreckage of the port. Do you know how many merchants lost their boats and all their wares?" Borleek's deep voice was thunderous with indignation. "If you weren't fooling around, we could have solved this before the monster came and drowned half the waterfront!"

Shenza felt keenly aware of Lord Aspace's dispassionate eyes on them, but she didn't dare look up to see his face. Sweat stung in the shallow cuts along her side. Stiffly, striving for calm, she answered. "Undue haste causes errors."

"My eye!" Borleek snapped. "Doing nothing is worse. The ship crews were going crazy with boredom, sitting in port. Now half of them are out of work. What am I supposed to do with them?"

"Perhaps you could put them to work helping with the salvage," she suggested neutrally, knowing it would not sooth his temper. Well, if he felt free to air all her shortcomings in front of the new ruler, there was no reason she should not do the same. "I have used my lawful discretion in this investigation. As for Byben of Cessill, he is guilty of no crime. There was no reason to keep him prisoner. Further, there was good cause to remove him for the sake of his own safety. As you well know, he suffered a severe beating when he was first arrested. No one is permitted to take justice into their own hands. Most especially not the peacekeepers who the populace looks to for order and restraint."

The muscles bunched in Borleek's shoulders and face as if he wished to strike her. "Don't try to tell me my job!" he bellowed. "I've been doing this for twenty years and I've never failed in my duty. Now this comes along, and you just sit on your hands. How do you think I feel when I can't promise justice for the death of my Lord?"

"That is not the issue," Shenza told him primly. "Premature sentence is not permitted." She blessed the mask that let her hide her feelings. In a strange way, the confrontation was exhilarating. Yet, at the same time, it terrified her. There was little professional in her conduct, nor in Borleek's.

"Chief," Shamatt patiently repeated, trying again to break the impasse. Juss, too, shifted restlessly, as if he wished to respond.

"So you say," Borleek growled, too exasperated for restraint. "I don't know why everyone is so worried about *you* when the first lord's killer is still loose. When are you going to do something about *him?*"

"Chief!"

"What?" Borleek exploded. Shamatt showed no fear.

"I have a question. Magister," he bowed slightly to Shenza, earning a new growl from his Chief, "didn't you say that you now have the means to locate the criminal?"

"Thank you, Sub-Chief. Yes, I do." Shenza nodded in return. Her whole body felt stiff. It wasn't that she cared what Borleek thought of her, but must he treat her this way in front of everyone? "I didn't wish to say so in front of Master Nurune, but I have captured the semblage which the killer used against my Lord Anges and me."

"Why didn't you say so before?" The words burst from Borleek like thunder from the sky. "I swear, you..."

"Because Master Nurune would be extremely interested, and it is none of his business!" Shenza told him, her voice rising despite herself. Nurune worked for himself and his family, and she would never again trust a Sengool. "Only those of us here need to know. I hope I can trust each of us not to repeat this."

Borleek's deep-set eyes glared, hating her for correcting him.

Turning a little toward the first lord, Shenza noted that he was gazing into his cup again, as he had during Shamatt's exchange with Nurune. What must he think of her? Her stomach churned, but she strove to explain calmly, as if no fear touched her. "This object, the semblage, incorporates a strong personal link to its owner, enabling him to cast spells at a distance. It was destroyed as I defended myself, but I have gathered up most of the fragments. When I have remade it, I will be able to use the link to find Makko, no matter where he is."

"That is very good news," Master Laraquies observed. He seemed completely at ease, unruffled by the confrontation. Shenza longed to feel so calm.

"Yes," Shamatt agreed, carefully not looking at his Chief. "I wish you had not risked yourself, Magister, but I am relieved to hear it."

He made her sound too brave. "I really did not intend to risk myself," Shenza told him. "I also thank you for your fine investigation, Sub-Chief. We now know the name of the enemy. With this and the semblage to act as a link, I should be able to conclude the inquest this evening, or perhaps tomorrow. If there is no further interruption."

"If," Lord Aspace mused to his cup. He glanced to Laraquies. "And what do you think?"

"My lord?" the old man inquired mildly.

"This." The Lord flicked long brown fingers toward the floor where Borleek and Shenza stood, his displeasure all too plain. "Is this the way you did business as magister?"

Shenza's heart sank at his words. How could he listen to Borleek's self-serving bluster?

Laraquies hesitated briefly. "Chief Borleek and I often disagree," he truthfully admitted, "although he has never spoken to me so discourteously." The peacekeeper grated his teeth audibly in an effort to hold his tongue. Laraquies continued thoughtfully, "It appears that the importance of this inquiry has unnerved everyone. Surely it is no shame upon the chief peacekeeper if his judgement has been affected.

"Also, although disagreements are regrettable, they may be quite natural. Any change of personnel at this level may create misunderstandings. The peacekeeper and the magister must have time to learn mutual respect before they can work together harmoniously."

Borleek bristled at this appraisal despite its diplomatic phrasing, and Shenza felt herself sharing his rebellious feelings. There was no misunderstanding. She knew Borleek for the bully he was. Mutual respect? There would be no harmony until Borleek stopped trying to dominate her independent judgement.

Aspace raised one brow at Laraquies. "And you consider it proper to take a prisoner from custody without notice?" His tone was stinging. Shenza felt her heart pounding against her chest. Was she to be dismissed as summarily as Nurune?

"It was within her legitimate authority," Laraquies said mildly. "We did discuss this between us. Your servant the magister was aware that Chief Borleek might be offended. Yet she chose to place the innocent prisoner's welfare first. Who is to say that is wrong?"

"And do you say so as her teacher and mentor?" the Lord drawled with dangerous softness.

"She is no longer my apprentice," the old man replied gently. "I speak solely as the servant of my Lord."

"Indeed," Aspace murmured wryly into his cup.

There was a pause, in which Borleek's chest seemed to swell with self-satisfaction. Shenza felt her initial flush of fear fading, replaced by cold tremors. It was all she could do to hold her place. She was relieved her master supported her position, but it didn't seem to be enough.

A veiled glance took in all of them on the floor. "I can see I have a lot to do," the first lord remarked, "if this city is to be governed as the citizens deserve. I may as well begin with you two." His tone was now crisp and decisive. "I am not pleased by what I hear. Each of you is concerned more with your own authority than with obtaining justice for my brother's death. This is unacceptable, and it will change."

Aspace leaned over to set his cup down with a shrill tap. Rising, he gazed sternly down upon the four of them. Magister Laraquies stood beside him, his wizened face bearing a polite expression of attention.

"Chief Borleek, I have received a complaint of police abuse toward a prisoner in custody of your men. The magister mentioned this, but the formal charge comes from a curomancer, who provided me with detailed information on the seriousness of his injuries. What do you say to that?"

Borleek seemed surprised by the question. "My men were very upset at your brother's fate. There was no reason to believe he was not guilty," he shot a self-righteous glance at Shenza.

"He was a frail old man," Aspace retorted with mockery that, Shenza suspected, concealed real anger. "He could have been killed. Do you think I want my public buildings to be haunted by ghosts of the unjustly dead? What kind of precedent does that create?"

"My Lord," Borleek fumbled, gesturing angrily toward Shenza. "How can you listen to this..."

Aspace raised his hand with a flash of gems, silencing him. "I have let you speak for yourself, chief peacekeeper. Now you will hear me." The big man shut his mouth, his expression bewildered but grim. "However guilty they may be, the elderly are to be treated with respect as due their age."

Shamatt, at Borleek's shoulder, bowed deeply. "It shall be as my Lord says," he answered, loudly enough that Borleek also bowed with a jerk.

Implacably, Aspace continued, "I don't know how much freedom Anges saw fit to give you, but I am not my brother. I am both interested in the welfare of the public and capable of governing. Your men are protectors of this city, not thugs who may act as they wish. Never forget this again."

Borleek's heavy features were darkly flushed beneath his brown skin tone, as if it hurt him not to shout back at his ruler. Breathing harshly, he stiffly bowed again. Shenza might have enjoyed this reckoning, except that the Lord's pale eyes now turned to her. "As for you..."

Suddenly, Shenza couldn't bear his disapproval. She bowed, her left hand clenched painfully on the straps of her travel case and her right knotted in the fabric that draped across her chest.

Aspace snorted lightly. "Well, it's nice to see some humility around here," he said with some irony. Shenza dared to straighten. "I have a good many things to ask you, magister, but it's not getting any earlier and my meal has already been delayed. You will join me. And you." His glance flicked to Laraquies. "But remember what I've said," he sternly warned. His gaze touched Shenza and Borleek in turn. "I expect you to work together, not against each other."

The sandals of Borleek and Shamatt hissed away behind her as Shenza stood confused. Chaotic emotions stormed within her, elation at the peacekeeper's well earned scolding, dread of her own coming rebukes, and over all the appalling notion that she was supposed to dine with the new lord. Her stomach churned as if she had drunk poison again.

"Well?" The first lord's impatient voice goaded her. Shenza took a shaky step forward. Each step toward the throne was an awkward and clumsy effort. She was hardly aware of Juss coming behind her.

When she reached the top, her heart was beating rapidly, and not from exertion. Lord Aspace studied her with his impossible green eyes, and she felt her knees weaken. Pressing her hand to her chest to stop its shaking, she bowed again.

"Oh, stop that. Stand up. I want to see." One hand on his hip, the first lord stared at her face. A moment later Shenza realized he was really looking at the damage to her mask. "My, that *is* impressive."

Shenza stammered, "Oh, no, my Lord. It did not hurt." His brows rose again mockingly. "But I was dizzy afterward."

Laraquies glided to stand beside the ruler. "You've been busy again," was his cheerful remark.

"It was unavoidable," she mumbled, embarrassed by the scrutiny. "Despite the appearance, most of the functions are still intact. Otherwise I could not wear it."

"It seems you wrought well," her teacher approved. She studied the brown toes beneath the open weave of her sandals.

"I told her not to go off without me," Juss put in, all righteousness. "She wouldn't listen, like always."

Aspace looked up at the much larger peace officer with wry amusement. "Do we need a chaperon? I'm not wearing any love charms."

Juss seemed startled, as if he had forgotten the first lord was there. He bowed nervously.

Lord Aspace wouldn't need a love charm, Shenza thought frankly. Then she seized on Juss's presence as a ward against her own anxiety. "It would be appropriate, even for my Lord. My mother is still upset about the incident with Tonkatt of Sengool."

"Officer Juss has been very helpful to us," Laraquies said. "He is aware of all the facts."

"My Lord," Juss said, embarrassed but sincere. "I've been in on this from the beginning. Every time I turn around, something happens to Shenza. Please don't tell me to leave."

Lord Aspace smiled strangely, and Shenza's pulse raced. "Well, then," he said, "for the sake of her mother, you may come along." His tone was once more blandly autocratic. "Let's go. I don't know about any of you, but I'm hungry."

Chapter Nineteen
~ Words, Like Thorns ~

Torch-bearing servants escorted the small party across the moonlit estate, beneath arbors draped with blossoming vines. In the town below, the streets would be shrouded in a brine-scented fog, but at this height the air remained clear. They passed the lighted pavilion where Lord Anges lay surrounded by his treasures, and soon approached one of the private dwellings set just apart from the palace.

"I hope you don't mind leftovers," Aspace told his companions drolly as they mounted the short flight of steps to the covered porch. "You wouldn't think people would leave free food behind, but they did."

Shenza sensed, more than saw, Laraquies' responding smile. "Whatever my Lord offers is sufficient."

"Careful what you say," mumbled Juss, behind them.

Lord Aspace threw back his head and laughed heartily. He deposited his head cloth and its plumed brooch on a wall hook just inside the door. Within, Alceme stood supervising as a swarm of maids laid platters of food on a long, low table in the entry chamber. They backed away, silently bowing, when the first lord appeared.

"This is fine, thank you." Aspace spoke casually, but still with more courtesy than Shenza had ever witnessed in his brother.

As the staff retreated, still bowing, the lord took up an empty bowl. He strolled along the table, bending briefly to take what he fancied. After a moment, Juss followed. Shenza set her travel case near the door and glanced cautiously around the room.

In truth, the building was no larger than her own borrowed residence. The basic arrangement of an open chamber for entertainment with a raised level containing private rooms and bath seemed nearly identical. Hanging screens, painted with jungle birds and flowers, had been lowered about the perimeter to keep out the night. There was little other furnishing except for the food table and a smaller one farther back from the door, with a few cushions for seating. After the dense decoration in Lord Anges' home, this chamber seemed practically bare. Shenza wondered if this was a reflection of Aspace's own taste, or if he simply hadn't had the time to decorate.

A gentle cough from Master Laraquies drew her back to herself, and Shenza quickly moved to the table. Aware that the others were already seated, she chose almost at random: gingered noodles, a pigeon breast coated with sea-plum sauce. In a separate bowl she ladled a chilled fruit soup.

The chamber was all too quiet as she joined the three men at the table. Shenza took the remaining place, between Laraquies and Juss and directly opposite Lord Aspace. She wished that she didn't have to look across at him, but neither did she wish to sit beside him. The recent experience of Tonkatt's illicit advances was raw in her memory. She settled with her dishes, knees tucked under neatly, but then shifted to smooth out a fold of cloth pinching her skin. Finally, hesitantly, she laid her mask on the floor at her knee. She felt naked and vulnerable without it.

A full stomach would set the world right, she reminded herself. And she was hungry. Nervous fingers lifted her utensils, and she ate determinedly.

Though served cold, Shenza discovered, the soup was also very spicy. She had to quench the fire in her mouth with a mouthful of blander meat. Really, she scolded herself, this situation was nothing like the one Tonkatt had thrust on her. Throughout her training, she had known she would work with the first lord one day. She could hardly serve as magister without doing so. She simply hadn't expected a lord like Aspace. His decadent brother hadn't appealed to her in the least.

Shenza dared a glance across the table, but instantly lowered her gaze when she found him gazing at her speculatively. She forced herself to eat slowly, as if unafraid, though her cheeks burned with warmth. Really, it wasn't fair. None of it was.

Silence reigned except for the quiet tap of utensils on porcelain and soft chewing. Shenza wasn't the only one startled when Master Laraquies remarked, conversationally, "Did my Lord have a pleasant journey home?"

"Pleasant isn't quite the word." Aspace sounded both awed and uneasy. "The water swelled around us like a great wave. It carried our ship all the way from Porphery of the Domes, but it never crested. And the wind was full of voices that I couldn't understand. I've never heard it sound that way."

He had a sorcerer's instinct, Shenza thought. It must have been spirit voices he heard. "Eleshouri," she said quietly. Surely Master Choruta had told him. As all eyes turned to her, she explained, "They have been very involved with this matter."

"If you say so," Aspace answered sardonically. "I never put much faith in those old stories, myself. Like that fable at the coronation." He waved his knife dismissingly. "It sounded romantic, but it couldn't be true."

Shenza remembered her neighbors at the coronation expressing the same sentiment. Then she recalled the cloying perfume, the whisper that was not wind, the monster's roar from the depths of the sea and legend. She filled her mouth with fruit soup and said nothing.

"Does that bother you?"

The first lord's directness nearly choked her. Shenza swallowed the cold burning in a painful lump. How should she answer? She didn't want to contradict her ruler. She settled for evasion.

"I also did not think of the spirits often, before all this," Shenza said. After her recent experiences, she absolutely did believe the legends. But it might be unwise to say so.

Juss was not so circumspect. "They've talked to her," he said with his mouth full. "And I saw the thing that wiped out the market. It was real."

Aspace seemed annoyed, but covered it with bland mockery. "And you?" He turned to Laraquies.

"I believe my student," the old man responded simply.

This answer appeared to displease him. The first lord turned back to her, demanding, "So what did they look like?"

She could not meet his gaze. "Frightening," she said in a small voice. "Like a human, yet it was no man or woman. I knew. It was like something not real to me. Or rather, I was not real in its domain. I felt like one of the thousand termites you see when the hill is broken open. How can you tell which is which? And what is one termite's life to you?"

"That's not very nice," he answered sharply. "I always heard they were beautiful."

"Oh, they are." She swallowed, no longer pretending to eat. "Its eyes were... " She groped for a fuller description, but mere words seemed too small to describe the terrifying reality. And Aspace was so much like them.

She tried again. "I could see from its eyes that it wasn't human, no matter its appearance. And I felt that it could kick our hill down at any moment, if it wanted to."

"As we have seen," Laraquies remarked as if to himself.

Aspace shook his head irritably. "There you go again."

Shenza paused with her fork at her lips, trying to understand his anger. It was more, surely, than merely being told he was wrong. Thinking to offer reassurance, she said, "But my Lord is different. You they know apart from the rest."

"Because we're supposed to be related?" he asked with an edge to his voice. "I suppose *they* told you that."

She quickly parried, "In truth, they said it of my Lord Anges. But, as you both share the same parents, I assume..."

"Oh, that makes me feel better." Aspace ground at his food as if it had become distasteful.

Shenza chewed a mouthful of noodles, wondering what she had said to offend him. After a time, she offered, "My Lord is very like them. Only, less so."

"Less?" He caught her up sharply.

"More human," she hastily amended.

He gave her a long, suspicious look, and the table fell silent. Master Laraquies sipped his tea thoughtfully. Then Juss asked, with an obvious effort to appear nonchalant, "So, Magister, what's been going on down at the docks?"

Shenza regarded him with surprise, and then felt foolish when Laraquies answered the question. She wasn't the only magister, after all.

"Oh, busy, busy," the old man beamed. "Any magician who can mend wood has been well occupied. Although in some cases it is difficult to tell which pieces came from what vessel. The wharves themselves require repair as well, I fear. Many of the spells to prevent corrosion have failed." Perversely, he seemed quite pleased about the calamity. "I, myself, have been engaged in truth-telling claims to the lost wares. The arguments must be heard in the heavens above us."

"I'll bet the Chief has his hands full," Juss observed neutrally.

"What happened, anyway?" Lord Aspace asked. His tone still bristled with irritation. "I wasn't here yet. Was there a storm?"

Again, Shenza sensed the others looking at her expectantly. "Someone tried to leave," she answered. She could not believe no one had told Aspace what happened. A supernatural creature such as Taisaris was not seen every day. There had to be rumors all through the town. Perhaps, with his aversion for spiritualism, he hoped for some other explanation.

"So?" He regarded her with bland contempt. "It's a port. The ships are supposed to come and go."

Striving for a factual tone, Shenza elaborated. "After my Lord Anges was killed, I ordered the port closed so that the killer could not escape justice. But at the same time, the tide fell very low. It seemed obvious we were expected to remain here until my Lord's return." She took care not to say it was the sea spirits who desired this. From his frown, she did not need to say it. "When the two ships attempted to set forth, the tide came back in very suddenly."

"Suddenly," he repeated drily, looking from her to meet Laraquies' mild gaze.

"As my Lord says," she murmured. There seemed no point in insisting.

"And forcefully," added the determined Juss. "Very forcefully."

"And you say there was a monster," Aspace mocked, keenly annoyed. "I suppose you're going to tell me that the monster caused the tide to come back in."

"Uh... yeah." Too late, Juss seemed to recognize Aspace's dislike of the supernatural. He glanced to Laraquies for help, but the old man was peering at the lord with gentle bemusement. Juss blundered on, "It, uh... jumped out of the water, just like a fish. A really big fish. The wave came from where it hit. It hasn't been back since, thank the sun."

Lord Aspace shifted, raking the black waves of hair away from his face. "So, a wave hit the town and smashed all the boats." Evidently he had decided to concentrate on the material facts and ignore the cause.

Shenza kept her eyes on her bowl, hoping to provoke him no further. "As my Lord says."

To Laraquies, he asked, "How long until the port can be restored."

"It is functional now, except that the tide remains low. The condition of the wharves does not prevent normal shipping. Many vessels will take longer to repair, and some merchants may find it difficult to pay for the mending or to replace their lost goods. Nevertheless, were Magister Shenza to lift her restriction, business could go on as usual."

"But that would be premature," Shenza inserted anxiously. "Clearly, the murderer remains in Chalsett-port. If shipping began to move again..."

"Who said anything about opening the port?" Lord Aspace interrupted, sliding in a moment from thorny annoyance to a languid drawl. "Your original reasoning seems sound enough."

Shenza paused, momentarily disoriented by his agreement. "I am pleased my Lord finds it so."

His mobile features twisted in another quick change of mood. "What would please me," he remarked grievedly, "is to be called by my name. I am not my brother. I do not require flattery to remind me I'm special." Taking up his utensils, he made a swift poke at the air. "This is my house, and I want to relax here. I don't need to be fawned on."

Shenza, once again, was caught speechless. Laraquies answered first, serenely, "If that is your wish."

"It is." He firmly drew a portion of noodles into his mouth.

Juss, who had not stopped eating during the entire exchange, shrugged across his raised bowl. "All right."

Aspace eyed him sharply, but then smiled sidelong. "And I, for my part, shall call you Juss. I shall call you Shenza." She flushed, unable to meet his emerald eyes. "And you..." he trailed off, gazing at Laraquies speculatively.

"Laraquies?" the elder suggested moderately.

The first lord smiled. "Grandpa."

"Grandfather," Laraquies countered.

"Geezer."

Shenza watched them askance, dismayed by the disrespectful tone. Laraquies, perversely, seemed to enjoy the banter.

Juss, too, chuckled. He rose and strolled toward the food table. "Anyone want anything?"

"No, thank you." Shenza demurred, since she had yet to eat most of what she had already taken. The conversation had left her with little desire for food. But, to head off her teacher's reminder, she began picking at the meat in her dish.

Aspace waved casually toward the long banquet table. "Whatever's over there is fine for me." Perhaps he meant what he said about too much deference. Even so, Shenza was startled when he abruptly turned back to her. "Tell me, Shenza, what do you think of the chief peacekeeper? I've heard his opinion of you, you know."

This time, she managed not to choke over the pointed question. And she could well imagine he had heard Borleek's opinion of her. One would have to be deaf not to hear it. Mindful of his lecture about cooperation, she chose her words with care.

"I have the greatest respect for Chief Borleek's position." His brows rose, and she could fairly hear the unspoken question: *Respect for his position, but not for him?* "Like myself, he holds a key position in assuring redress to the citizens for any wrongs they may suffer. However, in order to fulfill his duties, I believe it is essential he remain within the proper bounds of his authority. And those who serve him, likewise."

The lord's pale eyes flicked over her shoulder momentarily, toward Juss, at the food table. Shenza wondered what his expression was saying that he did not speak aloud. She heard only the clink of utensils against dishes, then the firm beat of his sandals returning to the table.

Laraquies murmured, "I fear we magisters often disagree with Chief Borleek on where the proper bounds of his authority lie."

"I remember," Aspace answered drily. He reached to accept the bowl of fruit soup Juss extended. "And I don't suppose my brother ever helped you to clarify them. So you're saying Borleek oversteps his authority," he said to Shenza.

She swallowed a mouthful of tea before replying. "It is simply that he doesn't care what his men do. My Lord, when your brother died, the peacekeepers seized the first suspect presented to them and..."

"Yes, yes, I know. They beat him half to death. Don't think I approve of it." The man waved his utensils, a quick jab in the air. Shenza remembered too late that she had used his title rather than his name. She quickly resumed.

"This took place within the confines of the ward. I do not see how Chief Borleek or Sub-Chief Shamatt could have been unaware, yet no effort was made to stop the assault. When I asked Borleek about it, he loudly defended his officers and did not acknowledge the beating in itself as a crime. And this is not the first such incident, merely the most serious." Drawing a deep breath, she prayed she was not sounding as righteous and self- serving as she feared. "Such conduct cannot be tolerated if the people are to have faith in your wisdom and accept your judgements."

"Are you advising me on my job?" Aspace smiled blandly, and Shenza felt a chill. Not waiting for a reply, he continued. "Borleek is a brute. Worse yet, he is a boring brute. I'm amazed Anges would put up with him for that reason alone. But he is also a well entrenched and widely respected brute, and my advice is to stay out of his way until I've decided how to deal with him."

"I must do my duty," she objected, though pleased to hear he did intend to do something about the chief peacekeeper. "I shall not try to provoke him, but neither can I permit him to abuse the helpless."

Aspace gave her a long, silent look, as if unable to believe her romanticism. Shenza flushed uncomfortably. Finally he said, "Well, I'm pleased to hear you'll stand up for yourself, Magister. Just don't do it at the wrong time."

"We are not always permitted to choose our battles," Laraquies put in with an obscure smile.

Juss, meanwhile, was shaking his head in wonder.

"Yes?" Aspace inquired.

"It's just..." The peace officer smiled lop-sidedly. "I never thought I'd hear anyone describe the Chief as boring."

The thin lips quirked in an ironic smile. "Honesty is a privilege of rank."

In the brief silence, Shenza wondered about some of his words for his older brother, which hardly indicated brotherly affection. Cautiously, she asked, "Is there anything else you wish to ask me?" This time, she remembered not to call him 'my lord,' though it felt strange not to do so.

"Is there something else you want to tell me?" he countered, taking a casual swallow from his bowl.

At least this time she managed not to blush. "It is simply that I also have things to ask you."

He shrugged. "Go ahead."

Shenza hesitated awkwardly. Her left hand patted the matt beside her and found it empty. She had left her travel case at the door. Well, she would simply have to pay close attention and record her observations later.

"Please tell me," she began, feeling her stomach flutter with nervousness, "about your relationship with your brother."

His gaze was wary now. "What about it?"

This response was not encouraging. She had the depressing sense that this conversation could sour her relations with the new ruler. But her own words, recently spoken, goaded her.

"Did the two of you get along?" she hazarded.

Again, he deflected the question, shrugging, "Do brothers ever get along?"

"I like my brothers," Juss pointed out.

"You're lucky, then," the lord snapped back.

"Juss..." Shenza murmured reprovingly. Would he never learn not to speak out during questioning? For, she had to admit, that was what this was.

He quickly stuffed food into his mouth. "Sorry."

Aspace snorted with amusement at the exchange. Shenza turned back to him, neutral and patient. "Then you and Lord Anges did not like each other?"

"How could we?" he snapped, more irritated than the question warranted. "He was the oldest. He would inherit everything, while I was merely insurance in case something happened to him. He never let me forget it."

"Surely Lord Asbel did not say that," Shenza said, shocked despite herself by the heat of his bitterness.

"No," he admitted. "But he didn't stop Anges from saying it."

It sounded as if she must consider Aspace himself as a suspect, and she dreaded that. Reluctantly, she asked, "Did you argue often?"

"Daily." He answered shortly, grinding at his food. "No, hourly."

"Did he ever threaten you, or physically endanger you?" she probed.

"No, that would have required effort," Anges sneered. "Besides, he had the advantage. He was the elder, the inheritor. If we fought, he could have lost that. No, I think he was hoping to provoke me into doing it. He went out of his way to taunt me, if he could. Especially if mother and father weren't there. Even after he did inherit, and we weren't kids anymore, he never stopped acting like we were."

His remembered contempt was palpable, but it also could be a one-sided emotion. Shenza wished she could hear Master Laraquies' opinion, but there was no time to stop and confer. She continued, "Sometimes a first lord takes his brothers or sisters as viziers. Was there ever talk of..."

"Ha!" Aspace's bitter laugh interrupted her. "He let me know plainly enough there was only one lord in Chalsett-port. That's why I left."

"Did Lady Izmay have any role in that discussion?" Shenza could remember very little of the widowed first lady.

"Of course. Mother was a little more aware of Anges' failings than father was, I think. She wanted both of us to be his advisors, but he refused. Anges never listened to anyone, not really," he said with fresh scorn. "Mother finally had enough of him and decided the two of us should go. She had her own money, you know. We didn't need to stay here."

"Where did you go when you left?"

"Porphery, City of Domes. Mother's family is there, and they have many friends. She helped me gain a place in the high lord's ministries." He seemed to emphasize his mother's involvement. Shenza found this interesting, but he was already continuing. "I had been trained for leadership, after all. Why should my talents go to waste, just because Anges didn't want them?"

"It is admirable to serve," Laraquies observed, "and all the more to serve without fame or glory."

Aspace snorted, seeming to recover his humor. "If you say so."

"Where is Lady Izmay now?" Shenza inquired, resuming control of the inquiry.

"Oh, still in Porphery. Or she was. She'll be here for the funeral, I'm sure, but she wasn't in as much of a rush." His tone implied a mockery of Shenza's assertion that the Eleshouri had lent speed to his journey.

"You must be looking forward to her arrival," she said.

This as meant as mere politeness, but Aspace nodded firm agreement. "Yes, I am. I recognize when I need advice."

Again he pointed out his brother's failings. Shenza wondered how deeply his antagonism extended. She could not imagine feeling such anger toward Chimi or Sachakeen, despite the quarrels of their youth.

Seeking a less inflammatory subject, she asked, "Which ministry did you serve in?"

"Justice. I was hoping to be a magister, at one time, but someone else was chosen."

He slanted her another sarcastic look. Shenza hesitated, realizing he must mean her apprenticeship with Master Laraquies. "A worthy choice. Did you enjoy the work?"

"Yes, actually. At first, it was mostly record keeping and searching for legal precedents. High Lord Hadseem is a great believer in precedent. But I enjoyed the research and writing recommendations." Despite this assertion, he sounded aloof and bored.

"How long did you work in that capacity?"

He thought about it. "Six years, almost. Most recently, I reported directly to Minister Ittaht. He asked my opinion quite a lot." Aspace said this matter-of-factly, not as if he were bragging. Still, Shenza wondered why he felt it the need to mention it.

"That must have been an honor," she said. "Did you feel that your prospects in that ministry were good?"

"Maybe. Who knows?" He shrugged yet again, grandly bored. "It was all political. I think I did well, but there were many others also seeking the Minister's ear. Some of them I could trust, others not." His mobile features hardened at some undescribed memory. Shenza thought she would not have wished to be his adversary.

"That is true in many fields, surely," she pointed out, thinking of her own troubled relationship with Chief Borleek. Watching his face carefully, she asked, "Then I take it you were satisfied with your position and not interested in returning to Chalsett-port."

He snorted at that. "Are you joking? This is a very little city on the outside edge of the world. I could have gone much farther in Porphery, much more quickly, and the work would be a lot more rewarding. Besides, they're at the heart of the realm. People come there from all over the Jewel Sea. There were more things to do in a ten-day than we have here in a year. So, no, I didn't have my brother killed, if that's what you're suggesting," Aspace said with some heat. "I want you to understand that I take my duties seriously, but I had plans for my future. Coming back here was not part of them!"

Shenza was proud of herself. She did not quail beneath his fierce gaze. "Every possibility must be eliminated," she responded evenly. "Frankly, the one most baffling aspect of your brother's unfortunate fate is its cause."

"I thought everyone knew he burned to death," he frowned.

"My Lord was burned," she agreed, and leaned forward a little, urgently. "But why? To burn someone alive must be the

result of a violent hatred. Further, it cannot be inexpensive to
hire a sorcerer-assassin of this kind. Yet no one seems to have
any reason to hate my Lord Anges enough to take such extreme
steps. Even you, who are still angry with your brother, say you
did not wish him dead."

"Maybe they lied about it," he retorted succinctly.

"Certainly they would, when their own motives are in
question. But, for instance, I don't believe Master Nurune
would lie to protect one of your brother's enemies. It served him
too well to be the first lord's vizier and have his friendship."

"I suppose." He leaned back into his cushions, as if sinking
with the tedium. "But I wasn't living here. How would I know
who his enemies were?"

"Did Lady Izmay ever mention any feuds with people or
houses outside Chalsett-port?"

"No feuds on our side." He sounded very certain.

"Did he have any personal quarrels or insults from someone
from outside Chalsett-Port?"

"Since he seldom left here, I doubt it." But despite his
apparent lassitude, his pale eyes were keen on her face.

With the late lord's gambling in mind, Shenza asked, "Did he
have business disputes, or any unpaid debts that you know of?"

"No, he handled his finances well enough, though the
Heavens know how."

"Did he have any romantic affairs that ended with threats of
violence?"

He frowned once again. "How would I know?"

Shenza felt morbidly compelled to ask, "Was there ever talk
of a marriage contract that later had to be broken?"

"Him?" Aspace laughed outright at that. "No!"

That ought to end Innoshyra's aspirations, at any rate,
Shenza thought. Then she scolded herself for even thinking
about the spoiled merchant's daughter. The stubborn absence
of information was what ought to concern her.

Juss seemed to sense her frustration, for he suggested,
logically, "Why don't you just ask the fellow when you catch
him? You've got his semblage thing. So you're going to get him
soon." Broad brown shoulders lifted in a shrug. "Ask him then."

"Believe me, I will," Aspace replied with a relish that belied his many disputes with his elder brother.

Before Shenza could answer, Magister Laraquies voiced her own thought. "He may not know. After all, who would give such information to an agent who can be expected to repeat what he knows in the event of capture?"

"Oh." Juss appeared abashed now. "Yeah."

"But that reminds me," the old man continued. "I'd like to see your mask, Shenza."

She winced, reminded how she had managed to crack the talisman that represented the greatest portion of her power—and all her official prestige. Reluctantly, she lifted the flawed countenance from its place beside her knee. The old man received it reverently. All three watched as he turned it over thoughtfully, ran his fingers over the cracks, peered at it in profile.

Aspace broke the intense silence with a repeat of Juss' earlier question. "I thought nothing could break a magister's mask."

"Normally, no one tries to," the elder responded with a soft chuckle. "That's part of its function. If everyone respects what the mask represents, there is no question of attacking the one who wears it."

And yet, Shenza thought, someone certainly would. Someone like Makko. Her head throbbed slightly in remembrance of the magic fire bolt that had knocked her from her feet. But the lord interrupted her gloomy musings.

"As long as we're on the subject, I wouldn't mind knowing what happened this evening." His cool eyes touched briefly on her injured shoulder, where the cuts were now crusted with dried blood. "This isn't something I take lightly, you know."

"Yeah," Juss agreed, jabbing his blunt finger at her. "And you've got to stop taking so many risks, Shenza. I can't turn my back without something happening to you!"

Laraquies looked up from the mask momentarily. "There was no reason she should have thought it was a risk," he pointed out mildly.

"I was just reading over my notes," she added defensively.

The peacekeeper snorted loudly. "How many times do you have to be attacked before you learn it's dangerous to be by yourself?"

"That's enough," Aspace sounded exceptionally weary, which Shenza was learning to interpret as a sign of impatience. "I asked for *her* story."

"Sorry," Juss muttered yet again.

Reluctantly, Shenza told them what had happened. Lord Aspace kept a bland face when she said she had been expecting a visitation from the Eleshi, and she quickly went on to the more exciting events that followed. She made the account as brief as possible. At least, she thought, the telling helped her to keep the details firm in her memory, for she had not yet recorded her notes of the incident.

Juss was the first to speak after her. "For someone who usually plans so well, he didn't seem to have much of a strategy. Anyone would have known by now it wasn't the first lord's ghost."

"But," Shenza countered, "he has attempted all along to maintain the story, if you will, of what he wants it to seem happened. He may have thought if I were dead, others would be more persuaded by outward appearances. It was necessary to continue the pretense."

"Also," Master Laraquies added, "it is far easier to ambush an unarmed man in his sleep than a fully trained and well equipped sorceress. He could not set all the terms of this encounter to his advantage, as he seems accustomed to doing."

"Luckily for us," Juss agreed darkly. "I still don't want you being at risk, Shenza."

"So, in essence," Lord Aspace mused, swirling the remnant of his tea, "you each robbed the other of a key weapon. He has lost his semblage, but you lost your mask."

"And my spell-breaker, and bottle of daylight." Shenza responded. Depression again weighed her spirits. If this continued for a day or two more, she would have no weapons left.

Strangely, Master Laraquies was smiling. "But the mask is not lost." He offered Shenza her talisman with an encouraging nod. "You did say the magic spells still function. It appears only the surface is damaged. I see no reason it should not continue serving you."

Juss released a gusty sigh of relief. "That's good."

Shenza nodded, regarding her talisman glumly. In a way, the marring of its glossy features seemed symbolic of the entire inquiry, and the confident smile a mockery of her many failures.

The old man went on. "Even if it had been destroyed, the loss would not make Shenza as vulnerable as her foe, since his talisman's capture makes it possible for us to find him."

That thought did cheer her. "I will need another vial of daylight." she pointed out.

He nodded. "We should have a spare at home. And the spell-breaker can be found as well."

"But from a different coven," Juss advised sourly. "Do you know what Nurune was asking for the fire charms he sold us?"

"And not tonight," the first lord interrupted after Juss. "I know your type, Magister. You'd be up until dawn chasing shadows, when what you really need is sleep."

She blinked, irritated that he thought he knew her after so short a time. "Don't you want to complete the investigation?"

"My brother has waited four days for his funeral," he answered crisply. "One more day won't hurt him."

Is it really only four days? Shenza wondered silently. No wonder she felt tired.

"And you'll get those cuts looked at, too." His tone permitted no objections.

"Excellent advice," Laraquies murmured, patting Shenza's knee consolingly. "Even when we've located our target we must still bring him in. There is no reason to think he will surrender peacefully. Whatever happens will be easier if all of us are rested."

"That's the truth," Juss agreed gruffly.

"Yes, it is," the lord agreed, setting his cup down and gathering himself to rise. "And, if I'm not mistaken, the staff is ready to clear the table. You'll return to your quarters, Magister Shenza, and Alceme will send someone to attend you."

"Not without me, she won't," Juss insisted.

"Whatever." Aspace waved negligently. "Then Laraquies will put his ward back up, and we can all sleep soundly tonight. In the morning, you'll coordinate with Chief Borleek and anyone else who might be able to help."

"As you say." It annoyed Shenza to be ordered to stop her investigation when a resolution seemed so close, yet she could also see they spoke sense. It had grown late, and she frankly wondered if she could even stay awake long enough for a healer's visit. In one motion, she bowed and rose from the table. The others were already doing likewise.

"Tomorrow, then," Laraquies said.

"Tomorrow," Juss agreed with anticipation.

Chapter Twenty
~ Downside Up ~

Shenza awoke with a sense of urgency and rolled to her side, swinging her feet over the edge of the hammock. She waited a moment to orient herself before rising.

The cottage was dimly lit by a pale glow creeping through the window screens. From the lower chamber, beyond the bamboo panels, she could hear a deep, slow droning. Juss slept soundly in his self-appointed role as her guardian.

As this information penetrated her sleep-fogged brain, she saw there was little point in getting up. The day had yet to begin. A host of small pains beset her, mementos of the previous day's battle. Slowly, then, rubbing at sticky dry eyes, she rose and padded through the darkened upper level to the enclosed toilet just off the bath.

Yawning, she returned to bed. More rest would certainly be welcome. Yet now, perversely, her mind buzzed with the many duties that lay before her.

Despite her best resolve, Shenza had not been able to record her notes on the chaotic day just past. No sooner had she returned to her borrowed quarters than a pair of maids had arrived with the first lord's authority to tend to her needs. After they passed Juss's inspection, Shenza's injuries were gently cleaned and bandaged. They had then insisted on massaging her feet and head with soothing oils. By the time they finished, it had seemed an unbearable effort merely to reach her bed.

And so she now lay with responsibilities pressing in on all sides. Yawning again, widely, Shenza pushed her reluctant form up from the bed. There was no better time to write out her notes. There would be few interruptions at this hour. Taking a small shell lamp from the bedside table, she settled herself and her travel case beside a low table. Quietly, to avoid disturbing Juss, she murmured, "Light."

It wasn't easy to maintain a professional detachment as she wrote of the savage attack and of Borleek's hostility. Many times Shenza paused, excising some emotional comment. She felt, somehow, that Lord Aspace would laugh at her for doing so. She couldn't say why, but she was sure of it. Nonetheless, this was an official document, not a private diary. Her personal feelings had no place in it.

In the outer room, Juss' steady breathing gave way to restless movement. Beyond the cottage walls, voices echoed faintly as the palace staff went about their duties. Soon the light filtering into her room was bright enough to be called daylight.

As Shenza recorded the final passages, plodding footsteps approached. Juss leaned around the corner of a screen. He peered at her from heavy-lidded eyes and mumbled, "How long have you been up?"

She shrugged. "Since dawn. Did you sleep well?"

"I thought you were supposed to be resting," he accused.

"I did." Shenza refused to be provoked so early in the morning.

An indistinct grumble came in response, and the peacekeeper shuffled toward the bath. Vigorous splashing soon told her he was taking advantage of the deep pool. Smiling to herself, she bent to her work. She hadn't thought Juss would be one to wake up sour in the morning. Perhaps the bath would improve his mood.

With quick strokes of the stylus she inscribed her final summation and carefully reviewed what she had written. Satisfied at last, she covered her ink and sealed the scroll inside her travel case.

The splashing in the bath had stopped. Shenza stretched her stiff knees beneath the table. Suddenly, she felt both hungry and tired. A cup of strong tea would be welcome. Rising, she combed the tangles from her dark curls and changed into a fresh white under-robe. Over it she draped her magister's robe.

"When did Master Laraquies say he would be here?" Shenza called across the small house to her companion. She recalled some discussion being held during the massage, but details escaped her memory.

"He didn't say." This response came in a much more civil tone. "I hope it's soon."

"I should send a message."

Returning to the table, Shenza knelt to retrieve writing materials from her travel case. But before she began, there was a sonorous chime.

"Good morning," called an unfamiliar voice from the direction of the veranda. Shenza set down her pen and rose, but Juss' long strides carried him to the doorway before her. From the top of the stair, Shenza saw a small group of servants looking into the house from outside the faintly glowing line of the ward.

"Mistress Alceme sent us to see if you are hungry," a young woman explained. All three carried trays with covered dishes, but they appeared daunted by Juss's appraisal.

"We are," Shenza assured them. A moment's concentration, and the ward stone dropped into her palm. The three servants set their trays on the low table, while Juss rolled up his sleeping mat. "This is very kind of you."

"Is there anything else we can get you?" asked another of the staff.

"No, thank you."

The servants departed with bows, and Shenza quickly poured the tea. It was a fair day outside the little cottage. The sun, just brushing the treetops, flooded the surrounding garden with its warm rays. On such a day, it seemed that nothing could go wrong. Or perhaps it was merely the hot tea that revived her spirits.

Juss insisted on serving Shenza a heaping portion, and he stared at her until she began to eat. He then made short work of the rest. Before long only crumbs remained in their bowls.

"Now," Shenza said as she refilled her tea cup, "I will send our message." She rose and returned to her private chamber to retrieve her travel case. When she returned, Juss was clearing the dishes and setting them out on the porch for the servants to retrieve later. Shenza penned the missive, requesting Master Laraquies to bring Sub-Chief Shamatt and the men he chose for the arrest. As she folded it and chanted the spell to send it flying, Juss prowled the exterior of the house.

Shenza moved around the table, sitting where she could see the doorway but not be distracted by ordinary comings and goings. With careful deliberation, she laid out her tools: a pair of bamboo tweezers, her scrying shell, several small chunks of wax and a small ivory bowl carved with runes. Concentrating, Shenza activated the spell and deposited the wax inside. The bowl's mystic heat would soon melt it. She set her mask on the floor beside her knee, in case she needed it.

Reaching into her travel case, Shenza drew out the leather pouch containing the remains of the semblage. "Release," she murmured, and the drawstring's twined strands whirled apart. Cautiously, the young magister poured its contents across the table top. Shenza set the stoppered bottle aside for the moment. Taking up the tweezers, she began to pick through the potsherds. Not only was she wary of sharp edges, but she didn't want her personal magical aura to muddle the enemy's traces.

Using the sigils baked into the shards as a guide, she patiently began to reconstruct the semblage. *Be my eyes and cast my strength afar,* the inscribed symbols read. This incantation matched what she recalled of the spells required to make a semblage.

As each piece matched, Shenza dipped an edge into the fragrant, warm wax and bonded the sections together. A short, fat tube began to take shape. If she hurried, she might be able to complete it before Laraquies and Shamatt arrived. She wanted to begin scrying as soon as possible.

"What's that?" Juss asked suddenly.

Shenza looked up, puzzled. "What?"

"I hear something moving. I'm going to take a look." Shenza stopped her work to watch as he strode toward the veranda. Spear in hand, he walked stiff-legged, like a fighting cock. The wall on that side was open to the sunny garden, where a light breeze stirred the treetops. Juss cautiously descended to the garden level and stopped, looking around. Then Shenza heard it, too—a muffled cry from the just outside the house.

Juss spun in that direction, and suddenly shouted, "Shenza run! Get out of here!" He charged, spear raised, toward a bank of shrubbery along the foundation.

She set the semblage down quickly but carefully and swept up her mask. Even as she lifted it to her face, she heard a strange snap, like the crack of a whip. Shenza jumped to her feet. "What's wrong?" she called.

"Run!" Juss cried again.

A coil of rope snaked at him, weaving in the air like a living thing. Magic! Too quick to see, it coiled about his chest and pinned his left arm to his side. A hard jerk pulled him forward, falling. She heard a grunt of pain as he struck the base of the steps.

A new voice shouted, "Don't move!"

Makko! Shenza knew his voice at once. As she hesitated, he emerged from the undergrowth. "Don't move," he repeated. Makko yanked on another rope, dragging a struggling form with him.

Shenza gasped. A hostage! One of the maidservants was bound with more coils of rope that held her arms tightly at her sides. Her hair was falling into her face, and her head cloth had been stuffed into her mouth. Shenza could hear wild protests behind the makeshift gag.

"Shut up," Makko told her. The girl resisted until he grabbed her arm and held a bronze blade to her throat. Trembling, she stood rigid at his side.

Shenza, too, stood still.

"Release her," she said with authority she did not feel. "Your quarrel is with me."

"First things first," he retorted. "Come here."

"Don't do it," Juss shouted from somewhere near Makko's feet.

Makko kicked at him casually. "You shut up." To Shenza, he ordered, "You heard me. Get over here."

Warily, Shenza approached. She could see, through her mask, the fiery purple of magic in the cords that bound the girl. It appeared to be an ordinary rope with runes sewn on using a heavy thread, probably the kind fishermen used to mend nets. A makeshift spell, but clearly effective. As she took one step, then another, she tried to reckon how long it had been since she sent her message to Master Laraquies. How long would it take him to collect Shamatt and his officers? How long would it take the squad, not knowing of any danger, to reach the estate?

"What do you want of me?" she asked tensely.

"We are all going to go for a walk," Makko informed her pleasantly. "Down to the docks. And then, you're going to get me off this sandbar."

"What?"

Makko regarded her a moment with utter contempt. "You magisters are all alike," he sneered. "You get your imagination sucked out during training. Fortunately for me, I don't have such limited thinking. So let me explain it in small words. I... am... leaving. Is that clear enough?"

"You can't do that," she responded numbly. How could he not understand? Taisaris was still there.

Then Shenza realized she could easily resolve everything. All she had to do was give Makko what he wanted—let him leave. Taisaris, the legendary instrument of the spirits's revenge, would be waiting. If she and Juss captured Makko, the sentence for murdering Lord Anges would certainly be death, so the final result would be little different.

And yet... It was her duty to apprehend Makko. She had no more right to kill a suspect than Borleek did. Nor could she allow an innocent to be harmed.

As if he sensed her thought, Makko drew his knife sharply under his captive's chin. "If you want her to live, you'll cooperate," he warned. "It's nothing to me what happens to her."

The serving girl's eyes were brilliant with terror. She flinched suddenly, and a trickle of blood darkened the gleaming blade.

Shenza had reached the top of the steps, directly above Makko. Juss lay on his side behind Makko, his bonds tight enough to dig grooves in his skin. Then her heart gave a leap— his right hand was free! With it, he had drawn his dagger and was sawing at the rope, moving slowly so he wouldn't catch Makko's eye. All he had to do was sever one of the stitched runes and the spell would be broken. But there was no way for Shenza to tell him. She could only stall long enough for Juss to free himself.

As her eyes turned back to Makko, she noted the bamboo charm he wore about his neck was glowing brightly. Some kind of talisman, and he was using it. Shenza stared intently, but could not read the markings.

"Well?" Makko demanded impatiently. "There are so many people I want to kill, and time is short. But it's fine with me if you want this sow to die first."

The hostage whimpered again, and Shenza cried, "No! Release her, and I will come with you willingly."

Makko sneered. "Come with me, and I will release her. Once I have a boat and supplies. Like I said, I don't really care what happens to her. You've the one who wants her to live."

Juss was making progress on the ropes, Shenza saw, but he needed more time.

Dry-mouthed, she delayed. "Tell me something first. Why did you kill Lord Anges?"

"Everyone is good at something," he smirked.

"How can you say that?" Shenza gasped. She had known he must be a heartless killer, but to speak so lightly of murder...

"I have power. Why shouldn't I use it?" he retorted. "I wouldn't expect a witless sow like you to understand, but a man can make a good living when he doesn't let everyone else decide what spells he should cast."

"Then who hired you?"

"That would be telling. Now come down." He gave his captive a warning jerk.

Reluctantly, Shenza descended a step. "If you cooperate, Lord Aspace may show mercy."

He laughed aloud, but with deepest malice. "If *you* cooperate, maybe *I'll* show mercy. Now get down here!"

There was a kind of pop, more felt than heard, and Juss suddenly twisted his shoulders. He was free! Even as Makko started to jerk in that direction, the peacekeeper kicked out at him. No, at the maid. His foot struck the inside of her knee—and passed through it.

"Ha!" Juss laughed, rolling to his feet in a fluid motion.

The hostage was a phantasm! Shenza jumped back up the steps. Could Makko's talisman be the source of the illusion? There was no time to analyze. His knife was real enough. Metal crashed against metal, Juss and Makko sparring. Shenza watched anxiously from the porch until Juss snarled at her.

"What are you doing? Get away from here!"

Shenza backed slowly away. She was no fighter, but she didn't want to just leave him. When she reached the table she grabbed her travel case, swept in everything from the tabletop except the bowl of melted wax, and sealed it all in. Then she stood wavering. There was no rear door to this house. The porch was wide, but there was only one flight of steps. She would have to pass Juss and Makko to escape. Or she could jump down into the bushes. Better try that.

The clang of weapons abruptly ceased. Shenza ran to the porch and saw Juss backing toward her, breathing harshly. His knife was at the ready. "Where'd he go? I can't see him."

"What do you mean? You were fighting..."

"But he grabbed that charm around his neck and disappeared."

Makko had invoked a spell of invisibility? No, it must be another phantasm. Shenza's heart sank. How many talismans did Makko have? But she refused to let him escape, not now. Carefully she looked around.

"There!"

A purple silhouette moved against the green of the garden. Then the warning tone sounded in her ear. A familiar flicker of blue-red fire was speeding toward them. "Look out!"

"Duck!" Juss shouted in the same moment.

Shenza was already running down the steps, when a blast of heat and force hurled her through the air. She landed badly and tumbled to a crash against something solid. A wisteria tree, from the soft petals showering her. Groggily she noted thick, black smoke rising through the bungalow's window screens, and flames licked about its eaves. Shenza's knees and elbows smarted as she struggled to rise. If she had been inside the building, she wouldn't have survived, not even with her mask.

She had no idea where Makko was. Shenza crawled into the trees, tripping over roots and feeling the prick of sharp twigs.

There was no sign of Juss, nor of her travel case. The blast had torn it from her grip. But before anything else, she had to find Juss. They had to retreat, find Master Laraquies and Shamatt.

There, on the ground! Juss lay crumpled, as she must have been, on the open grass. He seemed unhurt, but he lay terribly still. Shenza hesitated to go to him—his position was so exposed—but she must. If the situation was reversed, nothing would have stopped Juss from coming to her aid. And yet... What if it wasn't Juss, but another illusion? No, it couldn't be. Makko didn't know Juss well enough to make it so convincing. Or did he?

As she gathered her courage, blue-red flames completely engulfed the cottage. The voice of the fire was eerie, animalistic, a guttural snarl mingled with erratic snaps and crashes from inside. Waves of dense black smoke boiled out, shot through with sparks. Shenza's mask protected her eyes, but she could still feel the terrible heat. She prayed to the heavens the smoke would give enough cover to reach Juss and escape.

Heart pounding, Shenza half-ran, half-crawled to where her friend lay. "Juss!" She caught at his shoulder and felt solid flesh.

With a groan, Juss rolled into a ball. He was alive! Shenza felt weak with relief, but she didn't dare let him rest.

"Juss, you have to get up. We can't stay here." She shook him harder, trying with all her strength to roll him over. His slack weight defied her. "Get up!"

Her mask's warning sounded again. Before she could react, something sent her bowling her across the lawn. Even as Shenza crashed against a low hedge, she clawed for a grip. Her hands slipped on the dense turf as some monstrous force lifted her into the air.

"Juss!" she cried in vain.

Shenza was wrenched upside-down, her robes falling over her face and leaving her legs exposed. Then she was whirled over and slammed downward. The jolt left her breathless. She struggled again to roll to her feet but was seized and hurled skyward a second time. The world spun madly, and she briefly glimpsed the burning cottage and leafy boughs tossed by the wind. The hard thump of another crash to earth drove those thoughts from her mind.

Before she could even try to stand, the unseen enemy threw her up once more. It must be kinesis. Makko had used it before, and she'd nearly died. Now, as she spun with ever more violent force, Shenza felt panic beating within her chest. She couldn't concentrate on any magic spells, which must be Makko's plan, but she had to take the initiative somehow. Shenza forced herself to hang limp and let her limbs flail as if she were unconscious.

It was hard to tell when the kinesis stopped, for her head continued to whirl on its own. Then she felt her head pounding as blood drained into it, and realized she was hanging upside-down. Her robes were bunched up around her knees. She doubted Makko cared for her modesty, but she guessed he wouldn't enjoy threatening her if he couldn't see her face.

It was hard to dangle there, like an insect caught in a spider's web. And it was very disorienting to see the ground above her and the sky at her feet. A thick black column of smoke rose past her ankles and above the tree tops. It met a dark sky. But it had been a sunny morning. When did this storm come up?

From behind her, where she couldn't see, came the shuffle of footsteps approaching. It had to be Makko. Juss would have been talking to her. The silence was unnerving. Shenza gave what she hoped was a convincing groan.

"Poor thing," came Makko's sarcastic voice. The sound moved as he circled her, and his chest came into view. He still wore a servant's garb, the short robe knotted loosely at the waist. Should she try to hit him? But she was no fighter. She hardly knew how!

"All your fine training doesn't prepare you for the real world, does it?" Makko gloated. "Oh, I know how it is. All that talk of honor and trust and responsibility. I heard it from my old man so many times I could probably say it backwards. Drove me half crazy."

Makko was a magister's son? It was all Shenza could do to keep still at the horrifying revelation. How could any child of a magister become so evil?

In her shock, she nearly missed the harsh fingers probing the edges of her mask. "First thing is to get rid of this. Now, let's see..."

At that Shenza twitched despite herself. Without her mask, she was as good as dead. She faked another feeble moan, and focused her will on her mask. Let it hold, by the heavens—let the seal hold!

She could not feel him touching her skin, but his hands blocked her vision. Then, suddenly, he punched her stomach. There was no trickery in her cry of pain.

"Waking up? I'm glad." Shenza had never heard anyone sound so vicious and smug. "I'm only sorry I don't have time to do this right."

Shenza hung panting, nauseated. What was that supposed to mean? She didn't want to find out. Makko went on, his voice chilling in its dry menace.

"There are so many things I'd like to do to you. These past four days, I've had nothing to do but plan it out." His hands gave a last frustrated yank and fell away. "Okay, you can keep the mask. For now. It'll come off when you're dead." Makko reached behind his waist and brought out the same knife she had seen earlier. "Besides, I don't have to use magic against you. Sometimes the simplest things are the best. Isn't that what they say?"

It was a common magister's proverb. Shenza would have choked with indignation at the twisted parody except the whole world had narrowed down to that terrible length of bronze. Her pulse pounded in her ears. She felt that she must move, must scream, must do something. But she couldn't take her eyes from it.

Then there was a wordless shout, a thump and a blur. Juss! Makko whirled, raising his knife in response. "You again!" he snarled.

Shenza could not see Juss clearly, but she heard him say in a businesslike manner, "Clouds and rain always come back. Just make it easy on yourself, and..."

"In your dreams, farm boy!" Makko snarled.

Seizing the moment of confusion, Shenza raised her body as best she could. "Get him, Juss!" She grabbed at Makko's waist, trying to confine his arms. Then she though better of it and groped for the amulet around his neck.

"Why, you—" Makko began.

And Juss barked, "Got you!"

Makko struggled, trying to break of her grip, and Juss closed the gap between them. Shenza felt her enemy's body jerk once, then twice, as solid blows landed. Her triumph was tempered by pain as the force holding her suddenly gave way. The two of them fell in a tangle.

"Let go of me, you sow, or I'll kill you!" Makko snarled. As if he hadn't meant to do that anyway.

"Cut the cord around his neck!" Shenza shouted at Juss.

"Get back, Magister!" Juss advised, both fists wrapped around Makko's hand that held the knife. "I can handle this now."

But Shenza couldn't do that. If she let Makko keep the talisman, Juss would be at a terrible disadvantage.

"Get off!" Makko snarled at her.

Her fumbling hands had found the narrow strip of carved bamboo. She yanked, felt the cord jerk taut. She didn't have the strength to break it. In desperation, Shenza focused her will on the leather cord.

"*Break!*" she shouted at it. And it did, a sudden release that left her awkwardly slumped against her enemy. Makko's elbow clouted her ear.

Now she was only too happy to put some distance between herself and the rolling, kicking brawl. With a frantic jerk she managed to free a leg that was pinned beneath Juss. Crabwise, she crawled a few steps away, turning to watch anxiously.

Makko threw himself backward, dragging Juss with him. The two men grappled, both of them giving inarticulate grunts of effort. Sprays of grass and earth kicked up as they struggled for control of the knife. Juss' own weapons were gone, and his broad shoulders bunched with the effort of forcing back the thirsty blade.

Shenza had never imagined she would be grateful to Chief Borleek for recruiting only the largest men as peace officers, but she was now. Juss had the advantage of size, but it wasn't enough. Makko fought with strength and cunning, and he still had the knife. As Shenza looked on he gouged at Juss's eyes with his free hand. When the officer jerked back, he gave an expert heave that pitched the two of them over. With a kick of his own, Juss continued rolling and ended up back on top again.

Shenza backed away slowly, wishing there was something she could do to help. Yet she knew her interference might only make things worse.

"Shenza, get out of here. I've got this... under control." Juss' voice was an uneven growl as he tried to turn Makko's wrist and make him drop his weapon.

Snarling with inhuman ferocity, Makko tried another kick to overbalance him. Shenza stared a moment in fearful fascination, until Juss grated out, "Go!"

Shenza did the only useful thing she could. Still backing away, she promised, "I'll go get Shamatt."

"Fine," he grunted. "Just hurry!"

Chapter Twenty-One
~ The Dark Beneath the Trees ~

Shenza ran, though she wobbled with dizziness from hanging upside-down and her body ached after too many hard falls. She ran as fast as she could. Makko was a professional runner in addition to his other skills, and he would waste no time in coming after her if he got away from Juss.

By now, Shamatt and Master Laraquies must be on the palace grounds. Shenza ran toward the buildings, thinking to find them there. The hilltop was thick with blowing smoke. She could not find a familiar landmark. Shenza slowed to a jog. The estate, for all its greenery, was not truly forested. She should have come out of the thicket, but the tangled undergrowth hemmed her in. And, she realized, it was darker under the trees than it should be.

A terrible suspicion came over her. For the scent on the air was not the stench of burning, but a cloying perfume. She stopped and looked around carefully.

A familiar, humanlike form swept the vegetation aside without touching it. The satiny stuff of its robe glimmered like moth's wings in the dusk. The Eleshi seemed to regard her from across a vast distance. Its fabulous eyes were as cold as the sea.

Before Shenza could summon the proper words, the spirit man asked simply, "That is the one?"

The one who had killed Lord Anges, it must mean. "Yes, great one," she stammered, "But..."

"Very well."

The wind gusted hard, tossing the branches and swirling a veil of smoke before her eyes.

"Patience, Lord of—Oh!" Shenza ducked as the fierce breeze whipped her robes into her face. When she looked up, the spirit was gone. Only a shaggy-barked fern tree stood before her in the filtered light of a normal grove.

Shenza stood with a sinking heart. What should she do? Keep searching for Master Laraquies, or return to help Juss? She knew he was in grave danger now. The spirits would not care who got hurt as long as Makko died. She couldn't even be certain they understood that Makko, not Juss, was the guilty one.

No, there was no time to go for help. Shenza fled back in the direction she had come, though her lungs ached and her legs trembled with fatigue. How she could stand against the spirits's terrifying power, she did not know. Somehow, she must!

The sky was nearly black as she returned to the clearing. Nothing was left of the guest cottage but a stony shell. Clusters of embers flew amid the smoke, thrown together with bits of leaves and branches. Despite the gusting wind, the choking fumes did not dissipate. Instead, the smoke was funneled into a roiling mass, a further blackness beneath the oppressive sky. Within that inky morass, Juss and Makko must be struggling still.

"Remarkable spell," said someone at her shoulder. Shenza started, and turned to see Master Laraquies surveying the scene with serene curiosity.

Farther behind him, Shamatt's squad was pouring into the clearing. Their weapons were drawn and they shouted to each other excitedly, but she noticed they kept a cautious distance from the smoke.

Shamatt himself jogged toward the two magisters. Gesturing to take in the smoky vortex, he asked, "What's happening? And where's Juss? He was supposed to be with you."

"In there," Shenza answered bleakly.

The three of them regarded the sinister, swirling cloud. "Why?" Shamatt asked incredulously.

"Yes, why?" another voice cut in. Shenza stood gaping while the others bowed before the first lord. Lord Aspace was not wearing his finery of the day before. In fact, he was was nearly as disheveled as she was. Not that this detracted from his beauty.

When no one answered, Aspace snapped, "Well?"

Shenza explained as quickly as she could. "Makko returned while we were remaking the semblage. We—"

"How did he get in?" Shamatt demanded indignantly. "I have guards everywhere."

"Please let me speak!" Shenza cried. She had no time for these interruptions. "He must have used a phantasm to make himself invisible. He also pretended to have one of the servants as his hostage. He demanded free passage from the harbor. Juss discovered the ruse, and Makko set the house on fire while he was trying to kill us."

Shamatt nodded. "We heard an explosion."

"I'm sure you did." Shenza hurried on, "Juss and Makko were fighting and I was coming to look for you. But now the spirits are involved..." She broke off with a guilty glance to Lord Aspace. "I came back to help Juss, but I haven't seen either of them. I assume they are both inside."

Shenza could see the lord wanted to argue with her about the spirits, but he stared at the sinister cloud and said nothing.

"Are the spirits inside?" Master Laraquies asked. The soft question disguised a keen curiosity.

She shook her head. "I don't know, but I have to find Juss, if I can."

The first lord's daunting frown snapped back to Shenza. "Why you? You're my magister. I don't want you going in there. It's dangerous."

Shenza heartily agreed, but it was too late for selfish concerns. "They know Makko is guilty, and they don't care about anything else as long as they kill him. Someone has to help Juss. I am the only one they might listen to."

Actually, Shenza was more certain the spirits would heed Aspace, but she was not about to suggest it. He, of all people, could not be placed at risk.

Turning back to Laraquies, she directed, "Master, please try to quench the fire. They seem to need the cover of darkness in order to work. Increased daylight might reduce their strength.

And keep this." She thrust Makko's talisman at him. "It's Makko's."

The old man bowed as if she were the first lord. "As you say." Hands clasped loosely behind his back, talisman dangling, he walked toward the burning shell of the cottage.

Aspace and Shamatt were staring at Shenza. It seemed there was more she should be saying, but there was no more time for words.

"I must go," Shenza said awkwardly, and turned away.

"Take someone with you," Aspace ordered behind her.

Shenza whirled back. "No! They are not prepared." Shenza wasn't certain she was, either, but she simply told Shamatt, "Just have your men circle the area, in case Makko breaks away from us."

Shamatt reluctantly nodded. Shenza turned from her ruler's fierce eyes to step toward the billowing cloud. The only sounds in the clearing were the snapping of the fire and Shamatt's orders.

"Magister, stop!" The first lord's voice cracked like a whip behind her. "You must not have heard what I said. I forbid this!"

Shenza felt herself go rigid. With an effort, she resisted her ingrained need to obey her ruler. She couldn't possibly take anyone else into such danger when she had no means to protect them. There was no time to summon another sorcerer, and Master Laraquies was still young enough to train another apprentice if the worst should happen.

Softly, not knowing if he could even hear her, she said, "It pains me to disobey my Lord." Then she walked into the smoke.

~

Shenza expected some sort of resistance, but there was none. The inky vapors swirled about her, cutting off the light and noise of the outside world. Even the wind died away, leaving the atmosphere oddly heavy and muffled. Shenza was afraid to go forward, dreading what she might find, and yet also afraid to stop in the eerie twilight. She advanced cautiously, the gloom rolling back in layers before her.

The green grass was gone from the ground, given way to a mat of rotted leaves that felt spongy beneath her sandals. Shenza felt she should have emerged on the far side of the cloud by now. Where were the trees? Where were Juss and Makko? She could pass within a few feet of them in this murk and never know it. She paused, fixing the image of Juss' broad face in her mind.

"Let me through!" she commanded between her teeth. She strode forward, willing herself to find him.

A low, dark shape resolved itself from the mists before her. When it moved, Shenza ran toward it. Juss! He and Makko were still on the ground, still fighting. Makko was on the bottom, half- buried in the crumbling soil. There was no sign of the knife.

"Juss!" she called anxiously.

"Get back!" He half-turned toward her. His face was covered with blood and twisted with an extreme expression she did almost didn't recognize. Juss, who was never afraid of anything, was terrified. "Get away from here, Shenza!"

It sounded like just the kind of stupid thing Shenza would say. She was so relieved to see Juss, she nearly laughed. "I didn't come all the way in here just so I could run away again. Let me try to get you out of there."

"No, I said. Stay back!"

Ignoring his words, Shenza stepped closer. She stopped with a gasp when she saw the true situation.

The two men were not struggling with each other, but against something that sought to drag them deeper into the earth. Roots!

Hairy filaments like the roots of trees writhed upward from the duff. They flapped like weirdly jointed hands as they searched for a grip. With a grunt, Juss pushed upward. Deep gouges cut into the skin of his back, and he fell forward with a panting breath. Shenza felt her stomach turn over as she realized the roots were digging into Juss' legs up to his hips. And Makko... Thick coils of roots invaded his stomach and chest, pinned all four limbs. Shenza tried not to look at him. Sickening though his fate might be, she had not come here for his sake.

Beneath the two men, she now saw, the soil was crawling with insects. All kinds of ants, termites, and spiders swarmed up from the earth below them. It must have been their tunneling that softened the ground. Now they were turning their attention to the trapped men. Indeed, something bit Shenza's ankle as she watched.

The pain roused her from her momentary paralysis. "I'll get you out," she vowed, hoping desperately it wasn't a lie.

At the sound of Shenza's voice, Makko's face came alive with hatred. "You," he grated, his voice barely recognizable. "This is your fault, you sow! If it wasn't for you, I'd be safe and well away from here."

"She's not the one who killed the first lord," Juss answered. Again he strained with his legs, trying to break the grip of earthen fingers, but it was obvious no mortal strength would be adequate.

Makko's grin was like a skull's. "Come down here and say that, big boy." But his eyes were fixed on Shenza, and they blazed with malice. "I don't know how you did this, but I know it's your doing. I hate goody-goody people like you. You make me sick, do you hear?"

He turned his head to spit out a bug. The roots tightened on both men, as if to avenge the insult. "Urrh!" Makko cried between clenched teeth. Juss, too, groaned as he strained against the confining tendrils.

Shenza stared at Makko, speechless. How could he think of petty things in a situation like this?

"Do you know... how long... I planned for this..." Makko rasped, still staring his fury. He seemed to fight for each breath. "And you... You..."

"Maybe you should have tried working at a different trade," Juss panted as the spasm eased.Makko ignored him, bitterly accusing, "Why couldn't... you just..." His words ended in a racking cough.

After the long days she had spent hunting this man, Shenza found she had nothing to say to him. He was obviously doomed, but there was still a chance for Juss. She owed the peacekeeper too much not to do whatever she could.

Saying nothing, she bent to seize the nearest visible root, which was clawing its way into Juss' back. The stuff was slippery despite its hairy seeming, as unyielding as bronze wire. It cut painfully into her fingers.

"Release him!" Shenza cried into the dreadful silence. A spider leapt onto her hand and immediately bit her. By force of will, she did not stop to slap at the burning pain. Shenza pulled again and again, crying to the rhythm. "Let him go! He is not guilty! Let go!"

"Good luck... sow," Makko rattled more faintly. A swarm of crawling things rose around him like a dark tide. She could feel them coming up her legs, too. The sensation lent impetus to her efforts.

I can do it, she thought desperately. *If I can break stasis, I can do this. I must!*

"Let go!" Shenza concentrated her will through the words as if they were a spell.

There was a slight easing of the tension. With a deep-throated roar Juss flexed his legs again. The roots gave way with a series of dull snaps. Shenza let out a harsh breath. He was free!

Juss tottered to his feet, nearly wading backward in the soft soil. Shenza could feel the slickness of blood on his skin as she helped support his weight.

"Lean on me," she told him. He did, and they both fell.

Shenza could feel tiny, prickling feet all over her, but no more bites. Was that a reprieve? She let Juss gather his strength for a moment, and she did the same. The impromptu spell casting had left her drained.

"Can you walk?" she asked.

"I'll have to." His fingers dug into the loam as he pushed himself up. "Let's go."

In truth, it was as much crawling as walking, but it was movement, and it was away from Makko. Shenza held back a surge of relief. If she could just keep her concentration a little longer —

Something jerked at her foot, and she fell forward. She twisted to find the source. A root? No, she felt warm, hard fingers. "Makko!"

"You die... if I do," he snarled. Only half his face and one arm were visible above the swallowing earth, but his grip was terribly strong. "You got him out. Get me, too, or you die here."

Terror made her blood beat in her ears. Shenza had no intention of helping Makko. She twisted and jerked, but she could not break his grip.

Then she stopped.

"Tell me the truth," she demanded. "Who hired you? If you tell me, I'll try to help you."

There was a silence. Shenza could see in Makko's eyes the war of desperation against his hatred of all she stood for.

"Ask your precious first lord," he bit out. "It's all his fault, anyway."

"Lord Aspace? What do you mean?"

"He was too good at his job, that one. He was poking into things he shouldn't. They warned him, but he ignored it. They couldn't kill him, it would have drawn more attention. They had to make him leave."

"What do you mean, they?" Shenze demanded. "Who did this?"

Makko ignored her. His voice was a dark thread, weaker as the moments passed. "If... if his brother died... he would be first lord... Then he would... have to stay away..."

"But who hired you?" Shenza shrieked.

"He knows," Makko rasped. He grinned like a skull and pulled on her ankle. "You stay... with me, sow..."

"Leave him, Shenza!" Juss shouted. "He's not worth it!"

It was hard to believe, afterward, that Juss found the strength to aid her. There was a loud slithering and he somehow pivoted on his forearms, lashing out with both scarred legs. Insects, blood and bits of crumbled leaves flew in a dark spray as Juss kicked Makko's face once, and then again.

At the same moment the earth shuddered, and Shenza could feel the soil giving way beneath her. Makko screamed, a hoarse cry of frustration and despair, and his hand slipped loose. Shenza wrenched free at last. Not wasting a backward look, she crawled forward, knees catching on her robe, until she collapsed onto firmer ground. Juss joined her, gasping for breath, even as the tremors stilled beneath them.

"Are you all right?" she asked.

His head jerked in a nod, but his eyes were wide and dark as a maddened beast's. "I want to get out of here," came a hoarse whisper.

Trembling herself, she answered, "So do I."

~

Once again, smoke rose from the first lord's palace. This time it was the controlled burning of the pyres which sent Lord Anges to the heavens.

The lord would lack for little in his life beyond, Laraquies reflected. No fewer than ten bonfires had been required to dispose of the mortuary offerings. The plumes of smoke lifted straight against the evening air, dark vapors dissipating into the tawny sunset sky. In the west, Inkesh finally lowered its crimson head. In the east, the heavens dimmed to purple set with the first glimmer of stars. Beneath the palace's proud roofs, the memorial feast was nearly over.

In contrast to the wild welcome Lord Aspace had received, the profusion of pyres was the only extravagance to this affair. Not even the wealth of a first lord could host two grand celebrations within such a short span of time, it seemed. The funeral could fairly be described as decorous and subdued. Laraquies could not help thinking that Lord Anges, the tireless reveler, would have been disappointed.

The feast was laid out within the central pavilion, now emptied of its riches. Lord Aspace sat on the dais formerly occupied by his brother's remains. He was truly resplendent in a full-length robe of red feather-flower silk shimmering with silver beads. On his right sat his mother, First Lady Izmay, who had returned to Chalsett-port just the morning of the funeral. Laraquies was glad to see the first lady looking well. She was aging, of course, and grieving for her eldest son, but she did not seem old. Izmay's return was welcome, for they had been friends and he missed her incisive wit.

Chief Borleek sat on Izmay's right. Personally, Laraquies didn't think the man deserved to sit at the high table. That honor should have gone to Juss, or even to Shamatt. Still, he understood why it would be impolitic to favor a junior officer above his commander.

To the first lord's left, despite her protests, sat Shenza. She looked downcast, no doubt because she had to borrow her robe, a gold fabric stitched with red blossoms. In Laraquies' opinion, she fretted too much over such things. Or perhaps she was still tired from all she had been through. Shenza did not complain of any injury, but he suspected from the way she walked that she was in some pain. In any event, she was much abashed in these grand surroundings.

The rest of the funeral guests were seated at tables on the floor of the pavilion. All the social elite were present, particularly the Houses of Kesquin and Sengool. The latter clan looked distinctly put out. Eespecially Lady Innoshyra, who shot eye-darts at Shenza when she thought no one was looking. Nurune, too, remained sullen over his demotion. Of the wayward apprentice, Tonkatt, there was no sign at all.

Laraquies was doubly glad of Shenza's fortune in attracting the first lord's regard, for it allowed him the luxury of choosing his own place amid the lower tables. He had been pleased to take his seat with Shenza's family. The House of Tresmeer was happy but awed amid the glittering assemblage. Chimi was fit to burst with the excitement of it all, sighing over the clothes and jewels of the Kesquin daughters adjoining them. Sachakeen was trying not to show how impressed he was. Only old Myri seemed to believe she truly deserved to be present at a state ceremony.

As for Shenza's mother, Giliatt had always appeared worried from the first moment Laraquies met her. Tonight was no exception. "Will Juss be all right, Master Laraquies?" she asked softly.

"Oh, yes," he assured her. "He is already healed, but Mistress Kafseet wants him to rest for a few more days. It was a difficult recovery." Between the poisoned insect bites and the tearing of his leg muscles, it would be some time before the peace officer walked again. The curomancer believed he would heal fully, however, since he was young and hardy.

"Oh, Arlais will take good care of him," Chimi said with breezy confidence. "She was a great help to us, you know. I hope we can see her and Juss again."

Giliatt murmured agreement, glancing briefly at Byben. The old man was oblivious to her discreet regard. Though the emergency was past, the elder seemed to have become part of the Tresmeer family. He hummed with wine and happiness, despite the solemnity of the occasion, and doted on Myri. Laraquies hadn't thought anything could soften that sour old woman, but it seemed he was wrong.

"But..." Sachakeen murmured with a wary glance around, "Is it really over? "

"For this time," Laraquies sighed. "If only Makko's body had been recovered, a necromancer could force his ghost to tell us the whole truth. As it is, we have little recourse."

"Is there nothing you can do?" Giliatt asked.

"Even sorcery is not all-powerful," he reminded her gently.

"Humph," murmured Myri, more from habit than malice.

"But what a way to die," Chimi shuddered with ghoulish empathy. Now that Makko was dead, Laraquies supposed it was safe to pity him. Better that, for some people, than to consider the implications of the half-solved crime.

It was not general knowledge that Makko had been a hired assassin. The public shock would be too great. That was a measure of how provincial Chalsett-port was. It was also one of the reasons Laraquies liked the City of Gardens. One should be shocked by murder, but citizens of larger cities became immured.

Few knew of Makko's troubling confession, that Lord Anges had been murdered simply to force his brother out of Porphery. Juss insisted that Makko was the kind of fellow to say the most upsetting thing, just for the pleasure of stirring up trouble. Shenza countered that Makko never shrank from the truth when it might cause pain. Beyond a question or two, Aspace said nothing. Laraquies did not know what to think of that.

There had been a tardy response to the inquiries Shenza dispatched to neighboring magisters. The day after the palace fire, the magister at Amethan had informed them, with deep regret, that the killer's tactics sounded similar to those of his own son. The young man, Geen, had been his father's apprentice, but Jiseppa was forced to expel him from training. He had not seen his son in many years. This might explain Makko's antipathy to magisters. Only a fuller exchange of details would confirm if Makko and Geen were the same person.

Even with this information, Laraquies knew the lack of a resolution weighed on his student. She had spent the days since Makko's death trying to find some shred of information that could further her probe. Thus far, her efforts were in vain.

Still, Laraquies was more than satisfied with his student's performance under the most difficult circumstances. The mere fact that Byben of Cessill sat among them drinking nut beer was a kind of triumph. It would have been easy to let him suffer the unjust penalties, and to leave Juss to his fate. Laraquies was proud that Shenza had not been content with those options. A magister without sympathy for strangers was a poor one, and one who would betray a loyal ally was no magister at all.

Of course, Laraquies expected no less from his own apprentice.

Moreover—and perhaps it was not his place, but an old man couldn't help speculating—he glanced again at the dais. Lord Aspace was slouched to one side, regarding Shenza. From their expressions, it appeared he was teasing her about something.

The young lord was unmarried. It struck Laraquies that he was taking more than a professional interest in the new magister. In time, Laraquies suspected Shenza would penetrate Aspace's jaded posing. He would have to sound Izmay out about that when he renewed their acquaintance.

But the future held its secrets, and the old magister knew better than to hurry them. He had already submitted a license request to the Ministry of Justice, along with his highest recommendation. He did not doubt it would be granted. Shenza Waik of Tresmeer would serve as an exemplary magister for many years to come.